NEWSREEL

NEWSREEL

by Irvin Faust

Harcourt Brace Jovanovich
Bruccoli Clark
New York and London

Requests for permission to make copies of any part of the work should be mailed to: Permissions, Harcourt Brace Jovanovich, Inc. 757 Third Avenue, New York, N.Y. 10017

Printed in the United States of America

Library of Congress Cataloging in Publication Data
Faust, Irvin.
Newsreel.
I. Title.
PZ4.F267Ne [PS3556.A97] 813'.54 79-3349
ISBN 0-15-165421-2

First edition

B C D E

For Jean

PART

Heroes on Parade

I have to get this right. I've started it three times. Here is the fourth . . .

I got out of the army on June 28, 1946. Of that I am sure; I have the discharge papers to prove it. I have no memory of the remainder of that year. I do have a twisted, writhing sense of 1947. It took place, as far as I can make out, in various hotels that seemed, for some reason, to be centered around Penn Station (Hellos? Goodbyes? Frantic connections?). Also in bars along Eighth Avenue; no mystery about that. Or the fact that I also frequented the ones on Queens Boulevard in Sunnyside, although how and why I operated in Sunnyside I have never been able to determine.

My perception of 1948 includes the addition of bars on Lexington Avenue; there are also flashes of the Hawaiian Room of the Hotel Lexington, with the Aloha Maids becoming a part of the writhing memory. I do believe that the Truman upset occurred there (Harry's Key West Hawaiian shirts?) because I have a loop of myself getting into a fight for my father. Reconstructing: if FDR had picked Truman, then he had to be all right, and the cigar and mustache beside me—clearly a Dewey man, therefore a *Hoover* man—clearly required a punch in the mouth.

So much for that. After the brawl, another writhing thing in my memory: I must have walked across town to my fleabag—surely no cab would stop for this ripped-up mess—because I recall that I was suddenly in my room on the squashy bed with the *Daily Mirror* in my hands (I had some need to check the race results every day). There, close to a dying neon sign, it was. *He*

3

was. Eisenhower. He was unquestionably in New York, because if you were President of Columbia you had to be in New York. He was only two miles away. The writhing ceased. I did not drink myself to sleep that night.

I think I may be getting it . . .

I did not instantly emerge into perfectly remembered action. No, felt, *experienced* action. I moved in flickers, like a speeded-up silent film. Jerky advances, holds, retreats. Yes, that's accurate. In one of those flickers I packed up and moved out. In another I found myself on Morningside Drive. Then a hold, a space, probably a retreat. Yes, a retreat. Then a flooding forward and I had a room in a residential hotel a block away from Eisenhower. I understand that it has since been exposed as a haven for pimps, prostitutes and junkies. Perhaps it was then. I didn't, *couldn't* know. That's a categorical statement. What I'm not sure of now is whether I ever really *saw* Eisenhower. For whatever reason, I always watched his house from across the street (probably still aware of the official distance between us); I'd pace back and forth for most of the morning, then break for lunch by creeping over to Amsterdam Avenue for a take-out sandwich and a carton of milk (no alcohol while on duty). Then back to Morningside Drive.

I can still see images of him: profiles, glances, D-Day sternness (I never thought of him as smiling in that period). Were the images real? Probably not. Yet I can practically swear that one of them was: a shadowy face above a trim Eisenhower jacket, gazing wistfully out over Harlem, east, east to the ocean, to England, to the Continent, to the life that had been so abruptly, cruelly cut away from us. Then it—he—disappeared, leaving me forever with the residual picture.

When my money ran down, I was somehow able to get on the subway and ride to the Bronx to dun my mother. (I was crazy, not stupid.) She always came through even though I was acting more and more like her brother who had dropped dead at the racetrack. In one of the frozen frames I can see and hear her telling me it was a blessing my father wasn't around. I'm quite sure I agreed, if only to get the money. (No, that's not fair to him *or* me. He had died one day after I got home; with Hitler wiped out, with FDR gone, the war won, his darling boy victorious and heroic, his life had no more purpose and he slipped away with one of his sighs. Happy? I think. I *know*. So yes, it was a blessing he couldn't see me now, the son who had conquered; and no, I didn't agree with her just for the money . . . There, that's better.)

Gradually, between times, I began to fan out to the west. Not that it was any big deal. I began, like a one year old, to take some faltering steps under daddy's careful arms. Eyes. Without alcohol, frankly, it was rugged. But whenever I ran down, *he* was there, so I managed to drag around the campus, then to move out, slowly, up and down Broadway, holding on to buildings and storefronts for dear life. I would catch a glimpse of someone in the store windows (that's when I started the habit, although now it's for admiration); I recall my surprise when that person's leg moved and mine did, too. It finally dawned that there was a connection between us, a kind of unity, and it was important that I study this phenomenon as I inched down to 110th Street and back up to 116th. The thing about those safaris is that I had proof in the windows that I still existed, even in no man's land. And whether or not I ever *saw* Eisenhower, there is no doubt in my body-sense that slowly, under his commanding guidance, I began to walk straighter and with something longer than six-inch steps. Looking and feeling my way back, I was ready.

Now let's see what I was ready for.

"Nuts to you, Captain."

That is what I heard. That is what the voice unquestionably said.

I was on Broadway and 113th Street, facing north. I had just passed an apartment house and was feeling a bit panicky because until I reached the windows of the Chinese laundry and the barbershop, I had to navigate past the yawning, windowless gap of the Hamilton Garage. That is when I heard it. I stopped, peered into the dimness. A jumble of cars. I crept on.

5

"Hubba, hubba," the voice said.

I stopped again. A smiling face, lit in some way from within like a Halloween pumpkin, came toward me. (From here on, the afternoon is sharp, sunlit and exact.)

"Can I help you?" I said. My father had taught me to use that whenever I smelled trouble.

The face bobbed in a little closer. It was cocked to one side on top of a dirty pair of coveralls. The face began to loom very large.

"Nuts," it said.

I stepped back sharply, the first clean movement I had made in days.

"Why do you . . . keep . . . saying that?"

"That's what McAuliffe said to the Germans."

Something twanged. I reached my right hand to my left shoulder: no railroad tracks. My father's sigh emerged. The voice said, "In the Bulge. I served under you." I stepped in, but remained balanced for flight. "Bastogne?" I said. The head bounced up and down; its face was a polished mass of acne in the dimness. I could think of only one thing to say: "What was your rank, soldier?"

"Yardbird," he said.

It was the most hilarious thing I had heard since the sex advice of the Mickey Mouse movies. I doubled over and guffawed until I was gasping. Then I straightened up and got very dignified. He said, "PFC, Captain."

I took another step. He was very thin, even had a thin head.

"Did you get enough to eat?" I asked.

"Nuts."

"Yes. Well . . ."

"You don't know me, but I know you," he said cheerfully. "You told me, 'Squeeze, don't jerk.' "

Twang.

"I did?"

"Yop. One day I'm in the motor pool cleaning plugs in Manchester, the next day I got an M1 and you're telling me, 'Squeeze, don't jerk.' It sure is a small world."

6

I brushed a hand against my eyes and said, "What's your name, soldier?"

"Monroe Meyer, sir."

"That's a very patriotic name."

"Not in Austria it's not. My father refused to fight for the Emperor."

"Monroe, soldier. *That's* patriotic."

"I was named after my grandfather, Moses Meyer."

"Yes. Well . . ."

"I seen you on Broadway a few times, Captain."

". . . I like Broadway. It's a good street."

"It has its good points and bad points."

"That's true . . . Would you like a cup of coffee?"

"I'm on duty. Vito would shit a brick."

Twang.

"That's all right," I said. "I'll square it with your commanding officer. Come on, Meyer, I'm in the mood for a cup of coffee."

We crossed Broadway, walked past 115th Street and entered Riker's. He plopped down on a revolving stool. I sat gingerly; revolving stools were making me dizzy in those days. A trim woman dressed in white, brightly made-up but caved-in around the edges, bustled over.

"Wadayou know?" she said.

"What's to know?" Monroe shot back.

She slapped the counter in delight. Coffee mugs jumped all down the line but no one looked up. Good old Broadway.

He said, "Rose, this is Captain Finestone." The face in the mirror behind the woman in white grew very red.

"Hi, Cap," she said. "You look pretty young to be such a big shot." I mumbled something about past history and water over the dam. Monroe nodded. "He got a battlefield commission. The brass was gettin knocked off left and right in the Bulge, so they pinned a bar on him. Dint they, Captain?"

"What're you having, Monroe?" I said.

"My brother got wounded in Sicily," she said.

7

"He taught me how to fire an M1," Monroe said.

"He still limps," she said. "You two guys are lucky."

"Coffee light, please," I said. "Two coffees. Doughnut, Monroe?"

"Sure. Sugar, Rose."

"Make it two," I said.

She bustled away. She had tremendous calves. To this day I can zero in on those calves. I began to relax a little. She bustled back with the coffee and. I bent toward the cup, caught the sad sack in the mirror hunching over and quickly brought the cup up to *me*. I even managed a quarter turn on the stool; my head did not spin. I drank. I made a half turn.

"Here's the thing, Monroe," I said. "You have to squeeze because that target sitting on your sights must be treated with care and affection. . . ."

We got back at fifteen hundred hours and Vito began immediately to chew him out with brilliance. When he paused for breath, I dived in.

"It was my fault. I accept full responsibility."

With his jack o'lantern smile, Monroe said, "This is Captain Finestone."

"I don't care if it's *Ei*senhower," Vito barked. He had the makings of an exemplary platoon leader. "You think a business runs itself? Now put them goddam cars away."

Squeal. Lurch. Gun. Whine. Roar. Whoosh. Squeal. Quiver.

Vito, shaking a khaki-capped head:

"That little bum. If car jockeys was a stock, he'd be A.T.&T."

That night has always been both hazy and clear, first one, then the other. I'll do the best I can . . .

There was, to begin with, my daily battle with gravity. With lack of same. As the sun dropped into New Jersey pulling its coverlet over the city, the laws of physics would stop working. Eternal equations would fall apart; the tides of the moon would fall asleep. Even as I would creep back to my room, lightness invaded the space that gravity had evacuated. My outer envelope began to fill with helium and I was convinced that this zeppelin that inched forward in vertical position must either soar into the lowering sky or disappear. No, *evaporate*. For whatever reason, probably Finestone's Returned Hero Law, it would do neither, but I couldn't be sure of that until dawn flooded the rooftops of Harlem, and apples again fell down and not up. So before the struggle each night, I would take one last look at Eisenhower's windows, lock myself in, and anchor the zeppelin beneath the hotel's dirty navy blankets. And shiver through the night without alcohol. I'm quite sure I began *that* night the same way. But this time my skin had taken too much helium. I resisted takeoff as long as I could, I'm certain of that. But the night-lightness was too strong. The next thing I knew I was dressed and standing outside on Morningside Drive, staring at E's windows. That seemed to help. I felt as if I could give it a fight. I squared my shoulders and began to walk. I don't remember the walk. I do remember that I found myself outside the garage, leaning in. Broadway traffic was swishing by. That was and has been constant background music, so it's no problem, except that it was terribly loud; but then everything was terribly loud for a long time after the war. I heard my voice in front of my head calling either "Monroe" or "Meyer," I'm very unclear which.

"Yo."

That I heard.

I repeated the name.

I know that a flashlight snapped on, picked at me. I stepped across the threshold and suddenly felt very solid, very real.

"Hiya Captain," he said, as if a visit from the brass were a nightly occurrence.

"What are you doing?" I said.

"This and that."

"Such as?"

"Oh keepin an eye on things."

"Don't you ever go home?"

"What for? Vito lets me sack in here and don't charge me no rent."

I was about to say so you found a home in the motor pool. I didn't. I inhaled oil, grease, Simonize, the one Esso pump.

"Am I barging in?" I said.

"Nah. I like a little company. You wanna sit in a jeep?"

"You have . . . a . . . jeep in here?"

"Sure. With a top and all. It belongs to Miss Donovan. She teaches art in Valley Stream on the Island. She's thirty-one and single and has an apartment on Claremont Avenue."

"You've got quite a file."

"I know my customers." He shared another piece of vital information: "She's a Jill in a Jeep."

"Yes. Well. . . ."

"You wanna sit in the jeep and shoot the shit?"

" . . . All right . . ."

"Follow the bouncing ball," he said cheerfully. He walked to the back and I followed. It was painted blue and did have a top and all. He opened the door on the passenger side and I got in; rank has its privileges. He got behind the wheel and switched on the radio; "It's a decent battery," he informed me. "Oh What a Beautiful Morning" came out of the dashboard followed by a deep, purry voice.

"Is that Lord Haw Haw?" I asked.

"Oh no. It's Symphony Sid."

"I see."

I sat back and let Sid introduce "Time After Time." Monroe spoke above the music.

"Rough duty, Captain?"

"What?" He remained quiet. I said, "Yes, rough . . ."

"The war's been over three years, Captain."

"I'm aware of that."

Sid said something about a dandruff shampoo and shifted quickly to Larry Clinton and a prewar "Dipsy Doodle." I sighed the way my father had sighed through the remilitarization of the Rhineland.

"The guys," Monroe said, "they said you hit the beach on D-Day."

"Plus one."

"You were a tech sergeant they said."

"Buck."

He was silent again and Bea Wain began to sing. I sat back and tipped a remembered garrison cap over my eyes. Bea Wain . . .

"I didn't think . . . I could do it . . ." I said. "But I did." I sighed again. "I never felt so confident in my life . . . Not since I was six . . ."

"Yeah?"

"Yes. They were dropping like flies, but nothing could touch me . . . I knew it . . . There wasn't even a letdown afterwards, like the textbook says . . . I felt even better . . ."

"Yeah?"

"And around Saint-Lo it got even better."

"Yeah?"

"I admit it. Christ, I admit it. Better. And *I* got better. Our half-assed lieutenant had to lean on *me*."

"I bet he was ROTC."

"OCS."

He nodded sagely; same difference.

"Speed this and Speed that, how do you read these gridpoints, Speed? What do you think, Speed?"

"Dopey bastard."

11

"We barreled across France and it was *me. I* took care of the men."

"The guys all said you wasn't chicken shit."

"I wasn't. I wasn't. Eisenhower took care of me; I took care of the men; it was simple."

"I seen him once."

"In England?"

"On Amsterdam Avenue and 118th Street. He was goin into a laundry with three shirts and a dress."

"Christ."

"He didn't look so hot."

"No? Christ, he knows, too."

"He does?"

"Yes, he does."

We were quiet. So was Symphony Sid.

"My buddy, Jackie Shadwesky, got one in the neck in the Bulge," Monroe said. "He was Soldier of the Month seven months in a row."

"Oh God. Do you hold it against me?"

"Nah, I hold it against Hitler."

"Would Jackie hold it against me?"

"I can't talk for him. I don't think so."

"Would he hold it against Eisenhower?"

"Hell*no*. He was taking orders just like you."

"But we *loved* it."

"Jackie loved bein Soldier of the Month. To each his own."

I slumped against the hard cushion. I breathed in motor pool and Miss Donovan's perfume. Upton, Benning, Sussex, Southampton . . . Sid. He was purring again. Larry Clinton moved over for Red Norvo. I kept sighing, unable to catch my breath. Czechoslovakia, Munich, Poland. Finally the breath came, I said: "After V-E I ran three towns, 250 square miles. I gave the nix Nazis democracy."

"They sure could use it."

"I didn't fraternize or touch their schnapps. My men didn't loot."

"I just got a camera. But I gave him a carton of cigarettes."

12

"That's OK . . . Then bang, it's over. Over. I'm in the Bronx, over a drugstore."

"All good things must end, sir."

"Looking down on Tremont Avenue. It wasn't *fair*."

"All's fair in love and war, sir."

"Bullshit. Excuse me."

"That's all right, Captain. You can't eat medals, can you?"

I sighed, for him and me. Red Norvo's xylophone rippled over the area. I shook my head, caught a breath, and said, "Did you enlist, Monroe?"

"Yop. I tried to get in the marines, but they turned me down."

I sat up. "Thank God," I said.

"Could be. I mighta got it in Guada-canal."

"Forget the Canal. Thank God you didn't serve under MacArthur, the sonofabitch."

"Yeah. I shall return."

"Don't say that."

"OK, Captain."

I turned off Red Norvo.

"MacArthur teargassed the bonus marchers in 1932, Monroe."

"Yeah?"

"Yes. *He* gave the order. Not Eisenhower. Eisenhower was merely taking orders from *him*. You said so yourself."

"I thought he took orders from Roosevelt."

"No way. *Hoover* to MacArthur, *then* to Eisenhower. Get it?"

"Sure."

"I'm going to tell you something, soldier. You think island hopping was such a brilliant goddam deal? Bullshit. Did you ever try to pull together a cranky fart like Montgomery, a pain in the ass like de Gaulle and a bunch of crazy Polacks?"

"Jackie Shadwesky was a Polack."

"Well, ask *him*."

"I can't. Anyways, you shouldn't get your balls in such an uproar, Captain."

"Well, just don't talk to me about MacArthur."

"OK, Captain."

"Fatuous sonofabitch."

13

"OK, Captain."

"Mama's boy. Goddam compensator."

"OK, Captain."

I sat back. Broadway swished its rhythmic tail. It wasn't all that noisy out there. I began to feel very tired.

"I think I'll take off now," I said.

"OK, Captain. Don't step on any mines."

Was he smiling?

I said, "I don't want to hear any more fucking nonsense about MacArthur."

He waved the bony shoulders.

"You can count on me, sir," he said.

I walked out swiftly, surely.

2

Two nights later. One? No, two. A heavy, opaque night. A night filled with M1s, carbines, panzerfausts, flights of P-38s:

"Hello, Monroe?"

"Who?"

"Monroe Meyer?"

"No way, this is John Q. Public."

"Sorry, wrong number."

"Wait a second. Is that you, Captain?"

"Yes. Is that you?"

"Sure. I was only kidding around."

"Don't kid on a communications device, Monroe."

"No, sir."

"What do you know?"

"What's to know?"

"What are you doing?"

"I was sacked out."

"In the jeep?"

"Nope, too hard. A '39 Packard."

"Who owns it?"

"Mr. Hilberg. He lives on Riverside Drive. He's got a very young wife."

14

"The old fart."

"He's a decent Joe. Minds his own business."

"Are you listening to Symphony Sam?"

"Sid."

"Yes. Are you?"

"For a while I was. Then I corked off."

"Great. While you're listening to Symphony Sid and cutting wood, I can't close my goddam eyes."

"There's nights like that."

"Not for you, dammit."

"I figure the world don't need me for a while, so what the h."

"Is that what you figure?"

"Uh huh. Jackie Shadwesky felt the same way."

"Why don't you leave Shadwesky out of this."

"OK, Captain . . . You still there, Captain?"

"Yes, I'm still here. Monroe?"

"Yeah?"

"Get into the jeep and drive over and meet me downstairs. I'll be on Morningside Drive and 116th, the uptown west corner. Got that?"

"I can't do that. Vito would have my ass in a sling."

"Monroe, what he doesn't know won't hurt him."

"In a way maybe . . ."

"That's an order, soldier."

Here is where it gets shadowy and dreamlike. Yet I know it happened:

To begin with, I got dressed in my uniform for the first time since 1946 (although I always carried it with me to all my fleabags, hanging it up carefully in a Val-Pack). Then with my security blanket on, I walked downstairs and my feet made terrific contact with the sidewalk. Yet I felt, I am sure, as buoyant and wise-guyish as in my palmiest days in Europe. (But not floaty; there's a difference.) Monroe was a good boy. He came careening around the corner and squealed to a rocking, grinning stop. I don't think he looked twice at the uniform. I glanced around; yes, I did that: there was a quarter moon hanging over Harlem, but

15

the Milky Way was very dim, the sky was low. I ground a cigarette under a buckled officer's shoe and climbed in.

"Let's head for the West Side Highway," I said crisply. "You know how to get on it?"

"Sure. Through the meat center."

True enough. Through the shadows of Broadway, down under the viaduct, west, twisting, spinning over cobblestones, past the huge parked semis, then like a cork under pressure, popping up onto the highway. He drove at about forty close by the river. I gazed at slices of it in fascination (which I do to this day), but now here and there it was gazing back.

"Jesus, the Rhine," I said.

"That's the Hudson, Captain."

"I know what it is, soldier."

I looked up ahead and the George Washington Bridge was a dappled streak against the sky. I felt for the railroad tracks on my shoulder. They were straight and cold.

"The bridge at Remagen," I said.

"Yes sir." (He did not inflect, clear his throat, grin.)

"Head for the goddam bridge, soldier; I want the bridge."

He nodded and gunned and we sped uptown and exited at 178th Street, looped up and around and approached the toll booth.

"Stop!"

We crunched to his patented, rocking stop.

"Go!"

He slammed gears and we shot ahead; he had read me perfectly. We barreled past the toll booth and a blank, staring face. "Step on it!" We fled across. He pointed up ahead to several signs.

"Which one, sir?"

I pointed to Route 4.

"That autobahn."

He hunched over the wheel and we accelerated down Route 4 through the black-forest night. Our tanks and trucks were behind us somewhere; keeping up was *their* problem. Everything was confusion here, but I was deadly calm. Lights flashed past, fingers

16

of flame licking at the B-17s which had done such good work. (Shadowy, dreamlike, *real.*)

Suddenly I reared up and yelled, "I don't want any looting or fraternizing!"

"You tell em, sir."

"No shooting of prisoners!"

"Hell *no.*"

"Show the bastards who *is* superior!"

"Show em in spades, sir."

"This is a goddam crusade, soldier, not a joyride!"

"And how, sir."

"Shadwesky's grandmother is in a goddam oven."

"You can say that again, sir."

"So is yours, soldier."

"Sure she is, sir."

"Shadwesky doesn't know it all."

"He'd be the first to tell you he's just a dumb Polack, sir."

"He was Soldier of the Month?"

"Seven months in a row, sir."

"I don't care if he was Jesus Christ of the Month. I've got my orders. A lot of good boys have bought it."

"Damn well told, sir."

"Don't run out of gas, soldier."

"I won't, sir."

"My ass is in a sling if we run out of gas."

"Don't worry, sir; I got a full tank."

I slouched.

"I don't want you to stop till we reach Frankfurt."

"What do we do then, sir?"

"How the hell do I know? I'll think of something."

He banged on the steering wheel. "Yes, *sir.*"

We reached Frankfurt—Paterson*—at approximately oh one

---

*I was able to transpose and *know* I was transposing with complete clarity; I've had that knack since I was four, but never with such power as in the winter of '48.

hundred hours. The lights of the city were spattered beneath us in the valley beside the autobahn. He slowed down and headed for an exit. And then I was suddenly, grindingly, excruciatingly tired. The sighing business started and I could hardly breathe. Between gasps, I finally managed: "Go back! Go back! Eisenhower wouldn't want us to outrun the column!"

(Head spinning even as I write)

I was shoving my nose above water. I was thrashing around down below. I was on the earth. The earth whirled and I grabbed. I was fighting. I was giving it one terrific fight, and because Eisenhower was in my corner (for all I knew, *also* fighting), I was hanging on—barely, but hanging on. This I know because I wrote it down in my little black book, the book that, after I had left England and crossed out the names and addresses of all my little lasses, was filled with my historic dates, towns, victories of the sweep across Europe. Now I was jotting down the sensations (mainly defeats) of *this* war. I think I had to pin it to the page to prove I was real. I must have suspected, even in the middle of this terrific turmoil, that someday I would require hard evidence of my reality down in the latrine. Over the years I have dipped into the little book, especially when the cat has grown too fat, and (wistfully?) reviewed the notes of the specific struggle. Here, for example, is a reality out of Dec. 31, 1948:

"Another *shvartz* year shot to hell . . . Grant in the bottom of his tomb could care less . . . Julia Grant is sad . . . Poor girl, married to a rummy . . . Riv Church ringing out the old, busting ears . . . Head exploding, aim head at church, topple same . . . Can clearly see left ear, congratulations . . . Can hear through nose, smell

18

through ears, wired incorrectly . . . Left knee snapping, shooting at right knee . . . What need shoulders for? . . . Why am I Finestone and not Geo Raft? . . . What has *he* done deserve being Raft? . . . Why Finestone in hell and Raft in swimming pool with starlet? . . . Georgie doesn't give shit for me, although saved his pool . . . Glad he didn't get lead in GWTW . . . Lungs falling out, bouncing on sidewalk, still breathing . . . Lungs ugly . . . M Loy's lungs ugly, she shouldn't look so superior . . . Left foot falling off, stomping on lung . . . Lung screaming . . . Hang on, buddy boy . . . John Jay is a snot . . . Battle of Harlem Heights . . . Washington does not give shit about me, only Eisenhower cares . . . Neck melting, how can head stay on? . . . Everything tall, thin, out of whack, am I El Greco? . . . Want my confidence, deserve my confidence . . . Faw down, go boom . . . Dogs big as elephants . . . Tongue burning up . . . Why tongues? . . . Tongues ugly . . . M Loy's tongue no bargain . . . French dirt no better than NY dirt . . . Skin peeling off, look like hell no skin . . . Want to spit out world . . . Finestone back, shithouse has him . . . Betrayal, Betrayal, Betrayal . . ."

That last was then a key to my condition. That betrayal. It shows up on page after page for almost two years; as I reconstruct, "Betrayal" must have undergirded the shithouse period. This is how I figure it: Creeping around, hanging on, even drinking and carousing before I moved up to Eisenhower country, all of this seemed to connect with my prewar days in the East Bronx, mainly my years at Morris High School. It was then that I would get my attacks of the adolescent blues and the only way I could comfort myself was with the thought that when I became an adult everything would be fine. Better than fine, *all right*. (In the war I wasn't an adult, I was a soldier.) I came to love the word "adult" in high school, and even on into NYU. (I didn't even accept the meaning of adultery until I was twenty.) Well, here I was now, an adult by any physical standard, and it was all wrong. It was a royal screwing. The ultimate bad joke: It was *adultery*. Thus: "Finestone up shit creek, no paddle . . . Betrayal!"

Ah well, at least I had the nights. That much had somewhat turned around. From being public enemy number one, the nights

19

had moved up to friendship. Helper. And very few people besides Eisenhower were helping me in those days, another part of the betrayal. I began to look forward to the nights as if they were the Saturday afternoon chapter at Loew's Prospect, except that I now knew how they would turn out; at last, for once since '46, here was something I could control (or so I thought, which was all that mattered). And this control gave the looking forward an extra dimension. So each night, wrapped in my uniform, railroad tracks burnished, I slouched beside my driver, the first person to listen to me, to obey, to give me no hard time since June, 1946. And as we drove deeper into enemy territory each night, I talked my exploding head off, which relieved some of the pressure.

Into the jeep, roarrrrrr, over the Hudson-Rhine, to Aschaffenburg:

"I have become totally pure over here, soldier. I am distilled water. Clean, pure and good. It rocked me at first because I was a thief before and I was used to that, comfortable with it. But now I am pure. I am honest."

"Honesty is the best policy, Captain."

The next night to *Wertheim*:

"I used ponies in high school. I copied Zack Levinson's homework. I let Mary Mahoney copy *my* homework. I lied when faced with those charges. I dissembled in college, used the same term paper for seven different courses. Santayana got me through Contemporary Civilization and I did *not* acknowledge. I touched four female thighs in Loew's Prospect, two at the Paradise, brushed a girdle as it squeezed by me to sit down. Each time I went home and jerked off. That is all finished. *Kaput.* As soon as I hit Omaha it was over. I have a brand new code, new standards, a blotless escutcheon. This is the real thing. I am virginally fastidious, I will not touch a drop of their corrupt schnapps, will not defile myself with their humped-out women."

"You keep your pecker in your pants and you'll never be sorry, Captain."

On to Bamberg:

"I was a misery as a son, a flop, a washout, a failure. They called

20

me their favorite son; and how did I pay them back? I tortured them. I sulked, I chafed, I wised off. I was a college man, I knew it all. I threw it up to them, I said 'I didn't *ask* to be born.' My father should have belted me; he bit his lip as it quivered. My mother told God she had been a good daughter so why was she punished? Don't you see, this makes it *up* to them. This purity, this goodness, this transformation is for *them*."

"They're the only mother and father you got, Captain."

Erlangen:

"But it is for me, *too*, soldier. I am too honest now to deny that. I *love* being pure, even though it was awfully rough at first. But nothing has ever come easy for me, soldier. So it is all the more precious. I love being the only guy in the outfit who will not fuck a German Wac. I love honesty; it fills me with true strength and joy. If Grable and Chili Williams both wanted to put out for me, it would be no contest, honesty and purity would win hands down."

"You get your gun off, Captain, and whadayou got? An empty gun."

To Nuremberg:

"Look at those flags, those banners, those fearful twisted crosses! Look at those mountains of light! Look at those bastards yelling their long heads off! Look at the pounding-cement heels! Look at the blond steel! Look at the thousand superior years! A bowlegged little *yid* has them all by the balls!"

"Bowlegged guys make the best shortstops, Captain."

MUNICH:

"Here's where it all began, soldier. Here. This half-assed city. Is this all? Is this what I shivered in my bed for? Is this why I prayed for the Russians to come in? Is this why my mother lit candles? Is this why my father rocked back and forth in *shul*? Look at those assholes swilling beer, lurching through the streets. Is this the cradle of the gods, the fucking wave of the future? IT IS A CROCK OF SHIT."

"Ain't it the truth, Captain?"

21

2

All right, I might as well get to it. I've handled a lot tougher things in my time (Let's hear it for the tough guy).

It was the day after we took Munich (which was Philadelphia). I decided I had to sack in all day in my furnished room. I had earned it, earned not facing the terrible-tasting world (I did much spitting in '46-'48, expelling an everpresent mass that was a cross between rotten eggs and mucilage). I was positive Eisenhower would approve my taking ten; he understood the importance of alternating advance with strategic hold. So I lay in my civvies on my mashed-potato bed, rested on battle-weary wrists, stared up at my bare bulb. I tried oh so hard, but never really closed my eyes. Here, from the perspective of fat-catness, is why:

I kept mixing my Finestone periods up. I would see myself in my room on Tremont Avenue. It was 1940 and I was listening to my mother and father talking through the night; then my father was crying and my mother was calming him, but he couldn't be calmed because Europe, *his* Europe, was gone and the end of the world was near. Then I was on Morningside Drive and my eyes were drooping, but my father was next door and I snapped awake. I spat on the floor beside the bed. (Come to think of it, that's what my father did, to my mother's horror, after the fall of France.) But now Manny had magically become Speed and was with Eisenhower in Europe, and my father at last was getting a decent night's sleep. As was Manny Finestone on Tremont Avenue. Then another leapfrog: to 1948, still with Eisenhower, and my breathing longer, deeper. And so it went: the phony war, France, the Crusade, Manny, Speed, my father, Eisenhower, victory, 1940, 1946, 1948, 1940. It became such a mishmash that I began to get the exploding head again. I got up, walked around the room, grasping for the necessary handle to all the bisecting, interlocking lines; it was like looking for the right geometry proof, only I had always been a rotten geometry student. But I also had always been a plugger, so I kept on pacing and grasping. And at eleven hundred hours, as it had nine months into the course at Morris, the handle, the key to the problem came thrusting through the wall from my father . . . I changed into my uniform, charged downstairs, marched over to the garage. Monroe was sitting in the '39 Packard. I smelled connections, solutions. He stepped out as I hurried up and tossed me a grinning salute; our rituals were precise and neatly worked out. I snapped one back.

"We gonna hit Austria tonight, sir?" said the acne child. I had him well trained by now, and he thoroughly enjoyed our nightly string of victories. (I always scrupulously paid for a full tank of gas when we returned; he told me that Miss Donovan never asked questions.)

"No. No more screwing around."

He stopped grinning. This was my no-looting-or-fraternizing voice. I enunciated very clearly.

"Listen to me hard, soldier. I have a very important question to ask. This fellow Hilberg, the one who owns this Packard; is he German?"

"He's a German Jew, Captain."

"Really?"

"Yop. Yes sir. He's a ref."

"When did he come over?"

"The early part of this year."

"You're certain?"

"Vito told me. He survived a concentration camp."

"Then he is not a refugee, soldier. Refugees came over *before* the war."

"Yeah? Well, he must be a displaced person then."

I reached back for my field commission face. He began to rock gently from one foot to the other.

"Soldier?"

"Yes sir?"

"Did you tell me he's got a young wife?"

"Yes sir."

"You know all about your customers. What's his wife's first name?"

"Dora, but he calls her Dawn."

"You're sure?"

"Sure. Vito told me. Dawn is more American."

"OK. What does Hilberg do for a living?"

"He manufactures ball-point pens."

"I see. Does he make these pens from scratch?"

"Sir?"

"Does he do everything in his own place, or does he farm out the work? Does he design them?"

"Well, he makes them."

"OK."

I walked to the Packard, peered in, walked back. I was fire and ice, I was filled with intelligence, I was plugged into my father and Wild Bill Donovan. I knew what I knew.

"Soldier," I said, "this man Hilberg is Hitler."

He continued to rock, like a child with a sore thumb. I said with excruciating calmness, "I do not want any nonsense about Berlin and bunkers and the like. I don't want to hear that. They live by the big lie. That's *their* code; if they live by it, do you think they *die* by it? The answer is no. So I don't want to hear any nonsense. Understood?"

"Yes sir," he said, "I won't give you any nonsense." He did a funny little thing then; he threw me a limp salute, then another, snappy one. As I review, as I push this spinning head, it occurs to me that I did not acknowledge that salute and I'm truly sorry (just one more of my truly sorrys), but at that moment I was preoccupied with the neatly dovetailing pieces of the equation:

"Hitler loved fancy cars and a Packard is pretty darn fancy. Plus it's a '39 Packard and that is the most significant year in his history . . . The young wife, Dora. Dawn. What is the opposite of Dawn? Evening. Eve. Eva. Try to follow me, soldier."

He nodded, rocked a bit faster.

"Ball-point pens. Little V-2s. And he designs them. Who else would design ball-point pens but a frustrated artist? Now then, what's his first name?"

"Arthur, sir."

"Of course. A. H. That kind of mind can never completely give up its identity."

Sliding around in my readjustment skin, I can still feel the strength in Captain Finestone that night. It is even helping my rotten head. The only comparable strength, the only equal power, drove my company through the Siegfried Line. Monroe was now lifting one foot, then the other, as if the garage floor were bubbling tar and he were barefoot. I continued to bore in, the strength accompanied by an all-over calmness.

"There's no problem in getting into this country," I said. "Didn't we let in Fritz Kuhn?"

"I guess we did, Captain."

"They never let go. My father could tell you how they never let go."

"No sir."

"Well, soldier?"

"It looks like you got a point, Captain."

"Thank you."

"Sir?"

"Yes, soldier?"

"What's Hitler doin here in New York?"

I was ready for that. I hadn't spent a whole day in the barracks not to be ready, and it had nothing to do with getting lost in the great city or planting a cancer in the Jewish population. It was quite simple:

"He's here to get Eisenhower."

He stopped rocking, planted both feet in the tar. He wiped his nose with the back of his hand. "Well," he said, "he came to the right place because New York is where Eisenhower is."

Out of the mouths of babes; the logic was impeccable. So was its conclusion:

"Soldier?"

"Yes sir?"

"We have to get the bastard before he gets Eisenhower."

"That's for dang sure, sir."

"I need your help, soldier."

"You name it, sir."

"You have the phone numbers of all your customers; get him down here."

"Yeah, I could do that, Captain."

25

"Call him, soldier. Tell him you ripped up his fender while you were parking another car."

Pain brightened the acne, and for that I have another truly sorry. He said, "I never ripped a fender in my life, sir."

"Tell him, anyway, soldier. If they can use the big lie, we can use a little one, a little white one."

"All right, sir . . . Suppose he don't come, sir?"

"Relax. He'll come. I know that mind. Our janitor was a Nazi. You busted a radiator, he came."

He smiled contentedly; oh, but I was the answer-man that night. I was fully prepared when he asked, "What's the deal when we get him here, Captain?"

Calm, so calm, but with a fire in the belly, I said, "We will go to Munich, soldier."

There was no confusion in my head, absolutely no confusion, and that absence of confusion is actually steadying my head at this moment as I reach back. I was an oasis, no, a parenthesis—pure, clean, filled with a clear liquid power that was ready to move according to the situation. I had that feeling of being a power-packed parenthesis as I hit the beach and for a week after. And that is what I was when Hilberg came hurrying into the garage. He made a bee line for his sweetheart. Monroe stood beside it, arms folded, as I had directed. Hilberg fondled all four fenders, returned to Monroe. (The only way to get the rest of this is to be terse, concise, specific, objective; well, not the only way: the easiest on me.)

He said, "Are you playing games mit me, Monroe?"

Monroe, under orders, said, "Call me Meyer."

"Vot?"

The power-parenthesis stepped out from behind the gas pump, one hand in his pocket.

"He said, 'Call me Meyer.' "

"Please?"

"Come off it," I said. "If the Luftwaffe doesn't knock out England, call me Meyer."

26

"Please?"

I stepped closer.

"Who said it?"

"How do I know?"

Closer still. I snapped on the flashlight; he narrowed the legendary eyes; they were bloodshot.

"Who said it?"

". . . Could Goering haf said it, maybe?"

"Cheez," said Monroe.

"Get in the car," I said.

"You vant money? I gif you my vallet."

"Get in."

Monroe opened the door. I took another power-packed step; he smiled politely and got in. I slid in beside him. Monroe ran around to the other side and bounced in behind the wheel.

"Let's hit the road, soldier," I said.

We backed out with a screech and he winced and I nodded to myself. We retraced the familiar dash to the bridge; this time, I paid the toll. We rolled across, got on the autobahn. He sat very stiff and straight. He didn't whine. I expected nothing less.

We drove on those smooth wheels for an hour and a half and entered Philadelphia-Munich.

"Where to, sir?"

"Just drive around."

We drove for another half hour. No one spoke, even when we stopped for a light. Munich whirled past. Finally I saw what I wanted. The Art Museum, brightly lit, high on its hill. Just what I needed. (I'm tempted to say I picked it for its Egyptian design, but that is modern me intruding; no, I think it had a chancellery look. But back to terse, objective:)

We drove up to the museum. "Hold it right here," I said. We stopped beneath the steep flight of steps.

"How do you like it, architect?" I said.

"I am in penss," he said. "In za morning I call my office and get you money."

"So you're in penss?" I said.

27

"Yes. I gif you a sousand free."

I was suddenly furious.

"I wouldn't use a ball-point pen if you gave me a million. I use nothing but *fountain* pens."

He smiled easily. "Fery nice, fery nice. No qvestion on qvality. I verk on folume."

Oh he was clever. I slouched back into my power, said, "Drive around to the back, soldier."

He drove behind the museum and stopped.

"Get out," I said, sliding quickly out. I waited.

He got out. Then Monroe. We stood in the moonlight behind the museum. My power-packed heart was beating.

"*Wie gehtz, Heil*berg?" I said.

"Hilberg," he said quickly.

"So Goering said 'Call me Meyer'."

"It iss logical. He vas head of za Luftwaffe."

"Jews know that, don't they?"

"Jews in par*ti*cular know zat. You take me back now? I promise I say nussing."

"Relax. Smoke an Old Gold. You survived a concentration camp. What can happen now?"

He shrugged. Oh, clever. . . .

I said, "How do you like Eisenhower?"

"A premier cheneral. A good fellow."

"I'll wager you think he's German."

"It iss a Cherman name."

"He's *half* German, buster. His mother was from *Switzerland.*"

"Dot's *gut.*"

Very cool. No ranting, no raving . . .

I tipped my overseas cap a little lower over my forehead.

"You were never a Nazi," I said. "Nix Nazi?"

He shook his head very firmly.

"A Chew iss not a Nazi," he said.

I slapped him across the face. The mustache-less area twitched. He glanced at Monroe. Monroe was rocking only slightly. Then he smiled. *Smiled.*

28

"All right, you got me," he said. "I am not a Chew." Monroe froze.

"Isn't that nice?" I said. "What else is new?"

"Vell listen, you do za best. It's easier for zem to come over here now, issn't it? Who could stay in East Chermany? Zo I said vat I said. No harm to anyvun, iss it?"

"Nix Nazi?"

"No, dot I svear. I neffer knew zose terrible sings, neffer."

"Hell, nobody knew. Did you ever help a Jew?"

"I should lie? I von't lie. Dot vas fery difficult. Mit za government. You belief *you* help zem?"

I slapped him again. He did not touch his face. He tried the stare. I stared back.

"How is Eva?" I said.

"Who?"

"Is it true you eat her shit?"

He trembled slightly.

"So the Emperor of the World eats shit," I said.

He turned to Monroe, Monroe turned away. He turned back, squared his shoulders. He was about my height. I stopped slouching. I said, "Hear this: You gave it to Private John Shadwesky. To his grandparents. To my grandparents. To Call-me-Meyer's grandparents. You ruined my father. I find you guilty."

I opened the car door and pulled out the can of gasoline. I unscrewed the cap.

"Vot's going on?" he said; his voice was quavering now. I stepped in and hit him from the neck down with the gasoline. I wanted the face to watch, to go last. He gasped, shivered, said not one word. The fumes wafted over me and I could barely breathe. I reached into the breast pocket of my Eisenhower jacket and took out my Zippo and spun the wheel. It flared.

"Chew bastid," he said.

I nodded and stepped closer.

At that precise moment, Monroe moved. He jumped between us, went for his neck, slammed him into the car and they went down. Monroe was clawing and screaming into his face.

29

I began to sail up, up into the moonlight, only it was now a black light and I was part of it and—

Balls. I fainted.

3

This is where objective gets shot to hell.

I was aware of an incredible amount of twisting and turning. The whoosh of cars. More twisting and turning. Then a long, blessed, leveling out. Then I was aware of nothing. The odor of oil, gas, grease, perfume must have brought me around. I came to on the front seat of the jeep. My tie had been loosened, the top button was unbuttoned, my collar was soaked with perspiration. But my head was not a balloon, nor was it exploding. (My mother's shock theory? She always claimed that if her brother had a big winner, it would cure him; he never had a big winner.) Monroe was sitting beside me. Symphony Sid was purring out of the dashboard. Monroe handed me my overseas cap.

"It got a little dirty," he said.

"Everything under control?" I said.

"Oh sure."

I inhaled a lot of garage. "Where . . . is . . . he?"

"I took him home."

I rubbed my face and smelled the gasoline; it reminded me of my father's first Nash. But my head was almost normal (as it is now). I looked around, at the other cars, the pump, looked back at Broadway. Something very odd: the distortions, the El Greco vision I had carried around for two years, had cleared up; everything looked right.

"I think I might have killed him," I said.

"It sure looked like it, Captain."

"Monroe," I sighed, "maybe he isn't Hitler."

"And maybe he is, Captain."

I thought that over as Sid purred away, I believe, about Boyd Raeburn.

"Then," I said, "why didn't you finish him?"

"Well, sir," he said, "I ain't a killer at heart. And this way, he can stew in his own juice the rest of his life."

Ah, acne child, the nix Nazies do not stew; dot's a fact. I didn't say it, for I could still see him clawing and screaming.

"Why didn't you let *me* finish him?" I said softly.

"They'd have cut your balls off, sir, seein you're an officer."

"I appreciate that, Monroe."

"Jackie woulda done the same," he smiled.

"I guess he would."

I opened the door of the jeep, the vehicle that had covered so much ground, and got out. I stuck my overseas cap in my belt.

"Be good now, Monroe," I said.

"If I can't be good, I'll be careful," he said.

"If you can't be careful, name him after me."

He slapped the steering wheel.

"See you tamorra night, Captain?"

"Maybe. I'll call first."

I walked out, Symphony Sid trailing after.

There it is . . .

I never called, of course. I sat on a bench across the street from Eisenhower for two whole days. Then I packed up my uniform and took the subway to the Bronx and after accepting my mother's money gave the uniform to her (but not the bars). She folded it up with camphor balls and put it away in the trunk with my first pair of longies and my *bar mitzvah* suit. Then I came back to New York and registered for an M.S. in business at Columbia under the GI Bill. I kept my room on Morningside Drive.

For about a year, I saw Monroe around the area, but we never spoke. I would nod, he would smile, but then he smiled at everybody; we would pass. Then one day I didn't see him anymore. I asked Vito about him and he said the little jerk had gone back to the army. (To Germany?)

A few times I saw Hilberg on Broadway. We didn't look, we didn't *not* look. We each walked into the Columbia crowds.

31

All very well, but *did it happen?* (Crazy is crazy, but *come now . . .*)

Fair question, but not at all pertinent. True enough, it did not appear in my little black book, so maybe it never did happen. But, as Monroe would say, might say, maybe it did. After all, far more implausible, impossible things had. Hadn't little Manny Finestone been plucked up out of his wet bed on Tremont Avenue and been flung across Germany? Hadn't he risen from nothing to stripes to bars? Hadn't he conquered the unconquerables? Hadn't he avenged his grandparents? Hadn't he given his father a little peace? Hadn't he turned into the slouchy, leaning-into-his-combat-boots Speed? Who would have believed *that?* Ah, one person would and did. And if Eisenhower could work such magic, if he could breathe not just life, but *living*, into the world's greatest yearner, couldn't he pull *this* off? Couldn't he set it up, then step in and save his boy? Wouldn't he?

So maybe it wasn't Hitler. Then again, maybe it was. And if it was, well then, forever and ever, he is doomed in the America of Eisenhower and Finestone!

Christ, I think I've nailed it down. . . .

32

PART

Foxholes in the Sky

Let's get to my father.

Shimon Finestone.

I remember him as a great reader, a fan of Abe Cahan and Sholom Aleichem; he liked Emil Ludwig and Lion Feuchtwanger; he had respect, if not affection, for Mike Gold. The point is, he read. Then all of a sudden he turned, he began to say the hell with them all. This was about my sophomore year at Morris. Oh, he still insisted on good marks, and all the "real" subjects; the "trade school" courses were for ditch-diggers. He bragged to all his brothers when I won a Regents scholarship and sent off a letter to Galicia, explaining how I was the equal of any of their talmudic hotshots. But he had definitely turned; he was against the liberal arts. And I think I have finally figured it out.

No, it was not the depression psychology which dictated *practical* college programs (he always agonized over the fact that he couldn't handle prescriptions in the cut-rate drugstore that saved our life). Nope, what turned him off the world of the cultured, well-stocked mind was his own sense of betrayal. He had put all his trust in Emperor Franz Joseph and the Kaiser, both of whom ruled the citadels of the finest in art, music and letters; he had trusted, even, I think, loved, because they were good to the Jews. And that trust and love had been assigned to the people of the Emperor and the Kaiser. Even the higher class bastards in Russia had their cultured points. Then it all collapsed. In the thirties his trust, his deepest heart, was broken. And the world of the mind, the humanistic spirit, was as lousy as a bad batch of Taystee Yeast. It was about then that he first began to spit on the floor, driving my mother crazy, but naturally he had to get that gall and wormwood up; he never did.

In the summer of 1939, I announced that I would major in English at NYU. He spit and said—and it was the only time I ever heard sarcasm from him—"Maybe you'll study how they gave away Czechoslovakia." I carefully explained that *that* involved political science and I was concerned with English *literature*. He walked away from me and never mentioned the subject again. Nor did he ever, I'm certain, veer back to the genteel world he had once loved.

And I began to agree with him. In the war, that is, as I metamorphosed into Speed Finestone and discovered the central truth of squeezing the trigger, not jerking, and learned that when I said something, which I rarely had up to 1943, the men around me tended to listen. *That* I loved. So I was ready when Eisenhower clinched the deal for me: if he could harness Montgomery, de Gaulle, Giraud, the Poles, the Dutch and the Belgians, if he could tame Patton, if he could mold all of them into victory, then literature was truly feces for the birds, and what my future needed—in 1949—was the handling of men. At Columbia Business I majored in Management Science.

Only one problem: I hated the courses. I hated Statistical Methods and Economic Research. I hated Applied Multivariate Statistics. I hated Policy Determination and Operations. But, and I quote the elder Finestone: "Who ever said you have to *love* school?" So I hung in, the way, at Morris, I had stayed with geometry and trig. And, as at Morris, I even developed a kind of satisfying martyrdom. I know it pleased my father then for he forever believed in "seeing it through." And I was sure, in a transferable way, that I was now pleasing the man across the street, who was putting up with his own obstacle course: if he could take handshaking, buttering up the alumni, bitching, backbiting, stroking the trustees, then I could plow through my tables and functions and utter, utter boredom. I got my Bs.

July, 1950.
Morningside Heights quivered beneath my solidly planted heels. Harken to the little black book:

36

"Whatthehell we doing Korea? . . . Would FDR go in? . . . Half-assed war, but. . . . Reenlist? . . . No . . . E here, so Speed here . . . Oh shit, MacArthur again, *he has returned* . . . Some joke, MacA. heads up *unified* command; *he* is command . . . very very pissed off HST didn't even *ask* E if wants job, genuine kick in ass. OK, see what Duggie does in war of attrition, just wait . . .

"Scrambled Eggs takes Seoul, bit g-d deal, so could my grandmother . . .

"Home before Xmas? In pig's eye! . .

"Aha, Chinx in, now see what Mama's boy made of. Home before Mother's Day? . . .

"WHAAAT? E BACK TO EUROPE? J. H. KREIST!"

I got that last item as I walked out of Managerial Accounting. A vet named Arnold Venturi told me and added, well that's one way to get rid of him. In the old days I would have swallowed it. I told him to go fuck himself and walked down to the Gold Rail and drank three bottles of beer.

From then on, Korea took a backseat. I watched and waited and fought it out on the home front:

"Doesn't *have* to accept . . . Done enough . . . Hell, duty is duty . . . E.T.O. primary theater, ask FDR, Marshall, Shimon . . . But can never go back, never same . . . So? Duty still Duty . . . OK, reenlist? Go with him? . . . Never work, MacA. grab you for Korea . . . Shit . . . He'll go, Finestones never have any luck . . . So what, GROW UP ALREADY!"

He went. In February of '51. Head of NATO. Somebody who never even heard of hedgerows took over at Columbia. I spent an afternoon staring out over the rooftops of Harlem.

2

I had steeled myself, thought I was ready. But you never are. Oh, there was no real danger of falling back into the shithouse; I was too far along for that. But I felt a sense of complete abandonment. The closest to it was the day my father took me to kindergarten and left me there. I remember punching the teacher, Mrs. Kelly, in the leg. I was really, Karen Horney tells me, angry at my father. Well *now*, to put it bluntly, I was pissed off as hell at Eisenhower. If I could bull my way through statistics and operations research, the least he could do was plug away at his miseries. The more so since I was where I was mainly *because* of him. *Unfair. Again.*

I withdrew from Columbia.

I looked around and discovered that an Admiral Connolly was the president of Long Island University in Brooklyn. Perfect. Sign on with the navy and give it to Eisenhower good. I went down to Brooklyn and registered, and, to grind it in some more, said the hell with business and management, and enrolled in the affiliated Brooklyn College of Pharmacy; *that* would have delighted my father, and it was suddenly very important to delight my father.

I answered an ad in the *Times* and moved out of Morningside Heights, another pay-back of sorts. A Mrs. Minna Cartwright, some kind of widow—maybe war, maybe grass—had a huge apartment on 58th Street off Sixth Avenue, rented out three of the rooms to "quiet, mature business men." She was so impressed with my combat credentials that she made an exception in my case.

Here we go again . . .

Pharmacy didn't thrill me either. Organic Chemistry bemused, eluded, bored. Ditto Zoology. I toughed out my grades—this time Cs—but for the first time in my academic life became the wise guy of the class, the Murray Hershkovitz of Morris, with a war under his belt. It would have horrified my father, whose head wagged with sadness when Mr. Hershkovitz told him of his burden; but I couldn't seem to stop myself even though I wanted to please Shimon so much in my LIU phase. My biggest *shtick*, in Pharmacology I, after a lousy recitation: "Yeah, but I make a great egg salad sandwich." It brought down the house and I got a glimmer of Murray's power. After class, Dr. Weissboard, a man who would have terrified me in the old days, noted that I was clicking on only fifty percent of my cylinders, but that I had the stuff in me and he knew I could do the job. I said uh-huh, we used motivational psychology in fighting Rommel, so *please*... turned around and walked out. He never brought it up again. Combat men in school had a sensational edge in those days.

Back on 58th Street it became increasingly clear that Mrs. Cartwright was available, willing and intrigued. Also not bad.* I had not formed any liaisons since my time in England before the invasion, and was certainly ready (even began to suspect that the automat on 57th Street, my personal mess hall, dumped the converse of saltpeter in its chicken a la king). But my wartime standards held fast. When her velveteen robe dropped open as she took my rent money, I gazed out the window. When she popped in all dolled up, with a hot cup of Ovaltine at midnight, I thanked her and said goodnight. The renewed sense of purity *that* gave me took some of the agony out of pharmacy and the daily safari to Brooklyn.

And something else. I was easing up toward Eisenhower. No question. I could see as the weeks and months slid by that no one else could possibly do the job in Europe. He was clearly the indispensable man, could even handle Zhukov if and when. I had to admit, too, that if Truman had tapped him (thus atoning for the Korean blunder), then FDR and my father would give him their blessing. So who was I to gripe? Yes, I was feeling good about him again. Best of all, I was blessed with one of my all-time favorite days. Here it is in black and white, one of the few times the book did not shout the outhouse miseries:

"April 11, 1951! Remember this date, buddy! MacArthur out on iron ass! HST shows what we're made of! Ridgway will do great job! Keep his trap shut! E never pull insubordinate horseshit one million years!"

I was flying. The night after oedipal old soldiers faded away I invited Mrs. Cartwright out to dinner. I took her to the Britanny

---

*During my pure periods, I scrupulously avoided "snatch," "pussy," "nooky," "poontang," "ass," "tail," "dog." I did, however, use "action" and "not bad."

on Ninth Avenue and on the wall posters I outlined with exquisite detail my role in the liberation of France (unlike the stereotype, whom I never met, I was not always a clam when it came to the war). When we returned to the apartment, I shook her hand, said *à bientôt* and retired gloriously to my room.

"SHIMON FINESTONE VINDICATED! 1933: BONUS MARCHERS FIRED ON! 'SOME DAY MACARTHUR WILL BE PUNISHED FOR BEING SO LOUSY TO POOR, HUNGRY VETERANS'!"

"THIS IS THE DAY."

I had read somewhere that Truman would have stepped aside for Eisenhower in '48. I had also read that there was a Democratic boomlet for him at the time. So I always took the stories about Republican interest in him for '52 as so many latrine rumors. Also, interest had to cut *both* ways; wasn't he Marshall's boy who was FDR's boy who was Shimon's boy? On January 7, 1952—I remember it like December 7, 1941—I received the news as I came up out of the BMT on 57th Street.

"IKE WOULD OK GOP NOD"

I went on a two-day binge. Most of it is a blank to this day, but the finale is not. I wound up at the bar of the Hawaiian Room of the Hotel Lexington. I would have to say it connected up with Truman and 1948 and the memory of taking on that Dewey-Hoover man; also, it must have been a reaching-back, to Pearl Harbor, where, despite MacArthur's intrusion, in the long pull, Eisenhower and I really began. I didn't get into any fights that night. I drank quietly, then shuffled back to 58th Street, studying the sidewalk. In my room, in Mrs. Cartwright's spotless, Republican apartment, I slugged at the book:

"Now on McCarthy's team! . . . FDR puking in grave! . . .
Shimon too, always said don't trust them . . . WHYWHYWHY?
Corrupted by big $? . . . Found out in Europe can never go back? . . .
Afraid MacArthur get nod? Love to believe, can't . . . No excuse,
none, none! WHY, E, WHY"*

The next morning I called the Registrar's office at LIU and told
them I refused to make egg salad sandwiches for the rest of my
life and hung up (I knew my father would understand). Then I
called Samuel Finestone a.k.a. Garth Lexington.

2

"Yeah?" he said.

"Samuel?"

"Who?"

"Samuel Finestone?"

"This," said the voice with icicles, "is Garth Lexington. I
suggest you have the wrong number."

"Wait, it's me, Speed."

"Who?"

". . . Manny."

"Holy Jesus! Will wonders never cease! To what do I owe the
honor?"

"Can we talk, Samuel?"

"If you will bear in mind that my name is Garth, yes, we can
talk."

"OK, Garth, now?"

"Sure now. We'll have coffee. Bless my miserable soul,
Manny."

"Speed. If you can be Garth, I can be Speed, goddamit."

I took the subway down to 14th Street, got out at 13th and
walked to University Place. My big brother lived in a dirty-
almost-brown graystone. I walked through a cement lawn down

*I never called him Ike. That was a superior, sneaky slap at our European
background, at the Jew in the woodpile.

41

to the basement apartment. I hefted the knocker, a gargoyle, beside the nameplate that in raised letters said GARTH LEXINGTON, MANHATTAN PLAYERS, and let it drop twice.

"*Entrez.*"

I walked into a huge studio decorated with Group Theatre heroes—Garfield, Luther Adler, Kazan, Franny Farmer. Garth-Samuel looked up, twisted his head with his onstage flick, set down the white enamel coffee pot, strode over and gave me a powerful, patting hug. We stepped back and looked at each other. He was a little taller—but I chalked that up to the elevator shoes—a bit thinner, and the head was just as large as I remembered; he always said it was his greatest physical asset, especially when the pricks tried to upstage him. The hairline which had once been smoothly widow-peaked was now high and jagged. Otherwise he was the Samuel who had had the leads in *Ah, Wilderness!* and *Having Wonderful Time* at Morris, the black sheep who had once caused my gently grieving father to ask my mother if she had ever given in to Harry Richman.

"Sit a little," he said. "Take Mama's chair."

I sat on the well-remembered green kitchen chair; I'm sure she gave it to him over my father's objection; Samuel was forever leaving home and coming back, then leaving again with a piece of furniture, a bribe—a remembrance of things past, my father would say to my mother. She would smile inwardly. She figured him to be another Muni or Schildkraut or at the very least Cesar Romero, the one movie hero who appealed to her. I always thought he was a natural Hugh Herbert, although I'd never tell him, for he considered himself—and looking back that must have been the problem—another Robert Montgomery.

"How's she doing?" I said, sipping his coffee.

He straddled her chair; he always straddled chairs.

"You might check once in a while," he said.

"I know. Don't lecture me."

We drank silently. Samuel—er, Garth—waited; he was a great waiter, often told me it was the key to his talent, long before Brando discovered the trick.

42

"Nice coffee," I finally said.

"Uh huh. How's school? She told me you went back."

"I quit."

He swallowed and waited. To his credit he did not say, again? Or, what now, professional student? He waited. I said, "I'd like to join Manhattan Players." He absorbed that, rolled it around with the coffee. Then he said, "What the hell can you do?"

"I don't know. Anything."

He did a little business with sipping and swallowing. He nodded professionally.

"I always said you were a good type. Didn't I always say that?"

"Yes, you did."

"Not that you ever listened."

"No, I never did."

"One thing I know is theater, Manny. Speed. I never knew shit about anything else, but *that* I knew. The old man wouldn't give an inch on it, but I knew theater. *Know* it. And you were a good type."

"What can I say? You must be right."

He tipped forward a little.

"Hit me, Manny, you never gave a shit for the theater."

"Speed."

"Yeah, Speed. You never did."

"Right is right. Again you're right."

"Well then?"

"Well what?"

"What's a war hero gonna do in the theater?"

"Fuck you."

He stuck his head high up on his neck, his Bob Montgomery thing.

"Bingo. I deserve that," he said.

"Ah shit, skip it," I said, getting up. He swung the chair out from under, thrust it behind him; it fell; I recalled that from *Waiting for Lefty.*

"Jesus," he said, "will you wait a second? At least you used to have a little patience."

"I used to have a lot of things."

43

He was using his inch and a half of elevator shoe now; he had always been a different kid in thick red-rubber-soled saddle shoes, and the Adlers gave him the same lift in the head.

"You will stay," he said. "I'm going to tell you something that's straight out of O'Neill. The old man made me promise to take care of you."

"Like hell he did."

"Well he did and you are not going to cheat me out of being a noble big brother."

Oh God, he could always zigzag, with just the balanced touch of truth and knowing grin; I don't know why he ever needed a plot. I shook my head, held out my hand. He grabbed it, gave me the firm, clean shake he had taught me when I was seven.

"Can I move in here, Garth?" I said.

Here is the size of it:

Eisenhower had conned, used, *betrayed* me. Above all that, a *basic part* of it, he was now on Joe McCarthy's team, and I do not mean the Yankees. That was the most bitter pill of all. He was allied with the man who accused my poor, sweet father, accused *me*, of twenty years of treason. I couldn't, *wouldn't* take that. OK, I'd move in with my conscientious-objector brother. Phase one. Phase two: I'd go to work for the outfit that would drive Eisenhower-McCarthy nuts.

Manhattan Players. They acted, re-acted, listened, prepared, related according to the Method as proclaimed by a *Russian*. Stanislavsky. On top of that, the Method was filtered down to us through the red-hot mind of Marge Wallabee who had knelt at the great one's feet in Moscow in 1925 and was the founding mother and money bags of M.P. And had given, worked for, fought for Tom Mooney, the Scottsboro Boys, Sacco-Vanzetti, the Bonus Marchers, the infant UAW, you name it. The one thing that convinced me McCarthy wasn't so stupid was that he never called her down to Washington; she would have murdered him.

All right, I was pushing back. I was a part of a Theater with Conscience . . . I was rooming with Antiwar Garth. He lost no time in assigning me *My Life in Art* and *An Actor Prepares* by Constantin S., also *Toward a True American Theatre* by M. U. Wallabee, published at the author's expense. He then gave me a three-page short answer quiz on each one. I had always been an exemplary test-taker, and got two 90s and a 95 on the Wallabee. I was ready. Garth slid into the elevators and took me down to Marge's on Fourth Street near Washington Square. She was little and round and crossed her dimpled legs up to here and smoked Between the Acts in a holder. She inhaled and coughed and looked me over as Garth balanced on his Adlers.

"He has a Nick Conte thing around the eyes," she announced finally.

I didn't know what to say, so I looked at Garth.

"Do that again," she said.

"What?"

"That."

"I didn't do anything."

"You glanced at your elder brother. Do it again."

I glanced.

"That is very spontaneous," she said to Garth, who nodded. "Even the second time. He won't have to unlearn any shit."

"Didn't I tell you?" said Garth.

She regarded me again.

"What do you think of periods?"

"What kind of periods?"

"The kind that writers burden us with."

"I don't think anything of them."

"I hope you mean that."

"I do."

"Then that's good. Always ignore periods. They are the actor's archenemy. Stanislavsky detested periods. How do you like Vincent Fremont?"

"Do you mean John Fremont?"

"I mean Vincent Fremont."

"I don't know any Vincent Fremont."

"He's you. How do you like it?"

I looked at Garth again; he was doing Robert Montgomery with his head. I said, "My name is Speed Finestone."

"No it's not, it's Emanuel Finestone."

I stood up and said, "Goodnight, Miss Wallabee, you can shove Manhattan Players up your ass," and headed for the door. Garth was there in a prance, corrugating his forehead.

"Je-*sus,* take it easy, Sergeant York. She was only testing, and you have to get a bug up your backside; weren't you only testing, Marge?"

"In a way," she said. "But Garthie, don't call him Sergeant York; he doesn't care for that, either."

I turned and walked slowly back. I sat down again.

"Miss Wallabee," I said, "I'm not so sure about this acting business. I just thought there was *some*thing I could do in your company."

"He's a neat little writer," Garth said quickly. "Reactionary, but clever."

"Don't worry your head," said Marge. "Everyone does everything in Manhattan. We dive in, we immerse, we grow, we blossom. This we do, or die."

"She's not kidding," said Garth.

"Thank you, darling," she said. To me: "You'll do whatever we tell you to do."

She waved a Between the Acts. Interview over. Garth kissed her on the cheek and steered me out. A few minutes later, at the Open Door over a beer, he said, "You're in; she's crazy about you. But, rule number one, absolutely no *shtupping.*"

"I'll try to restrain myself."

"I mean it. I know some nuts who think she's the greatest fuck in New York. Don't ask me why. But they don't last one week

46

after they get in. She's a Venus fly trap. Just remember."

I drank my beer. I sighed a little. Counterattacking wasn't going to be all peaches and cream.

2

Eisenhower's campaign proceeded apace and so did mine. I threw myself into deep water, soaked, kicked, began to swim. And, as Marge had promised, I did a little of this and a little of that. Everything from sweeping up in their building at 16th Street west of Fifth to writing blurbs, to going to classes run by Marge, Garth and a Lucille Ostrow. In addition to the Method, I was drilled on the function of an antiimperialist, antiwar, antiexploitive, people-yes theater. As at Morris, I always made eye contact with my teachers and nodded a lot. I got along fine.

In June, in a 14th Street cafeteria, I read in the *Post* that MacArthur was slated to be the keynote speaker at the Republican Convention. I went to the men's room and threw up. That night I read *The Lower Depths* over and over until I was vaguely aware that Garth was sliding it out from under my forehead. The next day, for the first time, I took a good look at Lucille Ostrow as she explained the anticlerical thrust in Odets. She had pulled-back hair coiled into a tight braid on top of her head, so tight it gave you a headache. No makeup. Huge eyes behind rimless glasses. Baggy, button-down shirt, collar buttons unbuttoned, baggy chinos, web belt, no socks, scuffed-up loafers. She was perfect, everything MacArthur would have detested. So would Eisenhower, his new *buddy*. After the lecture, I went up to the teacher and asked if I could take her to lunch, strictly dutch. She thought it over very carefully, as if I had asked about Brecht's hidden agenda, then said, carefully, "Why not?"

We walked to a coffee shop across the street from Barnes and Noble. We ordered hamburgers and she studied every bite; I began to wonder if she was telling me something about concentration. When she had finished and was studying the coke glass, she said, quite casually, "Well, do you feel you're making progress?"

I drank my coffee and said I didn't know.

47

"That's honest at least."

I set the cup down. "Honest," I said. "Spontaneous. Real. Is that the only kind of shit you people talk?"

She fingered the glass. She absorbed, sifted, dissected, reflected.

"Well well," she murmured. "So, the fires have been banked."

"Have they?"

"It would seem so."

"Don't worry so much about me, OK?"

She leaned forward on her elbows.

"Of course we worry about you, you idiot. Do you think we're the uptown bastards?"

I gave her one of my spontaneous looks.

"I didn't mean to yell," I said.

"Oh for heaven's sake, Speed, don't apologize. Spit it out and don't apologize." She touched the back of my hand on the table. She had a surprisingly sweet smile. "Use it."

"Use what?"

"Your resentment. We piss you off. Use that hostility. It's a gift, but don't waste it."

"Oh shit," I sighed.

"Speed, honestly, do you think we're exploiting you? Conning you?"

"Christ, I don't know . . . Christ, I came to *you* . . . Maybe . . . I don't know . . ."

"How do you *feel*?"

"Honestly?"

"Lovely. Yes."

"You're all a pain in the ass. Especially you."

"Lovely."

"Oh shit, lovely."

She touched the back of my hand again.

"Would you like to work on a scene with me?"

". . . I don't know anything . . ."

"Would you? I don't ask *every*one."

"Then why ask me?"

"You're real, Speed. Speed, you are Moe in *Awake and Sing*."

I walked from Garth's to the apartment she shared with a genuine working girl, Alicia Fargo, on the fourth floor rear at Sixth Avenue near 12th Street. Alicia was at the Sheridan squirming over Brando as Marc Antony, so the place was ours. They went in for much Diego Rivera.

"Let's not worry about the script," she said.

"Whatever you say."

"Don't be so damn accommodating. Let's establish a working base, a spine."

"OK."

"It seems to me," she said thoughtfully, "that you would have perfect emotional recall as Moe."

"Why should I?"

"He is a bitter veteran."

"I'm not bitter."

She gazed at me through the magnifying glasses and assimilated.

"Maybe you should be," she said.

"I don't agree with that."

"Are you always so resistant? Never mind. Eliminate that question. Grasp the resistance. Infuse it into Moe."

"How the hell do I do that?"

"Don't you listen to me in class?" The sweet, petite smile.

"Yes, as a matter of fact, I do. I still don't—"

"All right, you're still holding back. No big deal. Let's improvise. You hate the world, Speed, especially my guts."

"You're a pain in the ass, but I kind of like you," I smiled.

"Don't be a smart bastard. Go out of the room and prepare."

"How?"

She was very patient.

"Reach back. Try this on for size. You are Dick Frankensteen and I'm Henry Ford; better yet, Ford's billy club, Harry Bennett. Harriet Bennett. All right, my goons have kicked the shit out of you."

49

"So?"

This time she sighed, neatly.

"You're Picasso," she said. "I'm a Fascist pilot diving on Guernica."

I thought of the picture at the Modern, but looked at her blankly. She nodded with great economy.

"I warned you," I said. "Zero."

"Speed," she said gently, "I am a great teacher. I will *not* accept that. All right, whom do you admire? Look up to? *Honestly*. I promise I will not hold it against you. Babe Ruth?"

"Shit no."

"Gable?"

"Come on."

"Lindbergh? I won't be insulted."

"I can take him or leave him."

"Loosen up, Speed, who?"

"Well . . . I served under Eisenhower."

"Oh God."

"I just said I *served* under him . . ."

"Oh Speed."

"I had to take orders from the man. Jesus . . ."

She lensed me, arms folded.

"You are Eisenhower. You are at the front. You are in a German farmhouse. You hear a knock at the door. You open the door. It is Eva Braun. I am Eva Braun. I am wearing a bathing suit cut down to my *pupick*. If you will repossess your German heritage and make a separate peace, I will put out for you—"

She was screaming for help when the two gentle boys from down the hall burst in and pried me loose.

We worked on *Golden Boy, Paradise Lost, Rocket to the Moon* and, to show me she wasn't married to Odets, *The Petrified Forest*. She told me it was the best thing Bogart ever did, far truer than the revisionist clowns he later played. That stuck an apple in my throat and I suggested I tackle the Leslie Howard part. No copping out, she said, Duke Mantee. Then she set it up.

"What do you know about Rasputin?"

"He was *some goniff*."

"All right, I 'll accept that."

"You will?"

"Yes. I *want* you to re-act. You have a good, natural reaction, but you must build on it. You will react to me. Duke will react to Gaby."

"How?"

"I'm getting to that. Please let me proceed at my own pace. I will be the Empress. Don't worry, I can handle it. All right. I have just summoned you. I want you to tell me how to run the war. That is surface. Beneath the surface is the scene. Now, go out and prepare."

I walked out of the room. I shut the door. I also shut out the *goniff* because by now I knew a little about emotional recall; I decided this was the time to use it. I dredged up little Manny and Merrill Pillsbury, the Student Council Secretary at Morris and the girl who was reputed to have the cleanest panties in the East Bronx but reserved only for the basketball team. Then I cheated. I grafted Speed Finestone onto the nocturnal emitter. I sank into the combination. I opened the door. She was reclining on the couch. I walked over.

51

"Nicholas is at the Front," she said, looking past my shoulder.
I ran an appraising eye over Merrill Pillsbury. I felt a twinge.
"Is that what you wanted to tell me?" I said.

Languidly: "How dare you?"

I knelt beside the couch. Merrill always wore a white blouse
with a lace collar. I unbuttoned the blouse. I reached a hand inside.
Merrill did not wear a bra!

"You disgusting whoremaster," she said. Merrill began to
massage my hand against her breast. I was definitely feeling
something. Definitely.

"Should we attack in Siberia?" she said, massaging.

"No, we should attack in the Black Forest."

Merrill's hands were on my belt.

She said, "I think the enemy will attack at Brest Litovsk."

I continued to massage as she unbuckled.

"I believe we can take the offensive at Brest Litovsk," I said.
The hands were massaging on their own. Gripping.

"At Brest Litovsk?" she said.

"We will be victorious at Brest Litovsk. You'll see," I said.

"Will you rewrite history at Brest Litovsk?"

"Yes, at Brest Litovsk."

Merrill's slacks were off. I could not check on how clean the
panties were because Merrill was not wearing any; Moe Axelrod's
cynical soul could certainly use *that*.

As she opened, continuing to massage with royal expertise, she
said, "If only we could develop an offensive strategy at Brest
Litovsk."

Manny gazed at Merrill. Speed reviewed all his conquests. Moe
thought: Student Council to Queen, they're all alike. Manny.
Speed. Moe. MannySpeedMoe.

I reacted.

"E nom'ted! MacArthur! McCarthy! Betrayal! . . . Capt. Speed Finestone: Betrayed! Shimon Finestone: Betrayed! FDR: Betrayed! Jackie Shadwesky: Betrayed! Monroe Meyer: Betrayed! . . . Hoover, Mellon, Martin, Barton, Fish seventh heaven!"

I was halfway down the latrine. But Lucille reached in and pulled me out. She cleaned me up, fed me, took care of me, never said a word about what I was going through, although surely she knew. She took me in between her legs and taught me things I never knew existed, things which showed Eisenhower what he could do with the purity he had given me in the Crusade. Things which made him spin in his buckled shoes and, head trembling, stride away to find the chaplain.

At the end of July, what McCarthy called the Democrat Party nominated Stevenson. To my surprise, and delight, Lucille suggested we work for him. This was in Jack Delaney's on Sheridan Square. I flipped her a look and she stopped chewing, then began again, then swallowed.

"What's wrong?" she said.

"Nothing. I just thought you'd want to work for Wallace."

"That was four years ago, baby. He was a disaster and I learn from disasters even if Marge doesn't. Hallinan will be a disaster, too. It isn't even a question of compromise. I *like* Stevenson."

"What about Sparkman?"

"Don't live with stereotypes, baby. The South is not bad per se. And Stevenson picked him."

I leaned over the table and kissed her.

"That was very spontaneous," she said.

"Also honest and real."

53

"Yes it was."

"So is this. Let's go to my place. Garth is working on high finance at Marge's."

"No, baby."

"What no?"

"You heard me."

"Is your friend from the country visiting? You know I don't mind that."

"Of course not, and please don't use those euphemisms, you know how I hate them. I mean no until Stevenson is elected and the country is safe."

"IF GET BLUE BALLS WILL BE E'S FAULT!"

She meant it.

The campaign was an excursion through another level of existence, in its way like the rush across France. I was elated, depressed, ecstatic, miserable, numb, sandpapered and forever in heat. We worked on the East Side, from the Village to 59th Street, ringing doorbells, smiling at GOP masks, jabbing flyers at them, shaking cannisters in front of the soigné antique shops. Then, exhausted, we tumbled into her bed (Alicia had long since accepted me as the third roommate). I could never touch her and after a while stopped trying, although I never stopped hoping. I kept thinking that some cataclysmic motivation might shatter the iron vow. In September I thought we had it:

"Nix! Is he *real*? White suit? Checkers? Cloth coat? Come on! Bigger *goniff* than Rasputin!"

She shook her head all the way through the speech and into bed, but her legs were as tight as ever.

"He's real ... E: 'You're my boy' ... Shit, I'M his boy ... *Was* his boy! ... F them both ... F Checkers; he is horseshit next to Fala!"

I really didn't think things could get any worse. But they did. In Wisconsin Eisenhower copped out on Marshall. McCarthy had accomplished what Rommel never could.

"SPEED THROUGH, FINISHED, DONE!"

I drank my way through the Open Door, Delaney's and the

Village Vanguard. She found me at the Vanguard bar heckling Irwin Corey, who was being very tolerant; but the bartender was making faces. With Alicia she dragged, lifted, pulled me up to their place. Beside her in bed that night, after the ceiling had settled down, I decided I was falling in love. Not only that; I was falling in love with my own Rayna Prohme, my intellectual dream girl out of Vincent Sheean's *Personal History* which I had devoured in my junior year at NYU. For, as with Sheean, our relationship—at least now—was on the highest, most impeccable cerebral plane—no sex, no physicality—yet, oh so passionate. As we approached November, and the fate of the nation hung in the balance, the intellectual penetration grew more exquisite—as pure, no, *purer*, than my Crusade in Europe.

As Rayna did with Sheean, she educated me. She showed me the interlocking directorates behind Eisenhower, introduced me to the long line of thieves in the night who carried back to Hoover to Coolidge to Harding to Taft to Mark Hanna and all the Mark Hannas. (To my great relief she did not linger over Teddy Roosevelt, merely said he was a psychotic infant.) Poisoned beef she taught me. And Triangle Shirtwaist fires. The evils of protectionism she taught me; what the marines did in Haiti she taught me. Taught me what was under the country club cheviot of the judge who had railroaded SacVan (instead of a heart, an arrogant ice cube). All this she taught me; all this I sponged up. When Eisenhower and Taft—*Taft*—sealed their bargain on Morningside Drive—*my* Morningside Drive, she taught me, with Rayna's bright certainty, that "If he wins, McCarthy gets ready for the *putsch*." I shivered with love.

And she taught me Stevenson. I began to appreciate him as she did, saw how head and shoulders above the miserable little hacks he was.

Rescuer, teacher, flame . . .

Into November. Very little sleep. Shaking cannisters. Ringing doorbells, phoning: "Waitaminute, *listen*, will you? . . ."

The night before election day I didn't sleep at all, although she did, peacefully, confidently. My father kept appearing, lecturing me, asking if I was aware that not since 1932 had the *goniffs* been in control. I whispered in the dark, yes, I knew. Twenty years, he kept saying, twenty years . . . I looked at my Rayna. I had them both . . .

At six I got up, dressed, slipped out and walked to Grand Central where I handed out leaflets to the fatcat commuters from Hoover country. They took Stevenson, did not glance, crumpled him up and flipped him into Lexington Avenue. If I didn't know before, I knew then what Rayna and Shimon were talking about.

I hurried down to P.S. 40 and stood behind an old lady in flaming lipstick and Enna Jettick shoes. I gave my name, signed. The old lady disappeared into the booth, clanged it shut. Ten years later she clanged out.

"All right, Mr. Finnstone," the inspector said.

I walked in, shoved the joy stick, pulled the shroud around me. I stepped closer, stared at eagles and stars and columns. The columns began to shimmy. I stepped back and Rayna and Shimon intervened; the columns stopped. McCarthy, MacArthur, Hoover, they thundered. *Bonus Marchers. Pencils. Apples.*

I gritted and reached. My hand swerved. I voted for Eisenhower.

It was over early. By eleven o'clock we were sobbing in each other's arms. We went to bed and lay there and let the mellow voices of doom wash over us as we lay naked, wrapped about each other. Once I moved, tentatively, toward the magic triangle; she snapped as tightly shut as the voting booth.

She was still sleeping when I slipped out of bed at five-thirty; I could hear the faraway voice of reveille. I gulped some lukewarm coffee and wrote a note saying I had to be by myself for awhile and

I was sure she would understand. I walked out into the Manhattan dawn and took the subway up to the Bronx. I got out and walked to the cemetery. It was the first time I had been there since the burial, but I did not make a wrong twist or turn. I walked straight and true to my father's grave. I stood before it for several hours at parade rest, sighing and asking for his forgiveness. He was always a good listener and around noon I felt peace and quiet descend on me. The sighs smoothed out, stopped. I breathed calmly and my heart didn't catch. I touched the stone and about-faced and, chin up, walked out. I subwayed down to 96th Street, changed to the Broadway line and came back up to 116th. It was my day for firsts: the first time I had been back at Columbia since E had flown off to NATO. I filled up on Shimon's forgiveness and stepped onto the campus. I survived. I lifted one foot, then the other. I traversed the campus west to east. I walked to Morningside Drive. Walked past his house, spit my father's disgust onto the sidewalk. I got a coughing fit, crossed the street, entered Morningside Park and wound slowly down, coughing all the way, hoping to get mugged, framing the headline in the *News*: "DESPERATE VET GOES DOWN FIGHTING." I saw no one; no one saw me. I stopped coughing, turned around and marched back up. No luck. I walked back past his house. Past my little room. Back through Columbia, to Broadway, past the Hamilton Garage. I didn't give it a tumble. I got back on the subway at 110th and rode down to 14th Street, got out, walked through Union Square with Sam Gompers, Bill Haywood and Joe Hill trailing me every step of the way, with the Triangle Shirt-waist girls pointing at me behind their flaming faces.

At ten o'clock I walked into the apartment. Lucille threw herself against me.

"Thank God," she whimpered.

"I left you a note," I said.

"I'm afraid of notes . . ."

I stroked the coiled hair and led her into the bedroom. I sat her down on the bed and she said, over and over, "It's so sad, so sad . . ."

"I know, baby."

"I feel so awful, so . . . powerless."

"I know."

"I feel so bad for Stevenson."

"I do, too."

"It's so sad, so sad . . ."

"We have to survive, sugar."

"Oh I don't know, I just don't know . . ."

We sat there and I stroked her hair and she cried very quietly. When my father cried at the fall of France, my mother said let him get it out of his system and that's what I did now. I let her get it out for at least an hour. Finally, when the Maginot Line crumpled, she quietened, lay against me, her chest gently rising and falling. God help me, I said, "Should we do a scene?"

She raised her head.

"I don't know," she whispered.

"Let's try."

"I don't think it's right."

"Stevenson will understand. Let's try."

"I don't know . . . What?"

"How about *Golden Boy?*"

"It just doesn't seem right."

"It is. I know it is. Go ahead, you set it up."

She firmed up beside me.

"Well . . . You are Juarez . . . I'm the Empress Carlotta . . ." Her voice grew stronger. "Maximilian has been lording it over you, but you don't care. You shrug him off and come to get food for the peasants. Carlotta is your last hope. Now—"

"No," I said.

"You don't want to do it?"

"No."

"Would you like to do *Lefty?* Maybe it's more appropriate."

"No. *Golden Boy* is OK. Only screw Carlotta and Juarez. Here is the scene: I am Speed—"

"But—"

"You are Lucille."

"Yes, but—"

"You've been waiting for me and I'm here."

She stiffened. "Sweetie, please don't try to overwhelm me. You know how I detest that—"

"Speed has conquered the Fascists and he is here."

"I'm asking you . . . Stanislavsky . . ."

"Speed will take on the werewolves and conquer again."

"Odets . . . Luther Adler . . . I cannot . . ."

"Speed will cut McCarthy's balls off."

We were down on the bed. The voting booth opened. I spent the rest of the night getting even with Eisenhower.

2

We hardly left the bed for over a month, except to gulp some food and buy Trojans. It was one of those parenthesis times and my sense memory today, if I were to do the scene, would be a convulsive, physical one within the space: The three of us: Lucille, the bed and I. Climbing, groaning, wrestling, creaking, gnawing. My recollected feeling also tells me that I was blocking on voting for him. When I finally came up for air, looked around and saw that our flag was still there, then and only then did I admit it to myself. That was very close to Christmas.

I sat up in bed and proposed.

"You're out of your mind," she said.

"I'm not. I mean it."

"But why? We're together."

"That's simply not good enough."

She gave me a preelection look—slick, tough, Roz Russellish.

"You're getting all the ass you want," she said airily, "getting your rocks off. Gratifying the inner hard-on. Why complicate things?"

"Don't give me any goddam nonsense. I love you."

Oh lord, the floodgates opened.

We were married four days later in City Hall. Alicia, the silent roommate, took us out to Lüchow's for a wedding brunch, then went to work while we hurried back to bed as if for the first time. When the bell rang at six, we oozed out of the sack and welcomed

59

Alicia and her bottle of California champagne; then we excused ourselves.

I didn't have to move in, I was in. Alicia offered to leave but we wouldn't hear of it, so we carried on as before, tightening shower and eating schedules, three busy people on the New York escalator. Not quite. Lucille and I were in the down elevator, for we had returned to Manhattan Players and found them white-faced and shaky. They murmured things like concentration camps and barbed wire and, nodding, the marriage rate and the Fascist parabola have a positive correlation: it is the last grasp for security. I said that's an interesting point; then we threw ourselves into the barricade that our work represented.

Garth thought it was essential that we make a statement, no matter how hopeless the outlook, and said *The Time of Your Life* was it. He cast me as the cop and I came through with what he called a basically competent performance. He and Marge then settled on a whathehell-1920s-Berlin attitude and set us to work on the *Iron Monger Follies*, which they informed the assembled company was a calculated risk in today's climate and they wouldn't hold it against anyone for copping out. There was a consensus mutter of "SHIT NO," and Garth said I love you all, now let's toss a spotlight onto the pricks.

He came to the house for dinner that night and asked me to write a fast ten minutes on the Martin Durkin-Secretary of Labor fiasco, assured me I could do it, and it was the opportunity we had been waiting for. I said I would do my best and he beamed who could ask for anything more? He then dug into some inner meanings and character exploration with Lucille who would prance through the whole thing as Mamie, Pat Nixon and Oveta Culp Hobby; they spoke their special lingo for three hours.

I plunged in. I wrote Durkin, the wide-eyed Union Man who had been jobbed by the fatcat (house) cabinet, as Mr. Chollinsky, a plumber who lived across the street from us in the Bronx, and who, according to my father, was a genuine prince. For my Eisen—er, Iron Monger model, I called up Judson Caraway, a smiler from Caraway Realtors located on Fifth Avenue, who, according to my father, were genuine bloodsuckers (as well as

hypocritical ones: their developments in Q[...]
the bastards). Sir Judson, as we had been [...]
was the perfectly groomed front man, a[...]
class that was out to screw the Chollinskys[...]
after they had done an honest day's work.[...]
scowling at the typewriter, I swung from the n[...]
Shimon. At the Iron Mongers of America who with t[...]
teeth and softly draped banker's gray fronted for all the n[...]
barons, the trusts, the monopolies, the architects of every rotten
Hooverville.

Halfway along, as I was setting up my Durkin-Iron Monger confrontation on High Bridge between the Bronx and Manhattan, and as Lucille dug into Oveta Culp Hobby's spine, Garth dropped in unannounced. I swam up out of emotional recall, yelled for Lucille, and we set a table with Royal Crown Cola which was out to break the Coke-Pepsi monopoly, Lucille's personally baked, unsliced bread and a tin of beef that was not from Argentina. Garth seemed especially animated—he almost had his onstage energy—and I concluded that all the other elements of *Follies* were progressing nicely, probably even beyond themselves. Then he said, with a Bob Montgomery head-cock, "Oh shit, enough of this French lovemaking, I have an announcement to make: As of last night, I have joined the bourgeois team."

"Meaning?" I said, exchanging eyes with Lucille.

"Meaning I am now a domesticated lovebird."

"Yesss?" I said, exchanging again.

"Yes. Marge and I."

"You're *married*?"

"Not yet. But I've moved over to her place."

"But you said—"

"Screw what I said. I was a reactionary anticipator when I said what I said. Since then I have learned what it's all about. I only hope, lil brother, you have learned or will learn such a lesson."

"Yes, but—"

"I told you, fuck the buts. I wanted you to be the first to know and also you can have my place if you want it." He said that with

61

dd shyness, as if he were giving me his reversible
berjacket, which he had given me, with the same shyness,
hen I was eleven. I said to Lucille, "Of course we want it, don't
we?"

"Well yes, that's very decent of you, Garth, but are you sure—"

A directorial hand. "Cut. I am sure. I'll *shmear* the agent so he'll
let you sublet till the lease is up. No problem. It's my wedding
present."

I held out my hand and he patted my face and shook my hand.
His eyes misted over. I noticed a new puffiness below them; the
hairline was a bit more jagged. I swallowed a sigh. We chatted
quickly, then he spun and strode out on his Adlers. We looked at
the door, at each other.

"Oh, I hope it works out for him," I said.

"She'll break it in half," Lucille said.

3

In July Eisenhower produced the armistice in Korea. I began to
feel hot and sweaty. A week after that we put on the *Iron Monger
Follies.* Halfway through my skit I walked out and kept walking
until I reached the Hudson—our river—paced up and down
beside it, finally around ten-thirty walked back. The audience was
straggling out. I walked backstage and found Garth, who was
sipping a Royal Crown and looking into the distance; lately he
had been wearing that searching, puzzled face a lot: opening
night, Marge, who knew? I had other things on my mind.

"I don't think I can stick with this," I said.

He stopped sipping and gently laid the bottle down. I had
never before noticed that his mouth and chin were assuming the
set cast Shimon's had in the early years of the war.

"What are you pulling on me?" he said, the weight of the
Western world on his shoulders.

"It's nothing about you. It's me. I don't like what I've just done.
It's raunchy and demeaning and I don't like it."

"You and your messiah," he said.

"He ended the goddam war. That's more than the Stockholm

62

pledge and all its hustlers ever did. Anyway, it's how I feel. Stanislavsky says be honest. I'm being honest. I really think I have to pack it in."

He got up and I noticed he was small; the Adlers had been replaced by Thom McAn. He put his hand on my shoulder the way he did when I was twelve and he was explaining the facts of life because Shimon hadn't. My eyes had filled and he had put the same hand on my shoulder, saying the exact right thing: "Don't worry, you can do it; if all the *schmucks* in the world can do it, *you* can do it." Now the omniscient one was looking up at *me* and the hand was on my shoulder and he was saying, "I can understand. I never told you, but the great hero of my life was Teddy Roosevelt; can you picture that?"

"No."

"He was. Then I discovered what an imperialist nut he was. Poof."

"I know what you're saying, I do. It's just—"

He said the exact right thing:

"Stick with me, kid; I need you."

My damn eyes started. I put my arms around him and hugged him; I felt as powerful as FDR, the *real* Roosevelt. And as caring.

"Do you want to move in with us?" I said.

He stepped back and patted my face (he was doing that long before Brando).

"I'm in too deep," he half-smiled.

"Pull out."

The Shimon-chin swiveled.

"Mama said it perfectly: You make your bed, you lay in it. Only, don't abandon me, OK?"

In 1940 when Hitler had danced on the Allies and Shimon's chest had caved in, I promised him that someday I would get revenge; all I wanted in the world was for him to be the way he used to be. And he had actually looked up at me with incredulous hope in his eyes. I felt that power now, craved that look.

"Screw the bastards," I said. "I won't abandon you."

I went back to work. In February of '54, we did *Machinal* and Lucille was fluid perfection, dominating every scene even when she stood still. (I did the Gable bit, the one that had sent him out to Hollywood in the '20s; I did not get a screen test.) I had worked with her every night, building, shaping the part with her, helping her find every point of contact, filling in for Garth as he retreated further and further into his puzzled, far-off face. It was during this period that Marge began to call me, to check on Lucille, to offer advice and finally to take some. After the five-week run, which received a rave from Vernon Rice in the *Post* and a strong, though more muted review from Calta in the *Times*, who, however, called Lucille a plebian Katie Hepburn, Marge took us out to dinner at Cavanaugh's on 23rd Street. I tried with everything I had learned to bend the conversation toward Garth, but I couldn't do it, mainly because he wouldn't cooperate, would not react to my action. In the end he was staring through the window at 23rd Street while Marge leaned in toward me. As we said goodnight, I whispered to him, "Hang in, forcrissakes," and he looked at me with startled eyes, as if Paris had just fallen. Lucille and I walked home arms around each other, as quiet as the 12th Street bookstores. I'm positive it was on that night that Hannah was conceived.

2

After *Machinal* I began work on a play that had been surfacing for the last few years: six GIs and their twenty-four hours before D-Day; I had first act problems, could get no further than the Brooklyn boy who was from the Bronx. Thankfully, the Army-McCarthy hearings intervened and I stashed it in the drawer. My wife and her tiny bun in the oven and I stared at Garth's fancy fourteen-inch Du Mont day after day after day. Lucille and I were both convinced that the baby's first cogent phrase would be, "Who promoted Peress?"

Even before it was over, Marge had me working on a reprise entitled *Mr. Chairman*. Everything pulled together in me for this: my father, Truman, my army worship, E. I worked fifteen hours a day and I told Marge that nobody except the author was going to fuck it up. Therefore, I cast Garth as Schine to Speed Finestone's Cohn, and with Lucille's help we worked out a truckin, peckin gallop through Europe that returned some intelligence to my brother's far-off face. (*Mr. Chairman* ran all summer and into the fall; I wrote McCarthy as a Stalinesque presence who never quite appeared, but whose imminent arrival cued every scene. It became the thing to see that season, and a variety of political types were photographed in the theater as evidence of their better-late-than-never courage.) Garth continued to make progress as my ice-hot pen churned out *Sing Me a Song of Massive Retaliation*. I took a giant step, cast him as E to the Dulles of Anthony Interwhyte, a splendid old fellow who had once had a long run with Philip Merivale in *The Road to Rome*. Garth played Tony absolutely even; to my sighing delight he grabbed E, plucked every ribbon off the vulnerable chest, left him alone and naked at the final curtain. The Village crowd loved it. Loved him. Marge, with some frequency, began again to say, "How do *you* see it, Garthie."

The baby—Speed's baby, not Manny's—was born on February 10, 1955. We named her Hannah for Chaplin's mother and also for the girl Paulette Goddard played in *The Great Dictator*

(again, surely his mother). I have always believed that life imitates art, so I was convinced Hannah had Paulette's face. Garth disagreed. Winking: "I think she's a dead ringer for Eisenhower." Lucille, the first breast-feeder in history, said, you are both wrong, she is Garbo as Garbo must have looked as a baby. Hannah, a born peacemaker, went along with everyone.

I took her up to the Bronx and showed her to my mother, who cried and gave me fifty dollars (she ordinarily gave me twenty-five). Then I took her out to the cemetery and showed her to Shimon. Perfect! Then back down to Morningside Drive, 58th Street, the Hotel Lex, Penn Station and environs, Queens Boulevard: all the places where her father had readjusted. I explained to her my part in winning the war and making the world safe for all the Hannahs. I made a promise. I promised her that no bastard, on pain of suffering a permanently broken ass, would ever call her snatch, pussy, poontang, or nooky. She listened very carefully; she nodded.

When she was five weeks old, I strapped her on my back and she, Lucille and I went to work. Marge had decided that a series of readings—bare stage, lecterns, quiet actors on high stools—would be the most pertinent way to light up the underworld we were passing through, and so asked—suggested—*recommended* that I do a series of adaptations of great books, said works to be democratically chosen by the Players and approved by her. I wasn't at all sure I could handle it, but the warm bundle on my back said of course you can, so I bought the approved books at the Strand and handed Marge the bill. I said I would have to determine our sequential order, that I would do so depending on my felt reaction to the material; she said, I would expect nothing less, darling.

I started with *It Can't Happen Here*, mainly because I had been crazy about Dorothy Thompson in high school and figured that any man good enough to chase her all over Europe and land her had to have magnificent liberal (and personal) credentials. I even wrote myself in as Sinclair Lewis, stage manager, and brought the house down entering with Hannah, sound asleep. I also helped

66

Garth along the comeback trail by casting him as Doremus Jessup; with support and applause from Lucille, Hannah and me, he rose to the challenge.

Thus fortified, I took a giant step: I combined Crane's *Maggie*, which the company naturally adored, with *The House of Mirth*, which I had read at NYU after getting hooked on Edith Wharton. Nobody had heard of it, and they kept asking me if I meant *The Age of Innocence*? I said I know what I mean and informed Marge that my artistic conscience had been engaged by *Mirth*; she told the company, this Speed will do. And this I did. And it worked. In all objectivity, I have to say I did a magnificent job of integrating the two books, and Lucille did an equally magnificent job, swinging with ever tightening parabolas from the girl of the streets to the high-toned but equally lost Lili Barth; in the end she achieved a chain-smoking, disassociated synthesis that slapped my palms raw. *Commentary* gave it a two-page essay-review, and Lucille got letters from 20th Century and Selznick; she tacked them both over the john. She also got three letters from Broadway; these she stared at and went back to once before tacking them up as well.

I was something of a stand-out now, in a company that must have no stand-outs. But between Marge and me and the approving lamppost, I *was*. I was also, in my lovely little family, a very remarkable fellow. Chico in *Seventh Heaven*. Lucille my Diane. Hannah the child they should have had. And all this reality stimulus made me work like a horse, write like a streak. I conquered *The Jungle. Nana. Christ in Concrete. Man's Fate.* Click. Click, click, click. I worked fifteen hours a day, and night, across the table from my attentive, studious wife and our approving baby, spotlighting for them, for us all, the shenanigans that floated by under the aloof nose of a man who had once been great, whom I had once known, who was now a stranger. We went into repertory. I exposed, admonished, scolded, raged, slugged, punished, avenged. This I did.

Sept. 24, 1955:
"OMIGOD E MORTALLY ILL AND ALL YOUR FAULT! NO
GODDAM EXCUSES, EVASIONS, RATIONALIZATIONS,
COP-OUTS. YOU! BIGTIME MURDERING SPEED (THE
GRATEFUL ONE) FINESTONE. OFFICER, GENTLEMAN,
PRICK.
THUS CRACKS A NOBLE HEART!"

I left a note for Lucille and Hannah and caught the train for
Washington, praying all the way. I pulled in at eight at night and
took a cab to Walter Reed. I got out and stationed myself across
the street with the other vigil-keepers and stared up at his
window the way I had stared up on Morningside Drive. All the
shit I had written, said, performed, tumbled around in my head
and I started the spitting business. I remained all night, staring,
praying, spitting. Willing all the strength and purity he had given
me up through that silent window.

This time I didn't desert or go AWOL. Did not forsake him.
Through the cardiograms, the peristalsis, the bulletins, I
remained, across the street, gulping a hot dog from a kid I hired as
a gofer, not talking to conserve our strength, staring up. Only
once, as the crisis approached, I sprinted to a nearby *shul*, swayed,
implored, sprinted back. Then I pulled out my book and ripped
into it:

"Will he forgive? Why should he?
Because he knows. Don't you wish!
I'll be good. Sure, after horse

leaves barn. Promise! Hah, your
promises, tell it to marines, to
MacArthur! PROMISEPROMISEPROMISE—"
I looked up. The cop was examining me with his hands on his
hips. I spit and wrote. When I looked up, he was still examining
me.
"What're you writing?" he said.
"The Communist Manifesto."
He took one hand off a hip.
"That's against the law," he said.
"No, it's not." I spit.
He swiped and picked off my little book. He opened it, *my*
book. I ran at him and plowed an enraged shoulder into a soft gut.
He whooshed and went down and I grabbed my book and began
flailing at him, screaming, "GODDAM FUCKING NAZI," and I
continued to flail and scream through the whistles and pounding
feet and Roman candles.

The iron door really did clang. And they really did say, "You
can make one phone call."
I said, "Thank you, how is Eisenhower?"
The cop really did smile out of the side of his face.
"Hey, did you call Carnihan a Nazi?"
"I think so. How is Eisenhower?"
"That's rich." The sidesaddle smile widened. "He's forever
tellin us how he won the war single-handed. If you don't believe
it, just ask him."
"That's a lie. *I* won it. How is—"
"He just took a good shit, he'll live."
I sat down in the iron bed and covered my face with my
treacherous hands. It was very important that he not see my face.
When my shoulders stopped shaking, I looked up; my face felt
clean. He said, "Well, you wanna make that phone call?"
"Are you sure?"
"Yop. One call."
"I mean Eisenhower."

"I don't believe in doctors, but if anybody got the best, he got them. They say he got a good shot. If you don't believe me, ask them."

"I believe you."

He gave me the twisty smile and winked. "Nixon's gonna race him all the way back to the White House. Come on, tough guy, make your call."

Garth said, "Holy jumpin Jesus, thank God, I'll be right down, keep your big mouth shut."

He arrived at four in the morning and a different cop came in and he really did say, "All right, collect your belongings." We walked out and I collected my belongings while Garth kept shaking his head as he helped me on with my jacket and brushed it off. I riffled through the book quickly; it hadn't been raped. I tucked it into my shirt pocket. I grinned at him.

"You look like Julie Garfield after *Body and Soul,*" he said.

I continued to grin.

"Ooh hah, the Bronx Bulldog."

"That's me."

"Are you ready to leave this establishment?"

"Ready."

He said to the cop that he appreciated their courtesy and the cop said that's OK, tell him to keep his nose clean and we walked outside into the Washington dawn.

"Let's get some breakfast," he said. "If I know you, you didn't eat as some kind of offering while Wiley Post flew around the world."

"Post made it."

"A fuckin nut I got for a brother, oi, what a nut." He slapped my back with the old-time authority. I didn't have to glance down; he was wearing the elevators. I knew I was in for it all the way back to New York.

Sure enough, outside of Baltimore: "I think it's time you came to grips with this aberration. Don't you think so?"

I turned away from the fascination of Maryland, considered

70

him with a reacting but bland face, and said, "Maybe."

He propped an elevator on a knee and massaged his ankle. "All right, let's start there. Look, loyalty is great in its proper context, but you have long since discharged your debt, assuming it *was* a debt. Actually, he has discharged *you*."

"Truman discharged me."

"OK," he sighed, "we'll play your game. The fact remains that he unleashed McCarthy. Now that is the record."

"No. He just didn't *leash* him."

"Balls, don't you see it's the same difference . . . All right, let's play it *your* way. The noble general let McCarthy crap on your beloved army. He let the bastard scream that your army, *his* army, was as bad as the Nazis, that it had tortured the poor innocent SS in Malmédy. More? Your hero screwed Marshall in Wisconsin; the Savior of the Western World couldn't afford to offend a shitheel senator. OK? Good enough for the accuracy expert? And please do not respond with your defensively hostile answers."

I wanted to respond with, and what did *you* do for the army? For Marshall? How did *you* take on the SS? But that was all very dangerous ground, so I let them slide by. I stared out at Delaware; I thought he might start on me with Du Pont and E protecting *their* interests. I closed my eyes. He didn't give me Du Pont; he gave me: "Dad would spin around in his grave."

I opened my eyes and turned. My hotshot brother. Yardley Aftershave. Neutral talc that hid the broken veins around the nose. Thomas Hair Treatment, but the line was still jagged. Douglas Fairbanks, Shimon had called him, called *after* him as the stiff back stalked away; all I could do was watch and get nervous. *Now*, I could do something.

"Do not give me the Dad shit. Not that. You never called him Dad in your life. Here is accuracy: His Master's Voice. Jesus Christ Almighty. Shimon Peter. Julius Bonaparte. Ol Massa. He. Him. So, please, *please*, do not give me the filial role-playing. Anything but that."

He concaved. Not much, but enough. I wanted to reach over and touch the Shimon chest, but I couldn't; he had started it. And

71

then he tipped me over, as he usually would: "You're right," he said quietly.

I knew I had to remain a hard guy.

"Damn right I'm right."

He leaned back against the cushion and said to the world, "*Schmuck*, it serves you right."

I concentrated on the Delaware Water Gap. Shimon had driven us to Washington in '35 in his Nash and detoured to the Delaware Water Gap; he had informed us it was one of the world's great wonders. Pure, clean, counterbalancing all the Du Pont exploitation. Shimon had said it. He. Him. Ol Massa.

"It just won't work anymore," I said. "I'm leaving the company. This time I mean it."

"Jesus Christ," he said, "ever since you were three, you over-reacted. Why does it have to be all or nothing?"

"That's the way I am."

"But you can *change*."

"Not in that I can't. There are certain things I have to do."

"Like enlist."

"That's right."

"And break his heart."

"In a way. In another way, it put him back together. Don't use guilt on me, please."

"I'm sorry," he said. I looked over and he *was* sorry; I could always separate bullshit from boy. "I take that back," he said. He was flexing the elevator shoe. "Screw all this," he said. "It is immaterial. Do you agree?"

"Maybe."

"All right. You don't quite trust me. I don't blame you. But this I mean: I *need* you."

I poured some concrete into the corpus.

"You'll get by," I said.

"Maybe," he said, "to quote a noncommittal person. However, this is qualitative, not quantitative. Getting by is not good enough."

"Look," I said, "I am tired of being a hypocrite. I will not go on convincing myself the man is a prick. I owe too much . . . I'm a lousy writer if I have to use phony motivation. . . ."

"You're a *good* writer. Or could be. Real motivation is *us*. You just keep missing the point."

"That's how I am."

He sat back. Dover faded away.

"Would you like a bite?" he said.

"No thanks."

"I'll get it."

"No thanks."

"I took you in," he said.

"I know."

"I gave you a job."

"I know."

"You were pathetic."

"I know."

"I put you on your feet."

"I know."

"I gave you my place."

"I know."

"You met your wife through me."

"I know."

"You're the world's biggest prick."

"I know."

Philadelphia. 30th Street Station.

"Remember when the Japs bombed Pearl Harbor? We went out and wound up on Jerome Avenue and found him and dragged him out of that gin mill? Remember?"

"I remember."

"He had never got drunk in his life until then."

"I remember."

"Christ he was sick."

"I remember."

"He always said, 'I wish I could drink and forget this *shvartz* world, but I get sick.' "

"I remember."

"When we found him, after he puked he said to the bartender, 'These are my two beautiful sons. I love them so much.' And we carried him home."

"I remember."

"And then Naomi brought that Hungarian home in '42. I kicked his ass out of the house. I'll bet you've blocked that."

"No. I remember."

And as Newark approached I thought: Yes, and when I enlisted you let her marry the Nazi.

"Remember when he wanted to buy a diner in Newark because we didn't have a pot to cook in, I told him forget it, you're a dead duck outside the Bronx?"

"I remember." And a dead duck *inside*.

"You won't have to do any more writing if it breaks you up so much. I'll put my foot down with Marge. You can stick to acting. You've got a nice realistic talent. You can pick your spots. Jesus Christ, I am *talking* to you, will you please respond."

I looked. I responded, gruffly:

"I've made up my mind."

The magic city rose up. We both looked at it.

"All right," he said. "I will make a major concession. You're in love with the fucking army. That is a given. I accept it. To each his own. All right, stick with me and I'll get you work acting in Signal Corps movies in Astoria. This I can do. From your point of view, which I assure you I understand, although I'm not wild about it, it will be the next best thing to being back in. I think it will meet your peculiar, nationalistic needs. So be it."

"Will it?"

"Oh Christ. Yes, it will. Please, no world-weary bullshit. You'll make some money. You'll make a contribution to your world. Eisenhower would love it."

74

I was tempted. I was. Had he finally pulled it all together, made it work? "I don't know. I just don't know . . ."

He was boring in, and we both knew it. I don't know why Shimon always said he was in a dream world.

"Look," he said. "This is strictly between us. Marge doesn't know. But I've directed out there. They love the Method and Method people. I know I can set you up. You could even work with me. I've made *Skirmish Line* and *How to Fire an M1*. If you think I'm shitting you, I'll give you the names of people who can verify it. We'll do *How to Fire a Carbine*. You and me."

I directed a Stanislavsky gaze into the moist eyes.

"We?"

"Yes."

"You and me?"

"Yes."

"*How to Fire a Carbine?*"

"Yes."

"Go to hell, you fucking conchie."

We didn't talk for thirteen years.

The big shot was home.

Lucille and Hannah welcomed me with tearful, noisy, encircling arms, said that although from any sensible perspective I was the world's greatest patsy, far be it from them to be judgmental, that if I saw things in such a crazy, distorted way, then by God that was the crazy, distorted way I saw them. I was moved, touched, torn, above all, grateful, for I was still feeling bitterly rotten about Garth and plain rotten about E and I said, don't worry, don't you *ever* worry, I'll work this out, I will, and I'll do it for *you* (my father always said being a family man was all I ever needed to give me the necessary get up and go). I tucked Hannah into her crib and read her the first chapter of *Moby-Dick*, which she loved, and then Lucille and I went to bed and I loved her as I had never loved before, coming as close as ever I had to the sessions Manny had conjured up with his ceiling-wife. Just before we dropped off, I said, "I have to quit," and she said, "Yes, I was sure you would."

The next morning I called Dr. Elias Damon at NYU, the most perceptive teacher since Socrates, the one who had said as I went off to war that I was so promising it made him literally sick that I had not yet delivered. I said to him, as if it were 1942, I am now ready to deliver, and he picked it right up and said, we ought to talk and I said, now? and he said, can you think of a better time?

Hannah and I spelled out *mazel* with her blocks, I kissed my beautiful little family goodbye, told them not to worry, and took the subway up to University Heights. After pacing through the Hall of Fame, filling up on *its* emotional recall, I walked into Damon's open door. He shook my hand with energetic delight, told the switchboard to hold all calls, pointed to the tattered, old violet chair, lit up the horrible old pipe and said, so?

"Yes," I said. "So."

"You've been working," he said.

"In a way."

"I saw your *Christ in Concrete*. It was quite good."

"In a way," I said.

He gave me the strong, Midwestern face.

"When are you going to do some original work?"

"Well, that's what I wanted to talk to you about. I'm thinking of journalism."

"I see." He relit the pipe and sucked on it. "Mmmm, you know, Emanuel . . . mmm, I always thought you . . . mmm, would do *the* war novel. Yes. Instead, I had to settle for Jones and Mailer." He played with the lighter; he puffed, peered at me through octagonal lenses.

"Well," I said, "my war novel would have been *From Here to Attorney Street*."

"I see." Puff, light, puff, mmm. "It's near Delancey, is it not? Abraham Cahan."

You never taught Cahan, I wanted to say; if you had, maybe I would have written the damn thing. I said, "Not many college teachers know Cahan."

"I should have taught him. I didn't." Puff, light. "Journalism, you said?"

"Yes."

"Nothing more . . . creative?"

"I think journalism can be. At least enough for me."

"Davis, Crane, Gibbons, Sheean. I see."

"I'm not looking for any trench coats or eye patches."

"I see."

"I was wondering . . . Would you have some leads . . . ?"

"I know some people at the *Home News*. You are wrinkling your face. Is that too provincial for you?"

"Frankly, yes."

"The *Home News* was very important to the Lindbergh case which so gripped you, Emanuel." I winced. "He was a hero of yours, was he not?"

"*Was.*"

"I see."

"I want to work in New York," I said.

"Ah, New York. The dream of the *uitlander*. Let me think. I know a chap at *Look* who knows someone who knows Fleur Cowles. Would you like me to give him a ring?"

I took a deep breath. "Would you know anyone at the *Herald Tribune*?"

He sucked on the pipe.

"Is this Rexford Tugwell speaking?" he said.

"That was a long time ago."

"Are you sure you wouldn't prefer the *Post* or the *New Leader*?"

"I'm sure."

"I see. *Tis* a new world. Brave?"

"I don't know. I can't worry about that. I was also a pacifist once. Things change."

77

"Yes. They do. I s'pose that's why I remain here; I detest change. But alas, I don't know anyone at the *Herald Tribune*. Oddly enough, I do know someone at the *Journal-American*. Would that suffice?"

"Christ, Hearst . . ."

"He's been gone these five years. Anyway, would that possibly be a problem for the new Alf Landon?"

"Yes, but Hearst . . ."

"Yes?"

"You're right. Reid, Hearst, what's the big difference? Please give your friend a call."

He wrote himself a note, said that is settled; shall we talk?

We talked about the great NYU-Fordham football games and about King Kong Klein and Al Lassman and we talked about the great NYU-Notre Dame basketball games and about Len Maidman and Ralph Kaplowitz and Irv Terjesen, who (with the likes of Bernie Fliegel, Ace Goldstein and Red Holzman of City) were, I explained, the Abe Cahans of the court when basketball was *basketball*; and we talked . . .

In 1939, when I won a state regents scholarship at Morris, *Look* did a photo story on the brightest kids in New York and posed us on Fifth Avenue between the public library lions. Shimon framed the picture, painted an arrow next to my brilliant head and sent it to Galicia with the caption in Yiddish: "Here you have the smartest of the smart." *Look* also printed my all-time favorite article, in 1942: "WHY I HATE MY UNCLE. BY ADOLF HITLER'S NEPHEW." So I was very tempted to call Damon and say, I've thought it over, yes, *Look*. But I couldn't. It just wasn't big enough punishment for what I had done to Eisenhower. The *Journal* and Hearst, even with Shimon frowning (perhaps *especially* with Shimon frowning), were. I let the perceptive Damon run interference. In October of '55 I found myself on South Street in the shadow of the Brooklyn Bridge, looking up at my hairshirt.

Oh, I knew the *Journal-American*, all right.

From '32 to '34 Shimon brought it home every night.* Sprawled on the floor, I pursued Secret Agent X-9 and the Phantom, I agreed with Bill Corum and Hype Igoe, I picked my movies according to Rose Pelswick, and I learned some history from the occasional editorials of the great man himself. That was when he was an FDR man. When he went berserk and broke with him, Shimon banished the imperialist rag from the premises and shifted us over to the *Post*. I knew the *Journal*, all right.

I walked in, through halls built by the blood of Santiago and Manila Bay. I stopped, knocked. A busy voice said, come in. I entered, politely introduced myself and said I had an appointment and the busy girl said, yes, Mr. Wortham is expecting you. She pointed a severe head at a frosted door; I knocked and entered. Mr. Wortham looked up from a cluttered desk, the kind they used to call battered—very un-Republican—and murmured, won't you sit down, Elias Damon has told me all about you.

"Did he tell you how good I was?"

"Yes, he did."

I sat down. The Brooklyn Bridge loomed. When he came over in ought-three, Shimon lived near its western terminus, on Pearl Street. Shimon and San Simeon . . . I shifted and said, "What else did he tell you?"

"He said you were a war hero."

"That's true. How about my work?"

"He said you can put words together in a reasonable fashion, spell and have a catholic view of the world, small c."

"All true."

"He also said you are—or once were—a Galahad populist."

"Correct. So was William Randolph."

"Quite so . . . I more or less handle the editorial page. Letters,

---

*It was then only the *Journal*. The *American* was Hearst's morning paper, which he later grafted onto the *Journal*. One day it would become a growth on a monster called the *World Journal Tribune*, but that is another horror story. . . .

cartoon, the party line. Does that appeal to you?"

"Yes, it does."

"You would be working with a Princeton man. Does that appeal to you?"

"Not especially."

"Does it bother you?"

"Probably, but I can keep it in check."

"Fair enough. He's on the brilliant side but does not excel in his native language."

Here was the ideal punishment: the *Journal*, Hearst, Princeton. I said, "I'm sure I can handle it. Would you like to see some of my work?"

"Elias told me about it. That's good enough for me now. I will see your work when you work; I've been victimized by too many splendid credentials."

"I can live with that."

"You are also logistically perfect. I need someone now. When can you start?"

"As soon as you want."

"Please walk back down the hall. To the door marked PERSONNEL. Enter and take care of the social security business. Then you will meet the illiterate genius."

His name was Spencer Carmichael and he was precisely the sonofabitch I needed. So was the *Journal*:

LET US BE CAREFUL

Now that the State Department has eased up on travel regulations behind the iron curtain, the business community can certainly anticipate thirsty and hungry markets. However, we must never sell our souls for a handful of silver . . .

Thirsty and hungry were Spencer's, the handful of silver was mine and Wortham liked it even as Old Nassau crinkled his patrician nose.

HASTE? WASTE?

The Warren court has acted, as it had to, and has desegregated public parks, playgrounds, and golf courses; and Joe Louis has laid another rose on the grave of Abraham Lincoln. Yet, let us remember, as the President has so often said: we cannot legislate love, we cannot pass a law that will create brotherhood . . .

That was a standoff: the first sentence mine, the second the prick's.

THE PRESIDENT OF PROSPERITY
It is pleasing to note that General Motors has declared earnings in excess of one billion after taxes over the past year. Now this cannot be ascribed to Eisenhower luck. It is, quite simply, a free economy in full flower. What then of the tired bromide: the Depression Party? Depression indeed!

What you did not read was a line about Charlie Wilson at Defense (out of G.M.) nodding in smug satisfaction, plus a note of caution re hubris going before a fall. Spencer screamed all the way to Wortham on that and Wortham, with skyward eyes, x'd it, but not before Shimon almost broke his nose with his magnificent snort of ecstasy. Shimon also confided to me (beneath a swallow-tailed Willy Hearst) that he hoped Marion Davies wore the red flag every night for a year and we both snorted all the way to the Brooklyn Bridge on *that* one.

Still and all, to be absolutely Method honest, Hearst and his paper were now what I needed. And at the same time (for motivational combinations have always been essential to me or I'd never have gotten this far) they were what I deserved after what I had done to E. Speed has always—*always*—paid his dues. Yet the fact of the matter—which Shimon did *not* appreciate, but which again showed the forgiving nobility in E—was that I was functioning surprisingly well. The world had not ended with a whimper, bang or howl; I was making decent money; I was supporting my family. I was, by the best of definitions, an adult. And above all, I possessed secret intelligence (well, not so secret, but information that spoke specifically to *me*) and this motivating knowledge allowed me—or so I think I thought—to function neatly, also picked me up and infused me with cleanliness every time I felt messy about working for Bill H:

81

Any day now, Eisenhower, holding the pieces of that wounded heart together, would, MUST step aside.

This meant:

    I.   My debt would be paid in full.

    II.   I would be forever off the guilt-hook.

    III.   My perfidy would turn out to be a blessing in disguise. For:

        A. Him.

        B. Me.

        C. Both of us. Because:

            1. We would have survived the testing of each other.

            2. This would permit:

                a. E to return to himself.

                b. Speed to return to uplifting gratitude. Thus:

                    i. I did first-rate work.

                   ii. I made Wortham happy.

                 iii. I aggravated the ivy out of Spencer Carmichael.

                 iv. *I inexorably began to reshape Lucille.*

"Baby," said the power-holder, "you have gone as far as you can with Players. With Garth the way he is, with me gone, there's nothing left, no one else to dig you. It is time to cut the cord."

"Oh shit, I can't do that . . . can I?" she said. The man with the knowledge saw a chink of daylight.

"Look," he said, "you are being wasted. Exploited. Wasted and exploited. And not appreciated. You know this as well as I." He nodded with spontaneous sincerity, he *did*. "Why don't you look into one of those Broadway letters?"

"God, Broadway."

"Do not stereotype. Remember what you said about Sparkman? Stella Adler played Broadway. Stereotyping is not playing fair with your talent."

82

"Oh, but *those* bastards."

"You're not listening. A good actress must always listen."

". . . I'm listening . . ."

"All right, what's to lose? You don't have to make a commitment, merely explore."

"Exploring . . . is the beginning of a commitment . . ."

"It doesn't *have* to be."

She now had Hannah's solemn face; that was a good sign. She said, "Shit, I'd feel like a traitor."

The man of savvy was ready. "Listen, you don't owe; whom do you owe? McCarthy's down the drain. Dixon-Yates is dead."

". . . I suppose . . ."

"I'll tell you something else and you know it: Earl Warren is doing a terrific job."

"Well . . ."

"The plain fact is we've come through."

"We?" she said, looking up.

"Yes, we."

"Tell that to Oppenheimer."

"He's a professor, he can read."

"Sure, he can read the want ads."

"Well, tell Oppenheimer to wake up and live. Tell him next time check up on whom he talks to. Tell him there's a ball-buster out there named Russia."

The Hannah face said, "Speed, whatever your personal motivations for tying up with Wall Street, don't try to shit me."

He became expansive again. "Why should I try to shit you? We're a team." He leaned in confidentially. "I'll tell you something: Eisenhower won't run again."

"I told you not to shit me."

"I'm *not.* Jesus, you've certainly been *hearing* it."

"Sure, everyone talks, no one knows."

"*I* know."

"Did your overseers tell you?"

The big man let that one go. "They don't have to. I happen to know what makes him tick. If he is not one hundred percent, he will refuse to do the job."

"What about the concept-of-duty horseshit?"

"That is exactly *why* he won't run. He loves this country too much to keel over and give it to Nixon."

"As a certain editorial writer I know would say, balls."

Drew Pearson-Finestone reached down and picked Hannah up and curled her over his shoulder and patted gently. He said calmly, logically, "Don't you see? He doesn't run, this locks it up for Stevenson."

She brushed a wrist against a sprig of hair on her forehead; she always did that when she was upstaged.

"Who . . . *will* . . . they . . . run?"

"Good question. You tell *me*."

"Oh Christ," she said, "you're making too goddam much sense."

"You said that, I didn't," said the expansive chap. "Just look at it and think. Dewey is over the hill. Taft is pushing up daisies. Wilson's a *shlemiel.* Clay? Gruenther? Forget it."

She said in a small voice, "What about the senator from Formosa?"

"Please. No low comedy. The Eastern establishment wouldn't touch Knowland in a million years. Neither would the country. Neither, to let you in on something, would *he*."

The voice was smaller. "What about the bullshit artist?"

"Nixon? No way. No goddam way." Leaning further: "OK, I'll let you in on the whole Stassen thing: Specifically, Eisenhower is not quite the *schmuck* you've all constructed in your hot little heads. Believe me, he knows Nixon for just what he is. So he maneuvers. He outflanks. He sweeps wide. Not merely to dump the S.O.B., but to set Stassen up to run. Not for V.P., but the *whole ball of wax*." He folded comfortable arms. "If Stassen runs, Stevenson is *in*."

"Well then," she said, face flaring, "he *is* a *schmuck*."

The G-2 expert blinked. "Is it *his* fault they don't have anybody? Jesus, he didn't create the fucking party, he merely *saved* it."

A long assimilation.

"Will you remain with the Duma?" she said at last.

84

"Oh Christ," he said. "That is so mugwumpish. I really don't know. I have a theory I might be able to bore from within."

She shook her head and said with a shred of defiance, "If it makes you happy . . ."

Which brought the big man full circle. "More to the point," he said, "is making *you* happy. No. Making you *productive*. You owe it to yourself. You really do."

"Do you mean that, Speed?"

"Yes I do." And he *did*. For he wanted the Finestones to be together, to be inside the gate, to know that it wasn't so terrible after all, to be together.*

"It . . . wouldn't be a sellout?" she said.

"Not just exploring the thing, it wouldn't. Think of it this way: Stevenson will be in. You'll have done your job getting him in. He'd *want* you to expand your talent. To *share* it. You might even be pleasantly surprised. I work for a man who is not a philistine. Give it a whirl."

She rubbed Hannah's back, absorbed, touched deep cores.

"I have to let it develop," she said.

Splendid, for now. Hannah bubbled. The integrated man breezed out for a walk.

While she let it develop, I went back to work. And so did the little black book. I can see now, as I reconstruct, that it was the little book that kept me in my delicately functioning stasis, as well as the anticipated Eisenhower abdication. That was my phony war period and the book the dueling, standoff big guns:

---

*You may say, to be in the same miserable boat; I (still) say, to be *together*.

"Oh that prick Dulles and his Brink of War . . . Hold it, buster;
E knows we must never take shit . . . But the sanctimonious
bastard will bring on the fry bombs; E, Speed can handle land war,
but *that*? . . . Stay loose, E still in charge; WASP preacher works for
him . . . But righteous S.O.B.s are goddam bulldogs, never let go,
refer you to MacArthur . . . Glad you brought that up; E topped
MacA in long run . . . Granted, but Reds cannot take shit either,
must prove can do without Stalin . . . Fine, E on top of that:
writing to Zhukov; even preachers cannot split wartime buddies.
Buddies will keep peace . . . Maybe, but E is sick man; when cat's
away, pricks will play . . . Hate to say this but King Prick actually
acting like *mensch* . . . Come on, he's no match for Dulles . . .
Never underestimate a prick. Besides which, can we let Asia,
Africa go down red tubes? . . . But Asia, Africa none of our g-d
business . . . Oh yeah? THAT IS ISOLATIONISM; if do not
believe, check with Shimon . . . Hold it, vital question: Is it
possible, could it be, SHIMON, E ON SAME TEAM?????? All
together now:
  "PLEASEPLEASEPLEASEPLEASEPLEASEPLEASE . . ."

On February 29, 1956, my phony war ended. Eisenhower
announced he would run again.
  "You peckerhead! You *schmuck*! You patsy!"
  "Prince Richard in heaven! E, S same team? Never, *putz*!"

2

I was in a fog, a daze, a blue funk, I was a zombie. How could he
do this? How? How could he turn the country he loved over to the
King Of Pricks?
  I began to make mistakes at work. Spencer, happily,
complained to Wortham, who murmured that my usual high
standards seemed to have fallen off a bit. I shrugged and said even
DiMaggio struck out, and went for long, lunch-hour walks across
the Brooklyn Bridge. I wanted to go back and tell him, you can't
fire me, I *quit*, but I couldn't. I didn't even have the strength, the
will to do that. I returned to the house that Hearst built and while

86

he sat there fondling poor, innocent Marion Davies, I worked on the necessity for Eisenhower to complete the vital work he had begun, the equally compelling necessity for all of us to put our trust in medical science, especially Paul Dudley White.

"NIXON LICKING GODDAM CHOPS ANTICIPATION!"

To Lucille's credit she did not rub it in. Nor did Hannah. If anything, they were kinder, gentler, more on my side than ever before. Which, of course, made it tougher. For I had been worse than a patsy; I had been a *fatuous* patsy, and if there was anyone that Shimon hated more than a patsy, it was a patsy who said a state of unemployment exists when people are out of work. I made more mistakes, I began to move around in slow motion. I could not even get it up. I admit it. It's all there in the book.

But on June 8, 1956, so was something else: "Tonight fucked her to faretheewell; she came three x, aaahed, gasped like no tomorrow, said over, over, Speed, you never better!"

Eisenhower had ileitis.

I was restored. I was even stronger, yet newly modest, and ... yes, pure. Again. I walked around briskly, head high, but not too high like some people I had known. I was also incredibly magnanimous, particularly toward E. For this time, it was *his* punishment. No argument. He had tempted fate, his, ours, mine; had gone against the Gods of logic, national survival and his own nature. And the tough V-E body had rebelled. But this V-E body (and soul) forgave him; this GI said, it's all right, we're all entitled. Because he *had* to step down now and pave the way for Stevenson. So I could be my old, decent self.

But first I had to get him over the hump.

I said to Lucille, "How would you and the kid like to go to Washington?"

"I don't know," she said. "Ask the kid."

"How would you like to go to Washington, Hannah?" I asked. "It's a fascinating city. My father took me when I was little and we saw the cherry blossoms and Rock Creek Park and the Blue Room and Huey Long; what do you say?"

"Gaaah," she said.

"Good, we'll go."

"All right," said Lucille. "At least now you're asking; that's progress. Do you think we could see William Borah?"

I took her to bed.

We stayed in a little hotel in Arlington, because it was close to the Unknown Soldier, and while Lucille visited Lincoln, Washington, Jefferson and Smithson, Hannah and I hurried to my post across the street from Walter Reed. We stayed there for two days, staring up, praying. I have always believed in the prayers of babies and sure enough she came through. E and the wounded heart stood up beautifully and I promised him that when David, the grandson, grew up to know what time it was, and *if* he shaped up, I would see that he had a shot at Hannah, providing of course he went through me and she was still available.

The police were fine, just fine. They came around and kept asking: and how is the little lady doing? One of them let her pat his gigantic horse on the nose; she was fearless and drew a burst of applause. I carried her in triumph to the steps of the Lincoln Memorial.

"How's your gut?" Lucille said.

"Our gut is fine. Come on, we'll eat in a restaurant my father took us to across from Ford's Theater." I looked up to Hannah straddling my neck. "You won't believe what happened at Ford's Theater," I said . . .

88

I returned to my desk above the East River and, smiling to myself, shaped Spencer's tribute to the dignified and effective performance of the vice-president in his second time of trial. I also added a sentence about the succession, slapping the low-keyed but jockeying contenders on their lustful wrists for showing such poor taste at this critical time. Wortham liked it; Spencer pouted. I gave him one, didn't change a word, only added a comma and a question mark as he panned the steel strike.

On July 10 he walked over to me and said, very softly, "Word just came from Washington; he's going to run." He turned around and walked out of the room.

I looked at the Brooklyn Bridge. I could not feel patsied, or anything else; I could only hear my father: "What did you expect when you trust louses?" I looked at the Bridge, sighed, got up, walked to the water cooler. I drank. I walked out and in the corridor passed Spencer, who was leaning against the wall. I stopped. "What's eating you?" I said.

"Nothing," he said quietly.

"Then break out the champagne."

"Don't give me any of your radical nonsense," he said. "I wanted Nixon."

"*Schmuck*," I said, "you'll get him." I headed for Wortham's office.

"I have to quit."

"You heard?"

"Yes. I've had it. I can't take it anymore."

"They're using him, you know."

"No. It's his decision. If he put his foot down, they'd scream and cry and bang their heels, but he wouldn't run."

"Maybe."

"No maybes."

"Well then, you're quitting."

"Yes."

"Let me buy you lunch."

"Why not? It isn't your fault."

In a shrouding silence we walked to Sweet's on Fulton Street. We got V.I.P. treatment and the waiter asked if we would like cocktails before lunch. I said no, just give me a martini. Make it two, Wortham said.

"Well," he sipped, "what are you going to do now?"

"Probably go to work for Stevenson."

"I see," he said politely. We both drank and looked at the river. He finished his martini and asked if I'd like another. I said no; he said, do you mind if I do? Why should I mind? He ordered and sipped delicately but efficiently. "Would you believe," he said as he waved for another one, "that I became a Republican at the age of fifteen."

"That's terribly young to get so stupid."

"I rather suspected you would say something in that vein. But you are wrong. It was a very good thing to be. I was at Horace Mann and everyone there was a flaming Wilsonian. But you see, I had discovered Andrew Johnson."

"Jackson?"

He shook his head and ordered another drink.

"Everybody makes the same mistake. Poor Andrew, they cannot even get his name straight. Johnson. Lincoln's successor. I loved that man. An illiterate tailor, a boozer. But honest and tough as nails. He stood up to the hardest of them. Stevens, that crowd. He made me a Republican."

"Every man is entitled to his fling."

He chewed neatly on his olive. "May I give you a history lesson?" he asked shyly.

"Of course."

"We were the New Dealers of the last third of the nineteenth century. We had a magnificent reform record. On up to 1912. Teddy was quite splendid, you know, when he wasn't sending fleets around the world; marvelous record at home. The elder Taft was far better than the history books have led you to believe. In many ways we were the equal, if not the superior, of Wilson.

Terrible bigot, Wilson; did you know?"

"No, I didn't."

"Oh, yes. Not half the man Hughes was. I worked around the clock for Hughes, as you probably will for Stevenson. My greatest hero after Johnson. Actually president for eight hours until California did him in." He sipped, quickly. "Then," he sighed, "we got Harding, Coolidge and Hoover." His speech grew a bit more precise; otherwise there was no sign of the martinis. "I like to think I discovered Willkie; I wrote his first editorial, was even up in the galleries chanting. But no one could beat Franklin. And rightly so. But I didn't give up, for I knew that inevitably it would—*had*—to swing back, that we would do the things Harry could not do, much as I liked the old boy. Enter Eisenhower. I was absolutely certain he could recapture the glory years and return us to our greater selves . . . Ah well . . ."

I ordered another drink.

"You were shafted worse than I was," I said.

"I suppose you could put it that way," he said precisely. He looked out at the East River. "I have always enjoyed this place. It reminds me of Johnson; he would have been an honest tradesman in one of those shops. Ah well . . ."

"Why don't you quit?"

"Oh, it's much too late."

"Then go out and work for someone else. Try Rockefeller. He looks like he could tell Hoover to go fuck himself."

"Oh dear, Rockefeller? What would Andrew Johnson say?"

"What would he say about Hearst?"

He cradled his drink.

"A valid point. But somehow I've been able to work that out. Believe it or not, as Bob Ripley would say, the old man had some quite magnificent moments. I rather think I've blotted out the rest . . ." He looked shyly out at the river, the clipper ships, his magnificent third of the nineteenth century. "I don't suppose you would reconsider?" he said.

"No . . . I'm sorry."

"Ah then. Let's order. I can't have Carmichael see me in this state."

I went for long walks around the city with Hannah. When she got whiney, I took her up to the Stadium and explained the game to her and she clearly understood. I showed her the corner that Red Rolfe owned, where Flash Gordon did his somersaults, where Joe D glided around on water wheels. She clapped.

In August, Stevenson was nominated and opened up the vice-presidency to the convention. Lucille went for Henry Jackson because he had been so great in the '51 crime commission hearings. I leaned toward Symington; he had refused to be sucked in by McCarthy's "Sanctimonious Stu" bullshit and not many members of the Democrat Party had been that resistant. Hannah kept saying ooooh, which was her way of picking Hubert. None of us went for Kennedy; how could you go for a glamor boy whose father could buy and sell a senate seat? When we all turned out wrong, we shrugged and rallied round the flag because Kefauver was a good ol boy. Lucille got up very early the next morning to work for the ticket at the East Side Democrats while Hannah and I slouched around the TV set in the dining room.

Six days later, in San Francisco, the Republican convention: We watched the magnificent grin, the victorious arms, the screaming hordes, the sweating mask of the crown prince. I clicked it off, grabbed Hannah, walked down to the club and said to Lucille, who was stuffing envelopes, "Put us to work."

After a week in which we did every conceivable kind of dog work, she said, "You're really serious, aren't you?"

"Of course I'm serious, what do you think?"

"I never know with you."

"Well I'm serious."

"Then I'm going uptown tomorrow morning. Broadway."

I looked at my wife; my guilty face sighed.

"I think you are wasted with the Players. I haven't changed on that. But don't go uptown because of what I said when I was crazy. That doesn't count."

"But you still want me to try the bastards?"

"Yes, I think I do. You can beat them."

She kissed me and with Hannah beaming said, "Yes, I think we can."

2

She took one of the letters down from over the john and journeyed uptown, to 53rd Street, just east of Fifth. She met a Cyrus Broadcutter, who had been an assistant producer to Jed Harris and Saint Subber and was now ready to step up in class. He had a "property" called *Brownstone*, written by a 4F from Rego Park named Frank Contino. It was Bill Inge transplanted to 75th Street off Columbus, agonizingly confessional, but not without some squirmy truth. Lucille read for Lolly, first floor front, an Indiana girl who daylights at Altman's, who knows she must become the next Lynn Fontanne and until she does will not permit Mack Farley, basement apartment, straight hoofer, to touch her. She got the part ("It wasn't even a stretch").

Meanwhile, out of the East Side Kids, a scratching, hissing reform bunch, I worked my *tochis* off for Adlai-Estes, and it was even tougher than in '52 when at least we had had the new and gleaming Adlai. At the end of September I was back in Damon's office. I asked him if he was collecting I told you sos.

"Only briefly."

"My father was right. Bums are bums."

"Does that include Henry Wortham?"

"No. He was all right. He's some kind of mutant. The rest of them. From the top down."

"The top?"

"The top."

"Well?" he said.

"So here I am."

"Well."

"Sadder, wiser, hat in hand."

"To what end?" he said.

"I want to return to my world."

"Rexford Tugwell?"

"And Ben Cohen. And Tommy the Cork. And PWA and NRA and CCC and AAA. I want to repay my dues. Am I making any sense?"

"I believe you are," he said.

"Then would you . . . I mean, do you think . . . Well, can you put me back in touch with *my* side?"

He would. He could. He did.

The magazine was called *The New Meridian: A timeless review*. It had been conceived a year before by some of the old *PM-Star* people who could not live with the third version called the *Compass*, but who also could not get the old dream out of their heads. A stand-up liberal bunch, clean as Fala's tooth, with the impeccable credentials that would let them take head-snapping but true shots at the administration and its allies, they had pulled the lovely old ideas together and placed Ellis Island above the masthead. With the dream almost reality, they had then gone out to scrounge for money. They had tapped every big contributor to Stevenson in '52 and struck gold with Harvey Levine, a paper-box magnate from Riverdale, a self-made man, a Roosevelt man, who believed as a matter of basic business principle in reciprocal trade treaties: "Sure, I'll back your magazine. My daughter becomes editor in chief or chief editor or whateverthehell—the boss." They had caucused, agreed, interviewed the daughter. Or, as I heard the story, she had interviewed them. In any case, *The New* (timeless) *Meridian* had been born.

Enter Elias Damon. He had taught a nonfiction workshop at Sarah Lawrence in the summer of '51 and his star pupil had been a Carla Levine. She had basic talent, had asked questions when

94

she had run into trouble, had kept in touch. And she had talked to people Damon had said talk to. As in the present case. As she sat on a black leather and chrome recliner behind a Norsk desk in a graystone in Murray Hill. And she was saying, "What in heaven's name were you doing on the *Journal*?"

"Spying for Henry Wallace."

She didn't blink, crinkle, shrug.

"Damon told me you were a cynical sonofabitch," she said evenly. "That doesn't cut any ice with me." She had a head of straight black hair that framed her face, a face carefully unmade-up, probably by Elizabeth Arden on Fifth Avenue.

"That's your privilege," I said.

"It certainly is. He also told me to look past the cynicism deep into your sensitive and talented soul."

"Oh shit."

"That's what I told him."

"Do you have a job?"

"I might. Damon told me you know theater. I need a reviewer; the one I have thinks he's writing for *Dial*."

"I know theater. Sometimes I write like it's for the *Daily Mirror*."

"I can live with that. Let me see something."

"Is this an audition?"

"In a way."

"I thought Damon told you about me."

"He did. I still like to see the goods I pay for."

"Oh Christ. The *Journal* didn't ask to see anything."

"The *Journal* doesn't know its ass from an artesian well. Have you seen *Long Day's Journey*?"

"No, I don't like O'Neill."

"That's all right, he probably wouldn't care for you, either. See it and turn in a review. Then we can have a substantive talk."

She stood and strode around the desk and held out an un-manicured hand. She was very leggy, more Smith than Sarah Lawrence. I took the hand and pumped once.

"Thank you very much, Miss Levine," I said.

95

I got tickets to the play but, an hour before the curtain, backed out. I sat down and pounded out a piece that I headed, *LONG DAY'S JOURNEY INTO NIGHT: Dulles and America*. It was gloom, doom, storm and stress, comparing our foreign policy to the way France fought her wars: always getting ready for the last one, with the same possible (probable) outcome. I mailed it off to Carla Levine, then went to the Eighth Street Cinema to see *Baby Doll* because Eli Wallach was in it and I'd go to see Eli Wallach even if he played O'Neill.

She called me a week later.

"That was an interesting piece," she said.

"Thank you."

"It wasn't your assignment."

"I didn't particularly care for the assignment. I knew I wouldn't like it."

"So your artistic morality told you not to review it?"

"Yes, and I didn't like being ordered to review it."

"Really? Damon told me you were a big shot in the war."

"Just a medium shot."

"Then you know how important chain of command is."

"Was."

"I am still in command, Mr. Finestone."

"Would you like me to work for you, Miss Levine?"

"In a way I would. Do I hear you saying, 'Only if I pick the plays?'"

"I'm afraid you do. I might also get compulsive and want to do something else on occasion. A *cri de coeur*? Of course, you may reject it."

"May I?"

"You're the boss."

"Oh, don't be such a sensitive shit. I'll have to mull it over."

Another week. Suez exploding. British bombs falling on Cairo airfields; Bengal Lancers, Sepoys, Ghurkas, Khyber Passes, Roberts of Kandahar, Kitchener of Khartoum. They must, of course, prevail. Besides which, how could Fuzzy Wuzzies run the Canal? Wrong. The British Empire flickered out: Fuzzy Wuzzies worked the Canal. Over in Europe the iron curtain ripped open; the Budapest rebels had a chance. Wrong. Listen, I told the East Side faces, Stevenson is not indecisive, unsure, unsafe, unstable, unlikely. Wrong, they told me. And she called me again.

"All right, I'll take a chance," she said. "You've got the job."

"What about the substantive talk?"

"This is it. There'll be a desk for you tomorrow morning. You can move it if you wish providing there is space. Good luck to us both, Mr. Finestone."

I hit a stride, found a groove overnight; everything must have been gathering, building during my time with the *Journal*. I took on *Separate Tables*, probably, I can see now, because I was so furious with England for collapsing in Suez, and in nineteen paragraphs dismissed the play as the archetypal fluff the colonies forever swooned over. I got mail. Then I charged into *Anne Frank*. I titled the review, "*A LITTLE GUILT COULDN'T HURT YOU.*" I got more mail, some of it quite rugged. I shifted gears, turning an obit of Louis Bromfield into a dissection of *The Rains Came* starring Loy and Power, detailing with inordinate pain how it so innocently mirrored our own *Passage to India*. Carla Levine did not quite understand it (naturally), but did not reject it, which surprised me. Others, with gratifying intensity, did understand and a lively little feud sprang up on the letters page between the E. M. Forster people and those I labeled the MGM IMPERIALISTS. The fight sold a few more magazines. I was feeling good now, although a bit remorseful for stomping

Britain, so I knocked out a piece called *A Farewell to Eden*, wherein I reminded all the simon-pure anticolonialists that Sir Anthony was once (along with Churchill) the loneliest voice in the appeasing Western world and that one would hope Dulles and sanctimonious company remembered that even as they jerked the rug out from under him. For the tag line, I inquired plaintively (I was doing much plaintive inquiring in those early days on the magazine), wasn't that what history was for?

Hugh Dischley, who handled foreign affairs—mainly from the U.N. Library—rather liked it. Carla Levine pursed an unpainted lip, said, I don't follow all of it, but you *do* seem to make a valid point. Again she did not reject and I got more mail, including a pleasant note from Bennett Cerf which said that if ever I had the urge to do a book on the appeasement politics of the thirties to keep him in mind.

So there I was, Speed again. Grinning crookedly, dangling a butt, looking bland, Front-Pageish. But I was also the involved Speed. Hustling from smoking typewriter down into the pits to do battle for Adlai. Also the caring, sensitive Speed. From Adlai to the theater for the final shaping and then the opening of *Brownstone*. Lucille had a last-minute attack of nerves, but I got her through it and five days before Election Day she opened. The play got mixed reviews, but not Lucille. The first stringers dipped shamelessly into the critic's handbook and came up with the gems reserved for Harris, Stanley, Stapleton, et al: "Sustained incandescence"; "Heartbreaking accuracy"; "Outrageously luminous"; "Plastic yet tough"; "Specific, unique, but reminiscent of: (Pick one) Ina Claire, Kit Cornell, Pauline Lord, Betty Field." I didn't review it for obvious reasons, but had to agree that, bullshit aside, they were all basically correct about her; the performance was simple reality, but true and interesting because she was.

After seeing her Broadway ship safely launched, I decided to bite the uptown hand that was feeding us so fatly. I looked around and settled on *Fanny*. I savaged it, not only because it was so savageable but also because it gave me the opening to tear into prewar France, one of my father's pet hates; using the play as metaphor, I summed up the cultural hollowness of the period, as well as its moral flatulence. This also eased the smart of our doing commercial theater, so in one review I killed three irksome birds, one of my more satisfying performances.

With that under my belt, with the old Speed in control, I went out to vote.

I wound up in the same school as in '52 and with the same old-timers handling the register. I signed in. Just before I entered the booth I dipped one last time into the little black book. Under "Ten reasons why you must not vote for him" I had listed:

1. Defective ticker
2. Bad plumbing
3. Fatuous Fink Foster
4. Aswan F-up
5. Shafting of Hungary
6. Shafting of Eden
7. Quemoy, Matsu horseshit
8. Nixon
9. Nixon
10. Nixon

I walked in and pulled the shroud. I dangled an unlit butt, relaxed and looked the situation over. I reached smoothly for the Stevenson lever, grinned, closed my eyes. When I opened my eyes, my finger was on the Eisenhower lever. I pulled it down.

Every time my father screwed up the deal, he would spit and sigh, "Ah, shit-uh," always hanging that little tag onto the sigh. When he did that, I always knew he was in trouble.

I went around spitting and sighing and saying, "Ah, shit-uh."

Shimon also did something else; he worked twice as hard in the store, sometimes even sleeping down there.

I plunged into a kaleidoscope of projects. Complaints. Agonies. Disgusts. Cheers, jeers, corrections. I slammed *Middle of the Night* and advised Chayevsky on the fine points of garment center activity. I got furious with *Auntie Mame* and kept asking how dare they? In a long, rambling essay-review I compared the relative merits of two newcomers, Callas and Presley. I called it *Rebels With a Cause* and showed with involuted care how both of them fit perfectly into the historical-revolutionary continuum that included Wagner, Ibsen, Duncan, Jolson and Brando. But that hard sour ball, the one my father knew, still lay there, lumped there, despite the work, the spitting, the shit-uhs. And here is why: there was something—*someone*—complicating my guilt, someone who clearly knew *me* as well as I knew my father. Dammit, *Hannah kept staring at me.* No matter how hard I worked, how much I compensated, how much I blocked out, she kept staring. Finally, unlike my father who really should have taken the bull by the horns when the spitting started, but rarely did, I couldn't take it anymore. After all, as Vincent Sheean would say, there was personal history here. I drank a bottle of beer and scooped the Scrutinizer out of her crib and plumped her down on the sofa. She sat there, a little butterball, quiet, demure. She stared. I paced up and down in front of her.

"Look," I said, "You have to understand what makes a person tick. What his internal motivations are, as Stanislavsky would say. That is a prime necessity, OK?"

She stared.

"OK. You know what I was before the General got hold of me? Practically nothing. That is what. I don't care if the world thought I was something, that is what *I* thought. So we begin there, do you see?"

She stared.

"Oh sure I was a hotshot in art and French and world history, so what? In my innermost soul I was zero. And you know why? I'll tell you. I was a *misser*. M.I.S.S.E.R. I was almost, nearly, within shooting distance, an also-ran. I broad jumped nineteen feet eleven inches at Morris, but not twenty, *never twenty*. I high jumped five eleven, just missed *six*. I weighed a hundred and *forty-nine* pounds. Get it? I made Life Scout, missed Eagle by one merit badge, because I didn't know the lousy birds. Who knows birds on Tremont Avenue? . . . All right, you must perceive the pattern. In college I missed getting laid three times by the skin of my teeth, the last time was so close I could smell it. Close did not count to yours truly. I missed. Do you understand that?"

Her blue-green pupils filled her eyes.

"All right, *he* got me over there. Reached down and got me over there. *Over there*. Me. I was less than Nixon and he did it. Set me down in England, just outside of London. This nothing, this misser. But now listen carefully. Gradually, inexorably, I TURNED INTO SOMETHING. And the pace accelerated as I realized what was happening. I looked at my khaki sleeve and I accelerated. I felt those combat boots and I accelerated. And in those magic clodhoppers I began to go to the dances they threw for us, to the dance halls where they waited for us. Over in Brighton. Right beside the wild, rococo palace. And from a chronic misser I became a clicker. I met those gorgeous limey girls who were crazy about Yanks at Oxford and before you could say "Woodchoppers' Ball" or "Moonlight Serenade" I had them down on the famous beach. Bing, bing, bing, click, click, click. When I set up my target for tonight, *I did not miss*. And so Speed was born. "Hey," the guys said, "the new land *speed* record." "Hey, *Speed* strikes again." "There he goes, *Speed*." "What's your secret, *Speed*?" "This is my buddy, *Speed*!" Overnight almost, that is who I was. *Am*. Get it?"

She stared.

"Ah, but I'll tell you something. It wasn't all peaches and cream. An epiphany never is. The old comfortable kid, the misser, pulled and tugged, he wanted me to play it safe. But it was too late. Speed was in the deep water and swimming. He would *never* go back. Well hardly ever. But in essence, no more missing, no more close-but-no-cigars. This he knew. This *I* know. And so

101

did the man who made it all possible. Even while I was worrying about the invasion, he reached down again, now that I was who I was, and planted me on Omaha Beach. Do you have any idea what that meant to a kid who was scared shitless of Lefty McDougall on Tinton Avenue? Nobody does. Correction. *He* did. He made me a goddam hero. That's right, a clicking goddam hero. And I lived up to the honor. I did not touch one iota of jerry contraband. I did not once dip my wick into Nazi strength through joy. Never. Not this boy. I'll tell you something else just in case you're wondering. Every time I made out in France or England, in addition to my own personal inspection I immediately checked into a pro station, so you don't have a thing to worry about. That's because he showed me, taught me, *allowed* me, to become who I am."

She stared.

"Now how can I go back on that man? How can I vote against a person who did all that for your father? Do you see? Do you understand? Hannah, please don't look at me like that, please say something, I'm *talking* to you."

She stared. Then she said, firmly, loudly, "Da-da."

"What was that?"

"Da-da," she said, even louder.

I got down on my knees in front of the sofa.

"Do you really mean that?" I said. "That this thing I've done means nothing, you don't hold it against me; it is *nonsense* as far as you're concerned? I'm going to test you, Hannah. Say Ma-ma, not da-da."

"Da. Da."

"Real true Dada?"

"Da-da."

"Oh thank you, sweetheart."

I picked her up and fixed her a whole new bottle of orange juice and tucked her in and read her a chapter of *Billy Budd*. By the time Lucille came home my sour ball had melted, my stomach was calm and we were both dreaming sweetly.

"1936 . . . . . . plus . . . . . . 20"
by Speed Finestone

"Was it only twenty years ago? That watershed year? Only twice ten that they were saying, 'As Maine goes, so goes Vermont'? Was there something in between called WW2? Was it a history book ago? Did a man named (the second) Roosevelt really exist? Did he, that man? Did that woman? Was there a sunflower named Landon? A Father Coughlin? If there was, did he ever shut up? Did the *Literary Digest* really and truly predict a Republican landslide? Did the *Literary Digest* ever exist? Did Al Smith really tell us to vote for Landon? *Our* Al Smith? Did Jesse Owens come out for the GOP? Jesse *Owens*? Did Mencken say they could beat Roosevelt with a Chinaman or even a Republican? Did Mencken ever shut up? Was there ever a Gerald L. K. Smith? You're kidding, there was? Did Hugh Johnson actually say that Felix Frankfurter's boys were Happy Hot Dogs? He did?

"Did Lloyd George pat Hitler on the head for solving Germany's problems? Lloyd George, who in 1918 shouted, 'Hang the Kaiser'? When Hitler marched into the Rhineland, could France have been so yellow that 35,000 troops scared off six million? Not to mention fifty million Frenchmen? *Clemenceau's* France? *Joffre's* France? *Foch's* France? Did the Nobel Prize for Literature really go to someone besides Hitler? Couldn't we have bottled that Swedish courage and shipped it to England and France? They wouldn't have let it in? How come Hitler only got 99 percent of the German vote? Was there really one percent of guts in *Uber Alles*? What happened to that one percent? When Hitler and Musso joined Franco, did the rest of the world really

103

let them? Did the same world actually let Musso waltz into Ethiopia? Did that world think 'sanctions' got them off the guilt-hook? Did an American volunteer regiment *fight* for Musso? *American*? When Haile Selassie threw a party in exile, did the U.S., France and Russia actually refuse to attend? Are you telling me the great powers were *that* yellow? Was Badoglio really given the title of Duke of Addis Ababa? Would you kindly call me the Count of Castle Hill?

"Was there ever something called the Black Legion? Did they make a movie about the miserable thing? Did young people actually account for twenty percent of all crime? Was marijuana as big a problem as the narcos said?

"How could they ever replace Irving Thalberg? Kipling? Gorky? Cyrus McCormick? Madame Schumann-Heink? Marcel? Who would wave all that hair?

"Is it true that the film of *Anthony Adverse* gave the author, Hervey Allen, a great idea for a new novel? What happened to Luise Rainer after her second Oscar? Was Freddie Bartholomew really kidnaped by his Aunt Cissie? Why was *The Children's Hour* renamed *These Three*? Would hep cats destroy popular music? Did someone really and truly write a song called "The Music Goes Round and Round?" Why didn't Negro musicians get the credit for creating jazz and swing? Was Simone Simon the next sex kitten? Was Mr. Moto sinister and Charlie Chan a nice guy? Or was it the other way around? Wasn't televising pictures through the air a form of black magic? Did performers on the Amateur Hour really get more votes than candidates in state elections? Why not?

"Was that stringbean King Farouk? Musso's son-in-law got his job as Foreign Minister strictly on talent, didn't he? Did Germany and Austria really sign a treaty announcing Austria's independence? Was that the greatest snow job since the top of the Matterhorn? Was Chiang Kai-shek ever a hero? Was Chiang Kai-shek ever? Was there an Oswald Mosley? An Edward VIII? Was he really such a good guy? Did 39,000 maritime workers go out on strike? Did Haywood Patterson, one of the Scottsboro boys, actually get *seventy-five* years?

"Did Alabama call Patterson's lawyer, Sam Leibowitz, a meddling New York Jew?

"When Hitler called Jesse Owens and company our 'Black Auxiliaries', did much of the world really nod in silent agreement?

"When two Jewish runners were left off the American Olympic relay team in Germany, was it because they had suddenly gone lame?

"When Schmeling knocked out Louis, did millions of Americans secretly applaud?

"SO WHAT ELSE IS NEW?"

Carla Levine said, "Are *you* hung up on the thirties."

"I liked them," I said. "They were personally significant." I didn't tell her I couldn't stand Manny, but I loved his decade and the whole thing was terribly complicated; whathehell business was that of hers, anyway?

"Like?" she said. "Hung up. Yes, hung up. Hell, I liked the forties, especially 1945, but basically I could take them or leave them."

I took a good fast look at Carla Levine. She was about as tall as Margaret Truman. I smelled her; she smelled like Sweetheart soap. I had known an opinionated, Sweetheart-smelling Margaret Truman in Atlanta in 1942. Her name was Bianca Winningham. She called me Manyul. She said I was deep. I decided to give Carla Levine-Winningham a tantalizing glimpse into my depths. "It was my ambition to be a grown man by 1936," I said tantalizingly. "My parents and the stars were not in congruence, but that was still my ambition."

She looked me over; she always looked people over. "If you

were a big, grown man in 1936 you could have gone to the Olympic Games, couldn't you?"

"That and other things. Actually, just being a big, grown man and in New York, that would have been sufficient unto my needs." I decided to close the transom into my heart and soul; she was getting a little too close. That seemed all right with her and she didn't push; I'll say this for Carla Levine: she didn't push, at least, not then. She said, still keeping the connection, but now making it hers, "My father almost went to the Olympic Games; he couldn't see spending money in Nazi stores and hotels, but he was crazy about a Gene Venzke from the University of Pennsylvania. He was sure Venzke would win the mile."

"He once," I said, "ran the mile in four ten."

"Very good," she said.

"Cunningham was better and faster, also stronger. He ran it in four four four."

"Yes, but it was on a phony track up at Dartmouth. So it didn't count."

I took another look at Carla Levine. She had pointy, intelligent boobs, like Maggie Sullavan's. She said, "My father predicted Gene Venzke would defeat Jack Lovelock in Berlin."

"Did your father also say prosperity was just around the corner, in 1930?"

"I'm quite sure he did not."

"Well in the athletic world he was as good a predictor as Hoover in economics or Neville Chamberlain, the political seer, who was very big on peace in our time. The only man who could beat Lovelock was Cunningham. This adolescent person could have told him that. But even Cunningham couldn't do it in '36. To say nothing of Venzke."

"Oh well, Venzke and Fenske," she said.

"What's that supposed to mean?"

She regarded me archly. "After Venzke my father was nuts about Fenske."

"Chuck Fenske," I said. "U. of Wisconsin."

"Yes indeed."

106

"He liked those middle European guys, your father."

"Yes. He thought they were Jewish."

"Sorry. Jews didn't go to the University of Pennsylvania back then."

"I dare say they didn't. Shall I tell you why my father hated Hitler?"

"He kept him out of the U. of Pennsylvania."

"Don't be an idiot. Of course there was the usual, the devil business and that sort of thing, which you touched on in your hot little cathartic essay, but the main thing, and this infuriated my father, was that Hitler ruined the 1940 Olympics in Tokyo, thereby preventing Fenske from wreaking revenge on Lovelock in the mile."

"I wish you wouldn't keep saying mile. It was the fifteen hundred meters," I said.

"Same difference," she said with her Maggie Sullavan upper-crustiness. "The fact is, we always managed to screw up the mile."

"Almost always. We won it in ought four and ought eight. But we have screwed it up since then."

"With one exception. This year, a sophomore at Villanova won it. Ron Delaney."

"That doesn't count. He's Irish. He won it for Ireland."

"But he's beautiful."

"Beautiful? He runs like a chicken."

"A beautiful chicken. And Villanova is very close to the University of Pennsylvania. I have a proposition to make."

"I'm listening."

She leaned back on a sensible heel and pointed an intelligent tit at me. "Would you like to see Ron Delaney? I have two tickets to the Millrose Games and my father can't make it."

"No thanks," I said. "Delaney's not American."

2

The next night Lucille said, and Hannah is my witness, "They want me to tour in *Auntie Mame*."

"What?"

107

"*Brownstone* is closing and they want me to tour in *Auntie Mame*."

"But that's a piece of shit."

"So was *Brownstone*."

"But it was an *honest* piece of shit."

Lucille picked Hannah up and patted her behind nervously.

"I knew you'd be like this," she said.

"How else could I be?"

"Like this."

"Then why in God's name do it?"

"I don't like you to tell me what to do."

"I told you to try Broadway, God help me."

"You *asked* me."

"Well now I'm asking you. Don't tour in shit."

"We can use the money."

"Fuck the money. This is a sell-out."

"But you said I should—"

"I know what I said. I repeat: Not in *shit*."

"Don't be a hypocrite, Speed. It's your least attractive quality. If you do a thing, whatever, do it all the way. Besides, I'm not playing Mame."

"Some great distinction. Now who's splitting hypocritical hairs?"

"I'll let that go. I think I can do this and retain my integrity. Cyrus will let me shape the part my way. Speed, be reasonable, it's only as far as Chicago."

"What about Hannah?"

She patted her behind again. Hannah beamed.

"You're not exactly helpless. And I've asked Mary Coogan to look after her when you're at work. Her show is closing and she loves Hannah; they have a marvelous chemistry. You and Mary can work out a schedule between you. It's only three weeks . . . Speed . . . Come on . . . There are worse things than *Auntie Mame*."

"Like giving Hitler Czechoslovakia."

She slammed out so hard Hannah's head bounced.

☆   ☆   ☆

108

Fifteen minutes later the big man called Carla Levine. He said very distinctly, so the whole world and its cousin could hear, "All right, let's go see Ron Delaney."

I hadn't been to the Garden in eighteen years, probably because the ghost of Manny still hovered somewhere in the balcony, in the Clyde Beattied, Art Concelloed air. In the old days Manny had gone with Yale Muttlach, who was a track and field nut in his geometry class at Morris. They would meet at Davega's, next door, then go up to seventh heaven to screech for Greg Rice, to boo the foreigners like Luigi Beccali and Taisto Maki in the mile and Suo Ohe in the pole vault (and sure enough, they rarely won a thing even though they had been such hotshots overseas; Nurmi, thank goodness, was a little before Manny's time).
I met Carla at Tony Canzoneri's and we had Manhattans while I tracked Tony around the room as he glad-handed the customers and I marveled at the enormous head and torso perched on the tiny feet that had waltzed Lou Ambers around for so many rounds in the days of Manny's years. I didn't say anything to Carla Levine about him, or Ambers, or Barney Ross, or Jimmy McLarnin, or Billy Petrolle; why should I share them with a wiseass from Sarah Lawrence? Instead I explained that Ron Delaney had developed his herky-jerky style by slogging through peat bogs. She considered and said, you're shitting the kid, Finestone, come on, I like to watch all the heats and the P.A.L. relays.
Which she surely did. We sat in the loge on the turn and the pole vaulters almost jackknifed into our laps, and she yelled and clapped and got studding neck veins as the runners kicked off the last banked turn and drove for the tape. And yes, the big man got caught up. By the time the tuxedoed crowd arrived for the Wanamaker Mile, I was sitting up and paying attention and checking times against the Manny-Yale era. When Ron Delaney pit-patted onto the track for his warm-up, I joined the boo-birds while she stood and screamed Ronnie-e-e-e-e. I booed some more and she looked down at me from a great height.
"Why did you do that?" she demanded.
"He never ran a fast mile in his life."

109

"He runs to win. What's wrong with that?"

"Nothing. But I like records."

"That's nonsense."

"Besides, he's not American."

"Again? What a schmucky thing to say."

She turned away and cheered for Ronnie-e-e-e-e.

It was no contest, of course. Delaney sat back in his rocking chair as they had taught him at Villanova, and at the end of the tenth lap he rose up on his toes and sprinted from fifth to first in twenty yards, won, easing up, by three. Carla Levine clutched her Maggie Sullavan chest and dropped down next to me as I booed politely and she murmured, "Oh God, I thought he might lose."

"Are you kidding? He had it all the way. He was toying with them. But he didn't break four ten."

He bounced around the track smiling, and they announced four ten three. I said, "Even Venzke would have taken him."

Carla Levine shrugged. "Nonsense. He would have run fast enough to win, and that includes your precious Cunningham."

After we left Al Mueller's, she said, "I'll race you crosstown."

"Don't be silly," I said.

"Come on, Cunningham," she said. "Put your legs where your mouth is."

She took off toward Broadway in a long, low lope.

"Hey," I yelled. "Come back here and behave yourself."

She stopped and high-stepped backwards. When she reached me, she took off again. Her Tailored Woman trench coat flapping in the West Side night. I started after her. When I pulled up alongside, she accelerated and darted across Broadway in front of a howling taxi and loped for Radio City. I sprinted across the street after her, but she stretched out and kept her distance. I pulled Avenue D'Americas to me, then Fifth, Madison, Park. At each corner, just as I began to close the gap, she shifted into her Delaney gear and sprinted away. I began to labor at Lexington. I said out loud, "Now you nail that goddam broad, you *putz*," and I reached down for all I had left. Apparently I had something, for I caught her in the middle of Second Avenue, flung my arms wide for the tape, turned and grabbed her as the traffic screamed around us. She threw her arms around my neck, pulled me down and kissed me and panted, "Oh, but ... that ... was ... *gorgeous*."

Then, arm in arm, to blaring horns, we walked to the curb and continued on to her place on 53rd Street off First.

3

The doorman gave her a quietly respectful hello. So did the elevator man. We got off at fourteen and walked down a tasteful hall and near its end stopped. She took a key out of her purse and handed it to me. Manny should only have had it so good. Speed inserted, turned, opened and said, "Thank you for Ron Delaney, I had a good time."

"Would you like to come in?" she said, turning to face me, propping the door open with a loafered foot. I handed her the key.

"No thanks."

"All right," she said.

She put her arms around my neck and kissed me with enough wetness for Manny to swim all the way to France. I kissed her back. She unhooked one of my hands and placed it on a Maggie Sullavan tit. Manny made a little circle. She ahhhed and reached down and gave my crotch a gentle squeeze, disengaged and slipped inside and gently closed the door without saying a word.

I walked home.

Lucille was in bed, face to the wall, breathing just a little too deeply. I washed and walked into Hannah's room. I looked down at the crib, bent over it.

"No action," I whispered. "I swear."

On Monday morning Lucille left with the company for
Philadelphia. Hannah and I took her to the Greyhound terminal
on 50th Street near the Garden, which I carefully avoided looking
at. I loaded her luggage and chatted calmly and professionally and
then Hannah and I kissed her goodbye and good luck. Hannah
and I took the 104 bus to 74th Street, got off and walked to West
End to Mary Coogan's. Mary was waiting with coos and juice and
diapers and I produced the four pages of instructions I had
worked up the night before: Feeding times, Nap times, Going-to-
bed times, Reading material, with emphasis on Melville and
Hawthorne, Exercise times, Speed's number at *Meridian*,
Pediatrician's number, Bureau of Missing Persons' number, Local
FBI number, three paragraphs on the Lindbergh Kidnap Law
with detailed explanation on how to read law aloud with proper
inflection for potential Hauptmanns. Mary seemed to
understand; I gave her an extra key to the apartment and had a
long, serious talk with Hannah about the importance of grace
under pressure, kissed her goodbye and went off to work.

On Wednesday afternoon, Carla Levine asked me if I'd like to
see Ron Delaney do it again.
"Which meet?"
"N.Y.A.C."
"Sure, why not?"
We met again at Canzoneri's and there was a slight tinge of
familiarity that resonated with dates in Atlanta, London and
Brighton: ordering our drinks, the chitchat, sliding her neatly
into the trench coat, feeling her hand tuck into my arm, having
her slip me the tickets. Looking back, I didn't even have the sense
to think, uh-oh . . .

We had the same seats (another checkpoint) and I decided to root for the (mainly black) Pioneer Club and as we moved from the sprints into the middle distances I had some exciting (and gratifying) winners. Then the mile. And she was right again. That darn Delaney just sat back, rocked along, suddenly came to life, kicked, shot from last to first and won in a trot in four nine and change and a scattering of boos. This time I applauded lightly because he had broken four ten, while she whacked her palms like pistol shots. I bought her a hot dog and a beer and in her program, after she had carefully recorded the winner and his time, I wrote, "You and your education . . . G. Cunningham." She pecked me on the cheek; I glowed, looked around, slouched down in my seat.

We raced across town again. I nipped her by a careful head on First Avenue. We rode the elevator breathlessly, giggling, leaning against the walnut paneling. We had another session outside her door, hot, wet, hard. I walked home with my overcoat carefully buttoned all the way down, bent slightly into the wind. I got the report from my NYU sitter, paid her and gave her cab fare. I checked on Hannah and wrote in the little black book: "Am definitely holding my own . . . HAH!"

We caught the AAU Championships and the IC4As and Delaney cakewalked home in each and we ran through our before-and-after ritual and the Crusader in Europe would have been proud of me; I wound up home, scribbling in the little book, assuring Hannah that she could always be proud of me. During the day, now that I was in shape, I trotted home to relieve Mary; I took over for two hours, feeding Hannah and walking her and reading a little *Marble Faun* to her. Lucille called every night and I gave her a solid report, right down to ounces gained and BMs.

Near the end of February—it was a Thursday night—she called and said, "Speed, they want us to keep going, past Chicago."

"So?"

"They've got bookings in St. Paul, Denver and Vegas. Caesar's Palace, believe it or not."

"I believe it. Well?"

"They need me, Speed."

"Well?"

"It'll only be three more weeks."

"Well?"

"I told them I would do it."

"*Mazel tov.*"

I hung up and called Carla Levine.

"You've got tickets to the Knights of Columbus, haven't you?" I said.

2

It was the final meet of the New York season. The boo-birds, the stopwatchers with their serious faces, the Catholic school brothers, the Garden-addicts, the high school kids, the familiar voices were all there. Carla was Carla, but I was a little noisier than usual as we worked our way up to the mile. Delaney, looking comfortable, waited until the last manageable instant, timed himself beautifully and won by two feet with his broad Olympic grin. This time I yelled, you're all right, Delaney, and Carla said, well, *that's* progress.

We raced home stride for stride. Outside her door, before anything got started, I said, "How about a cup of coffee?"

"Are you sure?" she said.

"I'm sure."

"Well well."

We walked into a low-slung apartment and I sat down on a leather director's chair while she made coffee. We drank silently and I looked out at the East Side pile. Then I made a clumsy pass and knocked over the coffee cups.

"Oh shit," I said. "I'll get them."

"No," she said, "I will."

She kneeled down and picked them up and blotted the coffee with napkins and looked up at me, one knee gleaming.

"Do you mean it?" she said.

"Yes, I think so."

"The hell with that. Do you or don't you?"

"Yes."

114

"Then for heaven's sake let's get comfortable. Couches remind me of the backseats of cheap cars."

She got up and walked with her proudly marvelous spine into the bedroom. I heard Sibelius and looked at the front door. Manny got up and stepped toward it; Speed remembered St. Paul, Denver. *Vegas*. I turned slowly and followed *Finlandia*.

She was long, smooth, lean, tan, firm. The Margaret Sullavans sat straight up and winked at me. I stroked. So did she and she was so very neat and deft and clean with each hand, each leg. I looked down at all the easily meshing parts; Manny shivered; Speed covered with a polite cough. She said calmly, "What in the world took you so long?"

"Tonight or in general?"

"In general, *schmuck*. All goddam winter. I'm spoiled; I'm not used to it."

"I'm a happily married man."

"I'm not asking you to compare."

"Why don't you shut up."

"Aye, aye, Captain."

"Wiseass."

She settled down to business and began to move a little harder. I was in pretty good shape after the crosstown run, so I moved with her.

"Pick it up on the back stretch," she breathed.

"Yes. OK."

Quietly. Stride for stride.

"The last turn. Go wide."

"OK."

"Wider."

"OK."

I went wide.

"Float, baby."

"Yeah, I'm floating."

"Get rid of that lactic acid."

"I am, I am."

115

"Yes . . . Glide . . ."
"What?"
"Glide, dammit."
"Yeah, I'm gliding."
On ball bearings . . .
"Now, dammit . . ."
"Yes?"
"Accelerate."
"Yeah. I am."
And so help me, I was. Accelerating.
"Pour it on."
"Yes."
"Shovel coal, baby, pour it on."
"Yeah."
"Don't get caught in a pocket!"
"No, I won't . . ."
"Blow past the bastards . . ."
"OK, OK."
"Lean."
"I'm leaning."
"Knees. Knees, goddamit!"
"Yeah, knees."
"High. Arms high. Head high."
"Yeah, high . . ."
"Pump."
"Yes."
"PUMP."
"I am."
"You're not, you're running in sand!"
"No I'm not."
"Yes you are. Sand!"
"I'm *sprinting*."
"Oh yes you are. Nail the bastards . . ."
"I will. Four, three, two . . ."
"ONE."
"Yeah, one."

"Kick, baby."

"I'm kicking."

"Kick."

"I'm kicking."

"KICK!"

"I *am*. I'm through the fucking pain barrier. I'm home free. I'm breezing. I'm hitting four fucking minutes!"

"What time?"

"Four minutes."

"What time?"

"Four minutes."

"WHAT TIME?"

"Three fifty-nine nine!"

"OhmyGOD.................!"

"Cheshire cat bastard," she said. "Take a victory lap."

3

When I got home I dismissed the sitter and wrote in the little black book: "Every action has an equal and opposite reaction. — Newton."

I tore out the page, something I had never before done, and placed it beside Hannah's folded ear.

Lover Boy plunged into the wonderful world of work: Broadway, Off Broadway, Awful-Off Broadway. I checked out Finch College for a student production of *The Women*. Passable, although one of the leads thought she was a junior league Joan Crawford playing Sadie Thompson. I hopped down to Textile

117

High School on West 18th Street off the West Side Highway for a community center stab at *Rocket to the Moon* ("Why can't community centers stick to folk dancing?") Anything. Everything. Busy, busy. Idle thoughts are evil thoughts. And evil hands. And the hands of Lover Boy had to stay away from that marvelous stretch runner.

With a jot of success.

I did not call or talk to her except in the strict line of business, and Carla, who was exemplary in picking up vibrations, did not push from her end; I will forever respect her for that, at least. Work, work: When the Chinese visited Moscow, I pounded out a feverish item called *Mao as Fu Manchu* wherein I cast Dulles as Nayland Smith. An editorial writer, whose name escapes me, said it was rather arcane and suggested to Carla that I clear with him. She said he clears with *me* and dropped a note on my desk that said, "cute but nice." I tore it up and went out to see *The Sun Also Rises*, and since I could now get into the ring with anyone, and that included Crowther, Agee, Knight, or even Manny Farber, I wrote my first movie review and called it *Papa Pukes, or Tyrone Without Power*. It was mainly about Errol Flynn, who stole whatever picture there was, and his career since *Captain Blood*, and some plans I had for his future, including Leopold Bloom. This time her note said, "Aren't you the one." I tore that up, too. I went home and worked on a few basic sentences with Hannah and read to her from *Typee*. At one in the morning Lucille called from Vegas and apologized for the time difference and said she just had to hear our living voices. I woke Hannah and she cooed into the phone, "Who Pwomoted Peh-wess?" and Lucille wept uncontrollably. When she regained control she said she couldn't wait to see us, and this place was not to be believed. She loved me goodbye.

I tucked Hannah in and called Carla Levine.

"I read that the Philadelphia Inquirer Games are this Saturday. How would you like a train ride?"

"Don't be silly," she said. "I'll drive us down."

I hadn't been to Philadelphia since my crazy days on Morningside Heights, and as we drove down I felt only the lightest touch of a connection with that wild time. Still, there *was* a connection, and it occurred to me that I might be in for some more craziness if I let this thing continue. On the other hand, there was no law that said Speed Finestone's wife had to play shit in Vegas. I walked us into the arena with the danger shoved down to my gastrocnemius.

We had fun. The faces, the styles, the performances were pleasantly familiar. Old friends did the expected: Johnny Haines, Lee Calhoun, Ed Collymore, Phil Reavis, Don Bragg all won in their specific, unique way. And of course, so did Delaney. Before a home crowd, the gallery on his side for once, he sprinted early and actually won by six yards. All the way back to New York Carla was full up with excited laughter and glittering, analytical conversation.

When we reached her place, I ran the mile in three fifty-eight, just nipping Roger Bannister at the wire.

Lucille came home at the end of March. The All-American husband greeted her with hugs and kisses and a three-pound box of candy from Fanny Farmer and, after consuming a half pint of scotch, was able to turn in a reasonable facsimile of lovemaking. Just before I closed my eyes, I saw hers widen as I kicked in the stretch.

She spoke very little about the tour, but bustled around the house with new and tremendous energy—cooking, baking, touching up furniture, reading to Hannah from Chekhov, fashioning slender, tinkling mobiles for her room. She insisted on our going out as a nuclear family, and so we visited the Frick, the Museum of the American Indian, Jumel Mansion, Trinity Church, Poe Cottage, at all of which she bought appropriate monographs so she could start a file she called *The Finestone City*.

She signed up for classes with Sandy Meisner at the Neighborhood Playhouse and, since I was now doing my writing at home, I worked with her on her scenes. It was, all in all, as close as we got to the old days.

In June, Sandy told her that some friends who had done *Endgame* were looking for an understudy. She read and was hired on the spot. That night I didn't need any scotch, nor did I run for my life. We slept, as the novels of Manny's formation were wont to say, wrapped in each other's arms.

A month into *Endgame*, going on just once, she said casually, as we studied an elongated Cervantes at the Hispanic Museum, "I've been asked to read for an adaptation of *The Man Within*."

"It's a pretty good book."

"It's by Graham Greene."

"I know who it's by."

"It's mainly two people and the woman really owns it."

"I guess you could say that."

"Sandy thinks I'll get it."

"Uh-huh. Who's doing it?"

"Well, it's going to be done on television."

"*Television?*"

"Live."

"Television?"

"It's a beautiful book."

"I know the book, don't sell me the book. What do you want with television?"

Hannah began to get nervous.

"Don't be such a snob," Lucille said. "If I can do Broadway, I can do television. You like 'Studio One'."

"I don't *like* it. I merely said it was a higher class of shit. What's wrong with *Endgame*?"

120

"Wrong? I'm no understudy."

"Oh pardon me, Miss Bankhead."

"Don't give me that, please. I would like to read for *The Man Within*. What about it?"

"You're *asking* me?"

"I would like to have a rational opinion, yes."

"My opinion is make yourself happy. Be a big fucking star."

"Thank you, Speed. I knew I could count on you to be utterly supportive."

Hannah tugged us toward Diego Rivera.

2

She signed for *The Man Within*, naturally, and while she worked on it, I prowled the city and the sports and obituary pages, the thee-a-tuh, the upper Broadway movie houses from the Regency to the Nemo near Columbia, but most of all I prowled the head of MannySpeed. Also every inch of the amazingly responsive body of Carla Levine. The night the Greene play came on with my dedicated wife acting rings around her leading man, I plowed Miss Levine into a new world's record and myself into the shithouse.

Yes, Speed was back and the crapper had him.

I had had indications here and there, such as the Philadelphia track meet, but arrogant wiseguy that I was, I was sure that the punishing condition was a thing of the past, an artifact in the life of Finestone that would one day be dug up in the time capsule along with my captain's bars. Wrong again, as I usually was when I got overconfident. It was 1946 all over again, but with a new dimension, as befit my newly acquired eminence: the shithouse was a beauty, a stainless steel bathysphere designed by Dr. Beebe, and as it descended into the snaking, steaming coils it gave me unshuttered windows which constantly beckoned, so that I always knew exactly where I was even when I told myself it wasn't so. And to make sure I doubly understood where I was and why, Dr. Beebe (who had an amazing resemblance to my father) threw in a passenger, no one else but Manny's old acquaintance Benny Leonard.

121

Let me tell you about Benny.

Benny Leonard was to Manny as (roughly) Jimminy Cricket was to Pinocchio; but to call him his—*my*—conscience is to hopelessly vitiate his role. He was spirit, goad, pride, ambition, cheerleader, taskmaster, skeptic, appreciator, memory, future and conditional tense. He was, in other words, Manny's yet to be realized Eisenhower. Above and beyond all that he was Shimon's nonpareil, the one athlete he could connect with, talk about, *understand*. (Benny was actually before Manny's conscious time; he could only hear, read and *think* about him. Perfect.) Here was the speed demon with the pneumatic-drill fists. Here was the avenger. Here was the fighting, winning avenger. Here was the fighting, winning, JEWISH avenger. And, as Shimon explained, eyes aglow, he did it *without ever getting a hair out of place and with a nice clean shave.* So Benny Leonard shaped Manny up. With his slicked-down hair, his Barbasoled face, with his dancing, bobbing, weaving deadpan. Whenever Manny, which was oh so often, screwed up the deal, Benny Leonard let him know it. In time the two names became one and Manny could hear him coming a mile away; when BennyLeonard began to tattoo the small bag, Manny shivered.

As now Speed did.*

For into the stainless steel shithouse BennyLeonard floated on his feather feet and with every slicked-down hair in place, cheeks shining, he gave me the holy hell I deserved. Month after month after month. Oh I functioned, all right, in an objective, busywork way. I was father, husband, provider (semiprovider; Lucille had caught on with *You Are There*), even in some reverse way a better, colder, angrier observer and writer. But throughout the rest of 1957 and through '58, the facts of this life were inescapably clear: I was down, down, down in the latrine and BennyLeonard was making excruciatingly sure I knew why.

ADULTERER, he hooked. I shook out the cobwebs.

---

*A number of Manny's parts never let Speed alone; why should they?

122

ADULTERER, he jabbed. I grabbed and hung on. ADULTERER, he uppercut. I spit out my mouthpiece and mewled, Jesus Christ, look at what my wife is doing, *television*; and with Carla Levine's gorgeous derriere dangling before me, do you think I'm made of iron?

I am, he sneered. Clip. I went down.

The spitting business started again. So did the little black book, Volume II . . . "Horny bastard . . . Only human . . . Tell to the marines . . . Cut me, I bleed . . . Rationalizer . . . Deep feeling for Carla L. . . . six inches! . . . Think alike . . . Hump . . . Must get BenLen off back . . . Sure, nobody pays dues anymore . . ."

I scotchtaped its goddam yap shut, pasted on my old crooked grin, treated Lucille with terrific consideration. She treated me the same way, and we slept two inches apart. I couldn't work at home, couldn't work in the office, so I packed a yellow pad and a dozen pencils and a hand sharpener and wrote each day in the library of the New York Historical Society on Central Park West. Fulton, Van Buren, Greeley, Peter and Fenimore Cooper all looked at me askance, but when I copped a plea, relented and admitted that yes, under pressure they too had dipped their wicks.

I produced. Down in the privy, with BennyLeonard ball-peening away, I produced. At year's end, I did an obit on Bogart and McCarthy, calling it "Two Soft-Boiled Yeggs," that caused a multitude of flags to pop out of patriotic lapels.* With the Polo

---

*Infamous last line: "And so we will never have to imagine how Bogart would have played McCarthy; in an otherwise innocuous item called *The Caine Mutiny* he cleverly, masterfully slipped him in on us as Captain Queeg."

Grounds and Ebbets Field sprouting weeds, with innocence gone
west along with the loot, I swung from the heels for all the
Mannys of the world in "Go to Hell, Giants, Dodgers, Tom
Swift!" It only made me feel worse, my steel prison dipping even
lower. I turned to Hannah; Hannah always calmed me.

My darling Hannah,

Well, time is flying as it has a way of doing, and you will shortly
be one thirty-third and a third of a century old. This is a milestone,
surely no light matter, and I would like very much for you to think
carefully and insightfully about the significant date and especially
about its implications for the future. You can be categorically
assured that your mother and I have been considering that future,
although your mother has been so wrapped up in the world of the
commercial theater that she cannot devote as much time as I know
she would like to this crucial matter. You can be very certain,
however, that I would never let my career interfere with my
parental obligations, and that is not at all said in a pejorative sense
about your mother.

Therefore, like Hemingway in Pamplona, I'll take the bull by
the horns and simply tell you what I have in mind in a number of
categories:

1. Your physical well-being . . . Hannah, health is and always
will be number one. Without it, all else is cream cheese; take care
of your body, and your mind, *and* your emotionality, and they will
take care of you. Get your eight hours sleep come rain or shine. If
your date wants to keep you out beyond eleven and you must get
up at seven, just say uh-uh, nighty night . . . Use dental floss, not
tape, each night. Read something light, such as Thoreau, to bring
on dreamless sleep . . . Above all, you must learn to swim; this will
surely contribute to *mens sana in corpore sano*. You need have no
fear at all about learning; old Jack Medica will teach you every
stroke in the book, including a few of my own. Swimming is like
an education: they can never take it away from you.

2. Grace, balance, rhythm, poise, confidence . . . You must learn
to dance, not because of social pressure, but because of the points
listed. You must learn the rhumba, mambo, peabody, conga, tango.

Don't worry about the fox-trot, you'll pick that up through osmosis. And forget the jump-jerk that passes for dancing these days; it has nothing to do with nothing. And bear in mind that 'it takes two to tango' is merely a bromide; Hannah Finestone can dance alone any time she wants, and to that end you must learn the basics of tap dancing. I might even be able to help you there.

3. Reading . . . You are no longer a baby, so it's time to move on. I would suggest Conrad, Flaubert, Balzac, and a personal favorite of mine, Marjorie Bowen, who at the age of thirteen turned out a very respectable historical romance. If Bowen can do it, surely you can also, although I would hope you would not deal with whipped cream, but would break new ground.

4. Marriage . . . This is a ticklish one. I know you will develop your own thinking here, but I do have a suggestion: I see no reason why we cannot tuck into our hip pocket to be pulled out at some future date President Eisenhower's grandson, David, whose genes should be Class A in a Mendelian sense (not that you are a piker in that department, oh my, no). I'd also like to mention a boy named Bobby Fischer who shows fine mental promise, although he is ten years older than you; this does not mean a thing, you can handle it with absolutely no sweat. The main thing is keeping an eye on his physical and emotional development. There are also boys yet unborn who could show great possibilities. I would hope, for example, that Major John Glenn, who recently set an air speed record from California to New York, might become infatuated with Maria Callas long enough to produce a son who might fit into the picture. Again, the fact that Glenn-Callas would be younger means nothing in terms of your ability to cope.

The above are simply a few random thoughts brought on by your natal date. I would like to point out, apropos of marriage, that after extensive inner exploration, if you should decide, like Susan Cooper, the daughter of Fenimore, to devote your life to your father, to type and edit his work, I would not oppose that decision; I know the decision would be yours and not lightly made. Let's play that one by ear, shall we?

Well, my darling, there it is for now. Ingest, absorb, ruminate. Allow some present, future and delayed learning to take place. Above all, bear in mind that you must never let any S.O.B. take advantage of you in any manner, shape or form, or by games which these bums love to play. Keep those antennae up and sharply tuned and always be alert for the old double X. If in doubt, ask the gov'nor; he can spot a rat a hundred miles away.

OK?

OK.

You get all the love I have,·

Daddy

I mailed it and took it out of the box three days later and started *The Hannah File*. On that day I sat down and wrote another letter.

Dear David,

How would you like to meet a girl who physically is in the 98th percentile? If you question that stat, I suggest you consult Dr. Jack Lorenzo at 581 E. 18th Street, NYC. My feelings won't be hurt; in fact, I'll respect your thoroughness. This girl's name is Hannah Finestone. Mentally, she scores 140 and 139 on two separate performance I.Q. tests. (Dr. Myron Kutner, Ph.D., of 410 Fifth Ave., NYC can certify.) The 140 is by far the more valid figure.

Now, David, if we consider your background, and your connections, and if we combine these with Hannah's excellent mental and physical aptitudes (she is also exceptionally stable, an unbeatable parlay), you can easily see that marriage at some future date could make a great deal of (un)common sense. Let me assure you that Hannah's stock, at least on the paternal side, is exemplary; her grandfather, for example, was undoubtedly that undiscovered genius of the Ozarks, except that in his case this genius functioned in the daily life of the East Bronx, as anyone who lived between 170th and Tremont Avenue east of the Concourse prior to 1940 can testify.

Take your time in thinking this matter over, David, but do consider what I have said. Naturally, any future arrangements must hinge largely on what Miss Finestone has in mind. I would never coerce her (and suggest you do not, either), but I believe, because she is eminently reasonable, that I can point out the advantages of an Eisenhower-Finestone combination ... Perhaps

126

you might even start a new House of David, sans whiskers, but let's play that one by ear, shall we?

With all good wishes, I remain

(Capt.) E. Speed Finestone

A week later I got a form letter from the President thanking me for my support.

The man in the outhouse decided enough was enough; it was time to bust loose, to shoot to the surface.

First of all he went back to his old *Infantry Journals* and studied up on how to handle fear. He litanied especially the rules laid down by a company commander in Tunisia in the June '44 issue which had launched him across Europe. Things like, THE ENEMY IS SCARED, TOO; MAKE USE OF YOUR FEAR; THE MESS SERGEANT IS SWEATING YOU OUT, TOO. SO WHAT DO YOU DO WHEN YOU'RE AFRAID? KEEP SLUGGING! . . . That last . . . that rang an old bell. Speed's bell. And Manny's. For oh yes, he had his little crappers, too, potties maybe, but rugged enough for those days. What was it he used out of J. Salwyn Shapiro's history book when he was down and almost out? HELLYES. The great Marshal Foch, the embodiment of *élan*, that is what. I am beaten on the right, I am beaten on the left, *J'ATTAQUE*. Thatwasit! Time after time, Manny remembered: *J'attaque!* 1938: Sore at Sam-Garth because he wouldn't loan his corduroy shirt, did he sulk? Not this *poilu*. (*J'attaque!*) He said, Robert Montgomery couldn't hold a goddam candle to Bob Taylor. Big brother was wild for three weeks,

127

wouldn't even talk. Then (*J'attaque!*) Manny relented and took it back. Sam-Garth was so grateful he *gave* the kid his corduroy shirt . . . 1939: The war approaching and with it talk of a third term. Shimon insisting he go to CCNY instead of NYU because smart FDR men like Senator Wagner had gone there. In a moment of utter venom and inspiration (*J'attaque!*) he riposted, "Maybe eight years of the New Deal is enough." Shimon was a raging bull for a month. Manny then regrouped, followed up the first thrust (*J'attaque!*) by going to work for Young People for Roosevelt. Shimon *helped* him with the NYU application.

J'ATTAQUE!

On the Lucille front I discovered John Kennedy; that is, I rediscovered him, recalling the '56 vice-presidential surge.

SHE: So you're abandoning Stevenson.

 HE: He's a loser. Kennedy's a winner. And a hero.

SHE: You poor, exploited sap. He ran a fancy PT boat. You slogged through shit. Who's the hero?

 HE: Both of us. He understands what our generation needs.

SHE: *Your* generation.

 HE: Ours. Yours, mine, Hannah's.

SHE: Tell it to the Pope.

I had her. It was Al Smith all over again. The Vatican will run the country. Kennedy's conditioned loyalty will be to ritual mumbo jumbo, not the Constitution. I said (*J'attaque!*) that is KKK mentality. We took off the gloves and came out fighting. God, did we fight. We were Lombard and Barrymore on the Twentieth Century. Beery and Harlow in *Grand Hotel.* We were Bogart and (first) wife, Mayo Methot. Fear (and BennyLeonard) began to tap out. Also, these, in the following order, began to wither:

1. Denial
2. Disgust
3. Disorientation
4. Damnation
5. Defeat

With my advance under way, the provocateur now went to

work on Carla Levine. Casually, oh so casually, I said to her as the indoor track season for '59 got under way: "The Hungarians are really showing us something."

"Are you *serious?*"

"Of course I am. Igloi has revolutionized training and mental preparation."

"Will you just listen to this one?"

"I think (*J'attaque!*) Istvan Rosavogli can take Delaney."

"Oh, please!"

"Yes, I think he can."

And we were off and running. Istvan Rosavogli, Istvan Rosavogli, he became my *élan*, my charge against hopeless odds. Even when he came over and Delaney beat him. I airily tossed off the logical reasons: jet lag, outdoor runner, poor tactics. And *she* went wild. She didn't let me in for weeks (though when she did, she was sensational; so was I: I defeated Cunningham, Venzke, Fenske, Bonthron and Archie San Romani).

I was on my way. John Kennedy and Istvan Rosavogli were prying open the shithouse and I was counterpunching and BennyLeonard knew that at least he was in a fight. There was a temporary setback when F. G. Powers flew over Russia and neglected to bite down on his cyanide and Eisenhower lied through his hound's teeth about the whole business. That really hurt. Not the U-2, but his dissembling, the Crusader caught with his pants down and dissembling. I had a few rugged days until I realized what a stroke, even a small one, can do to the straightest of us. I forgot, forgave, worked harder than ever for Kennedy and Istvan Rosavogli.

But after everything had been sorted out, I could see that my main Fochian offensive had to be the election itself. For, despite my baiting of Lucille, I knew, deep down where it hurt, that I would not, could not, when the crisis point arrived, vote for Kennedy. Much as I was coming to idolize him—and I *did* think there was a difference long before Schlesinger's book or the debates—I knew that E simply would not permit it (and Shimon, who hated Joe Kennedy like poison, wouldn't be too happy,

either). As for Nixon, forget it. Not on personal grounds alone—
I probably could overcome that (although it would be some
battle)—but because, deep within, I was sure that E—despite
Checkers and "You're my boy"—couldn't take him either. So no
last-minute power would seize this hand and force it into the
mastodon column, not this time. But then where was I, besides up
shit creek without a paddle? It was, to paraphrase Churchill, an
enigma wrapped in a wickedly neat dilemma. I brooded on it for
two weeks . . . then bingo! *Voilà.* I hopped down to the 42nd
Street Library and looked up all the third parties that had been on
the ballot, anywhere in the country, in 1956. I found:
  The Constitution Party
  The States Rights Party
  The Socialist Labor Party
  The Socialist Workers Party
  The Socialist Party
  The American Third Party
  The Christian Nationalist Party
  The Prohibition Party
I immediately x'd out States Rights, Socialist Labor, Socialist
Workers and just plain Socialists. Also Christian Nationalist with
Gerald L. K. Smith. Constitution and American Third waved too
many flags. That left me with one choice: Prohibition. And that I
liked because I was sure Eisenhower's mother would have liked it.
Old-countryish, bible-reading, saintly, she would have definitely
approved. Therefore, so would he. The Prohibition Party also
had the aura of discipline, of sticking to its guns even when the
whole world was going to hell in a gin bottle. And a President
named Enoch A. Holtwick surely would exercise that discipline (I
have no patience with the "wasting your vote" theory; you vote
your conscience).

Next I looked up the New York State ballot for 1956. No good.
No Prohibition Party, only Constitution, Socialist Labor and
Worker. That meant it undoubtedly wouldn't be on the ballot this
year. That didn't faze me; I went to the neighboring states, the
only ones with track records on the Prohibition Party going back

to '48. I found New Jersey and Massachusetts. I could not completely desert Kennedy. On September 3, I flew up to Boston and found a small furnished flat with a Murphy bed on Commonwealth Avenue; I talked my way into a six-month lease and established Massachusetts residency. Then I went down to the local Democratic Club and explained that I had just moved in and I was a Kennedy man and a writer; could they expedite my registration. They could and did; Tammany would have done no less for R. W. Emerson. Just to keep everything honest, I spent every other weekend in Boston (telling Lucille I was gathering background material on Kennedy).

On November 8, 1960, I shuffled into a voting booth in Back Bay and looked at my choices. I had nothing to worry about: sure enough, there it was: the Prohibition line. (You simply cannot beat research.) Not Enoch A. Holtwick. Better. Rutherford L. Decker. That Rutherford clinched it, told me my instincts had been perfect. With Eisenhower's mother beaming down (plus Shimon, whose head got funny after a glass of schnapps) I reached and plunked down my lever.* Then I strode out into a sunlit world. Rutherford L. Decker and the Prohibition Party had broken me out of the shithouse.

I went on a two-day binge. When I made it home, Lucille said she couldn't take it any longer.

*That joyful sound also said congratulations; against all odds, E has come through!

131

PART

Holding Patterns

When my cousin Renee got her divorce from that phony Lou Pomerantz, she went out to Reno like all normally pissed-off women did in those days. But not Lucille. Oh no, Reno isn't good enough for my wife. Her television crowd has educated her to the classier things in life, so right after the Bay of Pigs, when I am at my most vulnerable, she becomes one of the beautiful people. There I am, apologizing to Stevenson for stringing him along, figuring out how to shape up the CIA, trying with everything I have to stabilize an administration, and my wife flies down to Costa Rica, says *si* seven times and turns me into a statistic.

I was frantic, furious, frenetic. Balls. I was terrifically relieved. As they say in rotten novels, it had been over for some time, only we didn't know it; but this flashy move of hers finalized it. I went around all day for two weeks sighing with relief, like Shimon after he had defeated Hoover. I didn't even put up a fight when it came to custody of Hannah. Why should I? You can say what you want, strap on a thousand million dildos, the mother is the mother, and she has to live up to her basic obligations during the formative years. As long as I could come and go when the need and occasion dictated, and Lucille understood that perfectly, I was reasonably happy. The only place I put my foot down was in the matter of school. Lucille, surely under TV duress, thought that a private school like Dalton or Ethical Culture was the place for my daughter. No deal. She could go to a private college, but now it was public school or nothing, and the public school I wanted was P.S. 6, which my research had told me was tops in all areas, especially the student population, which, when all is said and done, forces the teachers to produce. I told her she had to move to the Upper East Side and I would even pick up part of the tab. She said she didn't want a nickel from me, wanted to move anyway because there were too many memories in this house, and that was that. I found them a place on 80th and Second, moved them in and enrolled Hannah in the first grade at P.S. 6 after thoroughly interviewing the principal, the teacher, the teacher's aide and six of the kids.*

I decided I needed a new village to live in, so I moved into a furnished studio on the West Side at 108th Street between Broadway and Riverside. Then I wrote Hannah a short letter in which I explained that this was the Twentieth Century, that her mother and I were mature adults, that Thomas Jefferson had urged the Pursuit of Happiness on all of us, and that there was more love than ever for her now that I did not have to share it with anyone else.

I also wrote to David Eisenhower briefly outlining the divorce and the splendid way it had been handled, and assuring him that I knew he was big enough not to hold it against Hannah, who in the long run—because she had such a great outlook—would profit from the experience. I mailed it to the White House and asked them to please forward. I never received an answer, but my letter didn't come back either, so I wasn't worried. With his grandfather out of the White House, he had his own readjustment problems to cope with and simply hadn't time to handle the postadministration mail. I was secure in my mind, however, that he knew Hannah Finestone existed, that he was aware of her qualitative preconditions for a future contract. I was as content as on the evening of V-E Day.

---

*She had been in a private kindergarten of sorts and it was all fluff—no Melville or Conrad, not even Richard Hughes—another reason I wanted to get her into real red meat. I also wrote her a long letter telling her to use her I.Q. to the hilt, but never throw it up to the other kids, that the bigger they were, the *nicer* they were.

136

I sat down in my new studio and with a sliver of Riverside Park smiling from down the street, wrote my first piece on JFK. I called it "Kennedy the *Mensch*" and hand-delivered it to Carla. The next day, for the first time, she said she *loved* something I had written. I said yes; then I said I had to quit. Another first: her face crinkled.

"*Why*, in heaven's name?"

"I want a change of pace. I need one."

"You've got a change of pace, for Godsake, you're a free man."

"I want to be a free man all around."

"Have I ever shoved a ring into your nose?"

"No, and I appreciate that."

"Oh, thank you kindly. Am I pressuring you now?"

"No. And I appreciate *that*."

"Will you stop it! What the hell is going on with you?"

"I want to freelance."

"As a writer or a lover?"

"Writer."

"Then," she said, and I know this cost her, "at least we can see each other; there are some interesting track meets coming up..."

"I think we should let that go, too."

She sat quietly.

"You are a very aggravating man."

"I know. It's the way I am."

"That's a rotten answer. That's one of the rottenest answers I ever heard. Is it this? You fuck me while you're married and now the thrill is gone? Are you that goddam immature?"

"No, that's not it. Definitely no. I don't think I can verbalize it..."

"You're a goddam writer."

"But not a talker. Well, not now. I want to start from scratch but it's more complicated than that... I can't verbalize it..."

She watched me thoughtfully.

"Is it the running thing when we fuck? Speed, I can play it perfectly straight. It will be just as good; it doesn't mean a thing, I guarantee it."

137

I leaned in, smoothed out her face.

"Carla, please. I need a change of pace, a change of exterior and interior scene, that's the best I can do with it. It has nothing to do with you. Well, in a way it does, but not the way you just said, not in any personal sense. You're the one woman in my life and it's me, not you. Let's try this: I want to make it all by my lonesome, I want to be a big boy . . ."

Smooth, calm, collected, she stood up. Her hips and flat belly were very close and I wondered if I had screwed it up again. She said from that Sarah Lawrence height, "I've never begged anyone in my life to get humped. This is as close as I've ever come, but I come no closer. Next time, you ask Carla and Carla will think it over. So long, Istvan Rosavogli."

I took a deep breath, flexed my head, set myself up on 108th Street, went for long walks alongside the Hudson, from the piers in the 40s up to Inwood in the 200s, and I opened up all my creative pores and invited my new career to step in. The only problem was that '61 was a tough year for America, which meant a tough year for Speed Finestone. Eisenhower was brooding down on the farm after blasting his bread and butter in the military-industrial complex, so you knew the condition was serious; Kennedy was still trying to pull out of his Bay of Pigs tailspin; the Nobel in Literature and the first space orbit went to the Reds; the Davis Cup went to Australia; Carry Back, my favorite horse since Equipoise, lost the Belmont and blew the Triple Crown; and Hemingway and Gary Cooper both made it to the barn. I began to get extremely itchy, to long mightily for a winner; Speed could only go so long out of first place. So on July 4,

I went up to the Stadium; there, at least, you could count on some victorious stability.

It was a doubleheader, and in the eighth inning of the second game, Roger Maris hit one into the right field seats off Frank Lary, an old Yankee nemesis. I ordinarily droop halfway through a second game, but this time I sat up. It was Maris' 31st homer and the season wasn't even half over, and the beer-barrel beside me said Ruth didn't hit number 31 until his 94th game (in a 155 game season against Maris' 163; no arguments yet, please). I had heard that Ruthian song before: Foxx, Greenberg, Mize, Kiner, plus many an early bloomer who would blast the record. Interesting; not critical. What got to me that day was the deadly serious crew cut, the lovely, level, equally serious swing. I got very intrigued, got caught by that one-note face, the straight-ahead intensity. I whistled my way back on the subway. The next day I went back, bought a seat as close to the first one as I could (two away) and Maris hit one against Cleveland. The papers screamed again as I rode home, and the next morning, but they were screaming as hard (harder) for Mantle, who had hit about as many as Maris, and I suddenly became aware—as if I were truly awake for the first time in months—that M & M did not refer to bits of no-smear chocolate, but to a pair of logical successors to Murderers' Row who were turning New York upside down. I also discovered that rooting for Maris was not an easy decision; internally, that is (I did not give a holler in hell what the world thought). I had been a Mantle man for years because he was, incredible as it seemed, the man who had *truly* replaced DiMaggio. The inheritor. How could I not root for that catapulting speed, that switch-hitting power, that taped-up, magnificently flawed body? The Mays, Mantle, Snider comparison was no problem for me; even with the infected bone, the pulled muscles, the torn cartilages, he won going away. He had long since captured me once I realized Joe D. could not go on forever. But there was something about Maris— that brush cut, the tight, poker face, the clothesline connection with the right field seats, above all, the categorical fact that everybody and his uncle was pulling for Mantle and hating Maris'

139

guts for daring to be up there with Mickey, for *daring to challenge Ruth*—that made me sit up and say, WHATDOWEHAVE HERE?

Something else:

Upstairs I said I did not give a hell what the world thought. Correction. The world goes one way, Speed goes the *other*. I felt—I *knew*—he operated in the same way, that he couldn't be appointed dogcatcher, much less get elected. We were brothers; Speed, too, had never run for mayor. He had kicked a plentitude of ass sweeping through Europe, with the same no-nonsense haircut, the same straight-ahead drive. Perhaps my hair was a bit longer now, eyes perhaps a bit easier, but I had still been the hard, deadpan driver with Manhattan Players. Even at *Meridian* where, although I had rarely associated with the big names, I had never given them an inch on a matter of principle. And I was still the pile driver. I had given up jobs, wife, sensational hump because—and here I realized I was *finally* verbalizing it—I was still driving. Where? I didn't know, and I was convinced that Maris didn't either except that, like me, he had to keep driving. Not for the record, although if that fell, so be it. He simply had to keep going, pushing, *driving*.

And one more thing:

I was convinced that Eisenhower was pulling for him; two straight arrows. Whereas MacArthur was unquestionably going all out for Mantle, for both were connected with mythical greatness, he with Napoleon, Mick with Ruth.

So yes, I was a Maris man. Proud of it.

However, there were problems, logistic problems. As follows: The Stadium was simple enough; I just organized my life around it. The real problem was going on the road; that needed much working out. For I would only go to certain stadiums, that is, the *true* stadiums. Not those ridiculous new mausoleums which housed strange new teams (ersatz, I considered them, although the players were real enough—a fine but critical distinction). I absolutely refused to travel to those peculiar places and their teams: The *Minnesota Twins*. The *Los Angeles Angels*, the *Kansas City A's* (poor Connie Mack), the *Baltimore Orioles* (a bit less venom there, for they had once been real). Even going to Washington was a rough decision because this was the second edition of the Senators, the first having absconded to Minnesota, but in the end I did it for Walter Johnson and Bucky Harris. (After a minor struggle I did deign to watch these creations at the Stadium.)* Thus I traveled to my *real* towns: to Boston, where Roger hit one off Monbouquette, to Chicago to see him do it to Early Wynn and Ray Herbert, back to Boston and poor Monbouquette, home for Chi and Frank Baumann and (gulp!) Don Larsen and Russ Kemmerer and Warren Hacker—these four on a double bill on July 25. That took care of July. Total: 40 homers, heading into the dog days. On August 4 I ignored Minnesota and Pascual at home, just to show I could do it, then went down to Washington for clouts off Pete Burnside, Dick Donovan, Bennie Daniels and Marion Kutyna, then back to the Stadium for the White Sox and Juan Pizarro and Billy Pierce (2). I hopped out to Cleveland and we creamed Jim Perry; I stayed over and read about L.A. and K.C. Total through August: 51.

In Cleveland at the hotel barbershop I got myself a brush cut and worked out a deadpan scowl and a ramrod stance before the full-length mirror in the john. Then I scooted back to New York. By now everybody's gonads were in a terrific uproar; Ruth had entered September needing 17 while we needed just 10. The world was more pissed-off than ever at Maris because now Mantle began to develop the miseries and missed games; when he played there was a throttling-down of the amazing, bullnecked power; moving into the home stretch, the poor S.O.B. began to fade. Maris and I were now barking harder at the f'ing world, the press, the fans, even ourselves. I told my neighbor across the hall who said if Williams played in New York he'd hit 75 to please perform an impossible anatomical feat. I even yelled at Hannah when she got only nine Winnie the Poohs out of ten on a spelling

---

*In no way did the existence of the new teams diminish his performance. And I do not offer on his behalf the problems of night baseball, the travel, the pressure of the record. Immaterial. He did what he had to do, when he had to do it. Period.

test. Maris began to lose patches of hair and on September 9 when he hit #56 off Jim Grant of Cleveland I noticed a huge wad of gray-black hair on my morning comb.

We hung in. Against all odds, all prayers, all superstition, against all the world, we hung in. I flew out to Detroit on the 16th and belted our 57th off Frank Lary. That night in my hotel room I wrote my first piece on Maris and what he represented to my generation and, to sock it to all the Babe Ruth bullshit artists, did it as a takeoff on Granny Rice, calling it, "The Maris is Flighty and Causes Travail."* I mailed it off to a fancy review, of all places, and naturally, the way we were breezing, they printed it five weeks later and sent me fifty dollars.

Another blast in Detroit the next day in extra innings (we could now do no wrong, except to the whole raging world).

Now a tough one: Baltimore and #59 off Milt Pappas; tough because for purposes of self-discipline I stayed home and listened to Mel Allen and his crazed "How about that!" on a portable in the bathroom in front of the full-length mirror.

On September 26, with my hair falling out in great clumps, I pushed through to Maris country in the Stadium and got set up for Baltimore. Portables bristled around me. Screw them. I settled forward. He hit a screamer, #60, just to the left of me in the third off Jack Fisher and caused a mild riot as the sonsofbitches fought for the ball. The man next to me said, "Bigfuckingdeal, it took him 159 games, it took Ruth 154." I swung at him and caused another small riot and they kicked us both out of the park and to celebrate I bought the guy a beer on River Avenue and said, "We're all Yankee fans, right?" The *schnorrer* agreed and accepted three more beers.

On October 1, I was again out in the right field seats. I had one jittery moment when it occurred to me that the big shots might think Maris was Jewish and send down orders to feed him nothing remotely hitable, but fortunately a classy WASP named Tracy Stallard of the Red Sox was pitching and class is a given no

*Rice's famous opener: "The Ruth is mighty and shall prevail."

142

matter what you are. He challenged us and Roger hit #61, as I knew he would if given half a shot. No fuss, no muss. I walked out and had ten quiet beers. That night I wrote a long letter to Hannah explaining the significance of the 61 home runs. I said that the important thing here was that it was a magnificent tangential bonus spinning off supreme drive and the will to carry on. I told her that she must never ever forget this lesson, whether it was in spelling, math, world history, biology or working her way through Proust.

On October 2, I went to the barber for a complete baldy; the best cure for falling hair is to shave it all off. Naturally, I couldn't let anyone see me in that condition as a cueball does nothing for my face, especially in profile, so I holed up for ten days and wrote my first piece of fiction. It was based on one of my nightmares, which I transposed into a detective story set in the thirties. I named my nonhero Morse Junko, after Maris and Eddie Lopat, the Junkman, but I modeled his intellect and emotionality after Moe Berg, the smartest no-hit catcher who ever lived. I had him solve the Chiang Kai-shek kidnaping via some high-level intrigue that utilized the services of the illegitimate son of Chinese Gordon and Florence Nightingale, a middle-aged gentleman who made his home base in Singapore and fired off consistently-ignored letters to the British Foreign Office warning how simple it was to capture the great naval base and bastion of Empire by a lightninglike overland thrust from the north and down the Malay Peninsula. I finished it in two days and sent it to the SATEVEPOST and they bought it for $1200.

So please do not tell me that the 1961 baseball season was shit for the birds, that Roger Maris was merely a surly, hard-assed interloper, that we can neatly forget him and it. Please do not tell me that. And as for the asterisk, the one that purports to explain away his achievement by telling you that he hit 61 in 163 games whereas the mighty Babe hit 60 in a 155 game season and therefore (smirks the asterisk) he will always be a second-class champ, even though he took on the whole hostile world and creamed it, as for that asterisk, you know what they can do with their asterisk? Here is what they can do:

143

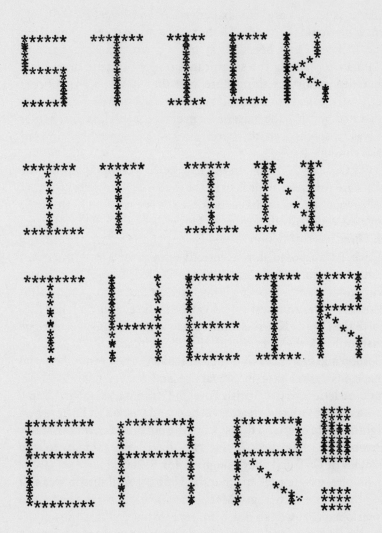

STICK
IT IN
THEIR
EAR

Maris did the trick. He got the administration off the ground. Kennedy told Roger Blough and big steel where to go and for once Shimon agreed with old Joe K. about the genealogy of businessmen. The steel confrontation touched off another Morse Junko story and the SATEVEPOST took it after I informed them that my price had gone up $200. Hannah went around for two weeks saying, "Never trust the sonsabitches."

The Cuban Crisis hit and I really took off. While everyone was defecating bricks I sat down and wrote a long story which detailed the exploits of one Saul Dréflique, a distant cousin of Dreyfus, and a man who combined the best of Arsène Lupin, Maigret and Simon Wiesenthal as he tracked down all the bastards who had framed his cousin. As Krushchev pulled in his horns, I had Clemenceau shaking Dréflique's hand on the Pont Neuf and sending him off to meet a dashing young officer named Foch who was trying to instill some *élan* into a colleague named Pétain who suffered from depressive nightmares about Germanic-looking dragons that were invariably called *Beesemarques*. I sent it to Elias Damon, not knowing what else to do with it, and he sent it to a friend who edited a prestigious magazine in Kentucky. The story got me $75 and letters from three publishers, all of whom asked me to let them know if I had a novel. I wrote back saying I did not have a novel, but could probably produce enough stories for a book. They wrote back saying they couldn't afford to publish my stories and I wrote back saying they couldn't afford not to, and that for the nonce was that.

I had a few bad moments when Kennedy said he was a Berliner, but decided that if he said it, it must be OK. To prove the point to myself, I wrote a Saul Dréflique story about a Russian pogrom, wherein Saul's father, who has seen and experienced everything, constantly reminds Saul, "Remember, sonny, Russians are lousier than the Germans even."

11/22/63.

PART

Charge
to the Rear

At three o'clock in the morning I found myself leaning on the doorbell of Carla Levine's apartment. She opened the door and took me into her arms.

I sat around for all of December and the first half of the next year, and the only writing I did was in the black book, where I filled up page after page of "Why?" and "NO!" I remember wondering one morning at around four as I prowled around her apartment if the Speed Finestones who had fought through the Civil War felt this way after April 15, 1865. Outside of that, I do not have a tangible memory of anything else except the presence of Carla, quiet, somber, carefully affectionate. Nor do I have a sense of any physicality except for a feeling that I was walking around the city during that time, although I can't remember where; I do know that from time to time I would ask myself if such and such a building didn't look like the Chrysler or the Flatiron or the Woolworth, my three favorite skyscrapers, but I will never be sure that I was actually in their part of town.

As noted, Carla applied no pressure whatsoever, was marvelously kind and gentle and when I said I wanted to watch

TV alone would walk quickly out of the room. I will always be beholden to her, will always in some pocket of my history be amazed and grateful for her splendid grace under pressure.

In the summer of '64 I looked around one day, saw some clouds, looked down and saw an unrolling map, heard a buzzing sound deep in my ears, turned to Carla and said, clearly, "Are we flying in an aeroplane?"

"Yes," she said.

"Where are we flying to?"

"Los Angeles."

"Why are we doing that?"

"Because we are going to the final Olympic trials."

I recall saying, "Oh," then settling back. I closed my eyes and pictures of people named Cunningham, Lovelock, Delaney and Istvan Rosavogli flickered by. I opened my eyes.

"Where are the Olympics?" I said.

"Tokyo."

"The *Japs* got the Olympics?"

"Yes."

I thought about that.

"They were supposed to get them in 1940," I said.

"I know," she smiled.

I thought some more.

"The German prick screwed them out of it," I said thoughtfully, "and they still fought with him."

"I know."

"The prick must have yelled at them."

"It's eminently possible."

"Anybody he yelled at folded up."

"I've heard that."

I settled back and looked out the window. Then I looked at Carla.

"I don't hold any grudges," I said.

"Beautiful."

"I had a Jap—Japanese—in my class at Columbia Business and he told me they had promised him Rita Hayworth on the White

150

House lawn. Whathehell, propaganda is propaganda, except of course for the little German bastard, then it was pure horseshit." She leaned over and kissed me.

In L.A. I took a giant step back to life. There we were, in great seats above the finish line for the longer races, and a gangly high school kid with a wobbling head named Jim Ryun burst past Jim Grelle at the tape and qualified for the mile—pardon, the metric mile—the race that had figured in so much of the real and dream life of both Manny and Speed. I yelled so long and loud that Carla thought I'd keel over. Instead, I kissed her through the yelling and continued to yell, "Wait till the Japs see him!"

We flew across the Pacific and I babbled all the way about the second coming of Cunningham, for weren't they both from Kansas? And she came right back at me about a second Lovelock from New Zealand named Snell, and we both smiled through the arguing, for it was clear to both of us that I was coming back to Speed and together we were coming back to Carla and Speed; above Pearl Harbor I leaned over and asked her if it was possible to screw in these goddam seats; be patient, darling, she said, we have a room in the Imperial Hotel and we can do it facing the palace if you wish.

"I wish," I Speed-grinned at her.

2

Peter Snell captured the Tokyo Olympics. He owned them, he will always own them with his incredible double victory. God bless him. It was Carla's Olympics, too. Her goodness to me had been rewarded by Peter. And by Speed. For I too was splendid. In the hotel, on the Ginza, all over the steaming town. I was funny, graceful, witty, magnanimous, exciting to be with. For I was truly grateful. Truly. But I must also tell you the whole truth: in the main I was such a great person because I had discovered my prodigy; I was Jack Kearns watching the baby Dempsey early on, MacGraw beaming at Master Melvin Ott. I had discovered him and he was, for me, the story of this Olympics even if he did get

151

sick and flop in the semifinals. As Hannah would say through high school: "No problem." Maris made me function again. Jim Ryun made me *Speed* again.

I was quiet at first on the flight home. Although I had four years in which to get Ryun ready, I then and there began to prepare mentally, which is how all victories are born. I sent powerful messages down to Kansas, instructing the coaches at the university he would soon enter not to fool around with his faraway look and wobbling head; if the style worked, it worked, and I pointed to such unorthodox winners as Crazy Legs Hirsch and Long John Woodruff. They seemed to understand.* I then proceeded to regale Carla with stories of prior Olympics, and she snuggled up. When we reached Idlewild, which was now JFK, I took a deep, prerace breath, said so be it, I'm going out and getting a job.

She was marvelous. She said nothing, absolutely nothing, about *Meridian* or for that matter any other writing job. I appreciated that more than I can ever tell you, much less her, for I didn't want any part of writing, could not consider any interior mucking-about. I called Damon and asked if he knew of any private school teaching jobs; I was a public school man but didn't have city or state credentials, so I had no choice. There was also something else: I felt that somehow I had to work against my grain—not as a punishment, but as a . . . *discipline* is the closest I can come to it.

He put me on to the Peter Minuit School on East 78th Street, called a Dr. Edison Birmingham and gave me a rave review. I was interviewed in September, after the year had started—one of their people had received a fancy offer from Great Neck and

---

*Although you always had to pay attention to Finestone's *Schmuck* Law: People rose to managerial—therefore coaching—positions in direct proportion to their gentile-ness and inverse proportion to brains. Nat Holman is the exception that proves the law.

grabbed it and they were in a hole in sophomore and junior English. I could take a #4 bus or the #104 on Broadway and then the 79th Street crosstown, or I could walk to work. I would be near Hannah and, after I had become a big boy and moved back to my place, not too far from Carla.

The idea of bailing them out appealed to me. I grinned at Birmingham over the phone: Finestone into the breach.

I became gradually aware of a man named Johnson and of the fact that perhaps we weren't a banana republic after all and that he had much to do with this remarkable condition. I recalled that Manny had once gotten a part-time job through the National Youth Administration and I learned that this same Johnson had run the Texas NYA, that in fact he had been one of FDR's boys. In August something called the Tonkin Gulf Incident came along and he handled it like a statesman with brains: he went to Congress, got practically unanimous support for his Resolution that combined *Peace* with *Honor*; FDR and my father said it together: Perfect! On top of which Kennedy had chosen him. Score three for Johnson.

I also became aware of a man named Goldwater. I became aware that he was too neanderthal even for Eisenhower, that he seemed intent on getting us into a land war in Asia (despite E's warning) and that he was fascinated with the idea of sawing New York off the mainland and letting it slide out to sea and sink. Above all, he had gone the route my father—therefore I— despised: a Jew turned *goy*. He clicked into *his* place. As I moved into my first months at Peter Minuit, checked on Hannah, got cozier with Carla, kept tabs on Jim Ryun as he settled into his freshman year at Kansas U., I began to feel for the first time since

Kennedy's sensational tour of Europe that my life was adding up to something.

As the election approached, I went to work for Johnson in the local reform club: I stuffed envelopes, licked stamps, answered questions in pidgin Spanish, turned out the lights at night. Carla and I went down to the Garden—I insisted on going by subway to be with the people—and we sang the hades out of "Hello Lyndon." I also shunted aside whatever reservations I had about Bobby because he had once worked for McCarthy (we're all entitled to blow one, especially as babies) and pounded my palms silly for him. We came back to my place afterward because it was more Johnson-ish than the East Side, more NYA-ish, and fucked with proletarian delight.

My world was spinning neatly: the private school kids were not all East Side money; some were even (potential) young Speeds. Hannah was moving in P.S. 6. Lucille and I were civilized. Carla and I were terrific. The campaign was swell.

Election Day, 1964.

I read all my campaign literature. I flicked on the tube and caught the commercial of Goldwater blowing up the world. I reread E's speech on the dangers of the military-industrial complex, plus the story of his nixing Nixon on getting us into the land war in Asia. Clearly, E abhorred Goldwater, too. (And because I knew where he stood—with *me*—this time I would not need Massachusetts, Rutherford L. Decker or the Prohibition Party.)

I worked my ass off at the Club. On election morning I went to *shul*. Then I started for the polling booth in my good Democratic neighborhood. I hummed "Hello Lyndon" all the way. This time, dammit, I would pull the necessary lever, and *he would approve*.

I got to within ten yards of the entrance, looked across the Hudson at E voting in Gettysburg: who was I kidding? He would never approve of Democratic giveaways; with eyes closed, he was pulling the *Goldwater* lever.

I stepped off the curb, felt my ankle snap, and as I settled nastily into the gutter, yelled "Thank God!"

I felt terrific. I was racked up with a broken ankle and it was killing me, and I felt terrific. By the time everything was completed at St. Luke's and I was plastered and codeined, was resting so bravely that the nurses were ecstatic, had read every *Time* and *Newsweek* in the place, it was 10 P.M., the polls were closing, and I was off the hook. And I felt terrific. I called Carla, who was afraid I had had some kind of relapse, told her what had happened, told her to come down and get me, and also to bring a bottle of champagne, for the Johnson victory was already in the bag. She bawled me out, said I had no business worrying her like that, that it was the greatest landslide since my beloved 1936, that she would be right over.

They had fixed me up with a mobile cast and I was sitting up in the waiting room, trying to talk an expectant father into naming it Lyndon or Lyndonia, when she walked in with a bottle of Mumm's, hugged and kissed me, checked me all over like my mother, a facet of Carla Levine she had never revealed before, but which pleased me no end; I hobbled bravely into the waiting cab. We started on the champagne in the cab and the cabbie said it's against the law, winked into the mirror and added, up Goldwater's. I tipped splendidly, clumped to the elevator, leaned on her and we finished another bottle of champagne in her beautiful bedroom. We flicked on her third TV and we made lovely love to "Hello Lyndon," and the walking cast was no problem whatsoever. Just before we exploded into our landslide victory, I said, "Thank goodness I voted before I broke the stupid thing."

2

Time passes. We are having Christmas and Chanukah dinner with Lucille and Hannah at their place. Very civilized; I am with Carla and Lucille has Cyrus Broadcutter, now a full-fledged producer who sees in Lucille his personal star-property. Hannah, who is an incredible nine and all bamboo legs, autographs my cast and sees me as her own star-property as Lucille smiles gamely. Halfway through dinner, at Lucille's prompting, she pipes up, "I am not an IBM card; do not bend, fold or mutilate." Lucille and Cyrus applaud.

Carla and I look blank and Lucille, at her most Odetsian, says, "The incredible stew pot at Berkeley." I still draw a blank. "Don't tell me you've forgotten your proletarian roots, Speed," she says sweetly. I hear Carla murmur, "Oh, yes." I am still stupid and Lucille purrs, "The Free Speech Movement? Mr. M. Savio? It would seem that the apathetic generation has finally awakened. Hannah?"

"I am not an IBM card; do not bend, fold or mutilate."

"Again, sweetheart."

"Yeah, yeah, I get the message," I say quickly. "U. of Cal. Sure. You said it very well, baby."

Hannah beams. Carla smiles politely. Lucille pushes a triumphant glance at Cyrus. Ah, Golden State Warriors, ah Mario, ah, Hello Lyndon, why couldn't you leave me alone?

Looking back, it is all so clear that practically nothing was under control as we moved into 1965, but please bear in mind that everything *seemed* under control. We were all (or almost all)

delighted with the man in the White House, and so it was with Speed. Everything *seemed* under control with him. And everyone in his immediate orbit was delighted with him, even Speed. So with the cast on—*especially* with the cast on—he began to hobble bravely around town. Museums, parks, movies, theater. There was a week when Carla and I went to the theater five nights in a row, the last night catching Lucille's latest, an updated *Anna Christie* on 12th Street and it wasn't bad if you can take *Anna Christie*. We were regulars on the indoor track circuit; I took Hannah with us to the AAU meet and she fell in love with the hurdlers and I told her all about Spec Towns and Bones Dillard and she loved that, too.

I couldn't hang onto the cast forever, so reluctantly let them take it off in March. I began some light heel-and-toe walking in Riverside Park to bring me back to my schedule for the Olympics; the first time I broke into a slow trot I was so excited I sent Hannah a telegram.

In April, to open the outdoor season, Carla and I drove down to Philadelphia for the Penn Relays. Not only did I root for the Villanova Wildcats, plus a coach she kept referring to as Jumbo Jim who by some mainline alchemy took in Irish plowboys and turned them into Ron Delaneys, I also pulled old Speed together and, at the end of the mile relay, proposed.

"Did you break your ankle or head?" she said.

"They are both in very good shape, especially the latter, thanks to you."

"Is that why you're asking?" she said quickly.

"Of course not. I love you, goddamit."

And I think I did. Yes, I think I did. Her eyes got wet and mine almost did too, for there was rarely ever a break in her smooth sheen except during the time after Kennedy that I think of as my zombie period.

"Well?" I said.

"Include me in," she said, the sheen intact.

We kissed hard as the crowd filed out of Franklin Field and we spent our troth night in a lovely old hotel near Rittenhouse Square. A week later we were married in an East Side temple, to

157

please her father and his first wife, Carla's mother, and of course my mother and father. At Dorado Beach in Puerto Rico, I pulled another one out of the hat.

"I want to continue teaching."

"That's up to you," she said.

"Well, I do."

"Fine."

"You don't care if I don't write?"

"I care, but it's still up to you. I hear you're a pretty good teacher."

"Yes, I think I am. Something else. I'd like to keep my apartment."

"Now, there I draw the line. Speed, it's much too small. You know all the junk I have."

"Well then," I said, smiling mightily, "suppose we keep both places? It'll be like living in two different towns."

She didn't even have to think.

"I *love* it. It's beautiful. How did you ever come up with that? You're usually so damn impractical."

I kissed her. "Stick with me, kid, Speed will show you a lot more." (Oh Lord.) We kissed again and sipped our piña coladas. I held mine up to the striped evening sky.

"The '68 Olympics in Mexico City," said the big deal.

"You got a date, boy-o."

We flew back in time for my first Monday class. There was no trace of a limp as I walked into 19th-Century English Lit.

How do I describe the next three years? The latrine? Below the latrine? Zombie? No, it was not '46-'47, it wasn't '61, it wasn't even the end of '63. It was, as I look, feel, grope my way back, a time-space thing, a kind of physical matrix which dropped down on me, in which I moved in slow motion that picked up—that is, grew slower—as what remained of the world hurtled by. It was a gooey, sticky mass, this matrix, that thickened and polluted everything around it, like motor oil in a car that is breaking down. From time to time, I would break clear, and there were stretches when a name, a persona would penetrate the mass—Carla, Heinz von Mulheim, Jay Milton, Red Baumgarten—yet the mass-thing continued to grow, continued, within the bits and pieces of my recollection, to entangle, envelop me. Slight, *critical* correction: one thing, one alone, held fast and gave me whatever basic stability I had in those years: Jim Ryun. The more the matrix thickened and boxed me in, the more I concentrated—*depended* on Ryun. But let me attempt some chronology:

Carla and I continued nicely enough following the marriage and the brilliant stroke of two apartments, two towns, two socio-eco-psychological settings. For a while *both* of us functioned in the two environments; for a while. The summer of '65 we went off to Europe and toured the battlefields and I handled them with a sad strength that impressed us both. We returned in September and as she hurried to *Meridian*, I clucked over civil disobedience and agreed with my colleagues at Minuit that Tom Hayden, Aptheker and Staughton Lynd and their "fact-finding mission" to Hanoi were some pain in the ass, practically treasonous (Lynd's parents, who had written my high school American History favorite, *Middletown*, *had* to be disgusted, too, along with Shimon). The only one who said, "I'm not so sure" was, of all people, the German teacher, Heinz von Mulheim. I had never before, on general principle, spoken to Heinz. As the swirling, looping mass thickened and the faculty split and hardened, Heinz became the only one there I *could* talk to. That developed toward the end of 1966, along with sit-ins, teach-ins, march-ins. Meanwhile: Jim Ryun.

As that year came off the launching pad, I began to work out after school. About one week before Ryun set the mile record, I, in my American Keds, had gotten down to 7:40 for the mile in

159

Riverside Park (106th Street to 96th and back). When he ran that sensational 3:51 and change, I knew we were both on target for Mexico City and for a few days did not even feel the swirling and the looping. The evening that I learned about his breakthrough, I ran 7:35, then showered, spiffed up and cabbed over to the East Side to tell Carla what Ryun had just accomplished. She did not faint dead away. There had been another bombing and she was proofing copy for an editorial on body-counts. I said it again, about Ryun. This time she raised her sleek head and gave me a neutral face.

"Congratulations," she said.

"Isn't it great? He's still a baby; milers get better as they get older."

"I rather think," she said slowly, in her rather-think voice, "that Keino may take the record away from him."

"Who?"

"Kipchoge Keino."

"The African?"

"Yes, the African. Is there anything wrong with that?"

"No, and please don't look at me in that tone of voice. Ryun, you may recall, is American."

"So?"

"He's still very young. He's still maturing . . ."

"So?"

"What is this African bullshit?"

"Ah."

"What ah?"

"You don't think they can last beyond a hundred yards? You think they're all Jesse Owens?"

"Sure they can last. Look at Abebe Bikila."

She looked at Abebe Bikila. "All right then," she said.

"All right then."

I walked to her magnificent bar and poured myself a Campari. I remember thinking as I belted the stuff and felt nothing, I should have stood in bed.

160

2

Things began to go downhill at Minuit. By the end of '66, as the Student Mobilization Committee began to hand out leaflets outside the school, we were divided, at lunch, into three different tables: Hawks, Doves and "I Don't Knows." By February of '67 the "IDKs" had dwindled down to Heinz, his pipe and me. The sticky mass swirled harder, grew ever more viscous. In March a history teacher and the Dean of Boys, both GIs in WW2, had a fistfight in the cafeteria. And in April, during Vietnam Week, Joel Feigenspan, my Fitzgerald of the junior class, came to me with a petition from SDS asking for an immediate end to the war, total withdrawal and a condemnation of American military and economic imperialism.

"I don't sign petitions," I said. "It's a matter of principle."

"So is this."

"I still don't sign petitions."

"Not even this one?"

"Not this one, or for that matter, one that wants us to accelerate or use the bomb."

He turned quickly and walked out, and I knew I had lost him. As I ran my fourth mile that night, I clearly saw Manny in '36 asking Mr. Talbot in European History, and a minor hero, to sign a petition from ADL of B'nai B'rith, asking for American withdrawal from the German Olympics; carrying that paper, perhaps shattering Glenn Cunningham's putative victory, almost broke Manny's heart, but he had to do it. Mr. Talbot squinted through his tan.

"We're not sure of the facts in Germany," he said; "bear in mind the propaganda of the Great War, and how it distorted all our perceptions and even governmental policies."

"You mean how rotten the Germans were in Belgium?"

"Among other things, Emanuel."

"But the propaganda never said that Belgium invaded Germany."

"No," Talbot smiled, "but atrocities were committed by both sides, the Allies as well as the Central Powers."

"The Jews are beating up the Nazis, busting their stores, kicking them out of school?"

"I'm not saying that. I am merely saying we must have all the objective facts before embarking on a precipitous course of action."

"This petition is a precipitous course of action?"

"Who knows where it might lead?"

"Then you won't sign?"

"I *cannot* sign."

I never talked to the asshole again.

The next day I said to Heinz, who was a kid in Cologne during the war, whose father was a party member and in the *Wehrmacht*, and who was the only poet that I ever knew who wrote in Esperanto, where the hell he moonlighted?

"How do you know I moonlight?" he said.

"You're never around at three o'clock, and you're also still pretty sane."

He thought about that with his pipe, then nodded.

"Maybe it does help," he said. "All right, I work on the *Evening Whisper*."

"What the hell is that? An Esperanto poetry journal?"

"The *Evening Whisper*, old man, is a cross between the *National Enquirer* and *Confidential*."

"Oh shit."

"Don't be so Godawful judgmental. It so happens that the *Whisper* performs a vital function. It needles, perhaps artlessly, nonetheless it needles. We are very necessary in this rather hectic time."

"There's enough needling going on. We need—*I* need—some common sense."

"But that is just the problem, old man; everyone has common sense, everyone is right. The *Whisper* needles on a basis of utter know-nothingness which is the only way that real needling can work. May I ask why you ask?"

"I'm getting out of Minuit; I've had it with teaching, with molding the young."

He nodded with his pipe; "Ah yes. Would you like me to talk to Red Baumgarten?"

"Editor?"

"Editor. Publisher. The most artless dodger of them all."

"Yes, talk to Red Baumgarten. Anything beats this."

3

The next time I made it to the East Side, which was about a week later, Carla was on the phone with Lucille. Yes, *Lucille*; they had discovered each other. It seemed they were both on a committee dedicated to kicking ROTC off every campus in the New York area. I waited patiently (I was doing much of that in those days) until she got off the phone, meanwhile pulling hard at a V.O. and water. When she looked at me with those sparkling eyes that always followed committee work, I said, with as much simplicity as I could muster, "I've just quit teaching."

She absorbed that, then said nicely, "Are you going to reenlist?"

"Up yours."

She smiled, her first interpersonal communication in four weeks.

"I'm sorry. I take that back. Are you finally off the goddam fence? That's what bugs me more than anything, you know."

"I know. Not completely. But I'm leaning."

"That's progress. Do you want to come back to *Meridian*? It might make . . . a difference . . . well, with us."

"Don't put a price on it, Carla. No, I don't want to come back."

Her eyes withdrew.

"Well then?"

"I'm looking around. I'll keep you posted."

"Yes, do that."

She returned to the phone. Something about a march on Brooklyn College.

163

36

Red Baumgarten was mister five by five, but he had shrewd, thin eyes.

"Sure I heard of you," he said. "You used to do bleeding-heart stuff for Levine."

"That's right."

"Is she still in business?"

"As far as I know."

"I give her six months. Her rag is dead."

"I'm not here to discuss *The New Meridian*. Heinz told me he had talked to you."

"Who?"

"Heinz von Mulheim."

"Oh, you mean Jay Milton."

"Is that his *nom de guerre*?"

"That's his pen name. You want a pen name?"

"You mean I've got the job?"

"Sure. I also read your Morse Junko stories. You got a funky head; I need that around here."

"Heinz . . . Jay . . . says you give him his funky head. Can I have the same deal?"

"Of course. That's the secret of my success. I ain't your father or mother or the government. If a person got the talent, I stay out of his way."

"Perfect. I'll keep my name, thanks."

It turned out that Red, whose version of yellow journalism would have blinded Hearst and Pulitzer, was a bedrock conservative. I discovered this on-West 72nd Street across from the *Whisper* office in a bar where he knew everyone and

164

everyone knew Red, especially on Saturday night (as a fat little boy he probably never had a date and so had long since established his social milieu). In the Jolly Mog he would turn his chair sideways at his personal table, lean against the wall, open the thin eyes and tell me what was wrong with the country. In the course of these seminars I learned that he had a love affair with the American Eagle ("Glaum the baleful eye, the glaring profile that could positively puke over what he's seeing"). His three greatest idols were Jim Thorpe, Irving Thalberg and Dick Bong, the World War II ace who was killed testing a jet plane in 1947. Red could devote an entire recitation to each one, return to the same one a week later and never quite repeat himself.

So it was that on a spring night of '67 he leaned against his wall-space and informed me that Norma Shearer, who could have had her pick of every stud in Hollywood, chose Thalberg, a little Jewboy who wore long underwear. He then plunked down his gin and tonic, swiveled about and said, you know why the country is so screwed up? I'll tell you why the country is all screwed up.

He then told me why.

It was, he said, the eyes almost wide open, the death of the studio system. That's right, the studio system. Without the stability of an MGM, a Warner Brothers, a Columbia, there is no goddam foundation. There is no—and he spaced out his words— no . . . established . . . or . . . predictable . . . way . . . to . . . raise . . . our . . . children. He let that sink in. Then: in point of actual and developmental fact, the *true* fathers of America were Louis B. Mayer, Harry Cohen and Jack Warner. Not Dagwood. They ran their families and their families were a real, true kibbutz. Everybody had a job to do and everybody knew where he stood. These men had rules, regulations. They spanked you if you got smart and that included Clark Gable or Bette Davis. And another thing, did your father ever tell you the facts of life?

No.

OK, these men, these *fathers* taught the boys of America the facts of life, including the crucial one of how to make out. And they taught the girls of America where they stood in the make-out process. But I'll clue you in to the most important thing of all:

they taught the children of America to *love* their country.

He sat back. Then he sat forward. In other words, he intoned, the studio-families headed by Mayer and Cohen and Warner told us who we were, where we had been, where we were *going* . . . OK, then what happened?

What?

Patricide.

Parricide?

Patricide, parricide, what's the difference? It was even worse than that, it was the murder of the entire family—

Universal, to name one, I ventured mildly, is still in business.

Hell, I'm talking about a real family. Not television and oil wells. I'm telling you it was the young devouring the old.

How?

Simple. The stars became the so-called independents and these independents destroyed the studios. Who created the star system? The studios. Now do you see?

I thought I did . . .

The end. Finito. Of Louis B. Mayer, of all Louis B. Mayers. The end of stability. The beginning of chaos.

Yes . . .

One man, one young man, sensitive, artistic, introspective, saw it coming. This young man was loyal to Louis B. Mayer. He died, supposedly of a heart attack. You know why I say, *supposedly?*

Why?

What do doctors know? This young man looked ahead and perceived the destruction of the family and all that would mean. Red pointed a stubby finger at me. Hear this and hear it good: *Irving Thalberg died of a broken heart.*

I walked very slowly from 72nd Street to 108th Street.

2

The following week he did a reprise on Dick Bong. He told Carmen, the waitress, and me that Bong could put Rickenbacker, Richtofen and Cobber Cain in his hip pocket and have room left

166

over for Don Gentile. His lip trembling, he talked about the crash that had taken Dick's life. Whyinhell, he demanded, enormous fist pounding his table, did he wanna test a goddam jet for? Carmen didn't know and neither did I. As she walked back to the bar, he asked me if I knew why the country was so screwed up? I thought about the death of the studios, said, lots of reasons.

Nah, not lots of reasons. Jets.

Jets?

That's right. Remember what Churchill said about Spitfires and Hurricanes? Never have so many owed so much, etc., etc.?

I remembered.

Jets are the opposite of that maxim. They are too much, too fast, too soon. And they're the opposite of something else. You know what obsolescence means?

I knew.

Well jets are superflessence. Remember that.

. . . All right . . .

Overkill. That's jets. Hey, they are screwing up all your Rusks and McNamaras and all the other brains zooming around the goddam world and I'll tell you why. Instead of getting ideas, these guys are getting jet lag. When it comes to making a goddam decision, all they wanna do is hit the sack . . . Did you, he asked, ever hear of *propeller* lag?

I couldn't say I had.

Darn tootin you haven't . . . He regarded his drink darkly. Then he looked at me with the widened, indignant eyes. Go ask the birds, he said.

Birds?

That's right. Don't give me one of those looks. I deal in facts. Birds. They tried their darnedest to help us. Threw themselves into the intake of those goddam jet engines. Caused all those crashes. They were telling us something and we wouldn't listen. Mother Nature is no fool.

I agreed completely.

All right, they sacrificed themselves. They looked at superflessence and they sacrificed themselves. Because we would

167

not listen. You know what the birds were saying?

What?

Bring back Yankee Clippers and De Haviland Mosquitoes and Lockheed Lightnings. Now he was slapping the table. His voice was a low rumble. The birds were saying, bring back to American speech, American spirit, the word you never hear anymore: CONTACT! Now don't let anybody ever tell you birds are stupid.

I sat around the park for a day and brooded. I was pissed off at Carla, Lucille, Johnson, the children of America, myself. I was working on a rag for a man about whom my father would have said, he fell out of his baby carriage. And yet, and yet, he had struck the ragged edge of a nerve . . . I clumped up to the apartment and began a two-part article entitled, "Why is America in Such a Mess?"

Red, who was all business on the job and never touched a drop till the evening, nodded not bad, let's do it. When the mail came in, it included a recipe for Louis B. Mayer's chicken soup and two budgies in cages.

Red turned out to be a splendid prognosticator. As we slogged into 1968, *Meridian* folded. It simply lay down, curled up its toes and died. Not that Carla was very concerned. She was too busy working (with Lucille) on the American Deserters Committee, Arms for Peace in Vietnam and a GI Coffeehouse she had opened in Fort Dix (where Harry Truman had discharged me and extended the "heartfelt thanks of a grateful Nation in bringing about the total defeat of the enemy"). In the middle of all that, *Meridian* just died.

By now I was spending five days a week on my side of town. It was soon six, then seven. For on January 30, Tet was on us. Carla and Lucille and their committees went bananas; Carla had absolutely no time for me. For my part, there were new problems because Tet had pushed rusty old suddenly-outraged buttons: We had been suckered. Suckered and clobbered. Suckered and clobbered worse than at Kasserine Pass, and God knows that was bad enough. But at least Patton and E and FDR acknowledged Kasserine for what it was: a complete stomping; Johnson un-hunkers and calls it a *victory*.

I began to run again.

I threw myself into quarters, halves, hard-slow 220s; I transformed Tets, Kasserines—defeats that were somehow victories—into a strict training routine that would put me back on target for the Olympics. By the middle of February I was down to 7:28 and thinking of nothing beyond my physical condition, which was as good as it had been in years. On Washington's Birthday, with that tightly focused strength under my belt, I thought I might try a visit to the East Side.

As I walked in, Carla and Lucille were working on a letter to the Fort Dix GIs, explaining the political and philosophical significance of Tet and advising them to address the enclosed list of questions to their officers. I walked to the bar and poured a Four Roses, neat, out of the pint I had brought with me. Then I walked over, drink in hand, and kissed Hannah who, like the good kid she was, sat in a corner and studied, this time for the tests she would soon take for Hunter High. I told her of my latest time for the mile and she congratulated me. Very solemnly then, she reached under her Barron's Guide and produced a piece of paper which she held out to me. It was, naturally, a petition; this one to impeach the Texas Ranger in the White House. I launched into a detailed explanation of why you just can't sign petitions without getting all the facts, that the facts were often mutually contradictory, and that when all was said and done, the man was still the only President we had. She didn't say anything, but continued to gaze without a single goddam blink. I walked out of the house; Carla and Lucille hadn't even looked up.

I walked back through the park, hoping that a mugger would start something, but the muggers were all home, celebrating the Tet victory. When I got to 108th Street, I walked upstairs and sat down at the window facing the slice of river and tried to write. Nothing. Not even a variation on the demise of the studios, or jets. At three o'clock in the morning I was running up the drive toward the George Washington Bridge, freezing my nuts off, but at least feeling that I existed.

2

I shall attempt, through the swirling thickness, to be terse, objective, factual about the following weeks:

J announces he will not run; students sprinting down Broadway celebrate. Speed writes postcard: "When the going gets tough, the tough get chickenshit"; tears up postcard.

April 4: Martin Luther King buys it. Speed rushes east and embraces tearful Carla. Twain spend one week before tube, sighing as riots flare, city after city. Slowly Speed and Carla begin to come alive, creep about apartment. She says nothing about war. Neither does he. The thickness: it loops, swirls. Speed lifts foot to take step, hears sucking sound, thinks of quicksand, banishes thought. Does no running in that time. Feels he is growing weaker and weaker, as if has walking pneumonia, which had in 1933. Takes temp. Temp reads 94.4. Of course, whole world subnormal. Fixates on Jim Ryun circling Kansas track mile after mile after mile. Turns to little black book. Nothing. Notes this with page of zeros.

Gradually, then, with ever increasing rhythm, Carla returned to the war. Returned to her Coffeehouse. Returned to Amnesty International. Returned to her phone calls. Called Lucille, Toronto, Halifax, Quebec. Her eyes clouded, filled with Hanoi, the Mekong, My Lai. I laced on my Keds and loped my way back to the West Side.

For three days, for a total of ten action hours, I ran myself into oxygen debt. On the night of the third day, as I was paying this debt in the apartment, on the floor, at eleven at night, the phone rang. I staggered up, gasped into it. Heinz sounded calm; he always sounded calm, so don't infer anything.

"How would you like to be liberated?" he said.

"That's my problem. I'd like a little captivity."

"I'm absolutely serious. SDS is liberating my building."

"Oh shit."

"Be that as it may, they are."

"Piss into a Trojan and drop it on their heads."

"I do not stoop. You know I do not stoop. Would you care to see this? It is remarkably organized bedlam below."

"What the hell; it beats what I'm doing."

"Which is?"

"Staring at a wall. Jerking off in slow motion."

"Sounds dull. You're welcome to come over. I believe you once said this was your turf."

"In another life. Should I come in the back way?"

"I'm afraid it's the *only* way."

"OK. Maybe there's a story in it."

☆　　☆　　☆

Heinz lived on 114th, between Broadway and Riverside, on the down-slope to the Hudson, off the southern border of Columbia. I walked to 113th and turned west toward the river. Three-quarters of the way down, I cut right into a sloping alley, walked under the budding trees of a courtyard and climbed over the fence. I slipped past garbage cans in the alley, entered his building through the laundry room and took the elevator up to four. I got out and rang his bell. Heinz, clamping an unlit pipe, let me in and handed me a beer. I sipped gratefully, then followed him to the window. I could hear the street noise below even though the window was closed. He opened it and motioned. I stuck my head out and the wave of noise, sweat and excitement slapped me in the face. I drew back, opened my mouth and breathed through it, again looked out at 114th Street. It was packed. From the church at the top of the slope down to Riverside. Beneath the street-lights hair, tee shirts, jeans, sandals and bare feet milled about. Some of the students carried candles and their faces flickered earnestly as they sang something to the tune of "When the Saints Go Marching In." Directly beneath me the singing, the hair, the tee shirts, the sweat were especially thick.

"They've taken over the building," Heinz said. "They have dispossessed Columbia, which apparently had no rights in the matter in the first place."

"According to who? Whom?"

"Their mimeograph machine. I will not have to pay rent."

"Says who? Don't tell me."

"Correct." He handed me his black-bordered writ of liberation. I folded it into an aeroplane and sailed it down into the pack. A man in a crew cut and plaid jacket reached up and plucked it out of the air. I noticed other men dressed like that one. Some wore incredibly thin ties and pointed black shoes. Old Siwash, '35?

"The *gendarmes*," said Heinz. "Perhaps they are fooling six-month-old children; no one else."

I pulled in.

"Do you think it'll get rough?"

"Can't guess. At first I thought yes, then I caught the sweet

172

aroma of grass. They are remarkably mellow, including some cops, who are smoking with commendable dedication."

I drank my beer and looked down with great calmness and detachment; I thought of Manny at NYU, counting the days until his enlistment physical at Grand Central Palace. Then I heard something. And to make sure I heard it, I leaned far out and looked down. I saw a sea of hair above a cordon of tee shirts that were locked together, facing the building. I heard the something again. And again:

"COLUMBIA GOES FROM JERK TO JERK, FROM EISENHOWER TO RACIST KIRK."

I leaned farther.

"Columbia . . . jerk . . . EISENHOWER . . . Kirk . . ."

I pulled in and said "Excuse me." I strode across the room, strode out, plunged down the stairs, three at a time. I ran down the hall, opened the outer door and barreled into the crowd. I smelled pot, sweat, dirty hair, garlic, bare feet. Then I was in the middle of it, surrounded by the chant: "EISENHOWER . . . JERK . . . EISENHOWER . . . JERK . . ." I reached for the first tee shirt I could see, grabbed, wrenched. I heard a scream. I grabbed another and twisted; I heard a snap. I began to swing and heard voices around me: *"Get that crazy bastard . . ."* A wave of tee shirts and jeans engulfed me and still I kept swinging. I heard myself yelling, far, far off: "TENACITY, ALWAYS TENACITY." Then the club.

They drove us in a van down to a precinct on 100th Street, ignored me for an hour, then drove us all down to Centre Street for arraignment. A judge in bifocals with the little halfmoons looked at my sheet, looked up and said I appeared to be a mature member of a minority group and that therefore I had a special responsibility.

"How come?" I said.

"It behooves you to set an example for others."

I stared at the neat halfmoons.

"Were you in the war?" I said.

173

"No," he said quickly.

"Four F?"

"I was deferred. I had a vital job and couldn't be replaced. The work I did was essential to national security. They wouldn't release me." He was breathing deeply.

"OK," I said.

"You seem mature and basically responsible. I will treat this as a momentary lapse in judgment, but will set nominal bail as a lesson to responsible persons who are tempted to forget their responsibilities as minority group members. Who is next, clerk?"

At one in the morning Heinz and Carla walked in. She hugged me, felt the lump in my hair, kissed it, said she had paid their blood money, kissed the lump again. "Oh those fucking pigs," she said. Heinz shifted his pipe and looked around. I kissed her and ran my hands along her satiny back. I didn't say a thing; why should I?

She kept filling the ice bag with fresh cubes, fed me aspirin and asked me over and over how many pigs I had taken out. I said only one, smiled crookedly and she kissed me and fed me some more aspirin. This continued through most of the night. Ice, aspirin, question, modest answer, kiss, aspirin. And the more it continued, the hornier I got (after all, it had been six months). Around four o'clock I tossed the ice bag across the room and reached for her shorts; she'd been nursing me through the night in shorts and nippled tee shirt. She caught my hands with surprising strength, quickly straddled me with those long, brown legs, gazed down at me.

"It's not good for your condition," she smiled.

174

"It's ideal," I said.

She dipped down and kissed me. "I respect what you did tonight," she whispered.

I took a breath and said, "It was a very fascist scene."

She kissed me again and I reached under the tee shirt. She grabbed my hand, pulled it out. The golden legs squeezed, she smiled down at me, crinkled her forehead.

"What was it they used to say in the army? . . . Oh yes, frig-it. Isn't that what you used to say?"

"Umm," I said, arching. She lifted.

"Come on, now," she said. "Frig ROTC."

"Ummm . . ."

"Say it, darling. Frig ROTC."

"Frig ROTC," I mumbled.

"I can't hear you."

"FRIG ROTC."

"Lovely. . . Frig Dow."

"Ahhh, frig . . . Dow . . ."

"That's it," she smiled. "Frig the Institute of Defense Analysis . . . Come on . . ."

"Frig the . . . Institute of Defense . . . Analysis."

"Frig Johnson."

"Shit. Frig Johnson."

"Frig Humphrey."

"Hey—"

"Frig *Humphrey*."

"Frig Humphrey," I said.

"Frig racist draft boards."

"And how. Frig racist draft boards."

"Frig the light at the end of the tunnel."

"Frig the light at the end of the friggin tunnel."

"Neat . . . Frig Westy Westmoreland."

"OK, frig Westy Westmoreland."

"Frig West Point."

"Frig . . . West . . . Point."

"Frig the Army," she said from on high.

I squirmed.

175

"Frig the *Army*," she said.
"Frig the goddam Army."
She eased down, touched me, slid once, twice.
"Frig Eisenhower," she said.
I looked away. She slid over me, nibbled at my ear.
"Frig Eisenhower," she whispered.
I closed my eyes. I felt her tongue.
"Furrriggg Eisenhowerrr," she whispered.
I opened my eyes. I closed my eyes.
"Frig Eisenhower," I croaked.
Then she put out.

For a solid month I lived on the East Side and we humped as if I'd be fleeing to Canada the next day. Not once in all that time did she push further on where I stood, or even ask me to leave the *Whisper* (not that I was doing any writing; Red merely shrugged over the telephone: "Funky heads write when they write"). And unless I imagine it in the remembering, the thick, swirling stuff that had coiled about me lifted in May of '68. From here I can see it was merely a gathering of powder for the next cannonball in the gut, but at the time I really thought it was a sliver of dancing light at the end of my tunnel.

For there was now Bobby Kennedy. And Bobby was winning primary after primary. And I was blinking, sitting up, taking notice. Not only would he forever destroy the Nixon Nightmare, he would restore us to the glory of 1960. But he would also do something else for Speed. For Speed, he would reforge the FDR (Shimon-Speed) coalition: bluecollars, blacks, Jews, eggheads. He *was* reforging it.

It would be 1932 all over again.

We had been down but we were on the rise. The depression might still be with us, but now there would be hope, brightness, excitement; my father would be rid of Hoover and fighting back; my mother would be smiling at him; Naomi, Samuel and Manny would be getting the marks they *should* get, listening to both of them. And Shimon would be reaching down for a few precious dollars and taking all of us downtown to the Roxy to laugh at the *shvartz* world with the Marx Brothers in *Horsefeathers*.

All this Bobby Kennedy would do . . .

June 6, 1968.

Clobbered. Again.

The viscous fog dropped down on me, ran in great contrails through my head. Carla and I were transfixed by the horror of Los Angeles. Huddling, again, we watched. The lovely moment of victory. Then the wildness. Bobby on the floor. We watched. All day, and the next. For an entire week we watched, did not leave each other.

At the end of that week I knew I must try something, anything, or we were finished. The crisscrossing contrails, the spitting faces, the guns would finish us off and we would never *leave* that room. The West Side; I had to struggle over to the West Side. There I could recognize Speed, I could be with Bobby's people, I could stay *alive*.

I had to leave, too, for Carla. She had to make it on her own or she would not be Carla. I did not give her what she would call a valid rationale, merely said, I have to go. I'm sure she understood; she said, all right, but do it fast.

I got myself onto the number 4 bus on Madison Avenue, wound up through El Barrio and turned west on 110th Street. Despite the swirling fog, the thickness in my legs, I made it to my place at 10:30. I ducked into my ancient building that was tenanted by black, brown, white, yellow; surely here, the blue-eyed soul brother would be at home. I didn't feel quite so heavy; I took the stairs, walking, two at a time, felt a shade stronger. I let myself in, leaned against the door, breathed. I locked the door, walked to the desk, sat, stared at a snapshot of Captain Speed in Salzberg:

combat boots, field jacket, stern V-E face. I pulled a yellow pad to me.

I stared at the pad for twenty-five minutes. Then I called her. She sounded trembly, but in Carla-control. I said, I'm trying to write and she said, I thought you would. I said, you can make it, but I'll be here; she said she loved me and hung up quickly. I returned to the yellow pad . . .

Between 11:30 and five in the morning, with time out only for coffee-V.O., I banged out a Morse Junko story. Literally banged out. For I shoved aside my pencils and sharpener and pad and broke out the typewriter and attacked it. I had never done that before; the few times I had gone directly to the typewriter I had produced a SpeedManny glossalalia. I have never been able to do it again. But as the sun lifted over the East River, I was able to pound out, "THIS I HAVE DONE."

Although I almost always have total recall of everything I've written, this one eludes me except that I sense it was filled with the murders of Matteotti, Jaures, Rathenau, Gandhi. I do know I did not change a word.

Totally exhausted, I crawled to the phone, called Carla. I said I had written something that would go into my drawer; she said, of course; said, good morning, Speed. I said good morning, hung up.

I returned to the story, breathed so deeply I became giddy, then again did something for the first and last time in my life: I tore up a piece of my fiction; tore it up for him.

Very carefully then, I gathered up the pieces and dropped them into one of the manila envelopes I used to send out my work. I walked downstairs.

I walked to Riverside, crossed, walked down into the park, across the softball field, jumped the iron fence, dodged my way across the West Side Highway. The Hudson was oil-shiny in the June night; the lights of the Jersey shore glittered beneath its film. I opened the envelope and scattered the pieces of my story onto the film. I watched the pieces drift down toward the bay. Then I turned and walked slowly back to the apartment and collapsed into a dreamless sleep.

She rebounded with her usual style. The sleek head, the magnificent neck, the smooth back straightened up, the proud mouth curled whenever it emitted Thieu, Westmoreland, McNamara, Rusk. Even Speed (*especially* Speed in this period) could see what was happening: the new respect for me, the delicate restructuring I had worked on our relationship that had created a subtle dependency, were beginning to wane, to disappear into her committees. Soon now we would be returning to the old Carla-Speed equation; that I could not accept. As horrible as the last month had been, it had at least revamped *that*, had given me the edge I had always needed with Carla.

I decided to make my decisive move, the one that must shake her loose from the props that had created and maintained the old balance.

On the 24th of June, I said, "Why don't we take a second honeymoon?"

She absorbed, wrinkled the ivory forehead.

"Speed . . . Really . . . This isn't the time."

"Why not? It's the perfect time."

"How in the world can you say that?"

"Because it is. Look, we've taken one shot in the *kishka* after another. We need a break. We owe it to ourselves."

She was beginning to think; her eyes were focused.

"You've got a point, but . . . now?" She was fingering a guide to the draft for high school seniors. I slid the book out of her hand and said, "Yes, now. Now."

"We've been to Europe, we've been to California."

I put my arm around the thoughtful, gorgeous waist.

"You are a real New Yorker, you know that? OK, let's go New York all the way. We haven't been to Niagara Falls."

"That's almost *obscene.*"

"Why, for God's sake?"

"It's what people did in another world."

"Perfect. Let's try that world. My parents always talked about it; now we can go and give them a wedding present."

"God, how corny . . ."

"Great. We'll try corn. No, wheat. The Shredded Wheat box was part of my childhood. Do you know where Shredded Wheat is made?"

"Oh God, don't tell me . . ."

"Right. There was a picture of the Falls right on the box. Come on, I'll rent a car and we'll do it in one week. I'll take care of everything."

". . . What's wrong with my car?"

It was working; she would do it, and for me. And once Speed was out on the open road, the old black magic would take over. I kissed her. "I'd rather rent one," I said. "Humor me."

"All right," she sighed and kissed me back. "Niagara Falls. What a cornball."

I wanted to rent a car because hers was a Mercury and even as Morse Junko I wanted nothing to do with Henry Ford. Especially not now. Not when Speed Finestone was newly courting Carla Levine. Not when the honeymoon machine would be the product of anyone so detested by Shimon Finestone. And that included the two other monopolists, Alfred Sloan of GM and Walter Chrysler, perhaps not as detestable as Ford, but bad enough. I decided on an AMC Rambler because American was the runt of the industry, and also because George Romney was something of a *shmegegge*, so there was a basic connection between us.*

---

*Some would consider Romney (and me) a *schlimazel*, i.e. the passive *putz.* Wrong. The *schlimazel* is the customer who gets the soup poured on his head. The *shmegegge* is the waiter who does the pouring. Therefore we both qualified as the active *putz.*

180

We started out on my project on the morning of June 29. I picked up the Thruway off the Saw Mill River Parkway and headed north for Albany and the turn west. It was a lovely, soft day and we drove with the windows down and she seemed calm and receptive to me and to this pleasant world as we rolled through the Hudson Valley. She stayed tuned to all-news WINS, but I didn't carp; I could not cut off all links to what we were leaving, not yet. Plus which WINS must fade out sooner or later.

We pulled in for a bite in a food-and-gas stop, then settled down for the long drive to the north. Sure enough, at the pivot point of Albany, the news faded and she turned the radio off. I started to run through *South Pacific*. When I reached "Dites-moi," I glanced sideways. She was reading a green paperback whose title glared at me: *4F: How to Avoid the Draft.*

I said, "Can you read in a moving car?"

"Sure," she said.

"I can't. It makes me nauseous."

"Not me. It doesn't bother me at all."

I stepped on the gas and pushed the speedometer up to sixty-five and began to weave in and out of the flow. She stayed with the book. We passed Schenectady and I said we were entering the Northwest Frontier and she said uh-huh. I weaved past Amsterdam, weaved south of Herkimer and she was still in the book. I said, "That is history out there. Revolutionary history. That town is named after General Herkimer. He died near here after the battle of Oriskany." She stayed with her book. "Lou Ambers, the Herkimer Hurricane, came from Herkimer." She read on, lost in the physical, mental and moral handicaps that would disqualify disgustingly healthy American boys, thereby handing Hitler, Mussolini, Tojo and Lord Haw Haw some horselaughs down in hell. "Lou Ambers," I said, "fought Tony Canzoneri a hundred times, or so it seemed." She plowed ahead as the patriots of the Northwest Frontier frowned and asked whatehell was going on? Near Utica I kicked us up to seventy and said, "Lou Ambers was no 4F, you can bet your life on that." I honked at a Cadillac who had clearly been a civilian from '41 to '45, screwing everything in sight on the home front while I was

181

getting my ass shot up for him. She finally looked at me.

"I presume," she presumed in her S. Lawrence voice, "that Tony Canzoneri was not 4F either."

"Correct."

She slipped a tooled leather bookmark into her place, closed the book and held it tenderly.

"Or Barney Ross," she said.

"Correct again. He had a terrific record with the marines." I looked over at her. She had her jawline composed the way it used to be composed before King and Bobby and the days of her dependency. I felt a spur of panic; this was not at all going according to plan; the old black magic was turning into the old thick, black fog. I slowed down to fifty-five, drove neatly.

"You know," I said reasonably, "this is very patriotic country up here. The settlers were isolated, they had to put up with the Iroquois, who mainly sided with the British; they were not on top of Washington's priority list, yet they hung in."

"Uh-huh," she said.

"They had a vision of what America could be."

"Uh-huh."

I wanted to stop myself, but I couldn't.

"General Herkimer didn't sit around all day figuring out how he could avoid the draft." (So I said it; was this a crime?) I waited.

"I dare say," she said coolly. I drove firmly, evenly; very well, Herkimer couldn't defend himself, but I could. "Jacob Herkimer," I said calmly, "could not *wait* to give up his life for his country, for his *vision* of his country."

"He had only one life to give," she observed.

"That's right. Plus a leg. He gave up a leg. The enemy shot it up. *He* didn't, looking for a deferment."

"I dare say," she dared say, "that Speed Finestone volunteered his own precious life."

"You bet your sweet ass."

"I dare say—correction—I am *certain* that 4F was a dirty word in Speed's lexicon."

"Give that little lady a ripe banana. Right, again."

She finally retreated. Silently she looked out at the lovely valley gliding by. She sighed. I sighed. We could both catch a gleaming patch here and there of the Mohawk River. I wanted to say, oh shit, forget it; let's start all over; who'll win the pennant? do you like McIntosh apples? New York wine is just as good as California wine. I didn't say anything; I felt the way Manny did after Samuel said he couldn't understand how anybody could screw up geometry so badly. Finally she broke the ice.

"Speed, what *you* did, what *Herkimer* did, is not what this country is now doing." She said it very gently. I didn't answer at first. To the north were two of the great places of Manny's career: Oriskany, Fort Stanwix. All around us were the heroes of his frontier: Peter Gansevoort, Marinus Willett, Herkimer, Sullivan, the splendid, early Benedict Arnold. "Maybe . . ." I said. "Maybe."

"No maybes, darling. We both know it. There is a higher patriotism, you know."

We sped past Oneida. The Oneidas were the one tribe of the six nations that fought with us. It was suddenly very important to stick up for the Oneidas.

"You don't have to tell kids how to avoid serving their country," I said.

"Speed," she said in her controlled voice, "please don't tell me what I have to do." She remained quiet, then said gently, "Darling, can't we just enjoy this trip?"

"Sure," I said. "Why not? Relax. Smoke an Old Gold."

2

Thirty miles on and we passed Syracuse which sprawled south of the Thruway. I thought about Syracuse and then thought that I might very well point out that Marty Glickman went to Syracuse. If I did, she might say, the sports announcer? And I would say, hell, he was a great *football* player and a great *sprinter* who came proudly up from the sidewalks of New York. And she would say, isn't that interesting? And I would say, Glickman made the '36 Olympic team and should have run on the winning 400 meter relay along with Sammy Stoller, but they didn't because they were nice Jewish boys and we didn't want to offend Hitler. And she would say, Oh for Heaven's sake, it's over and done with, stop living in the past, and I would say, it's *never* over and done with, shall we look at where Marty Glickman went to school, and she would say, what for?

I decided to say nothing about Marty Glickman.

We stopped briefly for a sandwich in one of those Thruway oases, then barreled west again, past Auburn and Geneva. We were north of Finger Lakes country now and she had left the draft and the 4Fs to gaze at the homegrown magnificence; if this were Europe, she and all the other visiting firemen would have been transported; they would be pointing and clucking and poring over the history of the Loire or Po or Rhine or Danube Valley. As it was, she merely gazed. I thought I might give her a little history lesson, go into what transpired here in 1779. I thought I might tell her about the Indian menace in the Mohawk Valley, that the Indians were in Sir William Johnson's hip pocket largely because he was married to Molly Brant, sister of Joseph Brant, the scourge of the Valley. I thought I might tell her that Washington finally realized the danger to his people here and realized, too, the strategic importance of upper New York. I thought I might tell her how he took the bull by the horns and sent General John Sullivan through this country with orders to destroy the Indian towns and to end once and for all the threat to the settlers. I thought I might tell her how efficiently Sullivan carried out his orders, redeeming himself after having screwed up at the battle of Long Island. All this I thought I might tell her.

But then she would say: You mean Washington ordered this Sullivan to search and destroy?

And I would say: Well, that is not the way I'd put it.

And she would say: How *would* you put it?

And I would say: We simply had to eliminate the Indian menace and to do this he had to order Sullivan to eliminate—

And she would say: *Eliminate?*

And I would say: Well, it was a matter of life and death for us and—

184

And she would say: But didn't the Indians live here? Wasn't it *their* country?

And I would say: In a way it was, but this was a matter of Manifest Destiny and—

And she would say: Body counts are Manifest Destiny?

And I would say: Stop putting words into my mouth; Washington knew that to win a war you had to be somewhat ruthless; I mean, all is fair in love and war; and if you burn their crops and villages, well, you eliminate the threat—

And she would say: Burn? Eliminate? Are you telling me that this Sullivan *defoliated* the area?

And I would say: No, I'm not telling you that, and please don't be so goddam judgmental as you glide along in complete safety from the Indian menace. Just remember that Sullivan made this condition possible, thereby allowing you to be so goddam judgmental on this magnificent Thruway.

And she would say: This was your idea, darling, and just bear in mind that in order to build this magnificent Thruway, your politicos defoliated this lovely country no less than your General Sullivan.

I decided not to tell her anything about 1779.

3

I managed to get past Rochester without stopping to pay my respects to George Eastman and American know-how and the box camera that was so much a part of Finestone history. I didn't even think I might tell her something about the camera and its place in *all* our histories; I just let it go and arrowed into the descending sun. By late afternoon we reached the western terminus of the Thruway and I turned north on 190 and entered the billboard approach to the Falls. I began to feel some of that honeymoon excitement, to feel a genuine part of the tremendous continuum of hump that stretched back to the first couple that made the journey. I didn't see how she could avoid feeling it, but I did not ask or press the point; she was wearing her calm, neutral face, playing it very close to the aristocratic chest. With a billboard announcing that Niagara was the home of Shredded

185

Wheat looming above us, she hit me with it out of the blue:

"The Canadian side," she announced, "is the side to see."

I thought, at least she is communicating, then observed, "I understand that *both* sides are extremely interesting."

"Yes, but everyone I've ever talked to says be sure to see the Falls—the Horseshoe Falls—from the Canadian side."

"I don't know who you've been talking to," I said mildly, "but I never got that kind of feedback."

"Then you simply do not know people who have been to the Falls and properly evaluated them. Actually, it's common knowledge."

"Is it? We'll see," I said with enough grimness to raise both eyebrows.

We parked and walked to the edge of the American Falls. I looked, listened, sniffed, swiveled my head in total astonishment and appreciation, cut my eyes at her. She certainly seemed impressed.

I said, "Isn't that magnificent? You know it's here, but you really don't know it until you see it. Isn't it magnificent?"

"It is rather," she said.

"Thousands of years. Pouring over that edge for thousands of years. That's a lot of hydrogen hydroxide."

"Yes," she said.

Her eyes crossed the Niagara River and she said, "The Sheraton looks nice over there."

"That's on the Canadian side," I said.

"Of course it is. Obviously, the Canadians have given this some thought and built a hotel that looks down on their Falls."

"There are hotels on this side."

"Do you call these hotels? Don't be ridiculous. The Canadians have simply looked at what they've got and we haven't."

Our Falls were plunging, rushing, working like hell only twenty yards away. I said, "We'll make out perfectly all right. I'll take you down in a boat if you have to experience the Canadian Falls, but we're staying on this side."

186

She looked me over and said, "I want to stay on the top floor of the Sheraton. On *that* side."

"What is this love affair with the Canadian Falls?"

"Why are you so pettily chauvinistic?"

"Chauvinistic? Marilyn Monroe stayed on the American side when she made *Niagara*."

"I don't give a shit where Marilyn Monroe stayed."

"Very nice. I suppose you think *she* was pettily chauvinistic?"

"I dare say."

I began to walk back and forth behind the railing. I stopped and said, "You have no business insulting Marilyn Monroe. She came a helluva long way with two strikes on her."

"Speed," she said, "will you stop this? Please let Marilyn Monroe R.I.P. Look, Sheraton is an American firm. Does that make you feel better?"

"No."

"I refuse to pursue this any further. I wish to have a top floor view of the superior Falls; I wish to ride to the top of their superior towers to look down on their superior Falls. Now will you please be reasonable?"

I looked at my Falls, doing the best they could, pounding away, rushing, gurgling, hanging in.

"Are you going to have evening meetings with your draft dodgers over there?" I said.

"Please get my bags out of the trunk and call a cab," she said. "You can reach me at the Sheraton."

I checked into the Cascade Motel and drank Taylor's New York State Dry Sherry until two in the morning, then read myself to sleep with *Drums Along the Mohawk*. The next morning I breakfasted on Shredded Wheat and walked over to my Falls and paid for a ride in the *Maid of the Mist* into their Falls. I haughtily refused the slicker we were supposed to wear and stood stiff and straight and soaking wet as we nosed, bucking and rearing, right up into their goddam horseshoe. Dripping but calm and quiet, I stalked back to the Cascade, sat on my bed still wet and called the Sheraton. She was out, probably *kvelling* over their rainbow, their plume, their record-breaking torrent from the wraparound top of one of their slick towers, so I left a message for her to please call me when she got the chance. Then I changed my clothes, walked to the nearest liquor store, bought two bottles of Great Western New York State Champagne and worked on those for the rest of the morning.

At one in the afternoon she called and asked what I had in mind. I asked her if she'd had enough and she said she had to buy a few souvenirs of the Falls and then, yes, she would have seen enough. She asked me how was Marilyn Monroe? I said, fine. Well, she said, you can pick me up at three o'clock. I'm not going to Canada, I said. I'm not going to your fleabag, she said. In the end, we met at the midpoint on the bridge between Canada and the U.S.

We drove in thick silence. The one time she spoke was to note that we had passed the Thruway. I said, I know, then announced that we were going into Buffalo as I wished to see where McKinley bought it and Teddy Roosevelt became President. I announced further that although I wasn't crazy about Teddy, a Roosevelt was a Roosevelt. She shifted slightly and dug into a paperback on the root causes of colonialism in Southeast Asia. I made my double pilgrimage, then drove within our silence back to the Thruway. We continued in silence to Rochester where I announced that we would visit the Eastman Kodak plant, or at least take a look at it since it was probably closed, but that this was a vital and necessary thing to do.

I circled my box cameras and Baby Brownies, then got back on the Thruway, this time eliciting a deep, thin-lipped sigh. At

Geneva I turned off again. After hamburgers (and a Genesee beer for me) I said we would follow a spur of General Sullivan's victorious sweep for a few miles, just to get the feel of it, and while she frowned at the French in Indochina I did just that. I swept down Seneca Lake as far as Dresden, commented in a very nice way on the appropriateness of this name, turned and reswept the area back to friend Thruway. The sun was dipping down in the rearview mirror now, so I hustled east to Syracuse, where we cut off and explored the campus that Marty Glickman had made famous. I carefully explained to her profile how explosively he had carried the mail for the Orange, that he was indeed a Jewish Jimmy Brown, with speed, and outlined briefly how he and Sammy Stoller had been jobbed in 1936.

She didn't sigh or respond; the head dropped farther into Western imperialism and stayed there until Albany. At Albany she switched back to the 4F book and stayed with it as we drove south through the night toward New York. We stopped once for a piss-call near New Paltz, then raced for the city. At one in the morning we were double-parked outside our East Side apartment. She closed the book she had been reading by my trouble-shooter flashlight and said, "It's not necessary for you to come up, just get my bags out of the trunk. Marvin will take them upstairs. Thank you."

I said, "You're welcome."

I wandered into the Jolly Mog and Red was sitting at his table, leaning against the wall. He waved me over. I didn't feel like a drink; he said, that's your business, took a gurgling pull of his gin and tonic. "Jim Thorpe," he announced, "got screwed." I sighed, said innocently, "How?" "How? They took his medals away from him after he broke his butt winning them, that's how." Still angry with Carla, Speed and the world, I said, "Maybe they had their reasons."

Red considered that with bland mildness and took another swallow. "Devil's advocate, eh?" I told him he could call it whatever he wanted to, Jim shouldn't have played pro ball. Red's jaw muscles fluttered, the giveaway that he was doing a controlled burn. He didn't answer. I plunged on. "Maybe he wasn't too smart. Playing pro ball in the summer wasn't too smart."

End of slow burn. The hippo body swiveled, the ham fist slammed. "Number one," he said, shoving his eyelids apart, "*Semipro*. Number two, it was baseball, and he won the medals in track and field. Number three, today's amateurs get paid by the goddam yard."

"The yard?"

"Come on. They run a hundred yards, they get a hundred dollars."

"Not Jim Ryun."

"Don't give me individual exceptions. Ryun's like Thorpe; he must have Indian blood in him. Anyway, number four, you said he's not smart?"

"Ah, I don't know," I mumbled.

"*I* know. He went to college, didn't he?"

"The Carlisle Indian School."

"Oh yes? That *school* played Harvard and beat their fancy pants off. Tell me Harvard is no college."

"You've made your point."

He called Carmen over for a refill. He said, "Don't do me any favors. You know what he said to King Gustav of Sweden in 1912?"

"What?"

"Gustav told him he was the greatest athlete in the world, and you know what he said?"

"No. What?"

190

"Thanks, King."

"So?"

"So?" The eyes sagged with pity, then clanged open. "A dumb jock would have said, I owe it to my teammates. Or my coach. Or I just got lucky. He said, 'Thanks, King'. It was pithiness. Shared information. Acknowledgement. Graceful frankness. He didn't have too much upstairs, eh? Don't knock me out. He was screwed. By the goddam bluebloods."

I sat up. He was *talking* to me now. He was saying, "They couldn't take this half-breed shoving it down their throats. Winning for America when they couldn't." He folded the enormous arms, shook the great head in wonder. "He never held it against America. Just the bluebloods. The true blue ama-choors." He finished his gin and tonic with a face of utter contempt and stared at the empty glass. "Taking a man's medals away from him," he said in the low, hard rumble. "What could possibly be lower than that?"

The piece was called "All-American." In it, I discovered Chief Henry Callaway wandering about town and, without too much trouble, drew forth his story. The Chief lived in Jim Thorpe, Pennsylvania ("the only town in America named for a gridiron star") and had played with the great one on the Carlisle Indians. Every four years, the Chief told me, he came to New York to agitate for the restoration of Jim's medals. He trudged all over the East Side of the city because he knew that's where the important people lived and he told his story, about Jim's great triumphs, King Gustav, the innocent semipro ball. The Chief was a Senecan Ancient Mariner. The big problem, which saddened but did not discourage him, was that no one listened to him but the doormen. To them he related the facts, as now he did to me, but he related much more. He told how Jim, despite everything, had always loved America, how he would always stand up and fight (cleanly) for her and, if asked, would have found absolutely no connection with what the white man did to the Indians and what America was doing in Vietnam. The Chief revealed that Jim bore no

191

grudges against the fancy college bluebloods who had done him in. That he just felt sorry for a bunch of spoiled brats who were 4F, meaning that they would F their country four different ways whenever they could. I then asked Chief Callaway if Jim Thorpe knew the meaning of 1A? The Chief, drawing himself up to his still imposing full, lean height, said: Absolutely: *Adore your country*.

With that, plus a few dollars from doormen and the present writer, the Chief went home to Jim Thorpe, Pa. for four more years.

Red said yeah, OK, but his eyes were misty.

The night the *Whisper* hit the stands, Carla sent her telegram:

MESSAGE LOUD AND CLEAR. YOU ARE IMPOSSIBLE. WE ARE IMPOSSIBLE. THANKS FOR THE MEMORIES, BUT IN FUTURE CONTACT MYRON WAMGANTZ OF JONAS, LEEKS, GOODMAN AND WAMGANTZ, WHO IS HAN-DLING DIVORCE PROCEEDINGS. BUENA FORTUNA IN MEX. CITY.

C.

My suitcases followed in a chauffeured limousine.

PART

Not to Reason Why

On July 15, I became a two-time loser. I fought it, fought what my mother and father would say ("I got Tommy Manville for a son?") by speeding down and back on my measured mile in Riverside Park a total of twelve and a half times. The swirling thickness came down hard anyway, now filling my legs with heavy doses of lactic acid, making the fighting back ten times tougher. And this time, as if to rub it in, I had gone down while thinking I was on the rise. This was mean, unfair and unjust, depriving me of the greatest piece of ass in my career, the one woman who had most satisfyingly met my psycho-sexual needs. So I ran, for all the good it did me. At dawn, high noon, sunset over the Palisades. Betwixt and between, I prowled: Broadway, Amsterdam, Columbus, 116th Street, Claremont. The Hamilton Garage, which now had new owners. Columbia. Especially Columbia, where I glared at both students and cops around the sundial, on the steps of Low, outside Butler Library. On the afternoon of August 8, I shoved the lactic acid down to my fingertips, strode along Campus Walk, cut right and flashed a Blue Cross card at the guard in front of Butler. He waved me through. Inside I turned to the right and walked up the flight of stairs to the landing that faced the full-length painting of Eisenhower. I pulled an envelope out of my breast pocket and placed it at his feet, saluted briefly, about-faced and walked back and out into the yakking, milling sunlight. In the envelope I had typed at the top of a Xerox of a page out of the *Infantry Journal*: "Crusaders must stick together . . . E.T.O. 1944-5."

I drank schnapps with Heinz von Mulheim until two in the morning and explained how we had rescued the Battered Bastards of Bastogne.

☆　☆　☆

The phone. It was cutting jagged flashes through my head. The phone was heavy so I placed it on the pillow beside my ear, not too close.

"JesusChrist, yeah?"

"Speed?"

"Yeah?"

"Speed Finestone?"

"Of course."

"This is Garth."

"Martha?"

"Garth. Garth Finestone."

"Samuel?"

"Garth. Garth Finestone."

I sat up. My forehead tore loose; I pushed it back, held the phone with my other hand; the phone was crackling. I cut into the crackling:

"Garth Finestone?"

"Yes."

"Jesus. Where'd you get my number?"

"It wasn't easy. You're a hermit, a regular hermit. I finally got it from the *Whisper*."

"You read the *Whisper*?"

"Occasionally, when *you* write something. You were very unfair to movie stars."

"Well, that's the way I am."

"That's the way you are, all right. I called to tell you Mama died."

"She what?"

"She died."

"Mama?"

"Yes."

"She died?"

"Yes. Last night."

"Last night?"

"Yes."

"I was out last night."

"That's when it happened."

"Mama?"

"Yes."

"Died?"

"Yes."

"That means . . . Mama and Papa are both gone?"

"Yes."

"Jesus, we're orphans, Samuel."

I could hear him crying.

2

I called Lucille and told her and she said of course she would be at the funeral and I called Carla and she said she would do her best to make it and I filed that under Forget but don't Forgive. I spent all of the next day at Levy's Memorial Chapel on Jerome Avenue, where they had taken my father. I put on their black paper *yarmulke* and with Garth said to the aunts and uncles and cousins, what can you say except isn't it too bad we only get together on these occasions? They said yes, ain't it too bad, and I said, but she would certainly appreciate, and they gazed and sighed the Finestone and Goodman sighs and signed the book and went home for another fifteen years.

I didn't have a chance to talk to Garth or to my sister, Naomi, whose Hungarian Nazi of a husband came for her after his taxicab shift at seven, put on a *yarmulke* and told a dozen hilarious stories about my mother's heart of gold, pure gold, finishing up with how happy she would be to see me doing so well. Naomi was looking puffy around the middle and had smeared too much black around the eyes ("my best feature"), but the face was basically still there, the face that was the pleasure of Shimon's brothers, the envy of their wives. She passed around a telegram from her Debbie who, by age twenty-six, was also a two-time loser, and who was practically destroyed that she couldn't be with us all at this time.

The surprise of the day, and night, was Garth's wife. Of all people, she turned out to be Alicia, Lucille's roommate when I

197

first knew her at Manhattan Players, and she handled everyone and everything with the kind of efficiency my mother would have loved even if she was a *shiksa*. Mama, as if reassured, slept peacefully through it all.

At nine o'clock Lucille came in with Hannah and Cyrus, out of whom she had finally made an honest man. Alicia chatted smoothly with each in turn, starting with Lucille, then sent them on. When Hannah went up to look at my mother I burst into tears and ran into the men's room. When I got back they were gone.

I got through the service on a Seconal as the house Reb extolled the tree of life that had been Sarah Finestone. Then we limousined out to the cemetery near Mosholu Parkway and placed her beside my father. Another Seconal got me back to Garth's apartment where he and Alicia were receiving. They lived near Fordham in a 20s apartment house that was still in good shape, that still had unbroken mirrors and mahogany paneling in the lobby. Alicia was a beautifully solemn, no-nonsense hostess: the corned beef, potato salad, sponge cake and wine were neatly lined up, and for the few *goyisheh* women who had known my mother from the old neighborhood she had little squares of egg and tuna salad Mama would have called itsy bitsy nothings. Family and friends drifted in and out and hit the chow line and congratulated Alicia on how tasty everything was and told me how well Mama had looked at the funeral home. Around eight I found myself beside Garth who sat with great dignity in a rocking chair I thought I recognized except that it was painted white. I thought I had recognized several other pieces, but they too had a twist of difference—new upholstery, or no more squeaks—and in the end I did not say anything such as, I guess you picked her clean before she went. In any case, I decided that it must have been Alicia's doing. I thought of several opening lines and finally came up with, "It's been a long time."

Garth rocked a bit, squeaklessly, and said with a smile that took in the room, "That it has."

"How long have you been married?" I said.

"Nine years."

"That's a long time."

"Not really . . . Hey, I didn't mean to dig you."

"That's all right. What about Marge?"

He sipped some Malaga wine and crossed his legs. Christ, he was wearing elevator *slippers.**

"A disaster," he said. "Sheer disaster."

He rocked some more and beamed at Alicia. I said, "What about the store?"

"You certainly have been out of touch," he said, rocking but looking at me.

"I know . . . What about it?"

"I've been running it for eight years. It's the smartest thing I ever did, next to Alicia."

"Well, it must have made Mama happy."

"It did. We gave her a few decent years."

"Yes . . ."

"We moved up here to be near her."

"She wasn't living with you?"

He stopped rocking.

"Was she living with *you?*" he said.

"No."

"OK then." He resumed the rocking. "You know her. She'd never leave her beloved Tremont Avenue."

"The damn house was falling down on her head."

He braked.

"How would *you* know?"

"All right, you made your point."

"All right."

"You couldn't get her into a decent place?"

"Come on, Manny. Speed. You know her. She says she has rotten memories in Tremont Avenue, so I say, leave them; and

---

*He must have picked that up from C. Boyer in *Gaslight*. Boyer had taught *me* how to sniff wine corks and cognac.

what does she say? Why should I leave them?"

"Yeah, I know her . . ."

I drank some Malaga. On top of the Seconal it made me dizzy and queasy. He started rocking again with long, smooth, confident strokes as if he were swimming in Orchard Beach, and that didn't help my head or my stomach. If you're going to rock, rock, like Papa; when he rocked, it was a hard, tough, jerking rock, especially when he was explaining the politics of a Horthy, a Ciano, a Laval (for Hitler, Goebbels, Mussolini and Stalin, he stood with his arms folded and spit on Mama's clean parquet floor). I looked away from Garth's rocking. I said, "I guess you cleaned up her place?"

"I don't know what you mean by cleaned up?" he said, still rocking, smiling imperiously.

"I mean," I sighed, "after she died. Winding it up. Her things . . . the furniture . . ."

"Well," he said, twisting it in neatly, "since you had very important things to do, I asked Nicky and he helped me. We broke our hump, but we got it done." The rocker swam easily, smoothly, out to deep water and back. I swallowed some of the rotten Malaga and looked around the room for the Nazi. He was feeding his face with sponge cake and jawing at Mama's sister, Molly, who was a little bird but could still handle a plate of corned beef and potato salad.

"Hunky prick," I muttered.

Garth shook his head in time to the rocking.

"Why don't you come off it?" he said.

"Off what? A fact is a fact."

"Don't you *ever* let anything go?"

I wanted to say, sure I do, I'm here, ain't I? I said, "All right, peace on earth, good will toward men."

"That's more like. You know how Mama hated us to fight. It always made her nervous."

I drank some fast Malaga.

"It's Naomi's bed. She's laying in it."

"Lying."

"Thank you. Lying."

"Oh, what a bulldog. Nimmi!" he waved. "Leave her alone," I said, but he called and waved again. She looked up from poor, twisted Aida, Papa's sister's girl. Garth gave her the imperial wave. He had always called us both over with that wave. "Leave her alone," I whispered loudly, "I have an appointment downtown." He flicked me off, called, waved again. Naomi patted Aida's emaciated shoulder; Aida was in heaven; Naomi walked over. Garth said, "Nimmi, this is Speed. You knew him as Manny, but them days is over. Now, you two behave." He suddenly rocked onto his elevators and bounded away. When he reached the food table, he turned and blew us a kiss, then began to talk with tremendous seriousness to Uncle Biggie, the village idiot. I turned and looked squarely at Naomi; she looked right back. She was carefully, skillfully made-up; instantly I could see her applying the thin brush to her lips, telling me a lipstick was from hunger, blotting, smiling brilliantly, asking if anything was on her teeth; there never was. She still smelled of Chanel Number Five, even through the crowd and the heat.

"Would you like some wine?" I said.

I noticed she was wearing drooping silver earrings. I remembered her getting her ears pierced by a gypsy in a storefront on 178th Street in 1935. Mama had cried all day and Papa had called her crazy and said she should only get an infection. She got infected the next day and Papa refused to call the doctor or to take her to the Board of Health and I rubbed zinc ointment onto her earlobes for three weeks. My left ear hurt; I scratched it, the way comics do when they're stuck for a line. I said, "Malaga or concord?"

"No thanks," she said. "They're both too sweet."

"Yes," I said, sipping my Malaga. "But they always loved the sweet stuff; I guess that's why Samuel got it."

"Alicia got it. She asked me and I told her."

"I see."

"They didn't even like sherry," she said.

"Oh, I can believe that."

"It's true."

I sipped again. The room was getting a little soft.

201

"I gave her a bottle of burgundy in '47," I said. "Very good stuff from Cucamonga. She said it had turned sour. I said, that's the way it's supposed to taste, but she insisted it had turned and I had to throw it out."

"You threw it out?"

"Yes. I told her I got my money back, but I threw it out."

Naomi nodded. She had my father's nod.

"She always knew what she knew," she said.

"Oh yes."

She folded her arms over her chest. She had done that since she was fourteen when overnight she had the biggest knockers on Tremont Avenue. Hubie Moscowitz bugged me crazy over them; I always came back swinging but could never catch up with the little speed demon. Now she nodded and the earrings jangled; my ears hurt. I sipped. I noticed that her hair was frosted; good thing Papa wasn't here; he'd have given her a bottle of peroxide for a present. I sipped. The room was even softer. She nodded Shimon's nod at Garth.

"Alicia is very good for him," she said.

"You're right."

"He deserves a little luck," she said.

"Well, it looks like he's found his niche," I said.

"Yes, it does. How about you?"

"Oh, I've had my ups and downs."

"So I've heard. It runs in the family."

"I think I'd have to agree with that."

"No question about it. Shimon and Sarah could tell you."

"Yes. They could."

"It definitely runs in the family," she said.

"Yes, I guess it does."

"No question. Don't ask me why. Somebody says Finestone? And somebody else says, oh yes, the family that gets the shaft."

"That's what Nixon said."

"The Finestones and the Nixons. The shaft."

"You've got a seemingly valid point."

"No question. And anyone connected with us gets the shaft."

"That's guilt by association," I said, trying a smile.

202

"I don't care what you call it, the knife is the knife."

My ears were really hurting now. I looked around the room and spotted her Hunky.

"How's Nick?"

"His blood pressure is up."

"He's too heavy. You better cut down on the dumplings." I tried another smile.

She shook her head, Papa's shake.

"It's his basal metabolism. His legs bother him also. They swell up at night."

I flexed my neck muscles.

"Exercise is very good for that."

At that moment Lucille and Hannah and Cyrus walked in. I wanted to dump Naomi and her fat Nazi, but her hand was on my arm.

"How can he exercise in a taxicab?" Hannah had on a heavy black dress. It hung loosely far down to her shins; oh, what Lucille knew about clothes . . . Naomi:

"Could you help him out, Manny?"

You would think the kid was right off the boat.

"Manny?" she said.

"What?"

"I said, could you help Nicky out?"

Oh what a *shmotte* . . .

"Could you?" She was smiling her thin-brush-lips-Ipana smile.

". . . What could I do for him?" I said. The poor kid must be sweating and itching like she was wearing a wool bathing suit. I wondered briefly if she was wearing bloomers.

"You could get him on your paper," Naomi said.

"My paper?"

"Yes, on the paper, Manny."

I pulled away from Hannah and said, "Please do me a favor. I'd prefer you to call me Speed."

"Of course. Samuel told me and I forgot. I agree completely. I always hated Naomi but never had the push or the guts to change it. Can you, Speed?"

I returned to Hannah. She was talking to Uncle Isaac, my

mother's brother. He would be asking her her opinion of the climate in California; he had dreamed of going to California since I was ten. Naomi was stroking my arm.

"Look, Nimmi, what can he do on a paper?" I said. "He could never get into the printers' union."

"Where there's a will, there's a way. You could get him in."

"You don't understand. I don't *have* any pull."

She reached up and patted my face. Oh, I remembered that one . . .

"You could talk. You could always talk. You lost your glasses and you convinced Mama W. A. Boody, the colored kid in your class, stole them."

Uncle Isaac would now be asking about Hawaii, his second choice of paradise. I looked at my sister.

"He didn't steal them," I said.

"I know," she smiled. "But you talked her into it. You could talk anybody into anything if you wanted."

I looked at her Hunky. He was *fressing* on potato salad; give him his starch and he was happy. He cut his eyes over the plate to us.

"What about Samuel and the store?" I said.

"He doesn't want to work in a cut-rate drugstore. Would you?"

"If I needed the job, I might."

"Talk sensible, Speed. Besides, how can a man work for his brother-in-law? You know what that is."

The room didn't look so good; my stomach didn't feel so good.

"Tell him to ask Horthy," I said.

She took her hand off my arm.

"Are you bringing that up after all these years?" she said.

"He likes the man; tell him to ask him for a job."

"So you want to start . . ."

"Start what?"

"My brother. My little brother. I took him to the movies; made him supper when his mother was sick; and he starts . . ."

"Start what?"

"What? You know what. I'll tell you, since the perfect memory

204

is now failing. Once in his life a man says something; he says Horthy has gotten the crooks out of Hungary, that's all he says; and for that you put a knife in his heart for the rest of his life. Is that so terrible, getting the crooks out of Hungary?"

"Mussolini made the trains run on time."

"Oh my God."

"Hitler ended unemployment."

"God."

"I did not see him on Omaha Beach."

"Where?"

"The invasion of Horthy's Europe."

"Samuel told me to be prepared, but I never expected *this*. All right, I'll get down in the gutter with you. Why not? I have told you before but I'll tell you again, as if you didn't know: He was *deferred*. He worked in a vital defense plant in Kearny. Does the perfect memory remember *that*?"

"Aliens could serve."

"Don't call him an alien, you son of a bitch. He's a citizen just like you and of course you're the perfect citizen."

"He was an alien. Aliens could serve."

"You really want to torture, don't you? He worked in a *defense* plant. In a *vital* industry. He might even have saved your life and *other* torturers like you."

"I'll bet."

"His employer *requested* his deferral, he wrote letter after letter."

"And Nick gave him some argument."

She sat down in Garth's rocker and looked up at me.

"Why don't you ever give in?" she said. "Once in your life?"

"Stick to the point."

"I'm sticking. This *is* the point. You'd get something into that little head and never give in. You would say black was white and I could shake you till you cried, but did you give in? Never." Her eyes were wet. "Was I so bad to you? I washed your stockings. When we went to the movies I took you to the bathroom. You urinated all over me that time at the Prospect, but I took you

205

again. It won't kill you to give in *once*, you know. For Mama's sake."

"Mama?" I shook my head and the soft room began to crisscross around me. I shook again and straightened it out. "Mama? You did what you did to her and *I* should give in?"

"What did I do?"

"Don't make me draw pictures. You know what you did."

"You mean, marry the man I love?"

"Oh shit, Fanny Brice. You married a fucking Nazi and broke her heart, and Papa's, too. That's what you did, and you know it."

"What a terrible thing to say. What-a-terrible-thing-to-say. You know as well as I do they never liked *any* of my beaus."

"Beaus?"

"That's right, my darling brother. There wasn't *one* they liked."

"Beaus? You brought home one gentile bum after the other. You couldn't *wait* to bring them home. I heard you out in the hall with those cocksuckers. I saw you with your goddam lipstick all over your face; you think I didn't see that?" I was looking down at the frosted hair. "Now you throw Mama up to me? You got *some* nerve, do you know that?"

She rocked for a good thirty seconds. Then she stood up and smiled. She put her hand on my arm again and pinched with all the strength she had; she always did that in the movies when the love scenes came on and I whined that I wanted to go; I never cried, but it shut me up. Now I smiled back at her and she pinched even harder. I smiled harder. She dropped her arm, spun around and switched away. She found her Nazi and whispered into his hairy ear. He looked at me and shrugged and ate some more potato salad. She pinched his arm. He nodded quickly and picked up some sponge cake. He was still chomping as they made the rounds and smiled their goodnights. As he veered toward me, chomping, she tugged him away.

"Hello, Daddy."

I took my time. When I looked up, Hannah was standing beside me with a glass of wine in her hand.

"How come you ran over so fast?" I said.

"You were talking to your sister."

"She's also your aunt."

"Yes, you were talking to Aunt Naomi."

"That was five minutes ago," I said.

"While you were talking, Uncle Isaac was asking me something."

"He was asking you about the climate in California."

"That's right; how did you know?"

I looked around for Isaac. He was asking Aida about California.

"I know how his mind works. Then he asked you about Hawaii."

"Honolulu to be exact."

"That's in Hawaii. Is that your wine?"

"Yes. Mama said I could have some."

"Why didn't she give you some Old Overholt?"

"Is that a hundred proof?"

"A hundred proof bottled in bond. How do you know about a hundred proof?"

"That's all Cyrus drinks. He says everything else is poison."

"Big drinker. Give him two drinks and he's dead. Big, big drinker."

"You don't feel so good, do you?" she said.

"I feel terrific. I got no more parents to bug me. Unlike you. I feel terrific. Where did you get that beautiful dress?"

"You don't like it, do you? I can tell by your tone."

"I love it. Who made it, Madame De Farge?"

"Is it that bad?"

"Couldn't your mother find a little number made out of burlap? With a hoop skirt?"

"Do you want a sandwich, Daddy?"

"No. Give me that lousy wine."

She handed it over and I gulped it down.

"What about your stomach?" she said.

"It's killing me, so what?"

207

She stood beside the chair quietly. She had always stood quietly, from the time she had learned to stand. Even when she first walked: three steps, stand quietly.

"Would you like some Gelusil tablets?" she said. "Cyrus always carries some in his pocket."

"No. I wouldn't take a Rolls Royce from Cyrus."

"I can understand that," she said ... my expression. Exact ...

"That makes me very happy. Very happy. Let's stand by the window and get some air. Your uncle has something against air conditioning."

"He says it emits a toxic gas."

"So does your uncle. Let's go to the window."

We walked across the room with Lucille tracking us every inch of the way. I pushed the window up with a bang and looked out. I could see the lights of Fordham.

"Have you started to think about college yet?"

"It's very early," she said. "I'm only going into the tenth."

"It's never too early. Not if you got the brains and the school. Hunter is a top school. You got the brains. Tell your grade adviser you want to discuss college."

"He's a guidance counselor."

"Whatever. Tell him. Tell him you can go *anywhere*: money is no problem."

"I know."

"Tell him you have a few ideas of your own. Tell him you're interested in Michigan, Pitt and Temple."

She stood quietly and considered.

"I know Benny Friedman went to Michigan," she said, "and Marvin Goldberg went to Pitt and—"

"Marshall."

"Oh yes, Marshall Goldberg. But who went to Temple?"

"Dave Smuckler."

She thought that over quietly. Then: "I'm not too sure the football alumni can tell you too much about a school."

"Have you got a better way?"

She thought *that* over. "I'm not sure. I talk to kids, but that's fallible, also."

"And how. What schools do the kids talk about?"

"Oh, the Ivies."

"Ivies? *Poison* Ivies."

"Don't say that, Daddy. They have some excellent alumni also."

"Sure. Kelly, MacCleod, Montgomery, LeVan . . ."

"What about Luckman?"

"That's the exception that proves the rule."

"Oh Daddy, you and your rules. He couldn't be the *only* minority star, could he?"

"You're right. When you're right, you are right. There was Jackson at Yale and Holland at Cornell. *Shvartz.*"

"Oh, Daddy."

"All right, let it alone for now; just don't come up with Texas Christian or Southern Methodist."

She shook her head and dug holes into the sides of her mouth. I reached down and smoothed them out. She shook her head. We stood there in the Bronx night and looked out. My mother had always looked out, especially when we were late. I was late because I played association or hockey under the streetlights. Not Naomi. Oh no. I looked out at the lights of Fordham, Naomi's lateness. Mama never knew, but I knew. I never said anything, but I knew. How Naomi walked solemnly with her brush-lipstick and mascara down to the lobby and how she met Miriam Lipshitz so they could study together and how they walked arm in arm on the campus looking for Catholic pickups instead of doing Biology. Oh I knew, all right. I rubbed my arm.

"Is there something wrong with your arm?" Hannah said.

"Nah. I played softball on Sunday and got hit by a foul tip."

"You're too old for that, Daddy."

"Thanks a lot. Bernarr MacFadden made parachute jumps when he was seventy."

"I thought you hated Bernarr MacFadden."

"I do. But he made great parachute jumps."

She did her mouth again and I smoothed it out again. She stood quietly and I looked down at her. Her face was shiny clean and her hair was pulled straight back and tied with a rubber band. Good

straight, brown, regular hair. So what if Lucille dressed her in
shmottes? I put my hand on the neck that had never reeked of
Chanel Number Five.

"Hannah," I said gently, "I've got something to tell you."

She looked up.

"There *is* something wrong with your arm."

"Forget the arm, will you? Nobody ever died from a foul tip." I
took a deep breath of Fordham. "I want you to take this in stride,"
I said.

She kept looking up.

I stroked the clean, unbobbed hair.

"David Eisenhower is engaged to Julie Nixon," I said.

She kept on looking.

"Listen to me," I said. "It can't *possibly* last. No way. I *know*
about these things. I know. Let nature take its course and it'll blow
over. You'll see. He has too much sense, you'll see."

She looked some more, then she finally said, "Daddy, David
Eisenhower isn't Jewish, is he?"

"Well, it's hard to say. Maybe way back—"

"Is he?"

"He could pass, Hannah—"

"Is he?"

"All right, so he's not. So what? I'm not a reverse bigot. Quality
is quality and he's got quality. Julie Nixon is merely a question of
proximity. That's all. You'll see."

"Daddy," she said, and she spoke with careful seriousness, as if
she were explaining the causes of World War I, "I'm sure he's a
very sweet boy, and I know how you feel, but really, I don't give a
shit about David Eisenhower."

I was aware, as at a great distance, of Johnson's Baby Powder
and Old Spice After Shave and Ivory Soap as I threw up. They got
all mixed up with my puke as I emptied myself of sponge cake and
potato salad and corned beef and bittersweet wine. I retched as if I
had just come off the roller coaster in Playland, until there was
nothing but green; and only then, cold, trembling, sweating, but

clean at last, I doused my head under one faucet, then the other, and toweled off with fluffy blue. I poured some Old Spice on my hair and rubbed it into my face and then gargled with it until my mouth was also pure. Then I opened the john door and, head proud and high, carefully navigated through every smiling, yapping face, and that included Hannah who was smiling seductively up at Cyrus who was chewing Gelusils a mile a minute, Lucille who was discussing the making of *shmottes* with Alicia, and Garth who was counting every piece of cut glass he had swiped from my mother, walked carefully through them all, opened the triple-security door, stepped through, closed it softly, inhaled the musty hall with all my strength and walked downstairs and through the deco lobby and out into the suddenly pure Bronx night.

I walked. I walked to University Avenue and turned left because left was downtown and downtown was where I had to go. To New York. I walked. I could hear some bongo music and a few kids were playing cards on the hood of a car. Otherwise it was quiet. I walked harder. A block past the kids a man came toward me, a white man wearing a jacket and tie and swinging a cane. He caught my eye and stopped. I stopped. He said, "Pardon me, but can you tell me where the subway is?"

I said, "You mean the subway *station*?"

"Yes, that's correct, the subway station," he said.

"You have to be specific," I said. "When you ask someone a question, you have to be specific."

"Well, the subway station is what I want."

"Dealing in vague generalities is tough on the questionee."

"Do you know where the subway station is?" he said.

"Where do you want to go?"

"Grand Central."

"Grand Central *Station*?"

"Oh, yes. Grand Central Station."

"That is a very large complex. They even have a shoe shine stand there. For all I know, you could want the shoe shine stand."

"No, I don't want that. I'm going to Grand Central *Station.* Maybe I could get a cab."

"That's difficult up here." I pointed at his cane. "Is there something wrong with your leg?"

He looked around, then leaned in confidentially.

"Not a thing. Carrying a cane simply makes good sense. *You* ought to carry one, especially around here. You'd be surprised at how much good sense it makes."

"There's nothing wrong with your leg?"

"Not a thing." He tapped each instep with the cane as if he were knocking dirt out of his cleats. "Not a thing."

"Did it keep you out of the army?" I said.

"The cane?"

"Your leg."

"There's nothing wrong with my leg."

"Then it didn't keep you out?"

"Out of the army?"

"Yes. It sounds like you weren't in."

He shifted from one good leg to the other. Then he smiled.

"Oh, I see what you mean. Sure, I was in. I was in the Korean War."

"Korea? War? Don't you mean police action?"

"Listen, tell that to guys who got killed. Tell *them* it was no war. A guy gets killed, it's a war."

"*You* didn't."

He rapped his cane.

"Knock wood," he said.

"Did you get to Korea?" I said.

"Not really . . ."

"You did or you didn't. Unless you suffered from combat amnesia."

"Oh no, I didn't have amnesia. Do you think there's a bus stop around here?"

"If you didn't go overseas, where did you serve?"

"Great Lakes."

"Great Lakes Naval Training Station?"

"Yes."

"You certainly like to avoid the word 'station'."

"That's where it was, all right."

"Uh-huh. So you were in the navy."

"That's right, the navy, at Great Lakes Naval Training Station."

"Stateside. You were a stateside commando."

"Hey, I was in the navy."

"A stateside admiral."

"Hey, I went where they told me to go."

"You didn't volunteer to go overseas?"

"Am I crazy? Did you?"

"We're talking about *you*. My conscience is perfectly clear. I can sleep nights. Can you?"

"Sure. Do you know where the Concourse is from here?"

"What did you think of MacArthur?"

"I know how to get downtown from the Concourse . . ."

"What did you think of MacArthur?"

"Of course I was in the navy, but I respected him. Maybe—"

"That's a waffling statement. What did you *really* think of MacArthur?"

"He knew his stuff. Nobody can say he didn't know his stuff. Is Webster Avenue around here?"

"Joe McCarthy would say you're being coy."

"McCarthy was peculiar. He did some bad things and he did some good things. He was peculiar."

"MacArthur. What did you think of *MacArthur*?"

"He knew the Pacific theater like the back of his hand. It's not a bad night, maybe I'll walk—"

"He was a good strategist, wasn't he?"

"Are you kidding? The best. The man knew his stuff."

"Next to him Eisenhower was just a personality boy, wasn't he?"

"Look at the record. Go look at the record. MacArthur was the best damn general we ever had when you look at the record. Eisenhower? No comparison."

213

"You really think so?"

"I *know* so."

"You do?"

"Listen. Anybody tells you Eisenhower could hold a candle to MacArthur, you know what to tell him?"

"What?"

"*Don't make me laugh.*"

I let him have it.

I began to run at all hours: four in the morning, midnight, the five o'clock rush hour through the exhaust fumes of Broadway and Amsterdam Avenue. When I didn't run, I rode the subway. Somehow the thick swirling stuff didn't reach down to the subway, so when it became too gooey and sticky up above and my heels killed me and my toenails turned black, I ducked into the comforting tunnels of Manhattan. Which is how I handled the next two weeks; not sensationally, but with a sense of some active control. Indeed, as I reached for autumn in New York I seemed to achieve a kind of inner and outer truce and, that being the case, I thought I might nurse it along by trying the movies; I was damned if lie-ins, sit-ins, coffee-ins, body counts or even Hannahs were going to do the job Hitler never could. I decided, too, that if I hung on—and *in*—Jim Ryun would come galloping to the rescue; ergo the flicks, which had always pulled me through in the Manny years. And that brought me full (or at least three-quarter) circle, for not any movie would do, I was not ready for *that*. No, revivals, I needed revivals. So I checked into the Thalia on 95th Street and the Elgin downtown and shivered my way through *China Seas*, *After the Thin Man*, *Tarzan and His Mate*. For, sitting there I could travel back to the little guy, taut and starey, at the Paradise or the Prospect or on sensational eleven A.M. Saturdays at the Strand. Only now, more than the kid: the kid with Speed's savvy, his biceps, his combat record, his worldwide conquests, his two beautiful wives (Manny had had a consistent vision of what he would do with the girl he would marry, especially as she stood washing dishes, back toward him; Speed had been true to that vision). So there I was in the Thalia-Paradise, the Elgin-Prospect-Strand, having fleshed out the little yearner's horniest dreams, yet *still* Manny longing wildly for Harlow, Loy, O'Sullivan, still making notes on Gable's raised eyebrow, Weismuller's knife-legs, Powell's *savoir faire*. And that fusion enabled me finally to sit back in those theaters, pull up my knees, calm my thudding chest. The revivals revived. So much so that I diagnosed I was then ready to try a *new* movie.

Here and there on my IRT safaris I had spotted ads for something called *The Graduate*, had seen a deadpan face staring at me through the inverted V of a smoothly rounded leg. I became aware that people were seeing this film, and once, riding south from 96th Street, had watched as a boy with a ponytail told a girl in khaki about *The Graduate*. Although I couldn't hear very much, I knew it was *The Graduate* because he kept pointing to the ad and saying Dustin (of course he meant Hoffman, but Dustin Farnum was a favorite of my mother's, which also told me I could handle it). At the end of his scenario, the girl squealed, "That's the best movie I ever heard about!" I decided to take the step.

Early in August I went to see *The Graduate* at Loew's 83rd Street on Broadway. 106 minutes later I staggered out of the theater. I made it to the 86th Street subway station. Clutching the railing, I somehow made it down the stairs, through the turnstile, found a bench. Three trains roared in and out before I managed to get myself on one. As we rushed uptown I hunkered down in a corner and tried, with the help of all that noise and power, to cope with the enormity of what I had just witnessed. Boy meets girl. Girl has mother. Boy meets mother . . .

At 125th Street, soaring above Harlem, I shook off a terrible question:

Would Mickey Rooney screw Ann Rutherford's mom?

As the train swooped down and rumbled toward City College, I slumped to the side for I had had another kick in the balls:

Would David Eisenhower screw Lucille?

I slumped to the other side. A first aid manual had once instructed me to tie my shoelaces if I felt faint. I untied, tied, untied, tied. 168th, 181st, Dyckman. At Dyckman I felt a little better and sat up, for my stubborn resilience had answered both those questions: *Never in a billion years!* But then at 225th Street the big one struck:

Would Nick the Nazi screw Sarah Finestone?

One station later I knew the answer. *Manny* knew the answer. Even the boy in the ponytail and the girl in khaki knew the answer:

HE WOULD TRY!

Ah, the only thing man learns from history is that he is doomed to repeat history ... I got off at 242nd, the end of the line, hustled to the downtown platform and clattered back to my 110th Street stop. The next morning I went to work.

PART

Champagne and Shredded Wheat

I wrote a story in which the daughters of four USO girls, who had entertained the boys in England, fly over the Mekong Delta in a P-51, in mint condition, that is piloted by an officer who had flown wing for Dick Bong, and I called it "Four Maids in a Mustang." I received thirty-nine letters for and against the war, thus assuring me I was alive and functioning, and I answered each one by informing the writer that the girls were neither hawks nor doves, but solemn sparrows, saddened almost beyond endurance by what they had seen down below, yet always faithful to the American fighting man, wherever he might be. Red said that was a pretty good answer.

Buoyed by the knowledge that I could still turn it on and get a response, I began to expand my running pattern. I had a desire to run over the GW bridge to New Jersey for no specific reason I can now recall except that it pleased me immensely to leave the city and pleased me even more to return to it after examining the skyline from the summit of the Palisades. I ran a bit farther each day, not west but south, and on August 10th I reached Bergen. On the 11th of August, at 11:35 A.M. I trotted into the Bergen Mall, and in Jerry's Ideal Footwear I saw a girl. She was standing behind the cash register reading "Four Maids in a Mustang" in the *Whisper*, which was spread out on the counter. I coughed and said, "Where are the Keds, please?" She did not look up (I found that quite pleasing) but pointed across the store. I stood my ground and inspected the area: She was the size girls had always been before vitamins and prenatal care stretched most of them into austere shears with a bump at the chest and below the coccyx. She was precisely cushioned and indented, with a high, firm pair that neatly nippled a yellow tee shirt, which I shall return to in a moment. Hair light brown throughout, clean, flipped up just below the ears. Eyes, nose, mouth neat with each other and with the whole. Touch of makeup, smudgeless eyes, no perfume I could detect, but no earthy aromas either. Blue skirt (not mini) showing an ample gastrocnemius. Now the tee shirt—the only thing that bothered me: It presented the petulant mug of Steve McQueen stretched between the firm anchorage of the nipples. Clearly, however, I could not complain. I coughed again, politely, and said, "Where are the Spot-bilt track shoes, please?" Without looking up, she pointed again. Incredulously, I asked if they really *carried* Spot-bilts. This time she looked up.

"What did you say?"

"Do you actually carry Spot-bilt running shoes?"

"I never heard of them."

"They're very good. Made in America."

"I didn't say they weren't good or they weren't made in America. I just said I never heard of them."

She looked at me blandly, head tilting up just enough. I said, "I suppose you don't carry track shoes anyway."

"We carry sneakers; they're over by the casual footwear." I was about to observe that sneakers were not, by strict definition, track shoes, but she had returned to the *Whisper*. A boy with hair to his shoulders and a muddy face wandered up, looked at her as she read, wandered away. I said, "I wrote that piece you're reading." She nodded without looking up. I asked if she liked it. She continued to read, turned the page, read on. I said, "*I wrote that.*" This time she stopped, looked up. Her eyes were a no-nonsense brown; not hazel, not flecked—clean brown.

"What's your name?" she said.

"Speed Finestone."

"Why is America in such a mess?"

"The studios are shot to hell, and jets have replaced props."

"Who is flying above the Mekong Delta?"

"Four Maids in a Mustang."

"Who is driving the plane?"

220

"A man who flew with Richard Bong. He *flies* it."

"Why is he driving a Mustang?"

"His parrot told him the Starfighter jet they assigned him was unsafe."

She folded her arms over Steve McQueen and nodded with thoughtful care, but didn't say anything.

"Do I pass?" I asked.

She nodded harder and the clean hair bounced. From the rear of the store, near the boots, a high, thin voice said, "Maureen, would you please come here if you're not too busy?" She rolled the no-nonsense eyes, unfolded a section of the counter, walked to the back of the store. A blondish man in a three-piece suit and high-heeled boots talked very seriously at her and she listened without responding. When he stopped, hands on hips, I heard, "He talked to *me*." Then she looked up at him as he spoke some more, quickly, quietly. He swiveled his face at me once, she bounced the clean hair and walked back and through the counter, folded up the *Whisper*, tucked it into a canvas bag with a shoulder strap, thrust the bag under the counter. Pointing the eyes up at me, she said, "He doesn't like us to converse with customers in a social way."

"I'll buy that." I took a gambler's breath. "When do you get off for lunch?"

"Twelve-thirty," she said precisely.

"Where do you eat?"

"The Coffee Shoppe Stoppe. Are you asking me out to lunch?"

"Yes."

"You'd probably prefer the Hawaiian Palm."

"Why?"

"It has more atmosphere."

"Do you like it?"

"I never ate there."

"Then how do you know?"

"*Maureen.*"

"I've been told it has atmosphere."

"Can I get in with a sweat shirt?"

"*Maureen.*"

221

"It's very informal."

"Where is it?"

"*Maureen, puh-leeze.*"

"Never mind, I'll find it. Twelve three oh."

I sauntered out.

I shaped up as best I could, drying off with paper towels, then hunted up the atmospheric restaurant. The title was spelled out in blue neon script in the window and below it a girl in a grass skirt and a *Noa Noa* face smiled out of a United Airlines poster. I stood close to her, shunting aside thoughts of being stood up, which had occurred four times in twenty-nine years since Manny's first date at the Paradise. At 12:30 on the dot she turned the corner. A white sweater was draped around her shoulders, half blocking McQueen. She held onto the strap of the canvas bag.

"We can still go to your coffee place," I said.

"I told you it doesn't have any atmosphere."

I grasped and steered her firmly padded arm that had resisted the dietary plots of the faggots who run nutrition in this country.

2

"Did you go to the University of Michigan?" she said, gazing at my sweat shirt in the glow of a blue candle. We were drinking Kona Coffee in wicker-encased mugs after a pungent barbecued sparerib lunch.

"No," I said, "but a good friend of mine did. Benny Friedman . . . No, I'm kidding . . . Benny went there but he wasn't a good friend of mine . . . well, not in a real sense . . ."

She absorbed that and I was afraid she was going to ask, then why did you say it? but she didn't. She did say, "Did Richard Bong go to college?" I was about to say, I hadn't the foggiest idea; then I thought, he *should* have gone. "He went to the University of Pittsburgh," I stabbed. "He didn't go to his graduation exercises, however; he was too busy enlisting."

The calm eyes absorbed *that*. Quickly I played with my coffee mug and said, "You know, I could have read everything in the *Whisper*—those things you asked me—then faked it."

222

"You could have, but you didn't."

"No, I didn't."

"I never met a writer before," she said.

I looked at her very carefully; her eyes were level, clear, *honest*. I wanted to say, very earnestly, Oh Lord, writing for a rag like the *Whisper* doesn't mean you're a writer. Well, maybe in a minuscule way, but in another way it's a kind of whoring of your talent so that you never truly come to grips with it; in fact, it's even worse than that, it's—

"I just happened to be in the right place at the right time," I said with a shrug. "I hear the right things from the right people and have a knack for getting it down on paper." I drank my coffee fast.

She nodded. "It's funny."

"What is?"

"Meeting a writer whose articles you've read. It's funny."

"Why?"

". . . I don't know. It just is."

My hand left the mug and touched hers, returned to the table and rested very quietly. She looked at my hand, looked up.

"Was James Bond a fag?" she said.

"What? Jesus no. Who told you that?"

"My father."

"Tell your father he's wrong, a hundred percent wrong. Dead wrong."

My hand touched hers again and she half-smiled in the blue light. I was tempted to blast her father for the smirk he wore when he smeared 007, but after what Hannah had done to me, fathers had to unite; she might also, although I doubted it, be daddy's girl; no point in risking it. She seemed to be thinking again; I let her think.

"Who is Renee Adoree?" she said at last. In my story, one of the Maids in a Mustang mentions Renee as they fly over the Mekong.

"A marvelous girl. She was in *The Big Parade* with Jack Gilbert. It was a famous war film."

"I didn't see it. Was it about Europe or the Pacific?"

'Europe. The first World War," I said with uncritical softness.
"Oh. I don't know that war."

This time my hand touched her cheek. It was very smooth and cool; she smiled and touched the palm of my hand with hers. I was tempted to squeeze her hand; I brushed back my hair. "I really don't know that much about it either," I lied. "Only things like Eddie Rickenbacker and Sergeant York."

"I know something about Sergeant York," she said. "Gary Cooper played him."

"Yup . . . What do you know about Sergeant York?"

"Sergeant York hated war."

". . . At first. Just at first. Then he realized he had . . . his duty . . ." I watched and waited. She seemed to review the Sergeant, to dismiss him, to make the next leap.

"You *do* know about the other war," she said.

"What makes you think that?" I said, feeling myself, incredibly, blushing in the blue light.

"From the way you write in the *Whisper*."

I webbed my fingers, pulled into Speed, felt perspiration drip down my sweat shirt.

She said, "Am I right?"

"Yes."

She nodded, then hit me again: "I don't care very much for wars."

I lifted my cup, thought, Christ, here we go again. I balanced on my elbows, waited. But that was all: She didn't care for wars.

"Well," I said, "there are wars and there are wars . . . Some are . . . were . . . necessary."

She seemed to take that in; at least no curtain had descended when I raised the flag. "Does it bother you," I said, "that I use the war in the *Whisper*?"

She seemed startled. "If it's important to *you*, that's what counts . . . I'm just the reader."

Cagey old Speed looked for the con; he saw sincerity; someone long ago had thought that about writers . . . Manny! I drank my coffee, not knowing what else to do. The reader looked at the writer and said, "I had an uncle in Okinawa. He was wounded in the leg. Were you all right?"

Was I? "I wasn't wounded . . . I was in Europe. The E.T.O., one day after the invasion . . . What rank was your uncle?"

". . . I'm not sure . . . Tech Sergeant?"

"That's right, Tech Sergeant." I paused. "I was a Captain." She didn't faint, but she didn't shrug either.

She said, "This is stupid; I know that's an officer and a well-known rank, but where does it come?"

"Most people don't know, so it isn't stupid. There's Second Lieutenant, then First Lieutenant, then Captain . . . then Major . . ."

"Then what?"

"Oh, Lieutenant Colonel, Full Colonel, Brigadier General."

She thought. "Only four away from General."

I held up a hand. "I ran out of time," I smiled.

She smiled back and said, "What did you wear on your shoulder?"

Again no con, search as I would. "A small pair of silver streaks. We called them railroad tracks."

She nodded. "I think I've seen them. Silver railroad tracks . . ." She was silent, looking at me. "Captain suits you," she said.

I began to blush again, drank my coffee, choked, coughed, smiled Speed's modestly acknowledging smile, drank, swallowed, said, "End of war talk. Eleven o'clock, November Eleventh . . . Maureen . . . It is Maureen?"

"Maureen O'Brien."

"Maureen O'Brien . . ." (Maureen and Manny? No. But Maureen and Speed . . . ? Sure, Speed could handle it . . .) "Does Maureen O'Brien go out during the week?"

"I'm out."

"I mean after work."

"Yes, I go out. Though not as a regular thing."

". . . What about tomorrow night?"

She didn't say, I just met you, or you don't even know me, or you sure are speedy. "Tomorrow is my late night," she said.

225

"How late?"

"Nine."

My reflexes were precise, honed. "How's this? Nine oh five outside the shoe store. Unless you don't want your boss to see us together."

"My personal life is my own."

"How about it, then?"

I leaned forward.

"All right," she said.

Speed sat back. He had sighted his objective, moved. The objective had responded. We had here closure, simple, complete closure. But with a glimpse of things to come. No maneuvers, no nonsense. He sat back . . . Too easy? *Too* simple? No. Never, when Captain Speed was clicking; not when he got lucky and pushed his luck . . . I slid my chair back quickly and stood so she had to crane up at me. "I'd better get you back," I said protectively. "I don't want Jerry to yell."

"That isn't Jerry. Jerry has his office in West Orange. That's Malcolm."

I turned on a wicked grin. "Was Malcolm in Okinawa or the European Theater?"

"Malcolm? Are you kidding? He was just a little boy at the time."

"Oh."

"Besides, they don't even want him in Vietnam."

That was the loveliest part: Malcolm and Vietnam. I glided back to New York, eyes high, shoulders back, belly in, heart soaring.

I go five ten and a quarter. That night and all next morning I had an overwhelming desire to be six feet even. To gaze down on Maureen from that magic plateau, to have her bend her lovely cervical column even further back, to tuck those clear brown eyes a good eight inches below my calm, controlled, E.T.O. gaze. The catch, the hook: I would have to wear elevators. Even as I came to grips with that, I got the hot, jolting slash I always got when I thought of Samuel in his Adlers; I felt the same (comforting) disgust I always felt whenever I caught him in his wedgies. Yes ... but ... yet ... And I permitted the slash/disgust to do battle with the overwhelming desire, until at three o'clock I figured whathehell and subwayed downtown to 42nd Street and twenty minutes later teetered out of old man Adler's six feet tall.

I practiced the rest of the afternoon ... growing ever dizzier as the day clumped by. By seven I was floaty and spinning. I was also ripping into the *schmucky* kid: phony, phonier, phoniest. Yes ... but ... yet ... Maureen over there, tilting, tilting ... I hung in through a giddy shave (dabbing furiously with the styptic pencil), hung in through the blue Palm Beach suit, hung in through the slide behind the wheel of the newly-rented Rambler. Hung in through the inspection of the half Windsor knot in the rearview mirror. That's when I saw it: the turned-down, milk-white face. I got out, teeter-tottered upstairs, shucked out of the stilts, kicked them into the corner where they cowered in defeat, slipped into the good old Nettleton Algonquins, buffed against each pants leg, strode to the door. Hesitated. Strode back. Flipped through a bureau drawer. Located my Captain's bars under a First Army patch, dropped them into a side pocket and, patting the pocket, strode back down and into the car, whistling Tattoo.

☆　☆　☆

227

Steve McQueen was gone. She was wearing a soft green dress that molded real hips, three-quarter heels that set off the round calf yet were still sensible and that still gave me a good four inches clearance. I asked how she was tonight? She was fine. She turned to a chubby, blushing girl and said, Mary, this is Speed; to me she said, Speed, this is Mary. I shook Mary's wet hand and she bustled away squeaking she would see Maureen tomorrow. Maureen tucked her hand firmly into the crook of my arm; patting the Captain's bars, I smiled down at her.

"Are there any movies around?" I said as we walked past the closing shops.

"It's too late for a drive-in," she said.

"I'm against drive-ins anyway, on general principle. Anything in Bergen?"

"Uh-huh. We can probably see the last show. Did you see *The Graduate?*"

"Yes, and forget it if you haven't. Anything else?"

"*Comedians?*"

I didn't say, you mean *The Comedians?* I said, "I read the book. It's fine with me if it's all right with you. It's not a comedy."

"Well, not everything that sounds like something turns out to be that something. *Bringing up Baby* was about a panther."

I didn't say, *leopard.* I said, "Fine, let's go."

Taylor and Burton were stomachable, the backgrounds were gorgeous and never once did she shift away from the technicolored magic. As for Speed, he fingered the R.R. tracks and thought of a hundred ways to hold her hand. By the time he made his move the picture was over. She stared for thirty more seconds, sighed, said to me as my hand drew back, "I liked it, did you?"

"Yes," I semi-lied. "Would you like some coffee?"

"All right."

She directed me to a huge, late-night drugstore with a circular counter. A girl in a smudged white apron walked over and gave her a pleasant hello. Hi Cindy, Maureen said and I had the sure feeling that they had played this scene many times; the green monster hit me; I touched the bars, assured myself that my predecessors had all been enlisted men (or had the e.m.'s mentality) and with that edge firmly in hand, ordered. As we sipped coffee and spooned ice cream, she asked if the book was like the movie?

"Not too far off." Oh Lord, a true believer: Was the *book* like the movie? "It's by Graham Greene. He's very good."

She dug seriously into her ice cream; then: "Did he write any other books that were made into movies?"

I thought of some, settled for, "Yes. *This Gun for Hire.* A long time ago." (Well, they used his *title.*)

"I've seen it on the Late Show. I like the way Alan Ladd combed his hair, with the wave off his forehead."

"In the book, the main character has a harelip."

"Alan Ladd was too beautiful for a harelip."

I felt a twinge of annoyance, wanted to say, art is more important than a sappy face, besides which, Ladd's wave merely covered incipient baldness. "Maybe," I said, "you'd like *The Quiet American* by the same author."

"Why?"

"Among other things, it's an antiwar book."

". . . Maybe I *would* like it."

I drove in hard. "It was made into a movie starring Audie Murphy."

"Who's Audie Murphy?"

"The most decorated soldier in World War Two."

"Really?"

"Yes. And he starred in this antiwar film."

She didn't blink. "He's a movie actor?"

"That's right. Mostly westerns. Some war films. And *The Quiet American.* Antiwar."

"The most decorated? In real life?"

"That's right."

She concentrated on her ice cream. After several spoonfuls, I said, "Look for *To Hell and Back* on television sometime. It's *his* war movie. From his book. About *his* war. About how he won all

229

those medals." I paused. "Then he made *The Quiet American.*" I paused again. "I guess you can preach against the evils of war only if you've fought and won the right war."

She dipped into her ice cream. When she looked up, she said, "Making a movie about himself must have felt very funny."

I was suddenly disgusted with Speed, his annoyance, his college-man one-upmanship. "I guess it did," I said. And with that profundity we both grew quiet. We finished our ice cream and coffee. She said goodbye to Cindy, I paid and we walked out, still quiet. I warned Speed to keep his brilliance to himself. We got into the car and she seemed to shake herself awake as she gave explicit directions to her place. My heart started up with the motor as I thought, for the first time in years, of what might or might not happen when that marvelous and mysterious goal, *her* place, had been achieved. The highway gleamed and shadows stretched away on each side.

"I wonder what it felt like . . ."

I turned down WPAT. "You still thinking about Audie Murphy?"

"Yes. Being there and going through hell; then making all that hell into a movie. I wonder what he thought . . ."

I saw the skinny little guy, a *goyisher* Manny, hurtling toward every medal in the book. Then doing it all over again in Hollywood, making out like a mink between takes. . . . I looked at Maureen. She was looking at me, waiting until I refocused.

"Could you do it?" she said.

"Make a movie about my war experiences?"

"Yes."

"I honestly don't know . . ."

She nodded as if that made sense, and we drove on in silence. I turned Mantovani up a notch to cover the silence.

"Speed?"

"Yes?"

"Have you ever written about your war experiences?"

"No . . ."

"Why don't you?"

230

"I thought you didn't care for wars."

"You certainly remember what people say."

"I remember *that*."

"Well, we're talking about *you*. Could you?"

". . . I don't think I could . . ."

"Would it be too painful? I've heard writing about it can get rid of the pain."

"Oh no, not that. Oh no . . ."

"Well, it's not for me to say . . ."

"Writers are always open to suggestion."

"I just thought if Audie Murphy can do it, why not you?"

"I didn't win as many medals."

"So what? You're a writer and you can write *your* story."

The big writer said, "Would you read it?"

"Of course. I'd be willing to bet it would make a darn good movie."

"Starring . . . Larry Parks."

"Starring Speed Finestone."

I willed the erection to behave itself.

"There it is," she said, pointing. I looked out at the lights, the sign. The bottom row of letters said, NO VACANCY; the top row said TRIPLE A APPROVED. I turned to her.

"That's a motel."

"That's right."

"You live in a motel? The Green Garden Motel?"

"That's right. Why do people always say that?"

"Say what?"

"You live in a motel?"

". . . I just . . . never knew anybody who lived in a motel."

"Did you ever know anybody who *stayed* in a motel?"

"Of course . . ."

"Well, substitute the word *live* for *stay* and it won't bother you . . . besides, motels are fun."

"Fun?" (Manny leering: *fun?*)

"That's right. I do laundry with a girl whose husband plays in a

231

combo in Paramus. Next week, they're going to St. Louis. I'll have new neighbors, probably from Jersey Bell, they stay here a lot, but maybe somebody else, it's fun . . . I'm in the back, take that half-circle."

I circled around. Four cars were nuzzled patiently against their rooms. "This is where the regulars live," she said.

"How long . . . ?"

"They stay as much as a year; I've been here five months. All right?"

". . . Sure . . . Fine . . ."

"The one on the end, number nine."

I swung in close to nine and we got out. My operations career reeled before me: apartment houses in the Bronx. The Taft, the New Yorker. Split level in Atlanta. Brownstone in Hampstead. A saltbox in Nantucket. Lucille's walk-up. Carla's castle. A motel? Never . . . Wait, summer, 1941, Lake Mahopac . . . Motor Inn . . . Same difference . . . *Oh*, what a night . . . *Stop it*!

"Well, here we are, all safe and sound," I said lightly. I got out, hustled around and opened her door. Regally, she descended, walked to her unit, Speed three paces to the rear. Slivers of yellow light filtered out of numbers four and seven; otherwise, it was dark and quiet except for the Jersey insect symphony. She clicked on the light above her door, turned. Oh Lord, Lili Marlene. I approached, halted.

She said in her most serious voice, "I had a lovely evening, I hope you'll call me."

". . . I will . . . so did I . . . Maybe I'll drop into the store . . ."

"Better not. Malcolm lectured me again."

"All right . . . I won't . . ."

I took out the black book, turned past the latest gripe. "What's the number here?"

"Area code 201. 835-4372. Clara will always take the message. Thursday is my late night, remember."

"I'll remember." I slipped the book into my pocket and fingered the railroad tracks. I gazed down at her. She tilted and gazed back. Compared to Alan Ladd and Audie Murphy, I was a goddam giant. She reached up and for an instant her fingers were lambent flames on the nape of my neck; I felt her pelvis sagging into mine and the flick of a wet tongue. "Bye now," she whispered. She turned, slid her key into the door and was gone.

"Firm, soft, resilient, real, yes *real*: real hair, real hips, real knockers ... Real tongue? ... Of course ... Slick, experimental tongue? ... Oh no, tender, innocent tongue ... How can flicking tongue be innocent, *schmuck*? ... Easy, one must not be cynic ... Cynic? Motel, hips, sag, tongue; *cynic*? ... Refuse to argue with resident of gutter ... OK (for now), tell me more ... Soft yet firm ... You said that ... Clean underwear ... OK, give you that; pink, white, black? ... Pink ... Pink step-ins? ... Balls, cannot talk to you ... All right, peace (piece?), back to tongues ... Seriously? ... Yop ... Delicious Doublemint ... Not shrewd, slick Juicy Fruit? ... Warned you ... OK, *schmuck*, luuuv? ... Anything is possible, why not? ... Why not Shirley Temple? ... Cannot talk to you, darkness in your soul ... Stiffness in your dick ... Oh shit ... Come now, could be sensational *shtup*, right? ... Perhaps, if I taught her ... Hey walyo, she'd teach *you* ... Filthy, rotten mind; two ships in the night that found each other ... Oh my, high school dropout? ... Nonsense, at least general diploma; anyway, swirling, coiling shit easier, looser, thinner, doesn't bug me as much, so don't you *dare* discourage ... Discourage? heavenstobetsy, dying to get in as much as *you* ..."

I slept badly but awoke refreshed. I suited up immediately and ran uptown over the bridge, stoking up on pure, existential power as I reached, touched, thrust off. I ran to Bergen, encircled the mall three times, giving her (and us) the gift of my final sprint. I tried to recapture her face, but as I ran I simply couldn't do it; not that it receded from my grasp; I just could not put the features together to form the picture that would click. I recalled feeling the same way when Manny had a twenty-four hour pass from Shanks two weeks before he went overseas. He met a Gina Grimaldi in Nyack, spent seven magnificent hours with her (even then he was metamorphosing toward Speed), yet never again could we recapture her face or even her feel. Ahead of Gina lay the fantastic Columbus void and that night was filled with unspeakable poignancy which stayed with Manny all the way across in convoy. Yet we could never quite pin her down. Nor did we want to. Wherein lay the difference between Gina and Maureen. Maureen's face, her feel, Speed *had* to pin down. Perhaps this time she and I would enter a new Columbus void together. Perhaps. Whatever, I had to recapture that face. I ran to the nearest phone booth.

"I would like to speak to Maureen O'Brien, please."

The voice was high, thin, querulous.

"Is this a personal call?"

I thrust the implications of that question aside and said this was a neighbor of her uncle in Jersey City. Uncle Sean had been taken to the hospital. Could I please speak to Maureen?

"Which hospital is he at?"

"I don't believe that is germane but it happens to be the Jersey City Medical Center, the one built by Mayor Frank Hague. May I please speak to Miss O'Brien?"

"Just a minute ... *Maureen*. It's your *uncle*, he's ill. Please make it short ..."

"Hello?"

"Maureen, your uncle is not sick, I hope he lives to be a hundred; he's actually in a P-51 circling the pontoon bridge of the Rhine."

"... I see. Will they have to operate?"

High school dropout, indeed!

"Yes. But he has to see you tonight or he will not make it to the Ploesti oil fields. Do you get off at five?"

234

"That is correct."

"Five fifteen? He'll make a three-point landing in front of Hawaiian Palm."

"It will be very difficult, I was supposed to be elsewhere during visiting hours."

"Name the time."

"What were those visiting hours again?"

"Six, seven, eight, nine, you name it. Eight at your motel?"

"No, I don't know that ward . . ."

"In front of the movie house in Bergen? Eight?"

"All right, I'm quite sure I can make it. Thanks for calling, Mr. Greene, I really appreciate it."

I slapped the phone. Windmilling happy arms, I circled the mall three more times.

She was twenty minutes late and I was beginning to squeeze the railroad tracks with sweating fingers when she walked up with shy Mary. She wore a pleated red skirt, a white blouse with a high neck, both of which molded the soft suppleness. She said hello, how is Uncle Sean? He had made an amazing recovery; hello Mary, have you been keeping Maureen out of trouble? Mary blushed and Maureen said quickly, she doesn't have to because I don't get into trouble. I squeezed the railroad tracks and grinned like an idiot. Maureen dismissed Mary, saying she would see her Monday, now remember what I *told* you. Mary would remember and ran off with a birdlike nod. Maureen took my arm and said we better see my uncle before they give him something to sleep. I looked down, stretched up, ventilated deep.

She said, yes, she *did* like human music, and directed me to the Starlighter Lounge in Belleville (the neighbor, with whose wife she did laundry, was strictly R&R). The combo was indeed human and raised ghosts of the places I had haunted in Queens after the war. I hadn't danced in years, but a smiling Les Paul guitar brought it instantly back with the first chords of "Strangers in the Night." To my surprised relief, she was not a very good dancer: too tight and earnest, with little awareness of the bass and drum. With great confidence I told her to relax, never look at her

235

feet, and let me do the work. After one daiquiri, she did all three, and we got along splendidly with my basic box step which could be shaped into anything the beat demanded. In between sets I memorized her face in the half light and Ohhhed?, Of coursed, Is-that-a-facted? as she rattled on.* She refused a third daiquiri with a firm bounce of the springy hair, and I led her onto the floor again for a modified tango. After she got over absolutely dying whenever they played Latin music, she relaxed and scolded me, with an approving smile, for pulling such a "ruse" on poor Malcolm; as a matter of fact, every one of her uncles was healthy as a horse. I suddenly bent over and kissed the smooth, clean cheek; I inhaled Camay. She pulled back and tilted up. "That was nice," she said. My heart clanged.

We remained until eleven and I listened, approved and reflected as she explained the interesting aspects of working in a mall, Bergen being her third in two years. There was always something new and different to look forward to each day, you were always mingling with people and surrounded by colorful places, like you were in a busy toy town; you could even say it was your own *Brigadoon*, a little village, warm and protected, while on the outside everything was so open and cold and impersonal . . . Oh, I don't know, you know? Yes, I thought I did know, or understand. She suspected I would; did you realize you could learn a lot about people from their preferences in footwear and hose? I had rather realized that about footwear, but was surprised to hear about hose. Her fingers stroked above my collar as I kissed her cheek again.

I drank Courvoisier out of a wine glass, with a graceful and elegant hand. Before our last dance, I taught her to swirl, sniff and taste; live and learn, she smiled. We danced to "How High the Moon"; I thanked Les Paul and gave him a five dollar bill. We

*Listening, approving, reflecting were salvaged from my personnel management courses at Columbia which in retrospect were worth the price of admission.

drove to the Green Garden Motel. We stood on the welcome mat to number nine in the quiet darkness and she thanked me for a lovely evening. She reached up and sagged into me and flicked the little tongue and started to turn away. But I had been thinking all the way back through WPAT. I stepped in, slid my arms beneath hers, pressed the elastic body so quickly and tightly to me that she gasped loudly against my mouth. Here too I was prepared: I answered her tongue with my freshly Binaca-ed one. She gasped again and tried to pull back. But the cognac had done its job; with an even, insistent strength I pressed harder, kissed harder. She struggled once more, then gave in. And Speed went to work. He did not loosen a hand and apply it to a pressing breast, or for that matter to the in-sagging behind. No, he roamed carefully and with all the experience he could muster over every other intervening inch. For several moments she seemed to be hanging on for dear life. Then to his amazement, she came back and in a flashing instant gave him as good as she got. They clutched, breathed, gasped. Then, finally, she moaned. Speed's head lifted and seemed to shoot up to the sky. He hadn't had a moaner in twenty-one years, and that included two wives. Then he did a violently strange thing; *he* moaned. Speed. And Speed *never* moaned. He felt a moment of panic; *crying* would be next. Even as they kissed he sucked in his gut to prevent *that* . . . Ah, he nailed it, regained control. Returned to business. Which, with her moaning, their writhing and clutching, was soon topping anything he'd had in the Bronx, Atlanta, or even with Gina Grimaldi. Plus which, the Captain now knew what to do with all this sweet wildness. Without missing a beat, he breathed into her daiquiried mouth, "Your key . . . give me your key."

She gasped, whispered back, "No, please . . . no, please . . ."

I pulled back hard and held her so she wouldn't fall. I smoothed her hair and twisted her dress back into position. She stood there, breathing, looking up.

I said, "All right, no further. All right." I kissed her on the forehead, turned and wobbled back to the car.

Saturday.

I didn't run over the bridge. Instead I ran up Broadway to Van Cortlandt Park and looped through the cross-country course, ran back on Broadway. When I reached the apartment, then and only then—for a little self-discipline had become urgently important—did I call. A terribly polite woman, obviously Clara, said there was no answer in number nine. I called back every fifteen minutes. At 1:30 I reached her. I knew it was extremely short notice, but was she free tonight? Oh, she was sorry, but she had plans. I see . . . I had a lovely time Thursday night, Speed . . . Yes, I see . . . Have a nice day, Speed . . . Yes, you too . . .

I tried the West Side museums: Natural History, the Planetarium, the Historical Society, absolutely determined not to call back. At five I called. George Clinton stared at me on the main floor of the Historical Society as polite Clara rang.

"It's me."

"Hello, you."

"I'm in a museum," I said. "The New York Historical Society."

"I'm not familiar with that museum."

"It's a splendid museum."

"I should know more about museums, but I don't."

"If it happened in or around New York, this museum tells the story."

"It sounds like a very thorough museum."

"Thoroughness is this museum's middle name . . . Are you free tomorrow night?"

"Tomorrow is Sunday."

"I know. Are you free?"

238

"Monday is Labor Day."

"I know that, too. We'll make it an early night."

"Scout's honor?"

"Scout's honor."

"All right. Seven o'clock in the McDonald's across the highway from the motel. See you then."

"Yes . . . seven . . . McDonald's . . . Bye . . ."

I hung up with great care and grinned at the frowning George Clinton. You hear that, Guv?

2

I had something to rev up for, look forward to, but I still had to get through Saturday night. It was rough. Noisy, tasteless bite hunched over the *Post* at the counter of a Broadway greasy spoon. Half a movie at the New Yorker: sliding, clashing images, ear-smashing sound; still cannot remember title. Home at ten. Pull out yellow pad, summon up Morse Junko. Refuses to appear. Saul Dréflique. Likewise. Rise, wander downstairs, wander across Riverside, wander through park, wander across West Side Highway. Stare hotly, icily at Jersey. Nubile, concupiscent Jersey. With plans. Malcolm part of plan? Hilarious. Who then? Hey, *beaucoup* studs working the mall. New wave. Laid six times before they're twelve. Have it out even as they say hello. Hi, I'm Dick. Plans. Studs. Balls, 4Fs! Faint dead away at sight of blood. Or snatch. Yeah, snatch. Whothehell is she, Queen of the hill? Tee shirt freak. Tee shirts. Steve McQueen sitting on boobies. McQueen. Hondo Heat. Cruising by on goddam bike. Glaums her. Hollywood prix love innocence. Vavooms in. Vavooms out, pliant innocence pressed into sweaty back. Draft-dodging back. Plans, lady? *That Kawasaki Krud Has Plans!* Ohhhhhh . . .

I sprinted back across the highway, scrambled up through the park, pounded up to the apartment. I grabbed the yellow pad and slashed through twenty pages of Morse Junko and Saul Dréflique taking on and leaving for dead Stove McPrincess, the international playboy with a yellow streak, who feeds the operational plans of the RAF to Goering and Erhard Milch. I finished it at three A.M., slipped it under my pillow and managed to get some closely guarded sleep.

3

Sunday.

I got up as late as I could. After toying with breakfast, I picked up another pad and walked up to my roof. It was a Hudson-crystal afternoon and Jersey seemed just a hundred yards away. Returning to it every time I slowed down, I bent over the pad and revealed the hitherto untold story of how Junko and Dréflique had infiltrated the Wild One Gang and nailed for the helpless authorities one Stave McDuchess, who had with utter duplicity taken over the gang from Marlo Brandone. Feeling at least fifty percent better, I walked back down, set this story alongside the other beneath my pillow, showered, shampooed, shaved, shined. I said the hell with the Captain's bars and walked down to the car. I got in and drove uptown. At 125th Street, I stopped, U-turned, streaked back to the house. Dashed upstairs. Ripped through three drawers. Found my E.T.O. ribbon with three battle stars. Ran down. Vavoomed off.

She was waiting under the McDonald's arch in a cream-white dress that the ads in the *Times* would call impishly clingy. White shoes with Jackie Kennedy heels. White bag, shoulder strap. I said, hello, I like your outfit. She thanked me and inquired about Mr. Museum. I was fine and dandy, let's eat. She took my arm and started us into McDonald's. I told her to hold it, that we were going some place with atmosphere. McDonald's had atmosphere, she assured me, if you looked hard; besides, you've been spending too much money on us. I *like* to spend on you. I know you do and I appreciate it, but I'll bet writers don't make a fabulous salary. We ate at McDonald's.

Over coffee I pointed out that with the money she had saved me I could afford to take her to the Lamplighter. She thought that over with careful eyes. Would I promise to remain within the minimum? I crossed my scudding heart. We got into the car and drove through a burnished evening to our Lounge where I nursed a Courvoisier and she played with a daiquiri. It was that night that I learned she was born on May 29, 1944, which meant, I noted quietly, that she was bawling at this cold cruel coil while I was gearing up for the inhospitable sands of Omaha Beach. She set her glass down. Reached over and covered my hand. We looked at each other. I broke first and said, "If my math is any good, that makes you twenty-four."

"Correct. One foot in the grave."

"Then what do I have?" I said.

"A very youthful appearance. If I didn't know you were in the war, I'd place you at thirty-five."

". . . Well, I was awfully young when I enlisted." (True.)

"How young?" she smiled.

I figured frantically, lopped off four years which the war owed me anyway . . . "Seventeen. In 1943."

"You must have been a cute soldier."

" . . . I guess I got by . . ." Jesus, what about now?

"And you're a cute forty-two," she said with a firm nod.

I grinned out of the left side of my mouth, sloshed my cognac and sipped with the expertise taught me by Charles Boyer, peered down from the heights of my cute but toughed-out forty-six minus four years. We thank you for that, I said; let's dance.

We danced and talked until 9:30, at which point Speed said, "OK Cinderella, time to get your beauty sleep."

She tilted a smile at me and said, "Thank you; you remembered."

We walked with encircled waists back to the table and in spite of her look, I left the waiter a hefty tip. We walked out with Maureen explaining that it was really time I started saving my pennies. I took the elastic waist around, squeezed.

The door to number nine. She faced me, looked up. I reached. She placed two firm hands on my chest. She said, and I stepped back at its force: "Would you like to come in?"

241

I actually said, "You mean come into the motel?"

"Yes," she said with no trace of a smile. "*The Longest Day* is the Ten O'Clock Movie. I saw it in *TV Guide*."

I shuffled incredulous feet.

"*The Longest Day?*"

"Yes. You never heard of it?"

"Oh yes . . ."

"Did you see it?"

"No."

"I guessed that. I thought you might like to see it. I mean, now . . . Unless you think it might be too painful . . ."

"Oh no, I'm a big boy now. I'd like very much to see it. Especially with you. I'm just surprised you'd like to see it."

"Well, wars are reality, aren't they? Anyway, I thought if Audie Murphy could star in *his* war, Speed Finestone could at least observe *his*."

". . . Won't it keep you up late?"

Her smile was solemn and sweet.

"What are a few hours compared to the longest day?"

Sitting beneath a print of a button-eyed little girl, sipping a ginger ale out of her half-refrigerator, I watched the longest day. With time out for less wetness under the arm, less wetness on the hair, I watched Wayne, Steiger, Ryan, Lawford, Fonda, Red Buttons and a cast of thousands take the coast of Normandy. Maureen sat beside me without moving, except for time out, when she would quietly fill my glass. I sat back, crossed my legs and observed that seventeen-inch invasion and told myself if Audie Murphy can handle it, so can you. But even as I talked to myself, I could feel the resolve ooze out of me as Zanuck relentlessly poured it on. Until suddenly I was in it. One minute I was up in the panning plane with him, the next minute I was in it. Carbine high, thrashing through the icy water, not feeling anything from the waist down. Aware that I had crashed through some kind of door, aware that my far-off legs were scrabbling over a different surface, aware that they were melting yet were

242

pushing me ahead on this surface, aware that even as they were melting they were thrusting me incredibly at concrete scarabs, aware that my numb arms were pointing the carbine, squeezing, aware that an insane screeching was piercing my ears, then as my legs evaporated, aware that the screeching came from me. Now, incredibly the legs had poured back into my skin, and I was up again, pressing into the rear end of a jeep as it whined in low toward a scarab; then pressed against the horrible insect, shoving my carbine into its eyes, squeezing . . .

. . . In the Green Garden Motel I was feeling nothing in my crossed legs and yet they had an overwhelming urge to pick me up and run through the wall, keep on running until I dropped. I think I spilled my drink as I fought to keep those legs where they belonged. I think I loosened my belt and tie as the silent struggle continued. I held the legs down through another reel as Sergeant E. Finestone plunged through the cast of thousands, knowing with total certainty that he could not do it, yet doing it, taking his first giant steps toward Captain Speed. I held the legs in place even into the house-to-house nightmare; then they began to quiver and filled from foot to hip with an agonizing pressure. I said, excuse me, please, gave in to the pressure, rose and strode to the bathroom. I turned both faucets on full strength, dropped to my knees and surrendered after twenty-four years to the rippling, up-thrusting power that was more than I could endure, yet had endured . . . When I had finally gotten rid of Normandy Beach, I gargled with her Listerine, soaked my head, and carefully cleaned up as if latrine duty were my basic training detail. Before I left, I sprayed the room with her Lysol freshener. When I walked back in, reasonably combed and scrubbed, a newscaster was soundlessly working his mouth.

"Are you all right?" she said from the audio dial.

"Of course."

I sat in another chair and she walked across the room, looked down and took my face in her cool hands.

"Are you sure?"

"Sure I'm sure."

Suddenly my head was against her stomach and I was sobbing. Captain Speed was absolutely astonished, totally dismayed, but I couldn't stop. I felt her hands stroking my hair behind my ears, heard through my sobs, "Poor boy, poor boy." I was sobbing as hard now as when Shimon had slapped me his one and only time when I was six and had sprinted across Tremont Avenue against the light. My arms were around her hips and I was pressing into her stomach as I tried to stifle the crying, but that only made me cry harder, until it was hard and dry and convulsive. I heard her voice murmuring above me, felt her hands stroking, felt the soft warmth, then slowly, very slowly, I began to quieten. Then we were very still except for the murmuring and the stroking. I began to kiss her stomach through the dress. I felt her breath pull in, felt a quivering against my mouth. I hesitated, then my hands moved behind her. She pressed harder into me. I drew away and looked up. Her head was thrown back. The murmuring had stopped, she was breathing now. I pulled her down on my lap and enveloped her, digging my head into her breasts and neck as her head curved back and I heard a gasping, "Oh, Speed ... Oh ... no ... Speed ..." Her breathing and her words restored all the power I had lost on Omaha Beach. More power. Geometrically leaping power as I moved and she responded. The power slid an arm under her thighs; I lifted and stood for an instant as she clung to my neck. Then I carried her to the bed that had a black and white panda on the pillow. The button-eyed little girl was smiling down innocently from the green wall and the newscaster was still silently mouthing the terrors of the day as I eased her onto the bed. (The motel bed.) With great care and dexterity I began to undress her. She did not resist, but lay there with her eyes closed and her chest rising and falling. Nor did she say anything, not even the dreaded "no, please no," as each neat, fresh item dropped away. When she lay gleaming and smooth beneath me, I paused. Her eyes opened. I sat on the bed and kissed along the gleaming length. Her eyes closed and the breathing deepened. I unzipped then and drew her hand to me. That's when she whispered, "No, please, we mustn't . . ." but her hand was

244

moving even as she said it. I said, hearing myself very distinctly,
"Yes, we must, we *must* . . ."
"No, we mustn't . . . *I* . . . mustn't . . ."
"Yes . . ."
"No . . . D . . . Day . . ."
"Plus one . . . D-Day plus one . . ."
". . . D-Day plus one . . . making us do it . . ."
My hand was exploring.
"We will consecrate D-Day," I whispered.
"Not . . . right . . ."
I kissed and explored.
"Yes, perfectly right . . . And more than D-Day . . . We both
know it . . ." I reached and touched the magic place. She
shuddered. "Say it," I ordered.
"More . . . than D-Day . . ."
I gently arranged the lovely legs, kneeled, lowered. She was
guiding me now and I heard, or thought I heard, "Our link . . ."
"Yes," I whispered. "We're linked forever."
"Protection," she gasped.
I reached into my back pocket, brought forth the wallet,
dumped everything out including the rubber. I leaned back, broke
it open, managed to get it on.
"Don't worry," I said. "Don't *ever* worry."
Her eyes opened.
"I won't," she breathed. "He'll . . . just have to . . . understand."
Her hand pulled me down. I pulled back.
"Who?"
"Linc."
"*Our* link?"
"My Linc . . ."
"*Your* link?"
". . . Not anymore . . . never . . ."
"Who . . . is . . . Linc?"
"Lincoln . . . I'm married to him . . ."
"Whathehell are you talking about?"
"I wanted to tell you . . . Well, now I have . . . I can't think of that

245

anymore, I just can't . . . You saw how . . . hard I tried . . . didn't you see?"

"Yes, I saw . . . Lincoln O'Brien?"

"Yes . . . never mind about Linc . . . I've discharged all my obligations to Linc . . ."

"You have?"

"Don't talk anymore, Speed."

"Wait . . . I have to . . . Obligations?"

"Yes . . . No matter what, I've been faithful . . . Until now . . . Well, this is a higher faith . . ."

"Us?"

"Yes, us . . . Don't talk, please . . ."

"Where . . . is . . . Linc?"

She brushed back my hair.

"In Nam."

I leaned back on my hams. Now both her hands were reaching, coaxing.

"He's in the Army, in Nam?" I said.

"Yes. He's a PFC."

"You're married to a PFC?"

She smiled as she worked.

"Yes. That's all he'll ever be. I know that now."

I reached down and with a rough strength peeled away her fingers. She blinked as I zipped up. I picked her dress off the night table and draped it across the gleaming body. She reached up and touched my face.

"Thank you," she smiled. "But it's all right. It really is. I'll go to confession. I'll write to him."

"A Dear Linc letter?"

She touched my face again.

"No, a Dear Speed letter."

I looked down at her, at the dress covering her thighs. I draped it below the knees. She sat up quickly and the dress slid off. She kneeled beside me and her mouth was against my ear. I heard: "Speed . . . I respect you so much . . . I didn't know men like you existed . . . someone who could be strong enough for two . . . to

246

want each other so much, to teeter on the brink, then to see your strength . . . Speed, it's so *beautiful*."

I finished that beautiful, sensational night in a Broadway gin mill.

I awoke at three, turned on the light and reached for the wiseass book:

"Well, *schmuck*, are you happy? No. Play with fire, get immolated, eh, peckerhead? No, no . . . Hey, *schlub*, remember Todd Brookfield outside Erlangen? No. Balls, you don't remember Todd, the Dear John letter, Todd bawling all night, remember? No, no, no . . . Shit, his hotshot Captain keeping his patsy hand from pulling the trigger; now, do you remember? No, no, no, no . . . Hotshot Cap'n vowing vengeance on all Jezebels and stateside fornicators, remember? No, no, no, no, no . . . Hey, *petzl*, she really respects you, doesn't she? No, I mean yes, I mean—You shitheel fornicator, she respects your six inches, doesn't she, *doesn't* she? No, she respects the beauty of it all, our lovely relationship, my strength, this bittersweet—Hey, Hard-on, you're talking to me; ain't *this* beautiful: Linc slogging through shit while you get bare tit? nonononononononononono-ooooooooooo000000000!"

I resumed training the next day and rededicated myself to Jim Ryun. I ran. I ran. I ran. I stayed away from New Jersey, stayed away from Riverside Drive, the park and the West Side Highway where I could see Jersey, even when I didn't want to see it. I didn't touch a phone for two days and two nights. I ran. I tucked the

yapping black book under my mattress and ran. When the pain
shot up into the gut, the chest, the head, I still ran. Not until I
piled up a dizzying oxygen debt did I take a break. At which point,
I sat down and wrote a story for the *Whisper*. It was an exposé of
the clandestine affair between Texas Guinan and Sergeant York.
The last page trailed off into a profusion of "HELLO
SUCKERS!" Doubly exhausted, I flopped into bed. At four I got
up and ran. When I returned, I knocked out Texas Guinan and
substituted Helen Morgan. I slept for another hour, ran
downtown and hand-delivered the story to Red, who observed
me in silence through his narrow eyes. I ran up the East Side, cut
through Central Park, worked my way home. The hell with
Malcolm and everything else; I called her . . .

With a handkerchief over the phone, I informed Malcolm that
an M. O'Brien had won thirty-second prize money in the Irish
Sweepstakes and after he grudgingly put me through, pounded
my head over her dialogue, wound up by telling her I would come
by that evening . . .

The next day I told Malcolm I was a skip tracer and Miss
O'Brien was in bad trouble, but if he let me talk to her, perhaps we
could work this out without a garnishee. He said ohforcrying-
outears, but put her on. I wrote *"SCHMUCK"* all over the phone
pad, said I would be over after she quit work, then ripped into
myself in the black book . . .

Thus we malled, McDonalded and movied for eight straight
days . . . On the ninth she told me she had plans that evening, and
I went out of my mind. When I calmed down, I said couldn't she
alter her plans since they weren't made in heaven; she said,
neither was calling her at the last minute. I said, I thought we had
a kind of understanding. Sure, for me to be at your beck and call.
Oh gee, you're absolutely right, I've been stupidly thoughtless;
please don't make plans for tomorrow night. Pause . . . Then: all
right, that's better . . . Ahhhhh.

(Hey *putz*, who would believe this?)

The next night as I drove across the river I vowed to myself
that enough was enough, that this night, no matter how she

looked at me, or what was said, I would screw her up to the moon and get it over with. Without doubt, Linc was a goldbrick, he was shacking up with a pubescent whore, he was a pushover for a bunch of undersized rice-burners, he was stoned out of his PFC head, he was up to his ears in the black market, he napalmed old ladies with parchment faces and no teeth, and above all: HE WOULDN'T HAVE COME WITHIN FIFTY MILES OF MAUREEN'S PANTS IF IT HADN'T BEEN FOR ME; I HAD MADE THE WORLD SAFE FOR FUCK-OFFS LIKE HIM!

But that night, and all the other nights, I would see her face, she would reach for our hello kiss, she would hang onto my (powerful) arm, we would go to one of our special places, she would listen to my long-playing record without looking at anyone or anything else, she would say what a beautiful story that was about Sergeant York and Helen Morgan and was I hinting that Gary Cooper and Ann Blyth had a thing going? And I would wink and say, *Quién sabe?* And she would touch my ear, which was set so remarkably close to my head, and say, I don't believe a word, tell me more. And I would grin crookedly, tell her about the night Dutch Schultz bought it in Newark as she stared with eyes all aglow, and that goddam Linc would be home free. Again.

Three times I broke the pattern and drove us back to New York, to the Thalia, to see *Broadway Melody of 1936*, *Bright Lights* and *The Magnificent Brute* and in a flash there was Manny lusting after Eleanor Powell and her delicious mouth, Patricia Ellis and her gorgeous gams, Binnie Barnes and her exquisite nose, and then presto, change-o, there he was, the kid, with Elly-Patty-Binnie, tasting, feeling, biting, also writhing, twisting, flailing, tonguing, fingering, driving himself and Elly-Patty-Binnie nuts, as well as to the teeter-totter edge, but at the last incredible moment pulling the string as he heard, "Oh Speed, Oh Speed, how . . . beautiful . . ."

And after driving her home, after returning to 108th Street, I would hear it again, smell her hair, her clothes, her gleaming body in my rooms, recall how Manny would curl up in bed and following Elly-Patty-Binnie beat himself to a pulp, and I would pace and drink and consider the whipping hand for the first time in thirty years, smash that hand against the wall, plunge downstairs and run myself so ragged that by Times Square I was climbing a rope of sand in slow motion.

"The old Finestone luck.
How's that, Dickie Dare?
Finestone's the name, shitcreek's my game.
Poor thing . . . Little man, what now?
Am I Einstein? I'm painted into a goddam corner.
You are?
Don't be coy with me. Finally meet a human girl. Clean hair, scrubbed face, Camayed boobies, spotless panties. Does not wish to blow up every campus in America, turn every vitamin-packed stud into 4F . . . And something else, something big . . .
We know that, don't we, Hard-on?
Screw you. Here it is: she is Manny's dream in the *flesh*.
Ah, that's nice.
Nice! *She is married to this goddam war.*
My piles bleed for you.
I knew they would . . . Finestone luck.
Oh well, as the articulate little lady would say, isn't it funny?
. . . What?
You're 4F after all: Finagled, Finessed, Fulsomely Fucked!"

Except for the terrible night she had plans, we saw each other night after night after night and drove ourselves wild, wild, wild. Hold it; perhaps I should not project; *I* was wild. Yet, despite the beautiful and sustaining strength of my nobility, I'm sure she was

250

going crazy too. This even Manny could figure out as we writhed and clutched in the Green Garden Motel or in my place. But with her utter faith in me as officer and gentleman, it was *my* job, my *duty* to find a sensible way out of our nightly torment. This, also, the transported kid with the swelling gonads knew. But the harder I pressed for the liberating flash of insight, the more elusive it became. When we were together, no solution was possible; for as we wrestled, the Captain's commitment to his men threw the Boulder Dam up against my six and a half inches. Our time apart was no better; I filled that with sledge-hammer-pounding at the little black book. I sprinted. Nothing. I loped. Nothing. I back-pedaled. Nothing. Nothing. Nothing. Nothing... Then one day the downstairs bell rang . . .

He was a gray-suited messenger boy and he had a package from Miss Carla Levine. I thanked him, gave him a dollar and unwrapped the thing: it was an attaché case. Half expecting an alarm clock with coiled wires, I opened it and gingerly removed the contents. It was Niagara Falls: postcards, key chain, bumper stickers, tee shirt, pen with bubble top encasing the *Maid of the Mist*, paperweight with the *Maid* sailing through the flaking cascade, serving tray with bas reliefs of the American and Canadian sides. Plus a note FROM THE DESK OF C. LEVINE: "Hope you can use this stuff; I can't."

I stared . . .

I pondered . . .

The Falls . . . The Falls . . . The . . . Falls!

The Crash. The Smash. The . . .

FLASH!

The irresistible force

that would

break open

the immovable objects

we had

BECOME!

"In other words," said the little black book,

"now you can hump in peace."

☆　☆　☆

251

The same night, as she reached for the key to number nine, I said, "Wait a minute," and turned her around to face me.

"Is something wrong?" she said.

"You know what's wrong." I decided to use her language: "We can't go on like this."

She leaned against the door. In a small voice she said, "No, we can't, can we?"

I took her face in my hands. It was very warm.

"You know we can't."

She sighed against my hands.

"I know."

I took my powerful, gambling breath.

"Let's go away, Maureen."

I rationed the air out of my lungs and waited for life or death. It was neither, but it was her:

"What would that accomplish?"

"It would accomplish a lot. For one thing, it would get us off dead center."

"Then what?"

"This: I don't want to go just anywhere. I want to take you to Niagara Falls."

She smiled with such tenderness that I hated ever having been married.

"If only we could," she said.

"We *can*. Don't you see? We would be *truly* committed to each other then. There'd be no reason to torture ourselves anymore."

She kissed one of my caressing hands and my heart leaped, then plummeted.

"Ah Speed," she said, "I'm married to Linc. It's a fact."

(Marshal Foch: I am surrounded on the left, surrounded on the right; *J'attaque!*)

"Do you *love* him?"

"I thought I did . . ."

"And?"

"And now I don't."

"Why?" I said mercilessly.

"You know why."

252

"*Why?*"

"... Us ..."

"Then that's it! We'll go for a week. Two weeks. Three. However it develops. Let the Falls tell us."

"Speed ... Speed ... it *would* be thrilling."

I winced, dropped my hands to her shoulders, pulled her closer, kissed her gently; even so, her tongue lapped; I kissed her hard; we started to breathe; I slid around to her ear.

"We could leave tomorrow ..."

"I ... have a job ..." She was moving beneath my hands. "So do you," she whispered.

"Red won't mind. I'll tell him I'm digging up new material ... You don't care for your job, you know that. You've wanted to quit."

"Yes, but for the Garden State Mall ..."

"The Garden State Mall won't run away. Maureen. Darling. We have to do this. We *have* to."

She leaned away from me. "Linc ... is still between us."

Then I said it: "After we come back, we'll *both* write to him. We'll ask him to set you free. We'll *insist.* Then ... we'll put our marriage on paper." (Maybe I half-meant it ...)

Her hand flew to my mouth; I inhaled the Camay.

"Oh, it's too fast, too fast, I can't think ..."

I opened my mouth; she closed it.

"Wait." She drilled her eyes into mine. "Are you saying you want to *marry* me?"

"Yes." (No ... Maybe ... Whothehell knows?)

She dropped her hands, her head, and studied the welcome mat. Then slowly she raised her head; I waited; till the end of time I waited. Finally, she said, with the saddest of sighs, "But ... All the while up there in Niagara Falls ... I'd still be married to Linc ..."

I stepped back, felt a fender, sat on it, buried my face in my hands. After many years I heard, with a soft vibrancy, "Speed? Speed?"

I managed to look up.

"Yes?"

"Listen . . . are you listening?"

"Yes, I'm listening . . ."

"You've shown what *your* strength can do . . . Now let me show you mine . . . If—together—we can hold out against the power of Niagara Falls . . . then *that* would be the test of tests, wouldn't it? . . . The supreme test? About how we feel toward one another . . . can you see that?"

". . . Not exactly . . ."

"It would prove us *worthy*, darling."

"Of what . . . ?"

"Each other. Of forsaking all others!"

". . . I doubt . . ."

"Wouldn't it?"

"I'm not . . ."

"Speed, *wouldn't* it?"

"I . . . yes, I . . . suppose . . . I mean yes, but—"

"Speed, listen . . . Then we would still be without taint. We would both be completely and totally pure. Then, I could write to Linc. *I* alone. I would be free to write and tell him the truth. Then truly, *truly*, we could be married. Don't you see?"

She was gazing at me with a thousand stars in her eyes.

I was frantic, wild, desperate and implacably horny. I had to get her to Niagara; later I would figure out something, but now I *had to get her there* . . .

"Yes," I said. "Yes, then we could . . ."

She cupped my face in her hands. I looked at her; I thought I might burst out of my trousers.

"I still have to think," she said. "Give me time. . . ."

I said, sure, take your time, ecstatic at the prospect of another night in a Broadway gin mill.

She called me at six A.M.

"I'll go to Niagara Falls with you," she said.

I went straight out and tore off six purifying wind sprints.

254

I buried the black book deep in a dresser drawer, packed my Captain's bars, several pairs of new Jockey briefs—thirty-two waist—two complete changes, running shorts, a new pair of Keds, plenty of sweat socks, my U. of Mich. sweat shirt and at the last minute dropped in a copy of the collected works of e. e. cummings.

I drove to the Green Garden Motel the next morning at seven and she was waiting outside number nine with a vinyl suitcase and a large canvas shoulder bag. She was wearing a white blouse buttoned primly to the neck and a blue skirt which flowed over her hips.

While Manny gaped, Captain Speed deftly loaded the suitcase and shoulder bag and helped the exquisite young thing into the newly rented car. When I brought up the subject of paying two weeks rent in advance, she said I was sweet but she couldn't think of it, and anyway she was paid up a month in advance.

We drove north on 17 and picked up the Thruway at the New York line; once again, as in days of yore, I was cruising up the Hudson Valley: *One of the world's most beautiful areas. The landscape is enchanting and the beauty of the region's highlands rivals that of the Rhine. In the 1880s the Hudson scenery inspired such distinctly American artists as poet William Cullen Bryant, novelist Washington Irving, and such painters of the Hudson River School as Thomas Cole and Frederick E. Church, who fixed it vividly on canvas. The sight-seeing possibilities are almost limitless: Wineries, pick-your-own cherry and apple orchards, gardens, manors, estates, antiques and art centers, museums, battlefields, state-park playgrounds, monasteries,* *retreats, waterfalls, covered bridges and exhilarating views can all be found along the magnificent Hudson . . .* *

And, ah, this one was a listener. She didn't lean into news of sit-ins, lie-ins, screw-ins; she listened; with the featherweight fingers on the back of my neck, she listened. And I gave value for value received. The Point and Benedict Arnold and John André, Fulton and Claremont and the Day Liners, Hilltop Castle, Olana, Hyde Park and the President of them all. She listened, straight and true, all the way to Albany. When we stopped for coffee she wished she had had me for history, Mr. Leverson was *so* boring; teacher kissed bright-eyed pupil on tip of appreciative nose.

When we were back in the car and buckled up, she noted casually that if we had kept on going we would have run into her home town. I pricked up my ears; she rarely talked about herself and this had been almost too casual.

"Where's that?" I said.

"Champlain. Snow country."

"Uh-huh. Near Canada, isn't it?"

"That's right. You *would* know about it. Nobody else in New York would."

"Geography teacher, also," I smiled. I drove silently, feeling the hand on my neck. I decided to push, just a bit.

"How did you wind up in Jersey?"

"Oh . . . it's a long, sad story . . ."

"We have a lot of time." I glanced. "I'm a pushover for long, sad stories."

"Well—I worked in a local store after high school. A kind of department store, but don't tell that to Bamberger . . ."

"I won't. And?"

"Well, my mother and father were pushing me to get married . . . to Bruce Riordan . . ."

"I see . . . What's your father's name?"

"Eddie."

"His last name?"

---

*. . . and I agreed 100 percent with the guidebook.

256

"Hallahan."

"Maureen Hallahan. At last I know."

"Oh gee, that's right. It just never crossed my mind to tell you my maiden name." ("Hallahan. O'Brien," my father would say. "Now you're the jazz singer.") "I'm sorry, Speed," she said.

"It's OK, it's OK. Maureen Hallahan. Tell me more."

"Are you sure? It's really very boring . . ."

"I'm sure. I'll tell you if it's boring."

"All right . . . Well, I couldn't stand Bruce Riordan. He wasn't bad looking, it was just that he was . . . so boring. Well, in this fancy department store, Linc worked in Jeans and Casual Clothes. And he wasn't happy either. He was always talking about his plans for the future. I guess I felt a certain sympathy with that . . . maybe it even sounded romantic. That groping . . . The future . . . with questions, but . . . possibilities . . . it's hard to explain . . ."

"I think I understand."

". . . He talked about doing so many different things . . . Maybe that should have given me a hint that he was . . . I don't know . . . a jumper—"

"A grasshopper . . ."

"Yes, that's it, he was a grasshopper. I mean, you know what you are . . . you're a writer, you know it in the center of your being, don't you? (Oh sure) Well, Linc was a grasshopper, a dreamy grasshopper. So there he was, hopping around in his head; there I was, unhappy and going nowhere, and I guess we were naturally drawn together . . ."

"That's logical. A mutual need."

"Yes, *exactly*. Thank goodness you're a writer; that's it . . . Well . . . my father couldn't stand Linc and pushed all the harder for Bruce. Steady, serious, quiet, all that stuff . . . To make a long story short, Linc and I got married and left Champlain for Trenton—"

"Hold it. Why Trenton?"

"He had this theory. He said if you picked out a state capital to settle in, there was bound to be more opportunity. He said the politicians made sure of that. Some opportunity. We lived four flights up in a firetrap and all he could get was a job in a drugstore behind the counter. That was a rude awakening. It showed me his

257

dreams just would never be realized. That's when I began to feel I had made a mistake, although I tried, I really did . . ."

"Knowing you, I'm sure you did."

"Thank you . . . Well, one day . . . this was a little over two years ago . . . he came home and said he had enlisted in the Army. I was really surprised, I didn't know what to think, be happy or sad, or what. I just said, why? And he said they had promised him a good deal in Fort Monmouth and that he'd get training in the vital area of communications and some day he'd buy his own radio station and be his own disc jockey in Boise or Phoenix and we'd have it made."

"But there was a war on . . ."

"Oh, he said they had promised not to send him overseas . . ."

"Uh-huh."

"He was so excited. It even spread to me, the excitement. He said we could get a place near Monmouth and he would be able to see me on weekends and later on maybe even live off the post; it would be a real step up for us at last . . ."

"And was it?"

"In a way. I want to be fair to him. They sent him to Monmouth just like they said, and I moved into a motel outside of Eatontown, my first motel, and got a job in a mall, my first mall. So *I* got something out of it. And so did he. He got his training, although it was Morse Code and not as a deejay, but he got really cheerful, and had his uniforms tailored—one thing he knew was clothes—he always had a button sewn into the back of his collar and a specially-made buttonhole, that was his trademark.Things *did* pick up. I loved motel living and working in a mall and—this is a terrible thing to say—Linc wasn't around all the time . . . I'm not proud of saying that, but there it is . . . not that I dated, I never even went out with anybody till he went overseas . . . but I started to like my life for the first time I could remember, and we didn't argue when he *did* come home; and then the Army turned around and sent him to Nam . . ."

"And he felt betrayed . . ."

"Exactly. He went on endlessly about that . . . About being doubled-crossed and what a lousy world this was and I was the

258

only thing he had to live for, but so what? He'd never make it back, and the better your record the closer to the front lines they sent you . . . I was so confused . . . In one sense I was almost relieved we'd be separated, in another sense I felt terrible about being relieved, and in a third sense I was feeling so sorry for him. He asked me to promise to wait forever in case of a miracle and he came through, and to write and tell him how much I loved him. I did . . . I guess I confused pity and remorse with love . . ." She leaned her head on my shoulder. "I don't want to talk about it anymore, Speed . . ."

I inhaled the fresh, clean hair. My Breck girl. I thought of the poor bastard sweating out his double X. Then I stiffened.

"Of course, baby. You did very well, very well. Just one thing. The Army didn't shaft Linc. His country had its needs, has always had them and always will. Those needs change, can suddenly become more demanding. When that happens, you do what you have to do, and you serve your country. You just can't pick your spot. It's not an individual thing. Can you see that, sugar?"

"Yes, I can," she said, snuggling closer.

2

RED DELICIOUS: *Crisp, sweet, and America's #1 choice.* ROME BEAUTY: *The mild flavored classic baking apple.* McINTOSH: *Eat raw, or save some for applesauce.* YORK IMPERIAL: *Scarce, winy, and fine for baking.* BALDWIN: *Rare, old, sweet-sour favorite.* CORTLAND: *Tart, snowy, versatile, great for pie.* MACOUN: *Best, most pungent local choice.* NORTHERN SPY: *Bittersweet, juicy rarity . . .*

I explained the significance of the Mohawk Valley during the Revolution. I told of old Jacob Herkimer's heroism, of the siege of Stanwix, of the Six Nations and Sir William Johnson and his Indian wife, Molly Brant, and the listener took it all in with thoughtful attentiveness. I described the campaign of John Sullivan. A bit apprehensively I dug deep into the destruction of the Indian villages and crops, but I should have known she was a hundred percent: Not once did she bring up defoliation or pillage and looting or: Whose land was this *anyway*? As we skimmed north of Syracuse, to my surprised delight I noticed that the thick coils of the black stuff had lifted, that indeed, now that I thought of it, not one strand had enveloped me since picking her up this morning. In fact, since our first date it hadn't really entered my consciousness except to be brushed impatiently away. It occurred to me that not only was she a splendid listener, she was good luck. I leaned over and kissed her and said, that's for nothing. She reached up and kissed me back on my close-fitting ear.

Syracuse touched off Marty Glickman: The relay team. Berlin. Marty and Sam Stoller. Their purge to appease Hitler. The disgrace of the '36 Olympics. She said loud enough for all domestic Chamberlains to hear: "That's *terrible*." Nothing more. Nothing more was needed. I smiled into the rearview mirror at the approving Manny, the surprised Shimon, the thoroughly remorseful Naomi. I reminded Carla that it pays *never to forget* ... I drove on contentedly and she asked if I had been a runner in college. I told her quite truthfully that I ran a respectable hundred, that Emil von Elling had let me run in some dual meet 880 relays, and that was it. I'll *bet*, she said ...

I headed west and introduced her to the most important college runner since Glickman, a Kansan named Jim Ryun, with a *u*. She had, of course, never heard of him, so I proceeded to trace his phenomenal exploits since his high school years, including his world records, and explained how all of this would reach a stunning climax in just two short days. At which time Ryun would win the Olympic mile, the only American in sixty years to accomplish that; and since he was a knowledgeable, studious young man, he would know he'd be avenging Marty Glickman; and somewhere, somehow, Schicklgruber and various masters of appeasement would also know it.

She absorbed it, quietly, completely. When I finished she said, "I guess you'd really like to be in Mexico City right now?"

I looked down at that face.

"Baby, Ryun can handle it perfectly, I don't want to be anywhere else in this world but here."

She snuggled.

3

The Falls are awesome, dramatic, and breathtaking. It is here that the Niagara River drops 200 feet in a single plunge—a stunning spill of 30 million gallons of water each minute over a series of ragged crests. There are three falls at which to marvel— the American Falls, 182 feet high and 1,075 feet wide; the Canadian Horseshoe Falls, 176 feet high and 2,100 feet wide; and on the American side, the somewhat smaller Bridal Veil Falls. The Falls deserve several days of your time. View them from above, below and both sides, in the daytime and lit up at night ...

At six o'clock we stared at the American Falls.

"I can hardly believe it," she said. "They're almost unreal."

"They're real all right."

"Well, I can still hardly believe it."

I stroked the back of her head and looked across the river. I took a deep breath of spray and said, "Do you want to stay on the American or Canadian side?"

"Is there a difference?" she said.

"Well—" another breath—"the Canadian side is supposed to give you a very spectacular view."

"This view is spectacular. Which side do you prefer?"

"I rather like the American side."

"That's fine with me," she said.

I squeezed her.

"I'll take you on a boat right into the Canadian Falls," I said. "They're really no big deal."

We checked into the Cascade Motel (which was a challenge from another life and still had to be conquered) and she leaned against me as I asked for a double bed and registered as Mr. and Mrs. S. Finestone. We walked into a blue and yellow room with prints of the Falls over the bed. Fingering my Captain's bars, I insisted she take the two upper drawers. She said I was sweet, that Linc had never even *asked*, and carefully patted wisps of this and that into each drawer, carefully shook out the cream-white dress, plus a new black one, carefully hung them up. I unpacked, tucked cummings into the drawer of the night table. We shaped up quickly and by the cataracts' mighty roar went out to dinner.

I bought a bottle of iced New York State Champagne and when we returned to the motel demonstrated how it should be opened without spilling one drop or denting the ceiling. I apologized for the plastic glasses, poured. She had drunk champagne cocktails before, but never absolutely straight champagne; her mouth puckered, her nose twitched, but all in all it was really quite pleasant. Then we finished the bottle; that is, *I* did. Then, even though I had promised myself to go slow, I leaned over and kissed her and tasted the champagne on the reflexively lapping tongue.

"Shouldn't you pull the blinds?" she said, her eyes a bit out of focus. I pulled the blinds down fast. Reaching into my pocket for a final stroke of my security tracks, I proceeded to unbutton the prim blouse. She regarded me gravely with the slightly unfocused eyes and said, "Let's get on the bed." I rose, took her hands and led her across the room, her head on my shoulder. I kissed her oh so gently and carefully arranged her on the bed. The huge, solemn pupils gazed up at me.

"Don't worry," I said, "I never take advantage of tipsy women."

"I'm not tipsy," she said, "and I'm not worried."

She closed her eyes, I said to myself, OK *Schmuckola,* and went into the undressing ritual, piece by sparkling piece, growing a half inch with each one. When I had finished and she was stretched out, gleaming beneath me, she opened her eyes and said, "Happy Niagara Falls."

"Happy Niagara Falls to you," I said. I leaned over her and began my kissing routine, the one that made her gasp and permitted Speed to work into Manny's old dreams. As I was about to cross over the line, I stopped, reamed myself out—again—and drew the coverlet across her up to her neck. Her breathing smoothed out and when we were both quiet she said, "That was sweet."

I raised up; some sweet; she sighed and touched the straining bulge.

"It isn't fair," she said, frowning. It sure as hell wasn't, but the Captain had better reject that if it meant what I thought it meant.

Tonight simply must *not* be the night. Besides, Linc was still in the room . . .

"I knew what I was doing. I'm a big boy," I said.

"But big boys have needs," she said. "Speed . . . if you want . . ."

I drew her hand away and said, "Yes, I want, but the right way. Someday it *will* be . . ." She reached up and touched my face and said precisely what I wanted (and half expected) to hear:

"I never knew anyone like you."

"Lucky girl," I grinned, looking down.

"Don't joke about that," she said.

"All right." I kissed the tilted nose. "Big girls have needs, too," I said.

The smile was now focused and oh so wistful.

"Don't tell that to Linc . . ."

There he was. I was suddenly furious with the goldbricking S.O.B. Not only had he had her, but clearly it had been wham, bam, thank you, ma'am. *Schmuck* of an enlisted man knew more about his own radio set than about the female body. I looked at that map of needs and desires and I was furious. But then I cooled down; after all, the Captain had had a bit of experience, had studied and understood what made all those glands, hormones, interconnecting nerves tick; what could a sad sack know? I smiled down tenderly and gently peeled the coverlet away. Then the knowledgeable fingers moved expertly, specifically to meet the needs of big girls. It took three and a half minutes, but by then she was jittering and twanging beneath me like a finely-tuned guitar (and Speed gave himself an A in physiology). In the end she burst into tears. I gazed down at my handiwork, stroked her hair, let the moment sink in. When she finally stopped sobbing she reached up and pulled me down beside her and whispered into my neat, glistening ear: "I never knew it could be like that."

I buried my head in the pillow. I arched up my behind because the Sealy Posturepedic was murder on my erection. I thought: OHGod, I must not laugh, not *now* . . . Then I felt myself getting a little pissed off; for she had gotten it all wrong: Oh, she had the line right from *Eternity*, but the interrelationships were ass-backwards; Lancaster, the operator she had said it to down in the surf, was an *enlisted* man, and the patsy, the guy they were putting the horns on, was an *officer*. A *schmuck* of an officer. I was pissed off all right, for in real life *Captain Speed* was doing it to the *schmuck* of a PFC. Wrong, wrong, wrong ... Then came the other line—the big line—and although it was half-anticipated, the way she said it, as often happened, turned the anger on myself: "Speed, I really love you."

I turned on my side, looked into the eyes that were now clear and calm.

The hell with Lancaster and Kerr and who did what to whom. "I love you, too," I said.

She took my hand. "Do it again."

As she breathed quietly beside me, I read *him* by cummings until two in the morning.

We had breakfast in the shadow of the Shredded Wheat plant and I told her about studying the Falls on the box all my years in the Bronx. She wished she had known me then; I must have been a darling little boy. Manny purred, leered, cavorted under the table until I kicked him into silence. Then we drove to the huge parking lot and got into line for the *Maid of the Mist*.

I made a pest of myself by rejecting three slickers until I found one dry enough to protect her. I buttoned it all the way up and told her to be sure and use the hood when the spray hit the boat. She complained that it would ruin her hair but if you say so: I said so. We stood in the bow and sailed past our American Falls—which we both waved at—and then into the big, bad Canadian ones. The little *Maid* bucked and heaved and moaned and I held Maureen tightly and braced hard against the foreign waves, and she screamed and laughed and we both faced everything Canada threw at us until the Captain finally had enough, circled around and headed back. As we walked off and turned in our slickers, she told the boy that it had been extremely enjoyable.

We browsed through the souvenir shops. I bought us each a tee shirt with the American Falls spilling over the left nipple. She picked out a paperweight of the *Maid* sailing into a rainbow, a hat that said "I've Been to the Falls" around the brim, and a driftwood tray that had both Falls plus the Bridal Veil done up in reds, blues and yellows. She wanted to pay at least half, but I said she was out with a rich American author. She said, maybe *some*day; anyway, I'm buying lunch. We settled for her leaving the tip.

Later I asked her if she'd like to see the Canadian side.

"If you like."

I said, "Sure, why not?"

I drove across the bridge to the Skylon Tower. We rode to the top and while I fought off my dizziness, she pranced delightedly around the enclosed circle, gushing over both Falls, pointing to the bouncing *Maid*, the Shredded Wheat Plant, our motel. Then we descended, I got my legs back, and we walked to the lip of the Canadian Falls.

Magnificent, sensational, spectacular, and at five P.M., rainbowed. We gaped in silence. But then, as we walked back to the car, she said, "They're certainly something, but the American Falls are cuter." Wincing, I hugged her.

We had dinner on the American side and I ordered a half bottle of New York State Chablis and said if she were going to be my girl, she'd have to learn to drink wine. She dutifully tasted, wrinkled her nose. I told her not to worry, she'd get used to it. Sipping slowly, I then reviewed the Revolutionary history of the Niagara region. I was, of course, stalling; all day, at both Falls, the motel had lain in my gut like bad Spanish-American War beef and I was postponing it as long as strategically possible. I had pushed it aside, but it had returned, was returning still through my story of Fort Niagara and its three flags. At one point, I had the certain feeling that she could see through my strategem, that any minute she would reach over and say, "Poor darling, we're just prisoners of love."

I managed to shake that off, but could not draw dinner out much beyond two hours. It had to be faced anyway. I paid and we drove back. We walked in and she turned on the TV, then disappeared into the bathroom. I looked at the postcard colors of the set. Early technicolor; I half expected to see *Becky Sharp*. It was *Gunsmoke*. I looked at Jim Arness. She came back and said could we watch something else? she didn't like westerns. I said sure, and she found, of all things, *The Glass Key*. She fixed up our chairs, reached for my hand (which I willingly gave, for it meant a two-hour reprieve), drilled her eyes into the set. She moved only during commercials, squeezing my hand, touching her hair. When it was over, she stared at the afterimage for another twenty seconds, sighed and got up. She stood in front of me, leaned in while I pulled myself together for the rest of the evening, and brushed my hair back behind my ears.

"Did you like it?" she said.

"I saw it years ago. It holds up pretty well."

"I loved Alan Ladd when he looked like that. Before he got a double chin."

I stretched my head back, firming my chin line.

"Ladd and Lake were a perfect team," I said. "Perfect miniatures."

"Did you like Veronica Lake?"

I took her hips, my hands moved; it was starting.

"I like girls who are fully packed," I said. "Miss Lake was a stringbean."

She tapped my interesting profile, the one Manny thought was such a horror.

"Oh gee," she said. "I forgot . . . Now, you sit right there and don't go way . . ." And before I could promise, she bounced out of the room and into the bathroom. I sat back and watched a wise-

266

guyish Johnny Carson with a blue face. I got up and turned his voice down; he seemed to be getting a bit too personal . . .

"What do you think?"

She was standing under the ventilator in a black, see-through, shortie nightgown with lacy red roses over the nipples. I was astonished. It was a complete and total lapse of the good taste she had always shown. Except for the McQueen tee shirt, everything had had quiet understatement, even her underclothes. Her pajamas the night before had been cool and neat and pink. Now this—which, clearly, she had bought for the trip—she stood there with one knee in and the foot turned out like the teenagers I had once seen trying to be Queen of Loew's Paradise. Like them she was blushing.

"You are a sexy lady," I said.

She took two beauty-contest steps, placed hands on hips.

"Can you resist me?" she said.

A moment, two . . . I said, "I'll have to, won't I?"

She was standing before me, brushing back my hair.

"I'm so sorry, Speed . . . I never want to be a tease . . ."

"It's all right, Maureen . . ."

"No, it's not."

She reached down, took both my hands and tugged. I rose; she led me to the bed. She lay back, and placed my hands on the roses. My fingers didn't move. I sat there and looked down. The nightgown slid up to her hips, revealing black bikini panties with a rose over the crotch.

"Speed, I said I was sorry."

"And I said it was all right."

"Show me it's all right."

She guided my hand down. I let her. Here it was . . . I drew my hand away and dropped it on my lap. She looked up, then nodded.

"You're perfectly right," she said. "I'm selfish."

"It's not that . . ." I looked at the ceiling.

"No, I'm a tease, I want it all *my* way . . . Speed . . . Speed, please look at me . . . Speed . . . I *want* you to . . ."

"Maureen, please . . ." I wanted to laugh, cry, laugh . . .

"No, I do. Listen. The Falls are just too powerful."

"Maureen, please stop—"

"I thought I could hold out against that power, but I can't. So it's not fair to make *you* hold out . . ."

"Linc . . ."

"Hush, forget Linc. He wouldn't understand any of this. Not you, not me." She touched me and smiled. "Take off your clothes," she said. "I hate buckles."

I looked down. She was right there, *it* was right there. Manny's dream of dreams. Hell, *Speed's* dream of dreams. I stood and actually began to unbuckle, to unzip. All right, pure and noble Speed had gone as far as he could and now he was off the hook . . . Ah . . . What ah? That was just it: the end of pure, noble Speed. Finito for the officer and gentleman; oh, it would be the greatest fuck in the history of Niagara Falls and she would come umpteen times, but in the end that's all it would be, great hump, sensational come. Ah . . . Again ah? Yes, WHAT THEN? The point exact: After we left the Falls and checked into the next motel, and the next, WHAT THEN? What? Another shack up, that's what; she'd look at me, I'd look at her, she'd look again and *pure, noble I-never-knew-anyone-like-you Speed would be shot to hell* . . . Her eyes were closed, her fingers rested near the magic triangle, one knee was drawn up. *What then?*

I walked outside, zipping up.

I walked to the Falls. I let them engulf me, let them shut out every other sound and sight and sensation. For ten minutes, fifteen, a half hour . . . I don't know. I do know that with terrible slowness something began to pierce the roar and to reach out to me. Something that was made up of bits and edges, and this something tiptoed up to me, touched, then ran, returned and ran again, but each time stayed longer, each time joined one piece to another piece. Until, ever so slowly, with the Falls rumbling away, the pieces remained and were joined, and the pieces changed to words, *sincere* words that even *I* could understand. I was weak and giddy and wet from the spume by the time it was all positioned and locked into place, but for the first time since the idea of this trip had struck, I felt *legitimately* pure (because my purity then was so different from all recent purity). I played it straight, however, waited for all the arguments to take over, even called up the absentee black book: But, and yes, and but, and no, and but, and but, and but and but . . . In the end, I spiked every goddam gun.

I walked back inside.

She was sitting cross-legged on the bed, the horrible night-gown barely down to her hips. She was staring at a sotto voce Johnny Carson. She didn't look at me. I kneeled beside the bed and took her hand. Slowly she turned, as if on a sandpapered axis. I don't think she had been crying, but her mouth was as thin as I'd ever seen it.

"Maureen. Listen to me. It's simple. So simple I couldn't even see it."

"What is?" she said tonelessly.

"Us. And Jim Ryun."

"What about Jim Ryun?"

"He's running in the Olympic finals tomorrow. *Tomorrow.* He's running for *America.*"

"So? I know that."

"Maureen . . . He's running for *us.*"

"I thought he was running for Marty Glickman."

"That's just to get even. The *constructive* thing, the *main* thing is, he's running for us."

". . . What do you mean, us?"

"That's just what I mean, us, you and me, *us.*"

"How?"

"It's simple. God, I've been so stupid . . . We haven't won the mile in sixty years, remember I told you that? Well, Ryun will win tomorrow and release us from our vow. It'll be all right then."

She stirred.

"I don't . . . understand . . ."

I started to pace. How *could* she understand? It was bound too tightly to Manny and Speed, but there was something in the equation that she *could* understand; the Falls and I had worked it

269

out. I stopped pacing and looked down at her, at the strategic roses.

"Maureen, Marilyn Monroe was here."

"I know that. She made *Niagara* here."

"That's right. Well, she's still here . . ."

"Speed? . . ."

"She is out there now, out over the Falls, I know it, like I know we're in this motel. Maureen, Marilyn reached out to me. To *us*. She told me that when Jim Ryun wins for America, we'll be free. We can then—" I took a deep breath—"consummate our love."

She sat up straight.

"Speed!"

"Maureen, she *was* out there; with the lights on, it was as if her face were on a technicolor cinemascope screen." (Naomi always said I could talk; I was talking for dear life now, except it wasn't *all* feces for the birds; something *had* happened out there). I think Maureen actually shivered. The torrent kept pouring out of me: "Maureen. Baby. He will win for America, therefore for *us*; he will set us free, we'll have *earned* it after all these losing years. And she will *bless* what we will do." She swung her legs over the side of the bed and stood up, head tilted back, as it had been when we first met. I grasped her shoulders. "Who was she married to?" I said quietly.

"Joe DiMaggio."

"Athlete. Ryun: great athlete. Dimag: great athlete. Who else?"

"Who else is a great athlete?"

"Who else was she *married* to?"

"There was a man who seemed nice enough, but it didn't last. They were both young and very immature."

"When she was *mature*. Who did she marry when she was *mature*?"

"Arthur Miller. But I think she always loved Joe—"

"Miller. Right. Maureen, Arthur Miller is a very sensitive man, you have to be to write plays. Maureen, Jim *Ryun* is a very *sensitive* man."

270

"I always felt Joe DiMaggio was a very sensitive man."

"He *is*. You're confirming the point. *Double sensitivity.* Maureen, I'll tell you something: Marilyn Monroe could *love* a man like Jim Ryun . . ."

"Speed, do you really think so?"

"I'm *sure* of it. He's as pure as snow. Deep in her heart of hearts, she was—*is*—pure . . . Maureen . . ."

"Yes, Speed?"

"Something else. Arthur Miller and I are *both* writers." I sat down on the bed, exhausted. I managed, "It's all connected. Marilyn, Joe, Miller, Jim Ryun, you, me . . . The race that will set us free, without a . . . taint . . ."

She sat beside me, put her arms around me, kissed me.

"I want to write to Linc," she said. "Tell him it's over."

". . . Hold it, Baby. Not yet. Not on motel stationery."

"Yes, on motel stationery. From the *American Falls*. From Jim Ryun's Falls. From Marilyn Monroe's Falls. From Joe DiMaggio's Falls . . . But all right, I'll wait till the victory is sealed. We'll watch it being sealed. So will *she* . . . Speed, do you realize what's happened? You've proven to be *stronger than Niagara Falls*."

"Let's just say," I smiled crookedly, feeling my strength seep back, "I'm at least even."

Johnny Carson gave me his sly-foxy grin.

At three A.M. I was still sending some of my Niagara Falls power down to Jim Ryun.

I got up very early and in my new Keds ran from the Falls to the Shredded Wheat plant and back three times. I showered very quickly and got back into bed beside her. She was wearing her neat pink pajamas.

We put on yellow slickers and walked in a long line down the face of the cliff and stood almost beneath the Falls. When I shouted above the roar, "HOW DO YOU LIKE IT?" she shouted back, "ARE YOU KIDDING?" The line snaked back topside and, looking down, still in our slickers, she said, "I'll never forget them."

I turned on the TV in the afternoon, fiddled with the color and pulled in a sunshiny picture from Mexico City. I remembered Carla's "Good luck in Mex. City," tossed it aside and we settled down in front of the set, champagne cooling in a styrofoam bucket of ice. I pointed out the importance of the warm-up, recollecting that as Glenn Cunningham prepared, he practically ran another race each night. I showed her our man, stretching, bending, loping in tall, inner-directed splendor. She squeezed my moist hand. Dutifully, I pointed out Kip Keino, definitely world class, but without the all-important finishing kick. My Captain's bars and a fresh box of Trojans were nestling in a drawer of the night table beside the bed . . .
The race.
It began quietly and we locked fingers. Jipcho, a *landsman* of Keino, bolted to the front and led the pack around the first lap, around the second lap. Then Keino shot past the rabbit and the

pack split into two smaller packs. Keino led one, pulling it along with an airy rope; Ryun and another rope pulled the second pack. I told her to take it easy, this was necessary strategy for Keino as he must try to draw the poison out of Ryun's final sting. But don't worry, Ryun is not only good, he's smart. She murmured thank goodness, for he was far back, well into the third lap. His head was bobbing, as usual, and the sensitive face was more detached than ever. I explained that this was his style. You cannot argue with results. Relax. She said, oh sure, relax . . .

Keino maintained his huge and precise lead—a good forty yards—and I was now unclasped and patting her thigh with a moist hand. Finally, finally, as they spun into the last lap, Ryun came to life. He seemed visibly to shake himself. I squeezed her knee, suggested she keep watching. He worked his way smoothly and easily through his subpack, attacked the first one. With confident ease he picked off each obstacle in his path, as I knew he would. I gently removed my hand and skimmed along with him. So did Cunningham, Bonthron, Archie San Romano and Peerless Mel Sheppard from 1908. So did Glickman. So did Manny. So did America. I stood as he stretched out, and I stretched out with him. The announcer, the crowd, were screaming, but we were in a gently smiling world of our own. The thin Mexico City air which was supposed to be murder didn't mean a thing. We were in front of the first struggling pack now and reaching for Keino. Keino was moving well, but was in range. We began to pull on the rope between us and excruciatingly, inexorably we moved forward. We came off the last turn, the one that always gave us such incredible acceleration. We accelerated. I ventilated deeply, kneeled down before the set. Thirty yards. Twenty-five. Keino was tough, mountain-bred tough, I gave him that. But so were sensitive American kids when the chips were down. In Normandy, Bastogne or Mexico City. I was pounding the paper-thin air now as we lifted and poured it on. Suddenly, behind me, I heard, *"Speed, the other one is winning!"* I glanced over my shoulder and gave her my smile of reassurance. Her cheeks were pink, her hair damp, her eyes huge; the first knuckle of her index finger was in her mouth. I winked and turned back. I picked up the action. Fifteen yards to go and Ryun was twenty yards back. I heard the scream taking off my head and I couldn't breathe and the track rose up to smash me in the face.

I knew with the utmost clarity that the next week existed, that it was filling up space and time on a stretched-out minute by minute basis and that incredibly important things were happening in those self-contained pockets of action. From here, however, that week was not a true part of my life as in the main I recognize that life. Unless in some split-off way, it was the truest, the most *honest* part I have ever lived; in that case, had it continued, I doubt that I'd be here to write about it ... But suppose I just settle for trying to pin that week to the board? Let it do its own struggling ...

In a spasm of northern-light clarity, I remember that Maureen packed us up and paid the bill at the Cascade. Next we were in the car and she was driving and telling me how cool and clear the air was up here and how lovely the sky. I remember agreeing; somehow I knew I must be very easy to get along with or something terrible would happen; I *knew* that with every minute I achieved. Then I remember our pulling into an area she called Fort Niagara. Then we were walking through the fort and she was asking me how the fort had protected us from the French. I said, "I'm not really sure." Then before I could stop myself, I was saying, "But I'll tell you one thing: I was scared shitless all the way down to Fort Benning."

"Were you?" she said with a smile.

That smile annoyed me, but I said, "Yes, like a lot of others. But I made it because it was unthinkable not to."

"Of course it was unthinkable."

I still wanted to be easy to live with, I truly did, but the next words came jumping out: "How would *you* know?"

She stopped smiling.

I then said, even as I tried to apply the brakes, "They cut off my hair and I was an ugly, plucked chicken and I shit green on the infiltration course and I pulled nothing but my pudding on a twenty-four-hour pass, so ... how ... would ... you ... know?"

"I know it was rough," she said quietly.

"Rough?" And I tried to zip the lip that was probably sinking the ship but I couldn't. "That's *wrong*, all *wrong* ... oh shit."

That cleaned me out for the moment and I was able to clam up. Now we were back in the car, she was behind the wheel, we were driving through the pleasant afternoon, we were surrounded by crystal airiness. Suddenly she was saying, "This is Lockport, Speed. It's very historic."

"Was history ever made at night?" I asked grumpily.

"I'm sure it was."

"Oh shit."

"Lockport is on the Erie Canal, Speed."

I looked at the eager, up-tilted face and I wondered whatthehell was I doing in a car with a chubby little mick, but I decided not to give her a chance to explain. I shrugged and said coldly, "Don't call me Speed."

She said nothing. Neither did I. She drove through Lockport and checked us into a motel with a swimming pool and she unpacked while I watched. I consented to join her for roast beef sandwiches in the mall across the highway. When we returned to the motel she asked if I'd like to take a swim. I said, sure, why not? We changed and she wore, I remember in another slashing spasm, a black bikini which exposed two little half moons below her ass; those little crescents were terribly irritating, but this time I was able to keep quiet because it was getting late and it occurred to me that if I was too wise, she'd throw me out and I must inevitably drown in the Erie Canal. As I obediently followed the stretching-contracting half moons out to the pool, I could

275

practically taste the dark brackish water, see the staring eyes of all the immigrant workers who had also drowned there.

I'm a competent swimmer but the best I could manage that afternoon was a pathetic dog paddle behind her: the runty duckling behind mama duck. We swam around for an hour—her smooth stroke, my pathetic paddle. Then she climbed out. So did I. We stretched out on webbed chairs to catch the late afternoon sun. In another jagged streak of clarity, I see myself looking at the sky, saying, "My brother Samuel once took me out into the deep water at Orchard Beach to teach me how to swim. I screamed like a banshee. My father rushed out and grabbed me and then he slapped Samuel's face this way and that so it looked like a rag doll . . . I kept sobbing, "It serves him right!"

She said, "It's very scary for a child to find himself out in deep water; that theory is not very good in practice."

I wanted with all my strength to ask whatehell she knew about theory and practice? Hadn't she ever heard about homeostasis, the wisdom of the body? But it was getting late and I would soon need her to face the night. I reined in, said, "Maybe." But I just couldn't settle for that; I added, *had* to add: "I learned one thing that day. I learned that I had shit in my blood."

". . . Don't say that—"

"Why not? It's true."

She was silent. Then: "You're too hard on yourself, Speed."

This time, night or no night, I couldn't stop. "Balls," I said. "Stop getting me off the hook. And I told you, don't call me Speed. My proper name is Emanuel Finestone. N.M.I. No middle initial. My father said, when I asked for a middle name, 'Shamusonhorseback, how's that?' "

She didn't ask me what that meant. She said, "My middle name is Agatha. I hate it . . ."

"Well," I said, still unable to apply the brakes, "Meet Manny. Manny. Go ahead, say it."

"Manny."

"Shitintheblood-Manny. Well?"

"A rose by any other name would smell just as sweetly."

I burst into tears.

276

2

Next morning. Looking down into the lock of the Erie Canal. I knew perfectly well she expected me to launch into a detailed history of the area. Clinton's Ditch. Shiny bridge to the west. The mick and guinea workers. I *could* have made it fascinating. But I had lived through the night and the morning sun was filling me with arrogant power. I said, "I had this friend named Sheldon Pincus. One day he moved to Brooklyn near the Gowanus Canal. He drowned in the Gowanus Canal. How's that for history?"

We move on. To the next town. And the next. Maureen does all the work. Finds the motel, registers, requests the double bed, lugs in the suitcases, unpacks. Finally, doesn't even unpack. Sometimes we stay less than one night; once we do three motels in twelve hours. I look around, tug at her dress: "I don't like it here, let's go." We go . . .

I had to keep going, had to . . . If I didn't, I'd float away, evaporate. The rush across Europe? Combined with the '46-'47 horrors? The ultimate synergistic outhouse? It's possible. Maybe yes, maybe no. I know only that this time had a life of its own. A thrusting, pushing life. Move. Pause. Move. No plan. No point. Not on my part, anyway. As for her, all I can now figure out is that she wanted to work our way east and check in close to a mall. I didn't worry about it one way or the other. I didn't worry about anything except whether I'd be alive for the next ten minutes. Miraculously I would be. And the longer I lived, the more I associated my survival with Maureen. Especially, as noted, at night. I'd slide under the covers, burrow up; she'd cuddle me and we'd watch TV until I would drift off. If I awoke because I had to go to the john, I'd suffer rather than leave the bed. The amazing thing about that time was that not *once* did I have any of my rotten dreams. I would get brave with the ascending curve of the sun. By early afternoon I was full of beans. King of the Northwest Frontier. Sir Speed Finestone.

I give you Big Speed in Canandaigua. Roseland Amusement Park. Insists on riding the roller coaster. Mama says he shouldn't, they even made her father sick and he had a stomach of iron.

277

Don't you think I can do it? Of course you can, but it makes no sense. *That is the best kind of sense.* He rides the roller coaster. He pukes all over fellow passengers. She had warned him. He is furious, yells:

"Sure, Manny can't ride the goddam whip at Playland without coughing up his cookies. Can't drive out to Long Island on Sunday without heaving all over the brand-new seat covers. Can't make it through basic, can't make it overseas. Can't hit the fucking beach. Can't make it through the E.T.O. . . .

"I got news for you. HEAR THIS: *I made it!*"

Suddenly he is heaving again. She holds his head until he is finished. People are looking. Never mind, she says. He winds up leaning against a rock looking out at Lake Canandaigua.

"I'm awfully tired," he says.

"It's no wonder."

He looks far out. "In the Bulge," he says, "There was this hole gouged out by a Panzerfaust. That's a German shoulder cannon. I was in that hole for thirteen hours with a dead Nazi. I know he was dead because his left eye was a hole in his head, but I stared at him for thirteen hours with my carbine pointed at that eye-hole . . ."

"No wonder you get nervous sometimes," she says.

He turns and looks at her.

"Please don't give me any Freudian horseshit. I don't want it. Please. I should have blown his fucking head off and I didn't. Don't tell me how humane I was compared to them. Don't tell me he would have done it to me. I should have blown his fucking head off. Even with the hole in the eye."

She holds his hand tightly.

The next town. Nestled against green hills that curved away into the hazy distance.

She said, "Believe it or not, this is Naples."

"As in Italy," I asked.

"Yes," she said, "I don't want to remind you of the war too much, but I've heard Naples is a lovely city. I thought maybe you were there."

278

The sun was high so I was hard and tough and brave. "Didn't you study World War Two in high school?"

"Yes . . ."

"If I was in France and Germany, as you well know, how could I have been in Italy?"

"Well—"

"These were *two . . . separate . . . theaters.* I was with the *First* Army. Italy was the *Fifth* Army. The Fifth Army had a terrible time making it in Italy. Once we broke out, we *breezed.*"

"Oh."

"Of course it's all ancient history . . ." And I was off and running. The foul-ups at Salerno and Anzio. The perfection of Normandy. Clark the journeyman; Eisenhower the *winner*. The symbolic difference between Rome and Paris. At that moment she got up and walked out of the motel. I sat stark still, then leaped up and ran down the road after her yelling, this was perfectly fine, the real Naples couldn't hold a candle to it!

One sunny morning I found myself in a town called Hammondsport in the Glenn Curtiss Museum. (She knew how much I liked museums.) After a calm half hour of studying Jennies and Curtiss-Wright engines, I saw a photograph and yelled. Several people headed for the exits. She came running, gasping, "What in the world is it?"

I pointed at the picture. The face with the stern mustache stared back at me.

"What's my father doing here?"

"That's Glenn Curtiss, the famous aviator."

"That's my father. I know my *father*."

"Speed . . . Manny. Look at the name under the picture."

I wiped my eyes and looked. I studied the name on the brass plate for a long minute.

"It says . . . Glenn Curtiss . . ."

"I told you."

"Jesus . . ."

"I told you," she said.

"But, he always *looked* at me like that . . ."

279

"Maybe he looked into the future like Mr. Curtiss."

"Yes. The future. He took me to see *Things to Come*. He spit on the floor of the Paradise and dragged me out ... The future ..."

"Come on, Speed . . . Manny. Let's look at the downstairs exhibit."

We walked to the door. I stopped and asked for one last look. She sighed and said all right, one. I held onto her hand as we walked back to the stern mustache.

"A mick?" said Glenn Curtiss. "I got no complaints as long as she's good to you. *But don't sign any papers.*"

Bath. Painted Post. Corning. Horseheads. Elmira.

In Elmira she said, "I have a surprise for you. Mark Twain's grave."

I shrugged my annoyance and said come on, that's in Missouri. She informed me that I didn't know *every*thing, that his wife came from Elmira, trust me. So, half-trusting and scowling all the way, I let her drive me out to a cemetery. We drove up to a huge, even expanse of white crosses, dappled here and there by a Star of David.

"What the hell is going on?" I muttered.

"They told me this was the cemetery . . ."

I looked, scowled. It was still early afternoon; I was still brave.

"You know what this is? This is a *national cemetery*. This is where GIs are buried. Why did you drive in here?"

"I was looking for Mark Twain's—"

"I *told* you, look in Missouri. Come on, why here? Are you telling me these guys did more than *I* did?"

"Of course not . . ."

"So Nazi lead didn't have my name on it. Do me something."

She didn't say a word. As I jawed away about various kinds of sacrifice, she backed out and drove around the outer rim of the cemetery. I told her it was her privilege to write to the War Department with my blessing and request a copy of my combat record. I asked what *her* father had done in the war except knock her mother up and produce a deferment—we came to Mark Twain's grave.

"You can drive back," she said, getting out.

I sat in the car for a long time. As the sun began to droop, I got out. I walked over and stood beside her as she looked down at the tablets.

"You can drive," I said.

"Thank you, can I?"

"Yes. Please drive."

"Will you behave?"

"Yes. Thank you for bringing me here. I always wanted to see Mark Twain's grave. It was a very pleasant surprise, finding it here in Elmira . . ."

I behaved up along Lake Cayuga, even though it reminded me of Cornell and the fact that Hannah was fighting me tooth and nail to go Ivy, someplace like Cornell. But I didn't say a word, merely sang Manny's version of the Cornell alma mater. But no smart stuff. Nothing that would bring on her, "All right, *you* drive." For I *couldn't.* Nor could I get on a bus, train or plane. So without her I was stranded. I needed her to save my life, resented her for saving it. She was America, I was France. I *hated* her for that. But the sun was low now . . .

Into Auburn where she thought a landmark called Seward House would be good for me. (Something like oatmeal?) That is where it happened again, only this time it was a *bust* of Shimon Finestone. I mentioned it quietly. She said it was William Seward, the man who bought Alaska.

"No, Maureen. It's Shimon Finestone. Look at that bugle. I'd know it anywhere." I pulled her closer. "You know why he's giving me the fish-eye?"

"Why?" she sighed.

"My sister Naomi. She's married to a Nazi and wants me to get him a job. Look, he *knows* . . ."

Instead of pulling me away or suggesting a cup of coffee, she said, "Tell me about Naomi."

"Why?"

"I'm interested."

"You got six months? All right . . . There was a girl with

281

everything. Brains, looks, even basically a good heart . . . Just one thing: she had hot pants for bums." I looked at her, she looked steadily back. I looked at Shimon's bust; he was glaring. I said quickly, "Step over there, so he won't hear me." We walked to a display case of Lincoln's letters to Seward. I whispered, "She *had* to marry him, I know for a fact. She put out for a Nazi, my gorgeous sister."

"Well, if she loved him . . ."

Then, as if that were the last word on the subject, she walked to the door, and stared out. I walked after her, worried that she'd pull another deal, leave me with a car that was as complicated as a spaceship. She was staring at a war memorial across the street. I suddenly got express-train mouth again.

"What kind of response is *that*?" I demanded.

She turned. "It's *my* response."

"Are you telling me that's all there is to it? Love, sweet love? That because she lu-u-uvs him I should now turn around and get him a job? The man who *knocked up my sister*?"

She looked at a point beyond my shoulder.

"Lower your voice," she snapped. "Your father will hear you."

3

We rushed east. Skaneatles. Cazenovia. Waterville . . . as the town fled past, I took a catnap, the kind of break I would take beside my jeep driver in the Rhineland. I had two of my dreams within dreams, but they weren't rotten, rather, kind of sad: First I was back on the North Atlantic and sea-green and empty from the retching and in *that* time dreaming, between heaves, that I was Drake, sick, old, demeaned, and on the last voyage, trying, with Frobisher, to recoup all, to climb back to the top. In that dream, I buckled on my armor for the last time, struggled up to the deck of the galleon, told the story of the Armada and Cadiz and all the glorious years to the listening wind. I awoke in '43

puking into my helmet, but I started to come around after that ...
Now in Waterville the dream shifted, to another one tucked into
itself. I was back on Tremont Avenue, and Ann Dvorak was
looking into my window from the taxpayer across the street
where Patricia Albertson lived above her father's hardware store.
Ann Dvorak, who looked amazingly like Patricia, had just been
told by Manny that he guessed he loved her. In the dream, which
Manny had ninety-seven times, she would say "Oh—" and he
would leap to fill in the blank after ruling out, Oh Manny. Thus:
Oh Biff, Oh Clip, Oh Dink, Oh Flip, Oh Hoot, Oh Jeff, Oh King,
Oh Lash, Oh Mack, Oh Nick, Oh Prince, Oh Quash, Oh Riff, Oh
Sock, Oh Topp, Oh Vic, Oh Whip, Oh Yank, Oh Zip! I awoke
with a crooked grin as she said, "Oh Speed!"

I saw sport shirts, shorts, short shorts, bellies, butts, beehives. I
turned to her smile.

"Cooperstown," she said. I must still have been on the North
Atlantic or Tremont Avenue. "James Fenimore Cooper," she
said. "*The Last of the Mohicans* ... the Baseball Hall of Fame." I
blinked, looked out at the touristy bustle, at miniature bats and
caps with real and ersatz names. I heard her say, "I thought I'd
surprise you. We can combine two of your passions, writing and
baseball; don't you think it looks interesting?" I let it register. I
wanted to say, what does a dumb little mick know about *my*
passions, but she looked so eager that I was able to hold down my
early afternoon annoyance. I nodded and told her Cooperstown
was a pretty good idea, but maybe with this crowd we'd better find
a motel. She smiled even wider (it occurs to me that this was the
first time I had thought about anything practical since leaving the
Falls, ergo the smile). It was Saturday. We tried seven motels, had
seven refusals. We settled at two o'clock for an upstairs room in
the Diamond Guest House, paying a Mrs. Hurlburt in advance a
rather tidy sum. The room was fairly cozy except that it had no
television set. I said, brusquely, we'll survive, and we walked the
three blocks to the Baseball Museum which she was positive I
wanted to see first. I shrugged and recited, "Jimmy Foxx of the
Boston Red Soxx can hit the ball a couple of bloxx." She said that

was cute and bought me a Yankees' cap which she set on my head with a slight tilt. I thanked her, paid, and we entered.

She remained beside me on each floor as I studied the pictures, the gloves, the bats, the tickets, the programs, the ghosted books. But she stood outside as I walked through the Hall of Fame room. I checked each tablet for the correctness of its facts, the aptness of its expression, then rejoined her. She asked if I wanted to see the Abbott and Costello movie downstairs. I said I knew who was on first, thanks, let's blow. She tucked a hand into my arm and we walked out into the sunshine. I asked her if she could describe a rounders contest in three words. Of course not, she said. "Rain, no game." Oh, she said, that's neat.

While she had been waiting, a guard had told her there were batting machines down the street beside the stadium where you could get any kind of curve ball thrown at you, would I like to try it? I considered, said not today, thank you. We continued through the students of the game who had never even heard of Cuddles Marshall.

"How did you like it?" she said.

"It was all right."

"Just all right?"

I looked at the eagerness.

"Do you really want to know?" I said.

"Of course."

"I mean *really*?"

"Yes, really."

I stopped.

"Why did you take me there?"

". . . I thought you'd like it . . ."

"Let me ask you a question. I root for the Yankees, right?"

"That's right, you told me . . ."

"Where are the Yankees?"

"In New York."

"In the standings. In the goddam *standings*."

"I don't know. They're the top team, aren't they?"

"Come on, Maureen. Don't play coy with me. They are down

284

the drain, up shitcreek, pay your money, take your choice, *they are dead*."

"... They are?"

"Uh-huh. You know that place we were just in? Well, the Yankees *dominate* that place. They have dominated, practically *created* the activity you refer to as my passion. And what do they get for that? Hatred, passionate hatred, that's what they get. Well, we are now shot to hell and everybody in that goddam building is coming in their pants. Did I like it? *Like* it? I ask *you*, lady: Are you rubbing salt into the goddam wound? Or are you asking me to face some kind of horseshit reality?"

Bellies and shorts were detouring around us.

"I just thought you'd like it," she said flatly.

"Oh? I'm ye olde masochist, is that it? Is that why you bought me the cute cap? If so, Miss Hall of Fame, learn about caps; they sit *straight* on your head." I swept the hat off and gave it to a passing ice cream cone.

"Speed," she said, "let's keep walking . . ."

"Sure."

I took her arm and it was very stiff. The express train was turning into old ninety-seven; Casey Jones roaring: "To use your sensational expression, it's really funny."

"What is?" she sighed.

"Oh sigh. I'll tell you, as if you didn't know. The Yankees dominate that place, as has been noted. But one Yankee will never appear there and we both know it."

"Joe DiMaggio?"

"Shit no, he's in. Roger Maris."

"I . . . never heard of him . . ."

"OK, I'll accept that. Know why he won't make it?"

"Why?"

"He's an asterisk."

She didn't ask what that meant and I didn't tell her. That was *my* business, not hers. We walked on. Somehow the asterisk had placated me and as we approached the guest house, I backed off and said, "At least you wanted to give me a little batting practice."

285

She looked at me warily, then said, "Yes, some physical exercise would have been nice; you could have worked off your mood hitting those curve pitches."

Oops. I stopped us.

"Fun? Curves, fun? Is that your idea of fun? Now batting cleanup for Murderers Row: Fabulous, Fat, Frantic, Foolish Finestone. Shit me easy, lady, you know as well as I do, *I could never hit the curve ball.*"

4

We took an hour to do Fenimore House. She wanted to meet in the bookstore, but I insisted on sticking together and as we walked through the house, I became the calm and witty docent. A change of scenery could do that during the incredible week. She flashed a look of surprise, then listened with her perfect attentiveness as I told her about Cooper's obsession with rent as well as Indians. That was fascinating and she didn't feel so bad about not being able to plow through *The Last of the Mohicans.* I told her (petit white lie) that I had only made it with the help of Classic Comics. She squeezed my arm and since it was getting late, I hung on to that squeeze.

At dinner, bellied up to a counter, I was quiet and behaved. She asked if I was thinking about Fenimore House. Yes, I said, it made me a little sad.

"Are you saying I shouldn't have taken you there?"

"No, I'm glad I went. It just made me sad."

"Because he had a hang-up on rent?"

"No. Because he had such a good daughter."

I then explained about Hannah. And me. Maybe I wasn't the perfect father, but I had *never* wavered in my devotion to her even when her mother was mucking about with producers and directors, and since I was the only father she had, one would think the attitude would be reciprocal—not that I expected her to give her life to her father's writing career as Susan Fenimore Cooper had—all I asked was that she keep an open mind on the boy I had carefully researched for marriage purposes, that's all I asked, but

all she could do was give me the modern rebellious horse manure
. . . I paused to gulp air . . . She said mildly, "Isn't that the old-
fashioned European system?" I said, so what? I had given it
modern American refinements. She considered that with
thoughtful eyes. Even if it was late, I was ready for *her* father. For
Eddie Hallahan pushing her toward Bruce Riordan. To which I
would respond triumphantly, "He couldn't have been any worse
than Linc O'Brien, could he?"

She said, "Let's see if we can find a movie."

5

We found, of all things, *Bullitt*. The theater was noisy and pop-
corned and McQueen leered at me behind her nipples on the
screen. I made it three-quarters through, then said, "I'm sorry, I
just can't sit anymore."

We walked outside and down to Otsego Lake, walked along the
shore, then walked back and past the mansions, away from the
bellies and the tee shirts, finally walked back to the guest house.

Ordinarily in those weeks we bathed together, but the tub was
half-sized, so she went first and I sat beside her and read Cooper's
Satanstoe, one of his antirent screams. Then she bathed me and
we went to bed. Without TV, she tried *The Spy*, which I
guaranteed would put her to sleep. I was right. I snuggled up.

At first I thought the television was still on. Then I
remembered that there was no television. I rolled over, reached; I
couldn't feel her. I looked around. A star-filled night held the
room with a light glow. Against the far wall an ancient winged
chair loomed in the pale brightness. The sounds were coming
from deep within the chair. They sounded like a child crying. I sat
up, shook my head. I saw something pressed against the wings of
the chair. I whipped across the room and knelt beside her. She
was wrapped in my jacket, knees drawn up, snuffling softly.

"Are you sick? Is it your rib cage? Do you have any referred
pain?"

She shook her head.

"Your stomach?"

"No," she whispered.

"Did you have a bad dream?"

"No . . ."

"What then?"

She shook her head. I took her hand; it was icy; I rubbed it. She stopped snuffling, began to breathe in tight little gasps.

"*Tell* me," I pleaded. "Don't hold it in."

She burst into gasping, convulsive sobs. I thought I must run downstairs for help; I looked at her; I couldn't leave her like this. I got up, sat on an arm of the chair, bent over, stroked her hair, murmured over and over, "It's OK, it's OK, go ahead, ventilate . . ." Each time I said it she would gasp and sob, then breathe, but each time she grew a bit more quiet, until only her chest was heaving. I stroked her hair and asked if she'd like to hear the history of Otsego Lake. She shook her head and I kept my mouth shut. We sat like that for an eternity, Maureen breathing deeply while I silently stroked her hair. Then she broke the rhythm with a sigh that frightened me; it was so deep and sad. I thought that she was going to start sobbing again and I stroked her face and said, inanely, "It's all right . . ." But she didn't cry; she shook her head and said, "I tried . . . God, I tried . . ." And breathed that sigh again. I took my hand away, but kept quiet. I heard, and it cut into my heart, "I thought it would be . . . good . . . for you . . ."

I suddenly felt the old Manny-hate for myself. "Ah Baby, it *was* good for me . . . it *was* . . . I screwed it up."

She shook her head. "No . . . It was all stupid . . ."

I punched my thigh. "That's not true," I said. I punched it again. "Maureen . . . Baby . . . I fuck up everything I touch. I always have. *Every*thing. Now *you.*"

"No, *I* ruined it . . . I was an idiot . . ."

"Maureen. Please listen. You did all the right things." I knelt down in front of her again and, miraculously, I wasn't feeling dizzy or light-headed; I was focused for the first time in ages; it was as if I had just dived into Otsego Lake and been revived by the icy water, had come up stroking powerfully. There was absolutely no con, no twist in what I then said that would evoke her pity: "It was *me*. Everything I come in contact with, I contaminate."

"Nooooo," she wailed, "I won't *listen* to that . . ."

"All right," I said, "but it's true."

She shook her head violently and covered her ears. I thought I was going to cry and the thought for some incredible reason made me feel terribly strong, again for the first time in ages. I stood up and reached down, removed her hands from her ears. She looked up, then held her arms out to me. I bent over and picked her up, walked to the bed and sat down with the sighing bundle in my lap. I stroked her hair, her face, kissed her eyes until her stiff back began to relax. We sat quietly until I heard against my ear, "I hate this place."

"Don't say that, Maureen. I told you, *I* screwed it up."

"No, I mean . . . this guest house."

I raised her head off my shoulder.

"Do you want a motel?"

"Yes . . ."

"With a TV?" I smiled.

"Yes . . ."

"We're getting out of here," I said. "Let's pack."

"It's two in the morning."

"Come on. Let's move."

I drove for half an hour and was given incredulous stares at three motels. The fourth one, The White Birch, was north of town, on the lake. The lady who owned it kept a unit for her son, but he hadn't come in from Troy, so if you and your wife are willing to settle for this one night since Axel would *never* pass up Sunday dinner, it's all right, especially since your wife isn't feeling too well.

I registered, carried in all the luggage, felt her inhale the motel aroma as we walked into a bright red and gold room. I snapped on the television set and unpacked toilet articles, located her pajamas in her bag, laid them out on the bed, shook out her dresses and hung them up. When I took a break she was raptly

289

watching William Holden and Capucine in *The Lion* on the late late show. I said she could watch from the bed, picked her up with a great surge of strength and carried her across the room and gently placed her down. She continued to watch Holden and I sat down beside her; it *was* warm and cozy here.

A commercial came on and she turned to me and said,"Thank you for finding this." She held her arms out and I reached over and cuddled her. With her head against my neck, I had a sudden image of a creature who had had some connection with me, but couldn't possibly have been me; the creature who had cuddled up to and desperately needed *her*. And she had *been* there. I kissed her forehead and thought, Thank *you*. I was suddenly angry with myself. Say it, I ordered, dammit, go on, say it. "Thank *you*," I said, and it came out with surprising ease. I kissed her again and she smiled and leaned against me and looked at *The Lion*. I found myself thinking of that creature who had been connected to me, part mule, part hyena, complete horse's ass. Yet she had taken the creature in, seen him through, *accepted* him. She had seen him at rock bottom, but no matter what he had done, or said, she had *accepted* him. *It*. I shuddered at what she had had to put up with. How had she been able to do such a thing? This pretty little face who had seen nothing, done nothing, *been* nothing . . . I flooded with tenderness and held her very tightly. Then I felt absolute amazement at the tenderness. Speed? Tender? Amazing. I said, and I remember exactly how surprised I was when the words came out, "I'll be a *mensch* for you."

And I knew it had nothing to do with needing her to save my life.

She looked at me, puzzled.

"A person," I smiled. "A man."

She shook her head. "You *are* a person, a man."

"No. I haven't been. But I will be now. For you." I was feeling a new strength while I was saying it. But she was still shaking her head. "Speed, not for me. For *you*."

The strength mixed with remorse and I thought I might cry. *Must* cry. But I couldn't, not now. I kissed her hands, her face, her neck. I was suddenly Speed again, but more than Speed had ever been and I owed this to *her*. My mind, after having been half-dead for years, was now working. Thinking. Gratitude. Yes, thinking gratitude. *Feeling* gratitude. Yes, one thing old Speed had always been able to feel was gratitude; through all the bitchiness, the selfishness, the craziness, gratitude he knew. Gratitude to anyone who could think, feel, say, you know, you're not so bad after all. Well, the working mind said, you never knew gratitude like this *existed*. And, it said, you'd better do something about it, or you'll burst through that beautiful gold ceiling.

I whispered into her ear.

She opened her eyes, looked at me and said, "Do you feel well enough?"

I spilled over again. "Yes ... Do you? You've had some day, and night."

"I'm all right . . . Yes . . ."

In a night of amazements I amazed myself once more. I did everything I had done a hundred years before when we were driving ourselves crazy, but now I did them softly and calmly and perfectly. Absolutely nothing was wrong, *nothing*. And when I went in, it was for her, for us and for this Speed who had become so much more than Speed.

And I never knew it could be like that.

We made one more stop in Livingston Manor, in the Catskills, where in July of 1940 I had worked as a waiter and never scored. I made love to her again and generations of secretaries on the two-week vacation ate their hearts out. On the last day of October—I was now back in the world of dates—we barreled for home, for New Jersey and the Green Garden Motel.

I drove hard but steadily, gluing the needle to sixty, with her hand on my unbarbered neck. We made only one pit stop and I pulled into the entrance to the rear units as the sun dipped below Montclair. I carried her bags inside and breathed the motel mustiness that had been touched up by the Airwick tongues she had left around and which were now almost completely dry. She turned on the TV and reached up to me. I kissed her with all my restored strength and tender purity; I didn't even *consider* staying overnight in a place where she'd be reminded of Linc or the old Speed.

"I'll call when I get back," I said against her mouth.

"Don't forget. And drive carefully."

"I will. You sleep late, you must be beat. Will you talk to Malcolm tomorrow?"

"Maybe. I'm sure he'd take me back. I said I had to go to California and he understood that; he went there after he quit college. Yes, he'll understand."

"Do you want to go back?"

"I don't know."

"No hurry. Take your time, we'll discuss it."

I kissed her again, felt the tongue. *That* definitely would require discussing. I placed daylight between our hips. "Sleep tight, Baby."

"You too," she said. "You've been through a lot."

"We *both* have . . ."

I walked quickly out. The TV was loud and bright behind the blinds as my headlights swept past.

I looked out my window at New Jersey and began to write *The Last of Moe Higgins*. An Indian private eye. Called in on the Judge Crater disappearance, he soon discovers that a gang from upstate New York led by a Linc Cooper has pulled the job because Crater believes in low-income housing which Cooper, a rich ne'er-do-well, considers un-American. Cooper's arch rival, Spud Finton, leader of the Hudson Kings, who came up the hard way, believes every family in New York State is entitled to four rooms for seventy dollars plus one month's concession. Spud hears of the Judge-naping, tips off Moe Higgins who has had it in for Cooper ever since the slaying of Baby Deer, a saloon-keeper with a heart of platinum. Moe straps on a lead vest and reaches down for his sawed-off piece which he has stashed away in his elevator shoe. (The *last* of Moe Higgins.) He heads for Newark where Cooper is meeting with the Dutchman and his (fruity) muscle, Malcolm Bumpeaux, from Vichy. He shoves his way into the bar of the Hoover Motor Hotel and—I stopped cold . . . I looked hard and long into the mirror, said you wiseass S.O.B., once, just *once*, don't be the arrogant hot shot when you're back on top.

I balled up Moe Higgins, looped him across the room for two points. I walked to the dresser drawer and dug down and yanked out the black book. I threw one yearning glance at the Palisades:

"Hey Yonkel, does love *really* conquer all?"

"Why not?"

2

I slept for twelve hours. When I got up, I walked up to Broadway for breakfast. Billy Grik said he never got no calls for Shredded Wheat so I settled for Rice Krispies. I then read the *Times* front to back, also the *News* and tossed in all the ads, this to give my willpower a nominal workout. When I had absorbed enough discipline, I called her. The polite Clara said, "Miss O'Brien has checked out."

"I want Miss *Maureen* O'Brien," I said.

"Yes. I'm sorry, Miss O'Brien checked out."

". . . How could she check out?"

"We have a very simple process. One P.M. is our checkout time."

"But she—"

"Sir, she checked out."

". . . Where did she go?"

"Do you mean did she leave a forwarding address?"

"Yes . . . that's what I mean."

"No."

"Did she go back . . . to Champlain?"

293

"I really couldn't say."

"California?"

"I'm sorry, but I have another call, sir. Have a nice day."

"Wait . . . Did she go to Jerry's shoe store? In Bergen?"

The phone buzzed politely.

I fled over the bridge without a glance at the ghost of Ben Marden's Riviera, cut south on 95 and screeched into the Bergen Mall. The car was still rocking as I shouldered through the revolving door. I found Mary in front of the store and asked her where Maureen was. She didn't have the faintest idea. Was she sick or something? She didn't have the faintest idea. Malcolm knee-actioned up and eyed me warily. Look, I said to Mary, if *you* were Maureen, and if you were very tired, and if you weren't here, where would you be? She thought that over and said it was an unfair question, she wasn't Maureen.

I inspected every store in the mall plus the coffee shop and Hawaiian Palm and didn't see anyone who came close. I asked a stout lady in a miniskirt coming out of the powder room if a girl with an Irish face had been sick in there. She stepped back and scuttled away. I stormed back to the car.

I drove to the Green Garden Motel, composed myself, and said to the lady at the desk that I had an urgent message for Miss M. O'Brien: it wasn't life or death but it was very close. Clara said, "Sir, I explained to you that she checked out, leaving no forwarding address." I slouched away, mounted up, drove around to number nine, peered through the blinds. The room was empty, the TV gray and lifeless. I slumped against the door . . .

I paced up and down on the lip of the Palisades, looked across at Manhattan, turned and looked inland. An hour of this and it finally hit me: she had been considering a move to the *Garden State Mall*. I slammed into the car, roared off.

In a GEM OF A PLACE I found her, bent over a display case of silver-plated charms, pointing to something that a girl with an edge of filigreed slip was purring over.

"I would like to see a diamond stickpin," I announced loudly.

She looked up, contracted. She nodded quickly, said, "I'll be right with you, sir."

The girl said in a stage whisper, "He looks like a sale, go on, I'm still looking."

"A stickpin," I said. "Diamond."

Maureen walked over with her back very straight, her mouth thin. She was wearing the white dress and her hair bounced. I leaned over a case of diamond rings and pointed.

"Please," she said in a low voice, "not now."

Conversationally, I said, "Yes, I think *now* . . . May I see *that*, please."

"That's a ring, not a stickpin."

"I'm quite aware of that. I also like rings. May I see that one. There."

She shook her head and reached down and gingerly lifted out a tray of engagement rings. They gleamed and blinked against the black velvet. In the mirror behind her a man with a pepper and salt toupee sat on a high stool and blandly appraised us. Maureen's mouth barely moved, like a ventriloquist's:

"This one? Please . . . *Please* . . ."

I picked a ring up and examined. "Well?"

"Simplicity," she said, "is always safe."

I squinted at the ring. I said to it, "That's my idea exactly . . . So what is going on?"

"It picks up the overhead lighting, which some people find most attractive," she said.

"I agree. Some people do find it attractive. They like light. Pure, simple light." I eased the ring into its slot, patted it, looked up into moist, blinking eyes.

"That's a very good rule," she said . . . Her mouth was almost closed again. "I had to think . . ."

"Let us not strain ourselves," I said loftily, smiling. "I'll smash this fucking case if you don't give me a straight answer."

She contracted again.

"Naturally it depends on the lady's taste in clothes and coloring," she said. ". . . The Café de France. On the end. Five-thirty."

"The lady had exquisite taste the last time I checked. And

295

exquisite coloring; that's because her conscience was clear. There's a coffee shop right next door."

"Also the shape of her fingers," she said . . . "No, no atmosphere. Café de France."

The toupee folded his arms.

I was polite. Polite. Polite. Friendly. Gallant. Polite. I seated her. Ordered in French. *Une bouteille de vin.* Chablis. New York State, *s'il vous plaît.* No? No, not French. California, *merci.* I tasted. Yes. A glass? Half a glass? Whatever you say, whatever. Are the crepes all right? I'll send them right back if you're unhappy. Oh no, there won't be a scene, perish forbid. Well, if that's better, I'm happy. I always aim to please. Mind if I have another glass? Oh no, it won't go to my head, I won't let it. Well now, everything is cozy and here we are, just the two of us, what the fuck is going on?

She swallowed, set down knife and fork.

"All right. What can I say? I should have called you."

"Now why in the world should you do that? You don't owe me anything, do you?"

"I didn't want to hear your voice," she said. "I was afraid I couldn't handle it . . ."

The idiot grin faded; I covered her hand; her other hand was on mine, stroking. "Ah Baby," I said, leaning forward. "What is it? You can talk to me."

She looked down at my hand.

"I was going to write, but I can't write . . . you'd laugh . . ."

Prick, I said to Speed. Prick.

I said, "Maureen. Baby, I . . . there's no *need* to write. I *love* you. I want to *marry* you."

She pulled her hand back, as if I'd thrust it into the candle flame.

"Don't say that," she said.

"Why not? It's true. You know it. Is it Linc? We'll handle Linc. *I'll* handle him."

"No . . . It's not Linc . . . Speed, I have to go to the ladies room, please . . ."

296

"Will you come back?"

"Oh . . . Yes, I promise."

I stood, the wine glass in my hand. She got up and I handed her her bag. She took it with a thank you and walked away. I felt dizzy, looked down. I was wearing the hated elevators. I looked quickly up, at Maureen. Walking away, she looked the way girls were supposed to look from the back. I sat down and shoved the elevators under the table and finished my glass of wine, poured another. I gulped down the building panic but then she reappeared. I jumped up, almost fell, and seated her as smoothly as my balance allowed. I touched her cheek; she leaned her face against my hand. I strode back to my chair, sat. I lifted the glass.

"Here's to you."

"I knew you would say that."

I felt warm. I drank. I kept my idiotic trap shut. It (apparently) worked.

"Is your apartment all right?" she asked.

"Fine . . ."

"Did you see your boss?"

"No."

"All right, Speed; I'm living at the Hudson Motel."

"Is it nice?"

"It's very nice."

"Is the toupee nice?"

"Mr. Berger? Yes, as a matter of fact. I knew him from Eatontown and he gave me a standing invitation to work for him when he moved to the mall."

"I see."

"I worked in Artcraft and Keepsake Diamonds in Champlain."

"I see . . . Do you love me?"

"Yes."

"Do you want to marry me?"

"Yes . . . But it's not for us . . ."

I took that quietly, finished my glass of wine. She was playing with the strap of her bag. I smoothed out her twisting fingers.

"Linc?" I said.

"Oh no, no . . ."

"Is it because you're Maureen Hallahan and I'm Manny Finestone?"

"I don't care about your name, although Speed is perfect for you."

"I mean . . . what the name represents?"

She looked at my well-placed cheekbones.

"Oh," she said, "don't be silly. My best friend in high school was Jewish."

My piercing eyes closed. Opened.

"What, Maureen? *Talk* to me . . ."

"Speed . . . we broke our vow."

"Our what?"

"Vow. We broke it."

"What vow?"

"That we would . . . consummate our love if Jim Ryun won the Olympics . . ."

The room began to circle about me, like a swinging lamp. I tapped my elevators against the shifting floor; the room held.

"Well?" I said. "So?"

"Jim Ryun lost," she said.

The room started; I tapped it to a halt.

"What in the world are you talking about?"

"He lost," she said.

"Ryun lost?"

"Yes . . . You took it very hard . . . I guess you don't remember."

"He lost?"

"Yes. The African won."

"Keino?"

"Yes, that was his name . . ."

I took her hands. I said in my deepest, softest whisper, "That is a shame, a darn shame, but all right, he lost. He'll go on; so must we." I realized that sounded like her; I smashed the realization.

"But we broke our pact," she said. He lost and in spite of that, we . . . I . . ."

"*We.* And whatever you did, you did for me. For *us.*"

"That's no excuse."

The goddam room. This time I banged it into submission.

298

"Maureen . . . What are we talking about? No, listen. I am crazy about you. Did you hear that? I never said that to anyone, not my wives, anyone . . . I'm saying it to you. I can *say* it to you—"

"Please, Speed. Don't make it any more difficult than it is . . ."

"Will you stop *talking* like that. If we broke our pact, we broke it. The history of the world is broken pacts. We're only human."

She shook her mick face, which was even more exquisite in the candlelight; the gleaming hair bounced.

"That doesn't make it right," she said with the thin mouth.

I tried to stay calm; I absorbed, reflected, assessed. I reviewed several options, rejected them all. Then I thought of the Northwest Frontier.

"Is it the way I carried on . . . upstate?" I said.

She shook her head firmly. "You had a terrible shock. It was as if you lost the war instead of winning it. How could I hold that against you?"

She stroked the hairs on my forearm against the grain, smiled sadly. I remained quiet and at last she said, "Speed, I put too much on your shoulders. I forced you to challenge Niagara Falls."

I had to handle that quickly. "I accepted the challenge. I *welcomed* it."

"And I respect you for that . . . But I didn't do *my* part."

I looked around the grinning room. I got up, walked to the left, the right, balanced, walked back, sat down. I looked at her and the twisting handbag. I had to come up with something, something, something . . .

"Maureen, listen . . . I remember now. For a long time I blocked but now I remember. Marilyn Monroe. She was there. I'm not going to snow you and say she is here *now*, but if she were, you know what she'd say? She would say: 'I forgive you both, bless you both. Now go ahead and make it legal.' Maureen, *this I know*."

The stubborn mick face was swinging.

"No, Speed. She wouldn't. She would know we couldn't build a marriage on a cracked foundation. She would never approve."

"Oh God, what in heaven's name are you *talking* about?"

"You know. Very well. All the time you were repressing your needs, you did it for us, our future. And then I spoiled it . . ."

"I wanted to *fuck* you—"

"Hush. We both know."

"Know *what*?"

"That you fought Niagara to the bitter end, but I folded up like a weakling and made us break our vow; I—"

"Oh God, Maureen . . . Maureen . . . Look, if you say Ryun didn't win, I believe you. But Baby, he *should* have won. That's what matters. The historical necessity. As it was, he did a great job. The air in Mexico City was just too goddam thin. Otherwise he would have walked away with it."

Again the swinging face.

"No, Speed. He lost for a simple reason. Just like I put too much on your shoulders, we put too much on *his* shoulders . . ."

"Maureen . . . Listen, I'll write to him. He's a nice guy. He'll let us off the hook . . ."

"No, Speed, we are *on* the hook."

I thought I was going to faint but somehow I didn't. This *had* to move away from quicksand, onto solid ground . . . "Maureen . . . are you trying to tell me something? Is it the age thing? The divorces?"

"Oh Speed—"

I leaned in. "Maureen, Charlie Chaplin was a *three*-time loser and he and Oona O'Neill are *ecstatic* together."

"Oh Speed—"

"Charlie Chaplin probably broke a *thousand* pacts."

"But Oona didn't . . . I'm positive she didn't. That saved them. I'm sure. One day you would look at me and think . . . and wonder what pact I would break *next* . . ."

"No, I wouldn't, I *promise*—"

"Ah, but you would."

I looked at her; the marvelous power that had filled every muscle fiber since the night of the White Birch Motel—Normandy and V-E Day combined—suddenly drained away . . . Why not, the name was Finestone . . . I began to cry. I covered my face with my hands and I was Manny when Naomi was in the hospital with ptomaine poisoning. She was in the huge bed, white and still, and I was outside on the bench, crying. Finally, I wiped my eyes and looked up and said to Maureen, "I can't make it without you."

Her finger was against my lips.

"Don't ever say that. Of course you can. You're a great writer."

My chest began to jerk; I swallowed it into stillness.

"I'm a fucking hack."

"Stop that! I'm not very smart, I know, but my *feelings* are never wrong. You . . . are . . . great."

I felt quiet now. I said, "Maybe I *could* have been . . ."

"Could? Your story about Gary Cooper and Helen Morgan made me cry."

"Sergeant York," I said.

"See? How good it was? You made me think it was Gary Cooper. You'll write the greatest war novel, I *know* you will."

"It's too late."

"No. No, no, no. That's not Speed."

"Oh yes it is . . ."

"No! Don't argue with me. I'll read that book someday and I'll say I knew him once . . ."

She took my hand. I looked at our hands, took a breath that at its deepest point had a sharp hook.

"Could we see each other?" I said quietly.

"No, Speed. A clean break is the only way."

"But why?"

"We mustn't prolong the agony."

"Oh Baby . . ."

"I'm going to Virginia. I have a girl friend who works in a mall there."

"Where?"

"No. This time for a change *I'll* be strong. I want to tell you, but I won't."

"I don't know if I can take that . . ."

"Yes you can."

"Will you live in a motel?"

"Yes. Sylvia says there's a lovely one a mile from the mall."

"What about the jewelry store?"

". . . Mr. Berger has a place in Virginia."

"Oh, I see."

"Don't say it like that, Speed. It's beneath you to say things like that—"

"Balls."

"Please, don't demean yourself."

"All right. I won't . . ."

"Promise?"

"Yes. Yes, I promise. Maureen—"

"No, Speed. Let's remember what we had. *Have.*"

"Oh Jesus . . . what about Linc?"

"That's all over. You showed me what two people can have . . ."

"Oh Jesus . . ."

We held hands and looked at each other. I tried to firm my chin line, but it was rough, very rough. Then she smiled and said she wanted to pay for dinner. Nothing doing, I said.

"Please," she said. "It would mean a lot to me someday."

"Oh Christ . . . all right . . . Christ . . ."

"Speed?"

". . . Yes?"

"I want you to do something for me."

". . . What?"

"I want you to get up and walk away and don't look back."

I was trembling but I looked at her as carefully as I could. She meant it. Speed always knew when they meant it . . .

"Is that what you really want?" I stalled.

"Yes. It is. I love to see your shoulders when you walk away."

Yes . . . meant it . . .

"I'm round-shouldered."

"You have *strong* shoulders. Now, do it. For me."

I looked at the face that in the beginning I couldn't pin down. I knew Speed: From now on, other faces would rarely, if ever, receive a fair appraisal. I looked at that face the way Manny looked at Patricia Albertson one morning and saw a new face above her new tits. I looked . . . Then with all the dignity I could muster beneath the wine, I got up, rotated carefully in my elevators, and walked out, tightly squaring my shoulders.

In the apartment I finished another bottle of wine, New York State burgundy, and began *Speeding Through the E.T.O.* I began it eight times and eight times I crushed it and fast-balled it into the round file. At three in the morning I pulled on the new Keds and ran down through the park and onto the West Side Highway. The traffic was light, but finally a tandem of cars came out of the darkness and charged at me. I watched them come on, but at the last possible second, broke. I wound up on the dog-dirtied hillside, gasping into the soft ground. I lay there I don't know how long, the cars wheeling by, the river gleaming beneath me, the Palisades hulking across the way. At last I got up and trudged back through the park and across Riverside Drive and up to the apartment. I took off the Keds and packed them away in the closet beside the elevators. At 4:30 I finally got some sleep.

[Tired. Very tired . . . Have just completed 150 push-ups . . . Do not run anymore (during waking hours); the whole world runs; Speed does push-ups (dreams are another matter; I can do a hundred miles per dream) . . . *Fatigué, très fatigué* . . .]

I spent the succeeding days alternating between the apartment and the West End Cafe on Broadway. Each segment of this new rhythm fed on the other like a hungry grinning snake. In the apartment I began page one of *Speeding* nineteen more times and nineteen times tore it up. Then I stalked angrily to the West End. To drink imported ale from England. To study the kids wearing soiled, unbuttoned Eisenhower jackets. To listen to them expound on how E, Speed, et al had fucked up the world for them. How dare they? E and Speed had not only saved their world, but made it possible for them to sit around, drink beer and bitch … And fuck up the world we had saved for them … Yet, these kids— who would have scared the hell out of Manny—did they know something I didn't know? *Had* I been a patsy? More anger.

How I stoked myself up on that anger. On the first Tuesday in November, as I marched into the well-remembered voting booth, I was ready to let it out. Absolutely, historically ready. With my furies. Furious with the kids who had desecrated the sainted garment and were telling everyone who had worn it to fuck off. But equally furious with myself because, quite possibly, I had been used. But my preparation did not stop there. (Did a Finestone ever stop there?) I was furious with Hannah for not calling me, thereby clearly joining those pricky kids. I was furious with Lucille and Carla for having given Captain Speed the business. I was furious with Naomi for being devoted to her Nazi for twenty-six years. I was furious with Samuel for needing elevators. I was furious with Elias Damon for not teaching Abe Cahan. I was furious with Wortham for not writing his book on Andrew Johnson. I was furious with Red for allowing me to whore my talent. I was furious with the Yankees for now being shit on a stick. I was furious with my mother for comfortably surviving my father by twenty-two years. I was furious with my father for packing it in so neatly at the end of the war and leaving me to fight on.

But most of all, of course, I was furious with the genius who couldn't get past the third paragraph of the book he had to write.

So in that voting booth, on that November 4, 1968, I was ready. Palpitatingly ready to get even, to strike back at all those I thought I had loved or needed or put my ass on the line for (including yours truly) and who had betrayed poor little Manny and all his dreams.

How? Simple: *Vote for Nixon.*

Oh, it was beautiful. The perfect, the ultimate revenge (also the final payment to E, who was now so old and sick and staring so wistfully out of the hospital window at Europe. His beloved David would soon marry Julie Nixon. As a good family man, he would close ranks. S.O.B. or no S.O.B. This I understood). I could hear all of them yelling in my head, carrying on so every neighbor on Tremont Avenue could hear: Not the S.O.B.! I actually smiled as I reached for the Republican lever.

But then the one person I had so carefully blocked out and had with all my strength shielded from the anger and disgust and despair—all the Finestone agonies—had to spoil it, had to ask in that quiet, serious voice, "Speed, I thought you said you were going to be a *mensch?*"

I sagged against the cold, uncaring columns.

I voted for Humphrey.

I walked home very slowly and for the rest of the evening sat at the window and stared out at New Jersey, stared and kept shaking my head. Only when the Palisades were a distant blur against a dark sky did I pull out a fresh yellow pad. Then, still shaking my head, but grinning Speed's crooked grin, I began *The Girl in the Mall.*